Days of Vengeance

RACHEL MAYS

Sometimes violence is the answer.

Author's Note:

This story contains content that may not be suitable for all readers, including but not limited to, graphic depictions of and references to violence, death, PTSD, sexual assault, non-consent and dubious consent. Please take care of your mental health!

Sage Habor
Fort Malek
Murvort
Osavian
Twin Beacons
Renoa
Dreslen
Lourova

Chapter One

Ladon

"Emilie," I choked out, reaching toward her. My limbs were so heavy, and it took an unfathomable amount of effort to grab her hand. Her eyes tracked my movement, but the rest of her body remained deadly still. Blurry figures circled us like predators ready to pounce, but the only face I could focus on was hers.

"Help," she said, wincing as though the words caused her pain.

I tried to move closer, to wrap my arms around her, but my feet were stuck to the floor, held by some magical force I couldn't fight. The harder I tried, the farther away she seemed to appear.

"Help," she cried again.

"I'm trying," I said, but the words were silenced as soon as they left my lips. It was like an invisible barrier had separated us and muffled my speech. Her figure turned distorted, like I was watching her through a rainy window. The need to reach her burned inside me, but I had no control over my body or my voice. There was nothing I could do but watch her slip farther away.

Those blurry figures began to swarm her body, and although the image was distorted, I could tell they were touching her. Tormenting her and violating her. Things I swore I'd never allow to happen to either of us ever again.

But I was helpless to stop it.

"Don't touch her!" I mouthed to no avail.

An unsettling chuckle sounded from behind me. I couldn't turn to see, but I knew who it belonged to.

"Reyna," I growled. "Let her go."

"I'd much rather watch. Aren't you enjoying the show?"

My hands clenched at my sides and I strained against the invisible hold on my body. "I'll kill you."

"Tsk, tsk. I would've thought you'd learned not to threaten me. Perhaps it's time I taught you what happens to my untrainable pets."

She snapped her fingers, and a warm sensation rushed through my veins and spine. The weight returned to my limbs—control over my body was mine once again. I bent my arms just to be sure before I sprinted toward the invisible barrier that separated Emilie and me.

I only made it two steps before my feet stuck to the ground again, almost causing me to topple over. Glancing down, I saw black vines growing out of the ground. They wrapped around my ankles and slithered up my legs.

I tugged and twisted, fighting their hold, but they continued to spread, sprouting thorns as they did so. The thorns pierced my skin, but I blocked out the pain. It didn't matter if they tore me to pieces; I had to reach Emilie.

As the vines wrapped around my waist, the impossibility of it all began to sank in. I searched for Emilie through the glassy wall, but the other side had gone dark. Those strangers and their sordid intentions had stolen her from me.

I screamed and clawed at the vines that were still growing, overtaking my shoulders and crawling down my biceps. The farther they spread, the more difficult it became to move.

Rough ivy squeezed my throat. Everything from my chin down was fixed in place, and the vines constricted tighter with each second.

Before they crawled over my face, Reyna stepped into view with a sinister glint in her eyes. "Such a shame you couldn't behave. I would've liked to play with you a while longer. Don't worry about Emilie, though. My friends will take good care of her."

My vision turned black as the vines consumed me at last.

Shooting upright, I clutched at my chest, my heart beating out of control. I grasped my neck, expecting vines, but only found heated skin and a raging pulse. Sweat accumulated on my brow, even though the drapes fluttered with the soft night breeze. Cool air rushed in, leaving goosebumps on my skin. A chill ran up my spine as I struggled to catch my breath.

I forced myself to look around—to remember this place.

I was home, not in the dark, decrepit mountains of Murvort. This was my room and my bed, my books stacked on a dusty desk across the room, and my wardrobe that was cracked open. Not the prison room with a lumpy old mattress thrown on the floor and barren stone walls that sucked the life out of everything within their confines. There were no vines around my wrists—though I still had the white scars where they once were—and no persistent leak dripping from an overhead drain.

Safe. I was safe.

Lowering my shaky hands to the black silk blanket, I ran my fingers over the fabric while I tried to bring myself back to this reality—the one where I was safe and sound, protected by the guards and walls surrounding our stone castle.

No one could touch me here. *No one.*

Since my return to Osavian, there hadn't been a single night where I hadn't woken up in a cold sweat, fighting shadows from my worst nightmares. Memories of unwanted hands and grating words infiltrated my dreams, chasing me until I couldn't outrun them. They left me feeling drained and haunted.

I pulled back the blanket and hopped out of bed. Stumbling in the dark, I felt my way to my private bathroom and lit a wall sconce, blinking at the sudden burst of light.

Once my eyes adjusted, I faced an unrecognizable reflection in the mirror. My face was gaunt and the bags under my eyes were more prominent than ever. A tinge of purple marred my pale skin, like I had bruises beneath my eyes. I'd always had trouble sleeping, but after being kidnapped, rest was a mythical creature I couldn't catch. It was as elusive as the gods who'd forsaken me.

I turned the faucet on and splashed cool water on my face, cupping it in my hands and taking a small sip. I felt like I'd swallowed fire and inhaled ash. It took more than one drink to soothe my burning throat. Once finished, I dried my hands on a towel and leaned against the counter. Gripping the edge, I stared into my own steel-blue eyes. The smart thing to do would've been to hop back in bed and attempt to sleep until morning light. If I didn't, I'd be in a world of pain, struggling to make it through another day of juggling my duties as Head Commander and filling in for Cyrus.

But a little voice in my head said to seek the only thing I knew would help put my nightmares to rest—the only person who understood, who'd suffered like I had.

Emilie.

Even the thought of her name brought a small curve to my lips, but it quickly vanished. I pictured her fighting demons in her sleep, blankets crumpled in a ball near the foot of her bed and her wavy brown hair in a tangled mess.

We were both struggling to return to normal. But wasn't that to be expected?

The two of us had spent months in captivity. We were tortured, starved, raped, and abused in every way imaginable. Wounds both visible and unseen had a habit of reopening when I least expected it, never letting me have a moment of peace.

It was impossible to live as though our trauma had never happened.

And my mother—she knew something was wrong. Every day I saw the concern on her face, but I didn't have the words to pacify her. I huffed a laugh, thinking of the moment she'd caught Emilie and me in the library a couple weeks ago. She had been so... disappointed. Yet she hadn't yelled or berated me. Instead, she sat me down and asked me to explain, but I couldn't do it. I just couldn't.

To tell her what Emilie meant to me would mean telling her everything we'd been through, and I didn't have the strength to confess. I'd choked up and dropped my head in shame. If my mother knew half the things we'd been through, it would break her heart. I was protecting her as much as I was protecting myself.

When she'd realized that I was incapable of recounting the events, she'd wrapped an arm around me and told me it would be okay. That she loved me no matter what, and she'd be there when I was ready to talk. She also suggested I see a mind healer like I had when I was younger, but I hadn't found the time or the courage yet.

The memory of that conversation left my eyes burning, but I pushed the feeling aside. She was unhappy with me, but her patience and love for me outweighed her frustration.

Since then, we hadn't spoken about Emilie. I wasn't sure what conclusions she'd come to, but for now, the subject had been put to rest. Probably for the best, since Emilie wanted to keep things 'friendly' until we could break the news to Cyrus.

But after two and a half weeks, Cyrus was still in a coma. Our healers had done everything they could, but they hadn't found the magical cure for his injuries. I tasted bile, knowing my brother had sacrificed himself to save me. I never would've asked that of him.

But I knew my brother well, and even knowing the outcome, he would've chosen this path a hundred times over. He was the most selfless person in the world, a trait I admired deeply but couldn't seem to emulate.

Turning around, I eyed my bed with irritation. The responsible thing to do, what my mother would want me to do, was to go back to bed. Stay out of trouble. But I'd always had a mind of my own, so I headed for the door instead, with only one destination in mind.

I made my way through the quiet castle corridors, the woven rugs dampening the sound of my footsteps. Mage light flickered on and off, sensing my presence and illuminating my route before dimming behind me. Without running into a single soul, I found myself in the wing that contained both Emilie and Cyrus's bedrooms.

I paused outside of Cyrus's door. He wasn't in there—he was still in the healer's ward where he could be monitored in case his condition changed—but that didn't stop me from placing a hand on the cool stone, like it might connect me to him in some way. I missed him so gods damn much.

On the other side of the hall, Emilie's door pulled me in like a magnet. I reached for the handle and wasn't surprised to feel it turn in my grasp. The perks of being a Castelli—this castle was enchanted to allow me access to any room I desired, including Emilie's. I'd never used it to my advantage so selfishly, but tonight felt like a good time to break my honorable streak.

Slowly, I pushed the door open, then quietly closed it behind me. It took a moment for my eyes to adjust, but once they did, I found Emilie in her bed, surrounded by a thin silver canopy that glistened in the moonlight. I inhaled a sharp breath as I watched her toss and turn, first on her stomach, then to her back with an arm slung over her forehead. It was just as I imagined she would be, with blankets pushed aside and her nightgown skewed and hanging off one shoulder.

Neither of us was adjusting well. Even though we weren't together romantically—her wishes, not mine—she still managed to find me every day so we could just exist together. No one else understood. They didn't understand how impossible it was to carry on with everyday life. But with Emilie, I didn't have to explain my hurt and she didn't have to hide hers. There was comfort in her presence.

From her place in the tangled-up sheets, she let out a small whimper. It was all I needed to bolt to her side.

Crawling into bed beside her, I reached for her hand and pulled it away from her face. "Emilie," I whispered.

Her eyelids squeezed tighter, and her forehead wrinkled.

"Emilie," I said again, brushing my hand over her sweat-dampened hair.

She stirred and, without opening her eyes, one hand reached for me and grazed my bare chest. Then she rolled toward me, her breathing erratic. Her nightmares were just as frequent as my own.

I cupped her face. "Emilie, love. Open your eyes."

She ceased her restless movement and slowly opened her eyes. She still wasn't seeing me, though. Her face was etched with confusion as her hand rose to my face. She traced my skin with curiosity.

"I'm real, princess." Gently, I laced my fingers with hers and waited for her to move past the midway point between sleep and consciousness. I knew she had when she pressed her body against mine and inhaled sharply.

"What are you doing here?"

My shoulders lifted with a small shrug. "I'm here for you."

She released her hold on me and leaned back, allowing me to see the uncertainty in her eyes. Though her room was dark, the moonlight was enough to paint her skin a milky blue, stars shimmering in her large hazel eyes.

She licked her lips, drawing my gaze there, and I tried not to think too hard about the last time I'd kissed them. It hadn't been that long ago. She had become my addiction during captivity, and the withdrawal was unbearable.

Damn Emilie and her ridiculous yearning to do the right thing.

As if she could read my thoughts, she pulled back. Resolve replaced her confusion. "You shouldn't be here."

"But I am."

She let a smile slip through, and my lips curved upward in response. Her body language and expressions spoke louder than any words she'd ever used.

Her fingers found their way back to my chest, drawing crooked lines down the length of my skin, ending just above my pajamas. She sighed and stared at me wistfully.

"Tell me something honest," I said, needing to know what was going on inside that magnificent mind of hers.

"I'm thinking about who we would've been if we were never forced to be together. Do you think we would've found our way to each other?"

The thought made me uncomfortable—that there was a world in which she and I hadn't had the chance to fall in love. Where she'd married my brother and neither of us had been the wiser that such strong chemistry existed between us. She would've borne his heirs, and I would've lived the bachelor life until the end of my days. Maybe I would've grown out of my hatred for her... or maybe I would've forever held a grudge against the woman who walked into Renoa like she owned the place.

I smiled at that first memory of her—so confident and optimistic. I'd been mistaken in my assumption that she was arrogant and flighty. She was simply a woman who knew exactly what she wanted and what she brought to the table.

Would I want to relive our time in captivity? Gods, no. But if it was the only option that led me to her...

No. I refused to believe that the only path to our happiness was through Reyna. Fuck that and fuck her.

Holding her tight, I said, "I would've found you in a hundred lifetimes."

She shook her head, and I could've sworn I saw her eyes roll. "You're so confident that you would've found me. What about me finding you?"

I pretended to consider this. "Hmm. Perhaps I'll leave, then, and wait for you to find me in my bed."

Emilie bit her lip, her eyes bouncing between mine. Gods, I'd never get over this feeling. This need to breathe the same air as her. To share every thought and impulse like she was an extension of me.

Reaching down, she pulled the blanket up around her shoulders and tucked it under her chin. I cursed the fabric that now separated us. But maybe it was a sign that I should return to my own bed and wait until she was ready.

I sighed and edged closer to the side of the mattress. But before my feet hit the floor, Emilie's hand closed around my wrist. Turning back, I found her gazing at me with hungry, lustful eyes.

Why were we waiting again?

There wasn't a single part of me that wanted to keep our feelings a secret. My mother already knew. Anyone else was inconsequential. The only other person who mattered was Cyrus, and he would know the second he woke up. I'd make sure of it myself.

"Why are you here?" Emilie asked again.

"I couldn't sleep."

She nodded, unsurprised. Then she lifted her blanket, making space for me to slip in beside her, and I wasted no time doing so. Her bed was soft and warm, just like her skin, and she happily melted into my embrace when I pulled her against me—back where we belonged.

Immediately, I felt at ease. It was odd how safe she made me feel. How comfortable I was around her. Not more than an hour ago, I'd been plagued with nightmares and anxious thoughts, but with Emilie, my muscles relaxed and my mind cut to more pleasant sentiments.

I tensed whenever anyone else touched me, whether it be a handshake or a pat on the back. My own mother couldn't hug me without summoning memories of a time when my body wasn't my own. Emilie's touch was the only one I could stomach. The only touch that didn't make me want to scrub my skin raw.

Brushing her hair aside, I placed a gentle kiss on her temple. Her body tensed for half a second, and I knew she was waiting to see if I'd push further. If I'd ignore her request to keep our relationship platonic until Cyrus awoke.

But I wasn't going to test the boundary—not tonight, at least. I just wanted to be with her and feel her presence. She relaxed again as I ran a hand down her back, nuzzling her head between my neck and shoulder.

For a second, I thought I felt her lips graze my throat, but it was hard to tell with her delicate precision. Maybe I'd just imagined it.

My eyes began to weigh heavily, and I welcomed the pressure of Emilie's chest against mine, her head tucked under my chin, her hand wrapped around my back. I waited until I heard her steady, heavy breathing before allowing myself to doze off.

With her, like this, everything was right in the world.

Chapter Two

Ladon

I skipped breakfast with my mother, as I had most days since returning to Renoa. Instead, I had a servant bring something light to eat before I headed out for my morning run. After I returned, I quickly washed up and got dressed in a pair of dark gray slacks and a black coat embroidered with the golden Castelli crest on the shoulder. The fabric itched against my neck, and I wished more than anything that I could change into my training gear.

But as regent, I needed to look the part.

I checked the mirror next to my bedroom door and attempted to smooth my white hair back and straighten my jacket. My reflection stared back at me with unimpressed gray-blue eyes. It mocked me and told me I looked ridiculous, so I tousled my hair and undid the top button.

Good enough.

My shoes clicked against the marble stairs as I climbed the tallest tower in the castle—the tower that held the King's Post. For as long as this castle had stood, all important meetings were held in the King's Post.

The stairs spiraled five stories high into the sky and ended in a circular room without walls—only a marble railing with six column posts that connected to the dome ceiling. In the King's Post, we were seemingly unprotected from the blue skies, but a magical barrier surrounded the tower and kept out rain and birds. There was only one record of attack against the King's Post in our history, and the barrier withheld a barrage of javelins, too.

As I made my way up the stairs, I suddenly understood why Cyrus never joined me on my morning runs. Climbing up and down these steps every day was a workout in itself. It also made sense why advisors in the King's Conclave stepped down while they were still fairly young. I couldn't imagine climbing these steps once I got to the age when my knees and hips began to ache.

I was the first of the Conclave to reach the top, and I took my seat in the chair that faced south. The other ten seats filled steadily as the other members appeared shortly after my arrival.

The room was quiet, and I couldn't help but wonder if this was how they behaved when Cyrus was in the room. Didn't they engage in small talk? Ask him how his day was? Or did they save this reserved attitude just for me? It was clear they didn't know how to react to me stepping in while Cyrus was bedridden.

To be fair, I didn't know how to react, either.

I cleared my throat, and the woman to my right gave me a curt nod while several other pairs of eyes met mine. "Shall we begin?"

Liam was the first to speak, passing out sheets of paper to each of us, filled with numbers and words that I didn't understand. "These are last month's financial statements. As you can see at the top, we brought in four percent more revenue than last..."

I immediately tuned him out. Listening to profit and percentages made my head spin and my eyes dry out. I understood the importance, but I simply couldn't make sense of the data. A lot of duties as king made me feel inept, but none as much as finance.

"Liam," I said, cutting him off as he began to speak about subsidies and vacant housing.

"Yes, Your Highness?" he said, pushing up his glasses.

I squirmed in my chair, and the fabric on my collar scratched my neck again. I resisted the urge to undo another button and loosen the aggravating material at my nape. Everyone else in the room sat straight with their attire all prim and proper. How did they do it? "I told you; you don't need to call me that."

While it was technically my moniker, it didn't suit me.

"Yes, Your... sir."

I reached into my pocket and fiddled with a ring—the one I'd kept from the child victim in Murvort. The idle movement helped calm my nerves.

"I think we all know that I'm not great with the numbers stuff," I said, looking around the circular table.

A few smiles and even a low laugh escaped the man sitting across from me. Liam only nodded. He was less than enthusiastic about my impatience for his area of expertise. Disappointment shone in his beady, dark brown eyes, but he held his tongue.

"I trust you, Liam. Whatever recommendations you have, I will approve them."

Liam sat up straighter and thrummed his fingers over the stack of papers in front of him. "Sir, I don't think that's a wise idea. I'm an advisor, not a king."

"And I'm not a king either," I said. My hands twitched and my hand reached to unbutton my coat, but I stopped myself just in time.

A few nervous glances were exchanged around the table, and I took note of every one. For every doubt these advisors had in me, I had twice as many. I knew I was unqualified, that my experience was severely lacking outside of combat. I was not a king. I'd never had any desire to *be* a king.

The woman next to Liam, Nicola, sucked in a sharp breath. "Sir, we know it must be hard being thrust into this position. I can't imagine how difficult it is taking over while King Cyrus is… away. But…" She looked around at the rest of the advisors, and I had the feeling they'd been talking about me behind my back. "We feel it would be best if you performed as if you *are* king. Just in case… you know, just in case King Cyrus doesn't…"

Nicola's words trailed off, and her face went unnaturally pale. I could see it in her eyes—she was calculating if she had said too much.

"Finish that sentence," I said, clenching my jaw. "Finish it."

Her mouth opened slightly, but nothing came out. In fact, she looked as though she'd lost the ability to speak altogether.

I had no intention of harming her, of course, but there was an unmistakable threat in my tone.

The entire room went silent—so quiet I could hear my throat working to swallow. As my eyes swept around the table, each person suddenly looked at their hands or out the windows or at their neighbor. None could hold my gaze for more than half a second.

Leaning forward, I rested my elbows on the table and touched my fingertips together. "Let me be crystal clear. I am *not* king, nor will I ever be."

After an uncomfortable pause and another round of exchanged glances, the members of the Conclave nodded in understanding. I hoped it was the last time we had to have that conversation, but something in me nagged that I'd have to hear it again soon.

"Now," I said with a sigh, leaning back in my chair. These meetings were exhausting. I was only interested in one subject... maybe two. "Can we talk about Murvort and any updates on Reyna?"

Xavier, my second in command, shifted in his seat. He pushed up the sleeves of his olive-green shirt, showing off his tattooed skin. Instinctively, I pulled at the cuffs of my jacket, making sure the scars from my former tattoos were hidden.

"Since Reyna and her immediate circle of supporters have fled, there has been a struggle for power within Murvort. There's been a lot of infighting, and various factions are all doing their best to kill one another to reach the throne. It wouldn't surprise me if a tenth of the population has been depleted.

"Our latest reports suggest that Jesse Holden and his sister Jade have seized rulership. This is good news for us because they are a young sibling duo and have been critics of Reyna for years. They'd been lying low since Reyna had their father beheaded, but with her disappearance, they've quickly gained popularity with the younger demographic who are hopeful for a change of pace."

I nodded. "Have we set up a meeting with them?"

The best thing we could do was to form an agreement quickly before Reyna made a return. We could help them keep power in exchange for their loyalty and peace.

"Not yet, but I can send a message if you'd like."

"Yes, thank you. And what about Reyna? Has she been found yet?"

Xavier's lips turned into a frown. "I'm sorry, sir, but no. We have spies scouring every town within a one-hundred-mile radius, but so far, she hasn't popped up. It seems she has left the continent."

"In that case—"

"You'll need to write to King Marsden," Nicola interrupted. "If she's gone to Wyland, then you'll need his permission to extradite her. I can do that, if you'd like. I've had years of correspondence with him."

Yes, as Osavian's advisor of foreign affairs, Nicola would have the best relationship with Wyland's royal leader. I didn't know him, but my brother did. And from what I'd heard, he didn't work well with others unless there was something in it for him.

"Please send a message to him as soon as possible. Thank you, Nicola."

After tuning out a few more sleep-inducing topics, the Conclave was dismissed. Chairs scraped the floor as members stood and the room emptied within a couple minutes. Xavier was the last to leave and took an unreasonable amount of time collecting his belongings, glancing around the room like he'd lost something.

"Is there something you'd like to talk about?" I asked. I wasn't in the mood for games and ambiguity.

"That obvious, huh?"

"As obvious as a beached whale, yes."

"Subtlety was never my strong suit, I guess. Sir, I wanted to speak to you about our guests..."

"Guests?"

"The ones in the dungeons..."

Ah, *those* guests. I'd almost forgotten about the monsters we kept below us—the handful of enemy soldiers taken after the battle in Murvort.

Xavier kept a blank face as he waited for me to catch up.

"What about them?" I asked.

"I don't think we're going to get any more information out of them. We've tried everything we can think of, but if they know anything else, they aren't breaking."

How was that possible? The only piece of information they'd given us was that Reyna had some important connections in Sage Harbor, but so far, our spies hadn't seen her in the town or anywhere in the vicinity.

I nodded as I contemplated. Perhaps they were telling the truth and didn't know anything else. If they had more information, surely Xavier would've been able to get it out of them. He was even more skilled in intelligence extraction than I was. "If they're no longer useful, then it's time to dispose of them."

Xavier didn't seem surprised by my order. The prisoners in the dungeon had committed heinous crimes. I wouldn't keep them around to suffer, like Reyna had done with Emilie and me. But I also wouldn't show mercy and set them free. Eliminating them was the only solution.

"It'll be done before the end of the day," Xavier said, collecting the last of his belongings and heading for the stairs.

I crossed the room, but before I headed down from the tower, I took a moment to look out across the shimmering sea. The sun was almost at its highest point, and specks of white reflected off the gentle waves. I had to squint to protect my eyes from the blinding glare.

The water seemed so peaceful from up here. Calm and still. Along the shoreline, I spotted a woman and her child searching for seashells where the waves met the sand. Farther along, fishers lined the pier with their poles, hoping to catch their next meal or a surplus to sell at this weekend's market. Closer to the street, a young vendor was setting up his cart, lifting the awning and tampering with his display of colorful boxes and bottles until he was satisfied.

From up here, it looked like they hadn't a care in the world.

I envied them.

If only I had the simple life they enjoyed. I didn't want to think about prisoners in dungeons and the change in leadership within our enemy's borders. I didn't want to rule over a kingdom. I wanted peace and quiet with the woman I loved.

The tower rumbled, the ground beneath my feet vibrating, and I released the railing with a wince. After being without power for so long, I kept forgetting to keep it in check. If I wasn't careful, I'd accidentally shatter the marble and stone that built this castle and plummet to my death.

Maybe it'd be a relief...

"No," I said softly, closing my eyes.

I had so much to live for, even if living was hard. These struggles were temporary. If I could survive Reyna, I could survive anything.

When I opened my eyes, my gaze was drawn to something on the horizon. It was only a miniscule white fleck, but it was quickly approaching. Time sped up as I watched, and eventually, the white dot turned into a full-sized ship.

I wasn't the only one who noticed. Folks along the shore were pointing and shouting, trying their best to see who was about to make land. It wasn't one of ours—it didn't carry the Osavian royal insignia.

I'd wasted enough time. Taking the stairs two at a time, I bolted down all five stories until I reached the landing, making a sharp right turn through an open archway and into the gardens.

A few servants jumped out of the way when they caught sight of my impatient gait. The last thing I wanted to deal with was an unexpected visitor. At least I knew they weren't a threat. Our naval fleet at Twin Beacons would've stopped them long before they could show up on the horizon.

I moved through the endless rows of blossoming flowers and perfectly manicured bushes, jogged down the stone steps and into the soft, white sand. The ship was close enough now that I could see a forest green flag with a silver cross through it.

Dreslen? Why would they send a ship...?

By the time I reached the marina, the ship had lowered its anchor and people were climbing into a smaller tender boat that could traverse the shallower waters. The pliable wooden boards beneath my feet creaked as I walked to the end of the dock. I crossed my arms, forced to wait for the tender to reach shore.

"She's a beautiful ship, huh? Don't see one like that very often."

I turned to find an elderly man with leathery skin and a missing tooth on the bottom row staring out at the massive vessel. He had one hand above his forehead, shielding his eyes from the sun pounding down on us.

"No, we don't."

The ship was far more ornate than most I had seen, with carvings along the bow and matching green trim around the portholes and deck railing. The longer I stared, the more intricate details I found.

Finally, the tender boat approached the dock and the man next to me tossed them a rope to guide them in. Once tied up, I smiled and prepared to greet the first individual to step off the boat—a familiar face I hadn't expected to see.

The man met my gaze with a crooked grin.

"Hello, Adrien. I wasn't expecting you."

Adrien ran a hand over his unkempt beard. He looked like hell—dirty face and clothing. His jacket had a rip on one sleeve and frayed edges around the collar. He was the exact opposite of the ship he captained. I wasn't sure how long he'd been at sea, but I knew why he'd returned to land.

"It's good to see you, Ladon, but I'm here to see someone else. Where's my little sister?"

Chapter Three

Emilie

"Have you seen the book about nocturnal flowers? The one with a black rose on the front... kind of dusty and falling apart?"

I looked up from my current textbook when I didn't get a response. The Harpy was around here somewhere, though it would've been hard to spot her through the stacks on the desk in front of me. I must've read through a thousand books from the Castelli's library, and none of them had led me to the cure for Cyrus. At this point, the search had become more of a distraction from unpleasant memories than a successful pursuit of knowledge.

I leaned over in my seat, searching beyond my cave of tomes to see where the Harpy had run off to. She was supposed to be helping me with my pursuit of an answer, but she was known to flit around while I stayed planted at the desk. Perhaps she had gone to another floor.

Placing a crumpled bit of parchment inside my book, I closed it and stood, stretching my legs. How long had I been sitting here? I yawned and craned my neck, searching for the gilded clock on the wall. It was still early, but I'd been awake for hours.

The room was quiet, even for a library, but I strained my ears and listened for the sound of footsteps or books sliding across a shelf—any indication that I wasn't alone.

When I heard a noise to my left, I followed without a second thought. Turning the corner, I found the Harpy sitting on the floor, her black wings tucked awkwardly between her body and the shelf she leaned against. Her feathers ruffled as her eyes roamed the pages of the book in her lap.

She didn't look up as I approached, nor when I took a seat on the hard floor next to her. "What did you find?"

Finally, she tore her eyes from the book and stared at me with big, haunted eyes. I often wondered what her story was, but she couldn't recall much before her time with Reyna. She couldn't remember where she was from or who her family was.

My heart broke for her. The only memories she had were of torture and captivity. Hopefully she'd be able to make new ones in Renoa.

She gently guided the book into my hands and pointed.

I skimmed the fable of a moon goddess sent down from the heavens to protect the innocent and heal the broken. My shoulders slumped, and I frowned. "This is children's story. I don't think we can count on an imaginary figure to heal Cyrus."

But the Harpy shook her head, pointing again to the ink on the page and then to her chest. She double tapped a word on the page and her eyes met mine, trying to convey a message.

I reread the passage. "Selene? What about her?"

She placed her palm over her heart, and a wave of calm washed over her face. Her expression was no longer haunted, but peaceful.

"Is that... is that *your* name?" I was under the impression that she couldn't remember her name—that it had been taken from her along with her memories.

She shrugged one shoulder.

"You're not sure?"

A curt nod.

"But... it feels right?"

She nodded again.

"Hmm." Maybe seeing the name had sparked something inside her, had called to her despite her forgetting. "Well, then, I think that's what we should call you. Selene."

Her eyes lit up at the sound, and I knew it was the right name for her. It was fitting that she be given the name of a goddess whose destiny was to protect and heal. Much of my survival in Murvort was owed to her.

Taking her hand in mine, I smiled. "Now, should we get back to our research?"

Selene looked embarrassed. Her cheeks flushed pink and her eyes pointed toward the ground, like she was foolish to be distracted by something so insignificant.

But it was significant.

"Don't be ashamed," I said. "This matters. You matter, Selene."

I'd say her name a thousand times until she understood that she wasn't small. That she wasn't someone's puppet. She was a whole person, and she deserved to take up space. Reyna had kept her on a leash, but she was free now. And I hoped she felt that every day from here on out.

I stood first and pulled her up, briefly exchanging a smile before we returned to the desk. The stack of books somehow seemed even more daunting now. Had it grown while I was away?

Before I could think too much about the long day ahead, the door to the library creaked open. It wasn't out of the ordinary—nobles visited the library every so often during the daytime hours—but it still made me anxious to share a space with them. They always stared and whispered whenever they spotted me. They didn't know everything that had happened in the confines of Murvort, but that didn't stop them from gossiping. Their gaping made me ill.

Footsteps echoed, coming closer until Ladon appeared from behind a towering shelf. His eyes met mine for a moment, and I would've gotten lost in them if Selene's wings hadn't fluttered at that very moment.

I cleared my throat. "Ladon, what are you doing here? Aren't you supposed to be doing... kingly things?"

Internally, I cringed at my lapse in intelligence. Between spending all my time in the library and Ladon's handsome face, I was all out of brain power.

Ladon only raised a questioning brow. "My kingly duties are done for the morning. How is the research going?"

He trailed a finger along the spines of the books closest to him, studying them with feigned interest. I knew he didn't think the answer would be found in his family's library. According to him, he'd already read every one of these books, but there was no way he could've retained all of that information. What if he'd forgotten the smallest detail that could save Cyrus?

For some reason, I didn't want him to know how unsuccessful we had been. Maybe I didn't want him to lose hope. "It's going well," I said, forcing what I hoped came off as a look of encouragement.

He glanced up from the stack of books, and his bright eyes bore straight into my soul. Then he gave me a knowing smirk that made my stomach flip. "Right... Well, I actually came here to share some news."

Wondering if this news was confidential, I turned my head to Selene. "Could you take this stack and put them back where they belong?"

Her mouth formed a close-lipped smile before she grabbed as many books as she could hold and set off to carry out her task.

"Thank you, Selene," I said as she walked away.

"Selene?" Ladon asked, stepping closer. His forearm brushed my hip as he reached for another book, flipping through the pages, though his attention never left me.

"That's her name."

"Since when?" he asked with an annoyingly charming grin.

"Since now."

"Hmm." He inched closer, invading my space until his chest brushed against my shoulder. Suddenly, the book in his hand shut with a thump.

I jumped. Something about his closeness put me on edge, but I liked it. I liked the way his voice made my heart race and my thighs clench together. But now was not the time for that.

"You said you had something to share?"

Curse the gods, he stepped away like he suddenly remembered we were in public and anyone could see the electricity that flowed between us. He placed the book down, nudging it until it was perfectly straight and in line with the rest.

"I did." He looked to his right and licked his perfect lips. "Actually, I think it'd be better if you just take a look."

He pointed his thumb over his shoulder, and I followed the gesture, walking around a shelf. My small study area opened up into the library's atrium, full of desks scattered about and mismatched mage lights floating above them. Near the door, the librarian was busy chatting with a male patron who leaned across the counter. She stared at him with wide eyes, appalled by the way he encroached on her space.

I knew the woman well. She liked her space to be neat and tidy, and this man was anything but. His hair was unruly and his jacket was worn out with a hole near his right shoulder. The boots he wore looked as though they'd taken him through a swamp or a pigpen. From here, I couldn't tell if he smelled like a pigsty too. He probably did.

But then he turned to the side, and I got a view of his profile—his defined jawline and the bump on the bridge of his nose, the crinkle near his eyes as he twisted my way.

"Adrien," I shouted, running across the atrium.

"Don't run," the librarian scolded.

Meanwhile, Adrien held his arms open to catch me. The moment we collided, he wrapped his arms around me and lifted me off the ground. "It's so good to see you. You had us worried for a moment there."

"What are you doing here? What about Mom and Dad?" I asked, searching the room. He had said 'us,' but I didn't see anyone else.

"What am I doing here?" he huffed. "I'm here for you, of course. You got kidnapped, and you thought I wouldn't be here to welcome you home?"

"Technically, you weren't," I told him, though it didn't bother me. Truthfully, I had needed a few days to myself before I was ready to see anyone. But he was here now. *That* was what mattered.

He waved me off. "Details. I would've been here sooner, but we came across a nasty storm. Waves twenty feet tall. I thought we were going to capsize."

"That sounds awful."

He rolled his eyes and let his head fall back, reminding me how much I'd missed his dramatics. "It was nothing. What's life without a little danger here and there?"

"Well, I'm glad you made it out alive."

"Likewise," he said, his eyes returning to meet mine.

For a moment, we stood in silence. I knew he was assessing me, expecting to see bruises and marks—physical signs of trauma. But aside from the faint white vines wrapped around my wrists and ankles, all my scars were internal.

I shifted uncomfortably. It didn't matter that he was my brother; I still disliked being observed. It brought me back to a dark, crowded room and a sea of eyes that swallowed me whole. The hair on my neck rose, and I had to look away.

Ladon stood nearby, leaning against a column with a book in his hands. I doubted he was reading it. Rather, he was listening to make sure I was okay. I appreciated that he gave me the space to work through things on my own but stayed close enough that he could be there in a second if I needed him.

I turned back to my brother. "Are Mom and Dad here too?"

He sucked in a breath through gritted teeth. "Afraid not. But you don't want them here anyway. Dad would be a bore, and Mom would fuss over your hair." Frowning, he reached out to touch a strand of hair. "When was the last time you got a haircut, anyway?"

I slapped his hand away. "You're not funny."

He grinned, and his eyes were full of youthfulness that reminded me of our childhood. Then we both burst into laughter.

"I suppose you're right," I said. "Mom and Dad would bring down the mood. How long will you be staying?"

"However long I want. Perks of being a captain of my own ship. I call the shots." He threw his arm over my shoulder and spun me toward the door. "Now, let's get out of here. I think if I stay any longer, the beauty over here might have a fit."

He winked at the librarian, and her ears turned red, her eyes narrowed to slits. She looked seconds away from throwing a book at his head—which would've violated her own moral compass.

I winced and tried to give her an apologetic smile, but she wasn't having it.

"Let's go," I said. "Before someone gets hurt."

"What about your friend?" Adrien asked, looking over his shoulder.

I followed his gaze to find Ladon still hovering nearby, but he was no longer alone. Selene was motioning something with her hands and Ladon was watching in confusion. He kept shaking his head, but that didn't deter Selene. She exaggerated her motions even more, ruffling her feathers and making Ladon jump back. It was a comical sight to behold.

I snorted. "He'll be fine here."

Adrien waved in front of him. "Then lead the way."

The cobbled streets were lined with tan stone buildings, vines growing up the side that were much more idyllic than those scarred upon my wrists. Colorful banners hung above the doors with advertisements while wooden signs displayed the name of each store we passed. Above us, strands of twinkling lights were hung across the pathway, though they were hardly noticeable during the daylight.

It was my first time walking through the city since I'd been taken captive, and thankfully, the streets weren't very busy. I didn't think I could handle a large crowd. Not yet.

"So, where do you want to go?" I asked my brother.

"I don't know. This is your city now, isn't it? Where would *you* like to go?"

It didn't feel like my city. I'd spent less time in Osavian than I had in Murvort. Everyone believed I was to be wed to Cyrus, but in my mind that engagement had already been called off. Would this city still claim me once they learned I'd turned my back on the king and chosen Ladon?

"What about... here?" I pointed to the first shop to my left.

Adrien took one look and frowned. "You want to go to a bookstore? Don't you already have every book available in the gigantic library we were just in?"

Fair point.

"Okay, then." I spun in a circle, looking for a better alternative, and gestured over his shoulder. "What about that?"

He turned around, and a smile replaced his frown. "Now you're speaking my language. I didn't realize you were interested in weaponry."

"It's a recent development," I said, my eyes locked on a sword in the window with emerald gems embedded in the hilt.

Inside, the shop was quiet and dimly lit. Spotlights hung above the most treasured pieces to ensure they glistened and lured in customers. It worked as intended. Adrien flitted around from pedestal to pedestal, examining each weapon with awe.

"Are you looking for anything in particular?" the shopkeeper asked, hidden behind the counter. When he stepped out and caught sight of us, he pasted on a smile. "Ah, Miss Emilie. It's good to see you out and about. Let me know if there's anything I can help you with."

"I'm just browsing," I said. Meanwhile, my brother asked the man for a specific type of blade. Apparently his was showing wear from the salty, humid sea air. He needed something more resistant to corrosion, and the shopkeeper was happy to help.

I aimlessly made my way through the shop, merely browsing until I reached the back corner. The wall held a spectacular exhibition of knives and daggers, each displayed in uniform rows and growing in size from the smallest at the bottom to the largest at the top.

My eyes caught on one in particular—a short blade with a black handle that looked to be the perfect fit for my palm. I reached for it, and I had to admit the weight felt exhilarating in my hands. It was just right. Not too heavy, but enough weight to propel it forward and hit my target.

I turned it around and admired the spiral design embossed in the handle that carried down to the blade—the dips in the hard material coated with amethyst. It was as beautiful as it was practical.

"Did you find something, milady?" The shopkeeper snuck up behind me. He must've finished helping Adrien while I was distracted.

"I did."

"Ah, excellent choice. It's part of a set of throwing knives. Should I pull out the rest for you?"

"Yes, please. Could you send the invoice to the castle? And for whatever my brother picked out as well."

Behind the shopkeeper, Adrien gave me a thumbs up, to which I responded with a grin.

It was the least I could do since he was the only one who had checked in on me.

Chapter Four

Ladon

THE HEALER'S WARD WAS bustling with staff. Not only was Cyrus injured, but other soldiers had sustained wounds from our latest battle, too, and it seemed like every healer in Renoa was on duty.

Of course, my brother was given his own private room down a long hall, around a corner, and farther down a second hall with guards standing outside his corridor. He would've been safe even without the extra precautions, but it eased my mother's nerves.

The guards gave me a small nod as I passed by and into the second hall. I stopped outside Cyrus's door, hand frozen on the knob, when I heard a voice.

I knew I shouldn't, but I leaned in closer to hear my mother speaking.

"He isn't doing well, Cyrus. None of us are. You're the pillar that holds this family together, and without you... I need you, Cyrus. Your family needs you. Ladon... he's suffering, too. He may not say it outright, but I know this is hard on him. And he hasn't even recovered from his time... well, his time..."

Her voice dropped to a whisper, and I strained to hear her next words.

"He won't speak about it, you know. I'm afraid we might've lost him forever. He's here... but he's not okay. And I don't know how to help him. So I need you to come back to us, because he listens to you and looks up to you. I need both of my sons to be okay again."

A lump lodged in my throat. My mother was sharp and observant, but I hadn't expected her to be so focused on me. Not while Cyrus was lying unconscious. My wounds were secondary.

I shoved my emotions down and arranged my face in a pleasant expression before knocking and opening the door.

My mother immediately wiped tears from her eyes, inhaling a shaky breath. Her gaze darted between me and Cyrus, who was in bed with a sheet pulled up to his chest and a fluffy pillow behind his head. "I didn't know you were stopping by."

"I hadn't planned to. It was a last-minute decision. Have you been here long?"

A tray of half-eaten food rested on the table next to her, and she had an olive-green blanket stretched across her lap. I could just make out the corner of a pillow placed behind her back. If I had to guess, she'd been sleeping here and having all her meals brought in.

"If you want to take a break, I can stay here with him," I told her. This wasn't healthy. Had she done the same thing while I was missing? Sat next to my empty bed and desperately waited for me to return?

"No, I can't. I have to be here."

Arguments with my mother never went in my favor, so I didn't bother. I took the seat next to her, and she pulled her blanket, stretching it over my legs too.

"How's he doing?"

"Same as yesterday. And you?"

I smirked. "Same as yesterday."

She gently swatted at my leg, and I grabbed her hand.

"I'm okay." I squeezed her hand to reassure her, but she only stared at me with glassy eyes. "Really, I am. I'm not the same as I was before, and I don't know if I ever will be, but I *am* okay. Promise."

Her eyes narrowed as if she were waiting for me to crack. When I showed no sign of breaking down, she finally relented. "You've never been one to show your emotions, but it's been even harder for me to read you since your return. You'll tell me if you're ever not okay?"

I nodded. "Of course."

"Anything else you'd like to share with your mother?"

"About...?" My pulse began to race as I imagined the questions she must have about what happened in Murvort. I still wasn't ready to talk about it, and honestly, I didn't think I ever would be. Emilie was the only one I felt comfortable confiding in because she knew how it felt. My gaze dropped to the white vines wrapped around my wrists.

"About a certain intelligent girl, brown hair, gorgeous eyes... You might've seen her in the library. I think she lives there now."

I was relieved she didn't want to talk about Murvort, but I kept my lips sealed. Something must've shown on my face though, because she carried on.

"Are we still pretending that nothing is happening there? That I didn't walk in on the two of you canoodling in the library?"

"Canoodling?" I couldn't keep the amusement out of my voice. She smacked my leg again, and this time I winced. "Ow."

"You know what I mean. Has that been laid to rest?"

I rubbed my hand across my face. Any leniency or patience I'd been hoping for was completely nonexistent. "We are—"

Immediately, I questioned my words, because her brows rose to an unnatural height.

"There shouldn't be a 'we.'"

"But there is," I said firmly, and she leaned back. "There is a 'we.' There is an 'Emilie and I.' I know that isn't what you want to hear, but it doesn't make it any less true. Cyrus will understand. He has to."

I glanced at my brother like he might be brought to life by the topic at hand, but he remained sleeping peacefully. I was so adamant that he would be sympathetic, but there was a very good possibility I was wrong.

My mother voiced my fears. "What if he doesn't? What if this tears apart our alliance with Dreslen? How do you think her parents will react if this engagement unravels? Are you willing to risk that for a girl?"

I resisted the urge to roll my eyes. Ignoring the fact that Dreslen brought nothing to the table through our alliance and wouldn't be missed, my mother was speaking as if I were infatuated with a childhood crush. But Emilie was so much more than that. "I'd risk my life for her."

The color drained from her face, and she blinked rapidly, at a complete loss for words. Then she turned to face forward again. Perhaps she couldn't bear to look at me after I'd disappointed her so thoroughly.

"You're truly in love with her."

She said it so quietly I almost missed it. It was a statement, not a question, but I answered anyway.

"I am."

Time stood still as she digested this information. When she finally looked at me again, it was with an expression of fear mixed with happiness. I saw it in her eyes—a paradoxical joyous sorrow.

I knew it all too well. I felt it every time I touched Emilie, knowing what it cost to call her mine.

Her bottom lip trembled when she spoke. "We'll figure it out."

I nodded because there was nothing else I could do. "Emilie doesn't think we should be together until Cyrus wakes."

"She's a smart woman." I made a disgruntled noise, and my mother huffed a laugh. "It's true. It's best for everyone if the two of you keep this quiet for now. Once Cyrus wakes—if he wakes—we can decide how to handle it as a family."

"Hey," I said, demanding my mother's attention. "He is going to wake up. You can't give up. You didn't give up on me, did you?"

She sighed and offered a half-hearted smile. "Of course not."

I wished there was more I could've said to her—to convince her that Cyrus would be okay—but I honestly didn't know. Besides, a knock at the door had us both turning to see who the latest visitor was. We'd given strict orders that only family be allowed to visit. The last thing we needed was to have nosy nobility and curious civilians hovering over him. Aside from my mother and me, healers were the only ones allowed to move freely where he was concerned.

The door slowly pushed open, and Emilie stepped inside. "Oh, sorry. Am I interrupting?"

I could practically feel my mother tense beside me. I muttered under my breath, "Be nice."

"Not at all," she said. "You're always welcome here, Emilie. I'm sure Cyrus would be happy to know you're concerned about his wellbeing."

Emilie's mouth parted slightly while I clenched my teeth. "Um, I do care very much for him, Sophia."

My mother hummed, and it was hard to tell if it was in approval or not. Rising from her seat, she walked around Cyrus's bed and crossed the narrow space before coming to a stop in front of Emilie.

"Come to dinner tonight. Both of you," she said, turning to look back at me. "And I don't want to hear any of your excuses. I'm tired of eating alone."

Leave it to my mother to make me feel guilty for something entirely different from what I'd expected. She could accept my feelings for Emilie but couldn't accept another meal on her own.

Emilie's face was full of surprise. "My brother is visiting. I'm not sure I—"

"Bring him too. I will see you all at dusk. I'm going to go freshen up."

I was too busy reveling in the fact that my mother was finally leaving the healer's ward that I didn't think about how uncomfortable this dinner was likely to be until the door closed behind her.

"Well, that was..."

"Unexpected?" Emilie asked.

"Yes."

"She knows, doesn't she?"

"How did you..."

Emilie raised her hands in exasperation. "It's obvious. Sophia has always been so kind to me, and now she's making pointed remarks about how *Cyrus will be pleased to know I care* and forcing us to have dinner together. What did you say to her?"

"I didn't say anything," I said defensively.

"You must've," she argued, brows pinched together with worry. "Sophia can't hate me. I couldn't bear it."

Sighing, I stood and crossed the room to hold her. She took a few steps back as I approached, like my touch might set her on fire, but eventually she allowed me to wrap my arms around her.

"My mother doesn't hate you. She's just trying to figure out how to navigate this, the same as we are. Trust me, she still adores you."

Emilie's shoulders slumped. "It didn't seem that way."

"She wouldn't have invited you to dinner if she didn't."

Emilie pulled back from me, and her eyes widened. "Oh, gods, dinner. Adrien doesn't know."

My lips curved into a half-smile. "Are you going to tell him before-hand?"

"No. I mean... I hadn't planned on telling him anything until we were ready to tell everyone, but I suppose this changes things." She frowned, and I could see the wheels in her brain turning, running through a thousand scenarios on how best to handle Adrien and breaking the news that she was ending her engagement to a king.

She looked up, and stress turned to exasperation as she narrowed her eyes at me. Her head quirked to the side before she asked, "Why are you smiling?"

I shrugged. There was no point in fretting when we were facing the inevitable. We'd faced much worse and made it out alive. "You're really adorable when you're freaking out."

Perhaps I could've done a better job at calming Emilie's nerves. She sat across from me at the dining table, clenching a fork like it was about to run away. She'd hardly touched her salmon, though she'd been pushing it around her plate for the past twenty minutes.

Under the table, I stretched my leg until I felt her foot. I tapped twice, and she looked at me.

Relax, I tried to tell her without words.

Her response silently screamed, *I can't.*

I wanted so badly to reach across the table and pull her into my lap, but that would hardly help the situation.

"Thank you so much for inviting me to dinner, Ms. Castelli," Adrien said. "The food is fabulous. I haven't had a meal this delicious in months."

"Please call me Sophia." My mother took a sip of her bubbling wine. She was already on her third glass, though that was standard for her.

"It's too bad your parents couldn't make it," I chimed in. But I wasn't sorry at all. In the time I'd gotten to know Emilie, I had started to loathe her parents. They sold her off to the highest bidder, and after she was taken captive and held hostage for months, living through the worst atrocities, they couldn't be bothered to make an appearance for her. They could rot in hell for all I cared.

Adrien nodded. "Yes, well, Father is busy running things and Mother couldn't handle the trip to Renoa on her own."

"Yes, the travel must be very difficult. Far worse than spending months locked in captivity, enduring abuse and things you couldn't imagine in your worst nightmares."

My mother coughed, and Emilie sucked in a breath. Immediately, I regretted my outburst. I rarely lost my temper, but it enraged me to see Emilie treated like an inconvenience rather than the goddess that she was.

"Apologies," I said. "I'm sure they'll visit another time when it's less troublesome."

Emilie's fork scraped across her plate, and Adrien watched her movements with concern.

"You're right—they should be here. There really isn't a good excuse for their absence. I told them as much in my last correspondence." He turned to Emilie and added, "I really am sorry."

Emilie forced a smile that disappeared as quickly as it came. "It's all right."

Adrien sighed. "It's not. But maybe they'll visit again soon when the wedding preparations continue. You know how much Mother loves that kind of stuff. She won't miss a chance to give you her opinion," he said with a soft chuckle.

An unsettling stillness fell over the table.

Emilie neatly placed her fork next to her plate while my mother's glass froze halfway to her lips.

I held my breath while I waited for someone to speak. This was Emilie's brother, and she should be the one to decide how and when he learned about us. I was ready to support her if she decided now was the right time.

But as the pink hue drained from her cheeks, I questioned whether I should step in to save her. I tried tapping her foot again underneath the table, but she didn't acknowledge me. It seemed she was tangled in her own thoughts.

I leaned down, hoping to catch her eye, but my movement only invited Adrien's attention. He followed my gaze, and his expression turned inquisitive. "What's wrong?"

My mother cleared her throat and drank from her glass again. There was hardly anything left, but she continued to sip slowly.

"Emilie," I said in a low voice.

She didn't look at me. Her eyes remained fixed on the plate in front of her while her chest rose and fell with strained breaths.

Afraid that she was about to have a panic attack, I rose from my chair, but that was the moment she finally looked up at me. She licked her lips and blinked away her unfocused expression. When she nodded at me, I took it as my cue to sit back down.

"What's happening?" Adrien asked, eyes flitting between the three of us.

Emilie took a few breaths, and I swore I saw her shoulders tremble, but she opened her mouth and calmly said, "The engagement is off."

"What do you mean? Why? Is Cyrus—"

"Cyrus will be fine," I said, coming off more defensive than I meant to.

Emilie covered her mouth with both hands, clearly stunned by her own confession.

Adrien leaned over to put his arm around her shoulders. "Hey, what's happened? Whatever it is, it'll be okay, Emilie. Tell me and I'll do whatever I can to fix it."

I couldn't help myself. The words were out of my mouth before I could stop them. "This doesn't need fixing."

Adrien looked at me, shaking his head in confusion. "*What* doesn't need fixing? Someone tell me what I'm missing here." He lowered his voice and turned back to Emilie. "You can tell me. Do you need me to help you out of Renoa? Did they do something?"

I scowled. He was only being a protective older brother, but I didn't like where his imagination had led him. I would never do anything to harm Emilie, nor would my mother.

Emilie shook her head. Then, with some hesitation, she turned to face her brother. Her voice was unwavering when she said, "I'm not marrying Cyrus because I'm in love with Ladon."

Chapter Five

Emilie

"That was awful. Could that have gone any worse?" I asked, pacing in front of the massive window in Ladon's bedroom. I ran my hands down my face before reaching behind my head and pulling my hair back into a bun. My skin crawled with the lack of control I felt, and I needed to get the hair off my neck.

"Adrien didn't take it that badly," Ladon said, kicking off his shoes and flopping down on the couch in front of the fireplace.

"He just sat there like I'd told him... I don't know... like I'd told him I was disowning the family. You don't know him like I do. Trust me, he was in shock. Maybe denial too."

My brother always spoke his mind. The fact that he'd been stunned into silence was alarming. If he took the news this poorly, how would my parents react?

I inched closer to the bar cart in the corner of Ladon's room and traced a finger over the top of each bottle. One caught my eye—a tall blue one with elaborate white lines swirling around the base. I picked it up and twisted the top.

Ladon's voice rumbled in warning. "That's strong."

"And?" I asked. I could hear the petulance in my tone, but I didn't care. I needed something to numb this feeling.

"Am I going to be carrying you to your bedroom?"

I shrugged my shoulders and tossed the lid aside.

"Emilie," he cautioned. "You don't want to do that."

"You can't tell me what to do."

"Technically, I could. I am king for now. My castle, my rules, princess." From the corner of my eye, I saw his smirk. He knew I loathed the idea of being obedient to him or anyone else.

But something else bothered me even more. *Princess.* That cursed nickname he'd given me months ago that had turned into something endearing. But it wasn't a proper title. It never had been. I was supposed to be a queen next to Cyrus, and now I was nothing.

I frowned and busied myself, looking for a glass to pour the alcohol into.

"What's wrong?"

I bit my cheek and ignored him, hoping he would drop it.

I should've known better.

His hand brushed the small of my back, and I let out a heavy sigh. "You're right."

Ladon cocked his head to the side, his silver eyes watching me carefully.

"I'm completely powerless. You could command me to do anything, and I would have to obey. Because I'm not a princess and I'm not a queen-to-be. I'm nothing."

Ladon shook his head. Slowly, he lowered to the ground, kneeling in front of me. He took my hands in his and let his head fall back, looking up at me through his dark lashes—a sight that took my breath away.

"What are you doing?" I asked, suddenly nervous.

He gently twisted my wrist and pressed his lips against my pulse, against the white scars that marked my skin. His eyelids fluttered closed, and somewhere in my belly, a pool of warmth and aching desire formed.

He hummed, and the vibration almost brought me to my knees with him. "You might not be royalty, Emilie, but you are my deity. You're the only thing I believe in."

The pale moonlight kissed his sharp cheekbones and twinkled in his eyes. I pulled my hand free and ran my fingers through his soft hair, pushing it back so I could see his face properly. He was so strikingly handsome—godlike, even. He leaned into my touch, eyes never straying from me.

Reaching for the liquor again, I drank straight from the bottle. Ladon watched with unwavering interest. It was strong but invigorating. It tasted like lightning and ice—the kind that was so cold, it led to frostbite in seconds.

He took the bottle from my hand and raised it to his lips. Those lips caressed the bottle in a way that made me jealous. Made me want to rip the glass away and replace the space with my mouth. My tongue.

Did he know how difficult he made it to stick to my boundaries? When I told him we couldn't be intimate until Cyrus was well again, I hadn't realized how badly I would miss his touch. I thought since I'd been deprived of it for my whole life, it couldn't be that bad.

But it was. Every day that passed made it harder to resist him. I longed for him. To be close to him. To give him every piece of me.

Maybe it was my attraction to him. Or maybe it was because Ladon was the cure for my dark thoughts. He was like a drug to dull the ache in my chest. No one understood the ever-present grief and heartache like he did.

I grabbed the bottle and took another long drink, shivering as the liquid burned down my throat and into my chest.

"Emilie..." he said, still watching me with reverence.

Rising to his feet, he tried to take the bottle, but I clutched it to my chest. Then I took another sip. I wasn't a drinker, and it probably wouldn't take long to dull my senses and inhibitions.

"I don't think this is a good idea."

Shrugging, I walked past him, taking another sip as I went. I let the burn simmer before I responded, "Maybe I don't want to make good decisions tonight. Maybe I want to be carefree."

I placed the bottle on the end table next to his plush couch. Before I could doubt myself, I grabbed the hem of my sweater and pulled it over my head, revealing a thin satin sleeveless top underneath. My skin was flushed already, but I picked the bottle back up and drank once more.

"Are you going to stand there and watch or are you going to join me?" I asked, settling onto the couch and leaning against the armrest.

Ladon hesitated, and I tried not to take it personally. It was my own fault for telling him one thing but leading him in another direction with my actions.

"Ladon," I said when he didn't move.

He cleared his throat and took a step toward me. "I'm coming."

The liquor emboldened me. "Not yet."

Ladon paused, and his lips curved into a playful smirk. He came around the couch and took a seat next to me, pulling my feet into his lap. "Give that to me," he said, reaching for the bottle.

I handed it over and watched him take another drink. It wasn't lost on me that he chose to set the bottle down on the table at the other end, rather than giving it back to me. Probably for the best since I was feeling the effects already.

I sighed and sank into the plush cushions while he massaged my feet. If I weren't so stressed and aroused, I might've fallen asleep. Instead, I squeezed my legs together as I imagined his hands working on other parts of my body.

Ladon, however, looked calm and relaxed. Unburdened. So different from how I was used to seeing him.

"Tell me something honest," I said.

"You first."

"That's not how this works."

He grinned and continued to squeeze and rub my muscles in all the right places.

"Fine," I said. "I miss your touch."

"I'm touching you now," he said, his voice a low rumble.

"Not how I want you to."

He stopped moving, and I watched his throat move as he swallowed. Then he slowly turned to look at me. "Honestly, princess, I'm not strong enough to tell you no."

A tingling sensation ran through my body, and I sat up, shifting until I was straddling him with my hands locked behind his neck and my core pressed against his groin.

He was patient, frustratingly so. I was used to Ladon being in charge and making all the moves. But he was doing his damnedest to respect my wishes when all I wanted was for him to rip my clothes off and cover me with his body.

His hands slid up my thighs and found a resting place on my hips, which he squeezed gently. I leaned closer until our foreheads touched and my breasts pushed against his chest. I was close enough that I could practically taste the icy liquor on his breath. It was tantalizing—delicious torture.

Wrapping one arm around my lower back, he used the other to cradle my head, bringing his lips to mine. I kissed him, forever crazed by the way our tongues collided and the way he moaned when he bit his lower lip. The sound of my own whimper caught me off guard, and I rolled my hips, aching to feel his hardening cock.

I tasted the liquor on his tongue, but it was nothing compared to *him*. Ladon was by far the most intoxicating thing I'd ever consumed. It had only been a couple weeks, but the withdrawal was unbearable.

I felt his hand slide down my back and grip my ass. The fabric of my pants was frustratingly thick—I would've preferred no barrier at all. He let out an exasperated sigh, and I knew he felt the same.

His lips traveled from my mouth to my neck, and my stomach tightened as he sucked and scraped his teeth over my skin.

"Emilie," he groaned, nipping at my earlobe and ripping a frantic moan from my throat.

I pulled back long enough to remove my satin undershirt, leaving behind a pink lace bralette. The fabric was so sheer, bits of flesh showed through the ornate thread work, and I watched as Ladon's eyes lit up. I cradled his head while he licked his way from my chest to my throat.

"Oh, gods," I breathed.

Wrapping his arms around my thighs, he stood and lifted me, carrying me to the bed. He gently laid me down, but I didn't allow him to pull away. I kept my arms and legs locked around him, keeping him tightly pressed against my body.

He felt so fucking amazing—his powerful muscles, his broad shoulders, his hard cock pressing against the seam of his pants. The only reason I released him was so that he could remove his clothes. I wanted to feel the warmth and softness of his skin, too.

Ladon took his time undoing his belt. He licked his lips and asked, "Are you sure about this? You're not going to regret it?"

I shook my head. "No, I want this. I promise."

"You haven't had too much to drink?"

"I wanted this before I took the first sip."

That confession brought out a soft smile, which he quickly masked. "Okay." Then, in a deeper, more sultry tone, he said, "Take off your clothes."

His command stole my breath, but I sprang into action, unfastening my pants and shoving them down my legs. Then I pulled my bra over my head. Before I could hook my fingers into my underwear, Ladon grabbed me by the ankles and dragged me to the end of the bed.

I sat up and reached for the button on his pants, momentarily distracted when he pulled his shirt over his head. I couldn't resist the urge to run my fingers over his smooth skin, tracing the ridges of his abdominal muscles. He flinched as though he were sensitive to my touch, and perhaps he was. He snatched my hands, placing them flat on his stomach and running them down his body until they caught on the hem of his pants.

Biting my lip, I finished what I'd started and unfastened his trousers, pulling them down his hips until they fell to the floor. Even through his dark gray briefs, I could see the outline of his cock, and it made my mouth water and my core throb.

I had barely touched him when he grabbed my wrist and pushed me back onto the bed. I couldn't help but feel satisfied with his lack of restraint. Whatever hesitation he had before was long gone now.

The weight of his body covered me, and he pinned my wrists above my head, marking me with kisses anywhere he pleased. I was at his mercy, and there was nowhere else I'd rather be. I craned my neck to give him better access. There was something about the way his lips nibbled at my skin that made me spiral out of control.

Ladon rolled his hips, and I whimpered, needing more of him. Needing to feel him inside me. Needing to feel the way his muscles tensed and trembled while he thrust into me.

"Ladon, please."

"Patience, princess."

He released his hold on my wrists and slid one hand between us, into my panties. When his fingers brushed my clit, I ground against his hand and squeezed my eyes closed until I felt him glide through my slick folds.

"Mm," I moaned, tugging my bottom lip between my teeth. I melted beneath him, molding to fit him perfectly.

His fingers eased inside my pussy, and I gasped, nails digging into his triceps. I was certain there would be red crescent marks when I removed my hands, but he didn't show any signs of pain. Or at least, he didn't stop the careful movements of his fingers and his thumb against my clit.

I was so wet and desperate for him that his fingers slid easily in and out of me. He gradually picked up his pace, and just when I was getting close to the edge, he removed his hand, pulling back to stare at me with a flushed face and hooded, lust-filled eyes.

He stopped only to admire me for a moment before his hands glided up my thighs and grabbed my panties, pulling them down my legs in one smooth motion. He dropped his own underwear and gripped his cock, working his hand up and down with slick fingers—slick with my arousal.

The sight made my thighs clench, but they couldn't move far with him standing between my legs. If he didn't do something soon, I would—

Oh. My. Gods.

Ladon thrust inside me with little effort; I was that eager for him. He fell on top of me, bracing his forearms on either side of my head and placing a quick kiss on my lips before he started to rock his hips.

His breath was hot on my ear as he said, "Fuck, Emilie. Do you know how amazing you feel?"

It could only be half as good as he felt, stretching me and creating the most delicious friction between us. He was as deep as he could go, and I still wanted more of him. I dug my nails into his back and closed my teeth around his shoulder. The sound of his sharp inhale made me smile.

Ladon was trying his best to remain in control, but I wanted him feral. So I moved my mouth to the sensitive spot near his jawline, alternating sucking on his neck and his earlobe. His throat vibrated with a groan of approval, and his movements became more frantic. Untamed and obsessed.

Thank the gods.

After a few moments, he pushed off of me, standing once again at the foot of the bed. Then he grabbed my legs, throwing my ankles over his shoulders, and dragged me down until my ass was practically hanging off the mattress. He leaned forward until the backs of my thighs stretched tight, driving inside me repeatedly.

I clutched at the sheets since he was no longer within reach. The new angle and tightness were almost too much—I didn't know it could feel this way.

His eyes bore into me, so focused, as if he were memorizing every curve of my body and every sound I made. It didn't take long before the muscle in his jaw clenched and his eyes rolled back. He groaned as his release ripped through him, his hands gripping my hips while he thrust inside me a few more times.

When he moved a hand between my legs and toyed with my clit, I easily came undone. Panting, I arched my back and clawed at the sheets. Ladon continued to circle my sensitive bud until I was trembling, lost somewhere between ecstasy and torment as he pushed me beyond my limit.

"Ladon," I gasped. With one hand, I reached down and pulled his hand away from my clit.

He chuckled. The deep rumble let me know just how pleased he was with himself. If I weren't half out of it, I would've smacked him for torturing me so.

He slowly eased out of me, and I rolled to my side, scooting up the bed until I could rest my head on a pillow. I must've closed my eyes for a moment because the next thing I knew, Ladon was covering me with a blanket and sliding into bed beside me. He wrapped his arms around my waist and cradled me against his warm chest.

A small voice in my head told me I should get up and return to my room, but what was the point? The boundaries I'd drawn were no longer intact. We'd just had sex, so was it really that bad to sleep in his bed too?

As if Ladon could hear my thoughts, he whispered against my neck, "Don't leave me."

I sighed, and my muscles relaxed. "I wouldn't dream of it."

Chapter Six

Emilie

"Are you sure you can't stay any longer?" I asked, neatly folding my brother's shirts before placing them into a worn leather suitcase. Adrien was distracted, searching the room for a missing item—a locket or a ring or some other piece of jewelry. I hadn't realized he was so interested in such luxury items.

"Adrien," I said, demanding his attention.

"What? Oh, sorry. I can't stay any longer, little sis. My crew has been commissioned for a trip to the east islands, and I can't refuse."

I sighed, disappointed. He'd only been in Renoa for a week, and I wished we had more time to discuss my situation. "Will you be back anytime soon?"

He only half-listened as he pulled up cushions and replaced them haphazardly. "If I have time. You know life on the sea isn't exactly made for leisure."

"I guess." I placed the last of his shirts into his luggage and then moved on to folding socks. Twenty-three years old and he still hadn't learned how to keep his socks in pairs. If he had, he might not be missing half a dozen. "I'm proud of you, you know."

He'd set off for Twin Beacons to appease our parents and build relationships with the troops settled there—allies for when he took over in Dreslen. Imagine our parents' surprise when, a few years later, he wound up with a ship of his own and a loyal crew who frequently took on private commissions for affluent treasure seekers. He hadn't outright defied our parents—he was still making friends with influential people—but I was proud of him for finding his own way.

"Aha!" he shouted, and I nearly jumped out of my skin. I turned to see him clutching a delicate gold chain with an ornate medallion swaying on the end. It looked heavy and gaudy. I'd never seen him wear such a thing.

"That's what you've been looking for?"

His eyes flicked to me and quickly back to his treasure. He slid it into his pocket and shrugged. "It's important to me."

Must've been a souvenir from one of his quests. If he didn't want to share more than that, I wouldn't pry. I knew what it was like to have your privacy invaded.

I returned to folding clothes. After a minute, Adrien flopped on the bed beside me, sending a pile of socks toppling to the floor. I shot him a disgruntled look. "Do you even care if your things are packed properly?"

"Not really. They'll be scattered about my cabin in less than a week. But I do appreciate the effort," he added at the sight of my irked expression.

Giving up, I shoved his suitcase to the side and took a seat next to him. "Fine, just toss everything in a pile and call it a day, then."

"That's the spirit," he said with a wide grin. His carefree attitude was contagious, and I smiled back. "And for what it's worth, I'm proud of you, too."

I narrowed my eyes. "I didn't think you were listening."

"Of course I was," he responded, hand covering his heart like I'd struck him with a dagger. Then he dropped his hand and his false pretense, replacing it with sincerity. "I'm proud of you for making your own decisions. This... *thing* that you have with Ladon—I can tell he makes you happy. I've been watching the two of you this week, and I've never seen you smile so brightly. Not since we were kids, at least."

"Thank you." I didn't hide the tremor in my voice. "You have no idea how much that means to me."

"Someone has to be on your side since you know Mom and Dad won't be. You really should've consulted with me before ruining their hopes and dreams for you."

I laughed. "You know all about that, don't you?"

"I do. You should've heard the way Mother spoke to me when I told her I was leaving Twins Peak. Well, technically she wrote a letter, but I could hear her voice through the angry scribbling."

My shoulders shook with laughter. "I expect a scathing letter myself."

"It would only be fair. Let me know when you do. I'll return as soon as possible, and we can have a bonfire to burn them together."

I lunged forward, and he caught me in a hug. "Thank you. Thank you for everything, Adrien. I don't know what I'd do without you."

Watching Adrien set sail was harder than I expected. I waited on the pier until the white sails melted into the clouds on the horizon, and even after, I stood hugging myself as the wind gently blew my hair around. It was hard to guess when I'd see him again—or if I'd see him again. The seas were unforgiving, especially when he ventured into uncharted waters.

The only reason I backed away from the old wooden pier and back toward the castle was because my stomach growled and I realized I hadn't eaten all day. I'd been so caught up helping Adrien pack that I'd skipped breakfast and lunch.

Servants greeted me as soon as I stepped into the kitchen.

"Miss Emilie, I told you we can bring something to you anytime you'd like. You don't need to come down here."

"That's all right. I—"

Another man interrupted, "We're preparing dinner, and you shouldn't be here. Fires are burning, and people are scurrying about without looking. It can be dangerous. Extra bodies create additional obstacles."

As soon as he finished his sentence, a clatter of dishes in the background proved his point. Two men had just run into each other, and one dropped a pot of steaming water.

"Right," I said with a wince. "Could you just bring up something for me to eat?"

"What will you have?"

"Surprise me."

After a delicious roasted chicken salad and creamy vegetable soup, I grabbed the new daggers I'd bought with my brother and set off for the training field. Most warriors practiced in the mornings, so I had the place almost entirely to myself—exactly how I preferred it.

There were two men fighting with wooden swords on the left side of the field, far away from the targets I needed to use on the opposite side. They didn't even look at me when I walked into the pit. I looked up at the stands, and no one was watching from above either.

My shoulders relaxed, and I took my stance in front of a set of three targets, each varying in distance and size. I warmed up with the one closest to me, and after a few throws, I struck the center with deadly precision and smiled.

I picked up another dagger and flung it at the middle target, hitting an outer ring. It took a few more tries before I was able to hit the center, but I was getting more comfortable with my new daggers. They were a perfect fit for my palm, and the weight felt like an extension of myself. Easy to throw the blade to my intended destination.

When I threw the next dagger at the farthest target, I struck the center on my first try and released a satisfied sigh.

"You're quite the natural at that."

I startled at the sound of Ladon's voice. I hadn't seen him enter the training grounds. "Thank you. Someone once told me to picture the person I hate and let the dagger flow through me. Turns out they were right."

I grinned, recalling the moment he'd taught me to throw, except back then he was throwing daggers at my imaginary face. Now, I was picturing Reyna and every single person who laid their hands on me. I wanted them to pay.

"You had a wise instructor," he boasted.

"True, though he was a bit full of himself."

Ladon looked away, but not before I caught his smile. When he turned back, he was biting his lip, stifling a laugh. He inched closer and noticed the daggers laid out on a stand next to me. Tracing the ornate details and gems, he let out a low whistle. "Did you get some new knives?"

"I did. Adrien and I found them at a shop in town."

"Bluebell's?"

"Might've been. I can't recall the name."

"It's the best place to find weaponry in Renoa—high quality and fair prices. And I would know since they sent the bill to me."

"Oh," I said softly. "I'm sorry if that wasn't okay. I just... Before everything happened, I—"

"Emilie, it's fine." He chuckled. "Regardless of your... agreement with Cyrus, you are still a guest here, and I will make sure you are taken care of. May I?" he asked, picking up one of the daggers.

"Go ahead."

He stepped in front of me and squared his shoulders. With perfect form, he flung the knife toward the farthest target. It landed so close to mine, the clink of the silver handles rang through the air.

"You're a natural," I said.

"No, I've had a lot of practice."

Since that had been the last dagger, I collected the lot of them from the targets and made my way back to Ladon.

I'd been so caught up in practice that I hadn't noticed the field had filled with over a dozen warriors practicing various skills—a trio taking turns with a bow, two pairs engaged in hand-to-hand combat, another couple doing a circuit of conditioning. And then off to the side, six more were standing around and watching... watching me and Ladon.

Immediately my cheeks heated, and I felt sweat running down my neck. Their eyes on me were like pin needles piercing my skin. Every move I made pulled at the wounds, slowly ripping them open until I was completely exposed. Not just my skin, but my muscles and organs. My bones.

I shivered and lost my footing, stumbling until I fell into Ladon's outstretched arms.

"What's wrong?" His voice was laced with panic, but I didn't know what to say. I didn't know how to tell him that the world was closing in on me. That I couldn't handle their penetrating glares.

"I think I'm going to be sick," I said, seconds before I doubled over and expelled my lunch.

Dropping to my knees, I felt Ladon lower beside me. His hand stroked my spine while the ground disappeared from my sight. It faded in and out, and I reached for him—reached for anything that would ground me and stop the world from spinning.

"It's going to be okay," he said, pulling my hair back while I continued to heave. "I'm here, princess. I'm here."

I wasn't sure how much time passed before my vision cleared. At some point, the vomiting subsided, and I found myself cradled in Ladon's lap. When I saw him clearly, his eyes were glistening—the silver blue almost completely consumed by black. The color in his cheeks had disappeared too.

"Hey," he said quietly. "Are you with me?"

I nodded, still queasy. I was afraid of what might come out if I opened my mouth. Although my body trembled with weakness, I found the strength to summon a light breeze, cooling me down and making it easier to breathe.

Finally, I sat up with Ladon's help.

"I don't know what happened. I just saw those people staring..."

The crowd of warriors were no longer looking in our direction, and I half-wondered if they ever were or if I imagined the whole thing.

Ladon followed my gaze and shot them daggers with his eyes anyway. "I can tell them to get lost."

"No, it's okay. I can't go through life demanding everyone to clear the room when I'm around."

"You could," he said with a half grin.

I found his hand and brushed the back of it with my thumb. "I don't want to."

He held me tighter, and if it weren't for the audience, I would've let him hold me forever. I dared to take another peek at the others training in the pit, and none of them were looking in our direction.

Sometimes, the memories felt more intense than living through the ordeal. It was as though my body knew I was safe now and therefore free to fall apart.

"Are you going to be okay?" he asked. "You know you can talk to me. If anyone understands, it's me."

"I know," I said, brushing dirt off my pants. We both stood, and I could tell he wanted to keep me close and be my support, but he gave me the space to stand on my own.

"You scared me," he admitted.

I had scared myself. I hated the feeling of disorientation, hated being taken back to that time and place when dozens of eyes were on me as I lived my worst nightmares.

We made it out. We were supposed to be safe and happy now, but the past still haunted us. It lingered like an unwanted shadow, darkening our brightest moments.

Pain tinged Ladon's voice when he spoke. "It brought me back to that first day in Murvort—the hedge maze. Do you remember?"

I wished I didn't. I remembered waking up in a fog-filled path lined with hedges. We ran from the beasts that chased us, but ultimately they won.

"I thought you were going to die in my arms that day," he continued. "You were in so much pain, and I could see the life fading from you."

I'd never asked what that was like for him. I remembered the pain of the venom from Reyna's snake, Vessina. The excruciating fire that ran through my body when her fangs sank into my skin. But everything after was hazy—I never asked what happened next.

"I swore I'd do anything to protect you," Ladon said softly. "To save you."

I didn't have to ask why. He might've hated me back then, but Ladon had never been a monster. He was heroic even when he didn't set out to be. It was in his nature.

"The amount of relief I felt when Reyna threw me that antidote... It was indescribable. Half of me wondered if it would even work, but I had no choice. You were seconds away from death, and I had no other options."

Something flickered in the back of my mind, like a long-lost memory trying to break through. "I was unconscious."

Ladon nodded. "That's right. You were barely hanging on."

"I was unconscious," I said again, a little louder and with more resolve. "Ladon, I was poisoned but still alive."

Just like Cyrus. It couldn't be a coincidence. How many varieties of poison did she have that resulted in the same condition?

"Yes," he said slowly, staring at me like I was about to have another breakdown. He hadn't made the same connection I did.

"Don't you see? I was unconscious. Cyrus is unconscious. Cyrus has been poisoned with Vessina's venom."

Chapter Seven

Ladon

I couldn't believe the solution was so simple. "I thought the harpy said it couldn't be Vessina's venom. That it was lethal, and those who were poisoned would've died within minutes."

"Did she?" Emilie's excitement deflated. "Right. I think I vaguely remember Selene saying something like that."

"It was one of the first things we considered. After all, Vessina's venom would've been the easiest to access."

Emilie tapped her index finger against her lip, lost in thought. I hated to disappoint her, but there was no way it was going to be that easy. She didn't give up easily, asking, "What if there was an additive? Something to slow down the effects?"

I sucked on my teeth. "It's possible. Anything is possible, but that doesn't make it likely."

"It still makes the most sense," she argued. "The key has to be something within Reyna's estate. She wouldn't keep a lethal concoction on hand without the antidote."

She was onto something there, but the conclave wouldn't send us into Murvort without concrete evidence.

"Do you recall seeing any greenhouses or gardens on the property? Other than the hedges?" she asked.

I shook my head. "Why?"

"I was thinking of possible herbs or plants that can be used to slow or dampen poison. Something like borealis root or pyxis balm."

Both were incredibly rare. For once, though, luck was on our side. "I don't know which Reyna had on hand, but we do grow borealis root in our greenhouses."

Emilie's eyes lit up. "Really? I don't know why I didn't think to check before. I just assumed since it isn't native to Lourova that you wouldn't have any. That will certainly make things easier."

I had a hard time not getting wrapped up in her optimism. "I'll summon the advisors immediately, and we'll make our way to Murvort."

Even speaking those words sent a shiver down my spine, and maybe that was why I'd been so reluctant to admit that Vessina's venom made the most sense. The idea of traveling back into enemy territory threatened to suck the air from my lungs. But Cyrus's life depended on it.

"Just like that?" she asked.

"We'll send a message ahead to let them know we're coming, but yes. I won't waste another day letting my brother rot in that bed."

Emilie seemed surprised that it would be so easy, but as Regent, I could do whatever I wanted. For once, I reveled in that.

True to my word, I left the training field and Emilie behind. I ordered the first servant I saw to round up the advisors and have them meet me in the King's Post for an emergency conclave. He ran ahead, and by the time I made it up the four flights of stairs, half the seats were filled. After waiting a few more minutes, the rest were occupied too. Conveniently, most of the advisors had been nearby when I called the meeting.

I began without fanfare. "I need a convoy to travel to Murvort."

Nervous glances were exchanged around the table, and Nicola was the only one brave enough to speak. "Your High... uh, sir. What would be the purpose of this excursion?"

"I believe the cure for Cyrus's ailment lies within Murvort's boundaries." More uneasy glances followed. I cleared my throat. "Reyna had a venomous snake—one that I've seen in action. Her poison can cause the victim to fade into unconsciousness, but there is a cure."

"Why wasn't this mentioned before?" Nicola asked.

"The idea was previously ruled out, but we've reconsidered and believe it to be the most viable solution."

"What changed?"

I explained what Emilie and I had discussed, and our conclusion.

Marco, a brown-skinned, middle-aged man with short black hair, nodded in agreement. "With the right ingredients, you could be onto something." He had a background in alchemy and held a decent amount of knowledge in concocting antidotes, so he would know. "And this snake... Could you identify it?"

"She was like nothing I've seen before. Certainly not native to Lourova. She was twenty feet long and had scales as black as night. Even her eyes were like shadows, and she must weigh thrice as much as I do. She would be hard to miss."

Marco nodded while a few others looked like I'd described their worst nightmare. Fear of snakes was common, but Vessina was on another level. She could paralyze a person using sheer terror.

"I'd like to join the convoy, if you don't mind," Marco said.

"Of course. I'd consider you an asset to the team." He was the only one to volunteer, but I wasn't surprised. The others were too comfortable with their pampered lives in Renoa.

"How many more will you need?" Xavier asked.

"A dozen," I said. Any more would be seen as a threat. I hoped to move into Murvort without an altercation, but I also didn't want to travel with any less. Not after our last incident at Fort Malek, which had ended in the capture of Emilie and me. "Can we spare them?"

Xavier made some mental calculations, and after a moment of deliberation, he gave me a curt nod. "Yes, but I am going with you."

"That's not necessary. I need you here."

"Sir, I insist. This is a dangerous mission, and you'll need the best of the best to protect you."

"I'm very well aware of the stakes, Xavier, which is why I need you here. Cyrus is compromised, and if something happens to me and the crown passes to my mother, she's going to need stability. I need *you* to step up and protect her and this realm."

His throat bobbed as he swallowed, and his brows pinched together. He looked like he wanted to argue further but thought better of it, probably realizing that I was right. I needed him in Renoa more than I needed him by my side.

"I will be okay," I assured him.

Finally, he nodded. "I will send a dozen of our best warriors to accompany you."

"Perfect. If there are no other questions or concerns, then everyone is dismissed."

My next stop to prepare for the journey back to Murvort was tucked in a private corner of the healer's ward. I didn't have to ask where my mother was holed up. I already knew she was still by Cyrus's side.

When I entered his room, her eyes met mine. "What is it?" she asked, clearly sensing a change in me. She stood slowly, as if her body had gotten too accustomed to her chair and struggled to leave it.

"It may be nothing," I said. "But we have a lead... for Cyrus."

Relief poured over her face, and she clutched her chest. "Thank the gods. Then why do you look as though someone died?" Her hand twisted in the fabric of her skirt, and I couldn't help but notice how clearly her bones protruded around her wrist and fingers. I wasn't the only one who'd lost weight over the past few months.

"Maybe you should sit," I suggested.

She frowned but returned to her chair, sitting on the edge while she waited for me to speak.

It was harder than I expected to get the words out. They seemed to stick in my throat. Was this what it had been like when Cyrus informed her that he was going to rescue me? One son in exchange for the other?

But that wouldn't happen this time. We would both come back to her.

"We think Cyrus was poisoned with the venom from a snake," I began, "and that an antidote exists for that venom."

"Well, that's good news. I understand you'll need to vet this lead before we celebrate, but this is... this is something," she said, cautious but hopeful. "We haven't had anything to go on in weeks. Why are you so nervous?"

"Because the cure lies within Murvort. And I will be going back."

I tried to swallow the lump in my throat as horror overtook her expression.

"Absolutely not."

"Mother—"

"Absolutely *not*." She stood and reached for me, wrapping her hands around my arms and giving me a shake. "Listen to me—you are not going anywhere near that hellscape ever again. You're staying here, safe with me. You are not to leave my sight *ever* again."

"Mother," I said softly. "I'm not a child, and you can't stop me from going. You need to trust me. Trust that I can do this and revive Cyrus. I'm going to put this family back together again. Okay?"

Tears welled in her eyes, and her bottom lip quivered. "No. *No.*"

Before her tears could streak down her face, I pulled her into a hug. "I'll be okay. I promise."

Xavier rounded up a dozen warriors in record time. After a restless night's sleep, I met them at the castle gate, where they loaded the horses with enough supplies to last us two weeks. The trip to Murvort shouldn't take more than a couple days, but I wanted to be prepared for any delay.

Given the early hour, the only people gathered at the gate were the warriors to accompany me, a handful of servants, Xavier, and my mother. For once, I wished she'd stayed in the healer's ward. Saying goodbye would be even harder than informing her of the mission.

"Everyone is ready and accounted for, sir," Xavier informed me.

"I appreciate you working so quickly to get this group of soldiers together. And fetching fourteen horses, too."

"Fifteen," he corrected.

I shook my head. "Twelve soldiers, Marco, and me—we only need fourteen." Hopefully he didn't plan on tagging along. I'd already stressed the importance of his staying in Renoa.

"And me," a voice like a song said from behind one of the horses. Emilie appeared, wearing leather pants that fit her like a glove, heavy boots, and a top with the long sleeves pushed up to her elbows. It would get cooler the closer we got to Murvort, but it was a pleasant morning in Renoa.

"No," I said plainly.

She quirked her head and narrowed her eyes. "What do you mean, no?"

"I mean, you are not coming."

Xavier shifted uncomfortably. "I'm sorry, sir. I thought you knew and had approved this."

"I don't need his approval," Emilie growled. Why did her attitude make my heart skip a beat? My brain immediately sensed it as an opportunity to push back until she snapped. I'd probably never get over the excitement of getting under her skin.

Xavier excused himself, and I moved closer to Emilie. Hidden between two horses, I reached up and tucked a piece of wavy hair behind her ear, then cupped her face. "Is there any point in my begging you to stay here where you'll be safe and I won't need to worry about you?"

"I think you know me better than that."

I did, but I'd had the tiniest sliver of hope that she might listen for once. "Fine, but stay close to me." When she gave me a look, I added hastily, "For protection."

She grinned. "For protection? Not because you enjoy my company?"

I chanced a glance around and, finding no one near, I said, "That too."

A short time later, our convoy was packed and ready to set off. Two warriors led the way while Emilie and I rode in the middle, with more warriors to our sides and following behind us.

Renoa was still quiet as we rode through the empty streets. Only a few lights illuminated the shops as the workers inside prepared to open. Farther away, stores gave way to houses of varying sizes but all in the same shade of sandstone. Doors and window shutters painted in bright shades of blue, green, and red broke up the sea of beige. That and the colorful flowers and trees planted between houses.

Slowly, the houses became scarcer until we crossed the bridge that marked the end of the city border. Here, in the cool morning air and wide-open space, a shiver ran down my back. It finally hit me we were returning to Murvort—something only an insane man would do.

My throat closed, and I loosened my jacket around my neck. Counting my breaths, I focused on the path ahead of me. On the sound of my horse's unhurried trot. On the pinks and oranges melding into blue with the rising sun. Anything but the mountains in the distance and the nightmares within.

I felt Emilie's presence and her gaze on me.

"I can't believe we're doing this," I muttered. We didn't have a choice, though. Cyrus's life depended on it, and he would've done it for me. He *did* do it for me, and my love and allegiance to him would keep me moving forward.

"We'll get through it," Emilie said just as softly. "She's not there. She can't hurt us."

"A shame she isn't. I could kill her and save my brother in one trip."

That earned a slight chuckle from Emilie, and I finally looked at her. The warm glow illuminated her skin, and her freckles were like sparkles across her cheeks and nose. Her eyes glistened as she studied me. "So is the new leader..."

"Jesse Holden."

"Right. Does he know we're coming?"

"Yes, I sent a messenger falcon ahead. He's been informed of our arrival, and I expect he will send a convoy of his own to meet us at the border."

"Oh?"

I nodded. "Can't let us run amok in his territory, now, can he?"

"Right…"

Silence filled the air, and I resisted the urge to fill it. I was curious about what else was running through her mind—if she was struggling like me—but I wouldn't push her if she wasn't ready to talk about it.

"What if he's worse than Reyna?" she finally whispered.

"He isn't." No one could be. "The Holdens have opposed Reyna for years."

"Is that enough to trust them?"

"No," I admitted. "But we also know their focus is on stabilizing Murvort. And if we can help, financially or otherwise…"

"Then they'll have reason to meet with us and give us whatever we ask for."

"Exactly."

I gave her a reassuring smile, but she seemed lost in thought. If only there were something I could say to ease her doubts, but everything was uncertain. My decisions were based on limited information, and I could only hope for the best. What other choice did we have?

Emilie and I took turns distracting one another during the otherwise dull ride. We stopped only once for a quick meal and to relieve ourselves before we carried on. Although we were safe within Osavian's boundaries, we still didn't want to travel at night. The closer we got to the border, the larger the mountains appeared—like giant beasts looming over us.

The sun was low in the sky by the time I caught sight of a structure in the mountain's shadow—Fort Malek. Its towers stood tall above the trees, and Osavian flags whipped in the wind on the tallest turrets.

Beside me, Emilie sucked in a breath. The reins slipped an inch in my sweaty palms, and I gripped them tighter. Visions swirled through my mind of the night Emilie and I had been taken. We were ambushed in Fort Malek after walking into a trap with bodies strewn about the entire place. It was the grisliest scene I'd ever encountered, and I'd seen a lot as High Commander.

The fort had been restored and the bodies laid to rest, but I could still feel the presence of their ghosts. Every life lost was personal to me. They were all reminders of my failure to keep them safe.

My failure to keep my brother safe... to keep Emilie safe...

Turning to face her, I noticed she'd gone pale. Was she even breathing? I nudged my horse closer to her. "Are you all right?"

Her lips pressed into a thin line, and she nodded.

"We don't have to stay inside the fort," I told her.

"Where else would we go?"

"We can set up a camp outside the walls. Have a couple guards rotate watch overnight." I didn't care if it made us look weak or silly. I'd do it if it made Emilie more comfortable.

She shook her head. "No, I think it's best we stay inside. It'll be practice for Murvort."

"Practice?"

"You know... entering the gates of hell will be so much worse than residing in an Osavian fortress for a few nights. If I can't survive this, then I have no business stepping foot into the territory of Murvort, let alone Reyna's estate in the mountains."

"I hadn't thought of it that way."

"So we'll stay inside," she said resolutely, her chin held high. It almost brought a smile to my face, but a cool breeze ran across my skin, and I swore it was the ghosts of those lost souls telling us to turn back.

I wouldn't. It might cost me my sanity, but I would save my brother one way or another.

Chapter Eight

Emilie

"It looks different than I remember."

Ladon's response was one of bewilderment. "Gods, I should hope so, Emilie."

It was clear I wasn't the only one thinking of the mutilated bodies covering the ground the last time we journeyed to Fort Malek. The welcome hall was almost unrecognizable now. Candle-filled chandeliers hung from the ceiling and cast the room in a warm glow. The dusty stone floor was a mixture of grays and browns, vastly different from the pools of crimson red I remembered.

Long tables were arranged in what had probably been neat rows at one point, but now they were pushed out of place and slightly crooked. Soldiers gathered around and talked loudly in groups. Some had pints in their hands while others were fixated on their dinner plates.

"This is where a lot of us hang out when we're not on duty," Ladon said as we approached the front of the hall. Some turned our way, acknowledging Ladon with a respectful bow of their heads, and I recalled that Fort Malek had been his home before my arrival in Renoa. Though he'd been absent for some time, he was their High Commander and perhaps even their friend on some level.

"Have you missed this?" I asked. I couldn't help but notice that some of the women here were quite beautiful. It wouldn't surprise me if he'd had relations with any of them. And yet, it was hard to feel any type of jealousy. None of them would ever share the bond that Ladon and I did.

Then there were the men. Surely some of them were friends with Ladon. I could easily picture him sitting at a table late in the evening, playing games and passing time. I wished I could've seen him back then, but perhaps I'd get a glance into his old life while we were here.

"Sometimes," Ladon said, pulling me from my thoughts. "I miss being on my own and not in my brother's shadow. And I love my mother, but some days it feels like I'm still a child with her around. I miss my independence, I guess."

"That's understandable." I chuckled. "The day my parents left me on my own in Renoa was one of the best days of my life, I think."

Ladon smiled and held back a laugh. I wondered if he was picturing that day like I was. It was the same day we'd trained together for the first time. Back when he was more likely to strangle me than embrace me. I had felt on top of the world until Ladon brought me down several notches. If that version of me could see myself today, she'd be in absolute disbelief to find I'd fallen for such a man.

We were almost at the front of the room when he spoke again. "What I miss the most is feeling competent. I was *good* at my job. Now, I feel lost every single day. Being a faux king is draining me. I'd give anything to feel like myself again."

And I'd give anything to reach out and squeeze his hand, but people were watching. I had a hunch that his identity crisis went beyond his temporary title. Living post-Murvort was like a foggy dream. Everything felt surreal, like this version of us only existed in my mind and I was still locked inside that mountain. Like everything that had happened since was just my brain's way of coping.

Was any of it real? Was this gathering hall real?

I clenched my fists so hard that I left crescent-shaped marks on my palms. The pain was sharp, but it didn't linger.

This was real.

I wasn't sure how long it would take for either of us to feel normal again—if normal was even possible—but I could see why returning to his old routine and home here in Fort Malek might be tempting. My life had been uprooted before our captivity, so normal was far beyond my reach.

My attention turned to the front of the hall, where three individuals sat at a long table on a raised platform. A massive circular wooden carving adorned the wall behind them, stretching at least four feet in diameter. The details were intricate and awe-inspiring, and it appeared to tell the history of Fort Malek. There were hordes of soldiers and battle scenes depicted. One corner had a sequence that started with the base of Fort Malek being laid—bare bones and simplicity—and moving forward in time until it became the massive infrastructure it was today. There were so many stories woven into the wood that I didn't want to tear my eyes from it.

But when the fiercely beautiful woman with dark skin and cunning eyes in the center stood up and spoke, I was forced to give her my attention.

"Well, you are a sight for sore eyes. Welcome home, Ladon."

"Aubrey," he said, taking a step closer and grasping her hand over the table. "I hope you haven't gotten too comfortable in my seat."

Her serious demeanor morphed into a wide smile, displaying perfect white teeth. "Just keeping it warm for you, sir." After releasing his hand, she pushed her hair, woven into dozens of long braids, over her shoulder and took a step to the side. The other two soldiers followed suit, making room for Ladon and everyone else in our traveling party.

Once seated, a few servers came out from behind a side door and set plates in front of us. Steam rose, and with it came the scent of butter, garlic, and other spices. My mouth salivated at the sight of a steak the size of my palm and roasted potatoes. A few of the soldiers closest to us craned their necks to see our meals, and from their frowns, I assumed we were being given special treatment. It was highly unlikely steak was served regularly to the fifty or so soldiers who were stationed at Fort Malek.

"Could you bring out the mead as well?" Aubrey asked. I had to lean forward to see her on the other side of Ladon.

"Is this how you use my funds while I'm gone?" Ladon asked, but there was only warmth in his voice.

"You said to take care of the place, and I have," she replied. Her eyes met mine, and she smiled. Reaching over Ladon's plate without a care in the world, she extended her hand to me. "I'm Aubrey, captain here at Fort Malek."

"Do you mind?" Ladon asked. The fork in his hand was positioned dangerously close to stabbing her extended arm.

"I'm Emilie," I said, quickly shaking her hand so she could return her limb to safety.

"Of course. The bride-to-be. I'm surprised to see you've come along on this excursion, but I suppose you're eager to see your fiancé healed."

I swallowed the lump in my throat as my cheeks flushed pink. I had no idea how to respond, so I shoved a bite of potatoes in my mouth instead and simply nodded.

"You didn't mention her in your correspondence," she said to Ladon. "If I'd known, I would've had another room prepared."

"She was a last-minute addition, but don't worry. She can stay in the guest suite next to mine."

Aubrey nodded.

"Speaking of correspondence, have we heard anything from the Holdens?"

"Not yet, though I wouldn't hold your breath. Every message we have sent in the past few weeks has gone unanswered."

"We've made several attempts to negotiate peace at the border since learning that Jesse has assumed power," Ladon said to me in explanation.

Aubrey leaned forward so she could see me. "They don't seem interested."

I grinned. Despite the dire circumstances and harsh conditions at the outpost, and the threat of attack at any moment, Aubrey had a way of putting people at ease.

"This time is different," Ladon said. "I am the one offering to negotiate."

"You think awfully highly of yourself," Aubrey said.

I chuckled, and Ladon shot me a glare. "Traitor," he mouthed.

Throughout the evening, soldiers came and went. Some approached the head table and greeted old friends. Others retired to their rooms for the evening as the hours passed. I had drunk enough mead for the room to spin, but at least I could blame my rosy cheeks on the alcohol and not the way Ladon kept sneaking sideways glances at me.

At some point, the tables had been pushed to the sides of the room, and a quartet of soldiers played string instruments and sang loud, drunken tunes while the others danced in wild circles. I watched in a trance. Their happiness was contagious.

"Do you want to dance?" Ladon asked.

"No." I huffed a laugh. The last thing I wanted to do was spin around like a fool and have everyone stare at me. I preferred to stay out of the spotlight. When I turned to look at Ladon, he was studying me with an unreadable expression. "Why? Do you?"

I didn't take him for the dancing type, but perhaps I didn't know everything about him.

He laughed and shook his head. "No, but I thought it would be impolite not to at least ask. Whenever you're ready to turn in for the night, let me know. I'll show you to your room."

I didn't tell him that I'd rather stay in his room, though it was my first thought. It would be highly inappropriate if anyone saw us together, and it went against our agreement to remain friends until Cyrus was healed. We'd failed to uphold that oath once already, and I had no intention of making it a habit.

I brought my heavy glass to my lips only to find that I'd drank the last drop. Setting it back down, I turned to Ladon. "I'm ready now."

Ladon led me out of the gathering hall, into the fresh night air and through a covered walkway. He opened another door and waved for me to enter first. It was dimly lit and lacked any notable décor, nothing like the grandness of the castle in Renoa.

It matched Ladon's personality. He was far more practical and indifferent to the luxury that Renoa offered. This place just *fit* him somehow.

We walked in quiet down a long, narrow hall and made a turn down a shorter, connecting corridor.

Ladon pointed at the door to my right. "That's yours."

He handed me a small brass key, and I fit it into the lock, pushing the door open to find a simple room with dark wooden floors and navy-blue walls. There was a single window with a long crack down the center that distorted the otherwise beautiful night sky. The furniture was limited to the essentials—a bed, a nightstand, and a dresser—but at least the bed was adorned with a thick comforter and plump pillows.

My bag rested on top of the bed; someone must've delivered our belongings while we ate dinner. I was eager to change into something comfortable so I could succumb to my exhaustion.

"There's a bathroom at the end of the hall. Unfortunately, only one room has a private bath," Ladon said.

"Let me guess—yours?"

He smirked. "You're more than welcome to use it if you'd like."

Then he crossed the room and casually leaned against the wall opposite my bed.

"What are you doing?"

His lips curved into a mischievous grin. What had gotten into him? Was he hoping that if he stayed long enough, I'd invite him into my bed? That something more might happen?

Or was he afraid of being alone? It was nearly impossible for either of us to sleep without the other, but it was a big enough risk to sneak into my room in Renoa. If someone caught him spending the night with me here, there would be more questions than we could answer.

As I stood trying to figure out what he was thinking, a dark outline appeared—two lines starting from the floor and moving upward on either side of him until they curved inward and met at a peak above his head.

As soon as the lines connected, a full door formed behind him.

My jaw dropped. "What is that?"

Ladon pushed away from the wall and laid one hand on the door. It disintegrated just as easily as it had formed, but this time, the wall did not reappear. This time, an opening was left where the door had been, and inside, I could see another bedroom, similar to mine in its simplicity but full of personal belongings. Like someone actually lived there.

"Your room is my guest suite," he said. "The connection is for convenience, but only if I allow it to be used."

Because it would be unwise to give just anyone access to his room, I surmised. The guests he had while on duty in Fort Malek varied from friend to foe, and the last thing he needed was to wake in the middle of the night with a knife held to his throat.

He walked through the doorway, and I followed, curious to get a better look at his bedroom here in Fort Malek. To see what glimpse it offered into the man I'd come to know.

The first thing I noticed was the walls. They were a matching blue to that in my room, but his were covered in paintings. Some were dark and frightening, and studying them made my heart race. Others were warmer, using reds and yellows that seemed to elicit hope and strength. Each of them depicted various scenery—the harsh mountains that bordered Osavian, the beaches back in Renoa, the forests surrounding Fort Malek.

I inspected the one to my immediate right, the brush strokes visible even in the dim light. In the bottom left corner, there were two initials.

L.C.

"You painted all these?" I asked.

Ladon's body slid into position behind me, his hands finding my hips and pulling me into his chest. He kissed the spot below my ear with such gentleness I thought I might melt.

"I did," he whispered.

"I never would've suspected you to be an artist."

I felt him shrug behind me. "These are old. I don't paint anymore."

"Why not?" I asked, spinning in his hold so I could see his face.

He shook his head, and his hair fell loosely over his forehead. "It was an exercise my mind healer gave me to cope with my father's passing. I enjoyed it for a while, but the older I got, the less time I had for it. Most of these I did on rainy days when there wasn't much to do. I honestly can't remember the last time I painted a scene."

"You should start again. You're quite talented," I said. "Have you ever painted people? Or only landscapes?"

Ladon flashed a devious grin that sent heat rushing through my body. "I've never tried to paint someone, but I'd be willing to learn. Are you volunteering to be my muse?"

"What would that require?"

His eyes took a trip down my body and then back up to meet my gaze. "Long hours. Just the two of us. In order to understand the proper proportions, you'd need minimal clothing. Maybe nothing at all."

I couldn't hold back a smile. "Tempting."

He looked at me as if he were ready to get started this moment, but I turned back toward my bedroom. I couldn't get swept up in his cyclone—not yet, at least.

"Emilie," he said from behind me.

I hesitated in the doorway. "Yes?"

"Stay with me."

Chapter Nine

Ladon

THE GATHERING HALL WASN'T nearly as crowded as it had been on the evening of our arrival. This morning, there were only a few soldiers present outside of our travel group. The others were busy with their regularly scheduled duties.

We'd only been in Fort Malek for one day and I was already getting anxious. I was impatient to move on and find the cure to wake my brother, but we were still waiting on a response from Murvort. It was unreasonable to expect them to reply so quickly, of course. Part of me wanted to waltz right into their territory without permission, but that wouldn't help us get what we wanted in the end.

Three dice clattered on the table, one landing right next to my empty plate. Marco and another soldier, Jensen, simultaneously moaned. Emilie held out her hand, and each of them took a turn handing over an item. Marco gave her a small leather coin purse—he'd already given her all the coins that it previously held—and Jensen handed her a pearl-encrusted pendant.

I watched as she cheerfully collected her winnings and slipped them into her pocket. "Do you want to play again?" she asked.

Marco's face fell, and Jensen searched his pockets for anything to wager with, coming up short. Then they made excuses for why they couldn't stay.

"I forgot I'm supposed to be meeting Dax."

"I'm going to grab something to eat."

They fled the table a little too eagerly, and Emilie leaned forward with her elbow on the table and rested her chin in her palm. She looked quite pleased with herself, and I had a hunch there was more to her cheery mood than her winnings.

"I thought you said you'd never played before."

She smiled. "I haven't."

I narrowed my eyes, but she remained firm in her position. "So I'm to believe that you cleaned out their pockets on pure luck?"

Her eyes twinkled in the most mesmerizing way, drawing me in. "I said I'd never *played* before. But I've watched my brother and his friends play many times. They never let me join, but I learned well enough as a spectator."

My brow rose in surprise, and a genuine laugh escaped my lips. "Emilie Duval, did you just hustle them?"

She shrugged. "Is it hustling, or did they simply not ask the right questions?"

"Remind me never to underestimate you."

"I would've thought you already learned that by now," she said with a subtle smirk.

Oh, Emilie. I'd learned a hundred things about her, and I wanted to discover a hundred more.

I shifted closer, leaning into her space. "I have."

Her eyes softened from mischief to something more contemplative, and I would've given anything to be inside her mind. To ask for a single shred of honesty. But at that moment, I glimpsed Aubrey approaching the table with a small envelope in her right hand.

Reluctantly, I put some space between myself and Emilie, and she noticed, peering over her shoulder to find the reason for my retreat.

"Aubrey," I said by way of greeting. "Do you have news for me?"

"A falcon just dropped it off," she said, handing me the letter. I ripped open the seal and let the parchment fall open.

"Well, what does it say?" Aubrey asked before I'd even made it past the first line.

Dear Ladon,

I would be honored to welcome you into my home and discuss important matters regarding our mutual welfare. However, I insist that you limit your entourage to no more than five individuals. I'm sure you understand how delicate our situation is, and we cannot invite discord into our region while we work to strengthen and rebuild. Should you accept these conditions, you will find guides waiting for you at the border near Fort Malek in two days' time.

Sincerely,

Jesse Holden

"He says he'll meet with us." I checked the date on the letter and added, "Tomorrow."

"That's great news," Emilie said.

"But only five can accompany me."

She narrowed her eyes. "That's ridiculous. It's not safe. That was the entire purpose of bringing a dozen with us this far."

I frowned and reread the letter. She was right, but what choice did I have? I couldn't say no, not when Jesse was willing to meet and discuss matters civilly. Saving Cyrus's life was worth the risk.

"You're not seriously going to wander into Murvort with only five soldiers, are you?"

"Three," I replied.

Her eyebrows rose to a comical height.

"I assumed you would want to come with me. And Marco needs to come since we'll need his expertise. So there's room for three soldiers."

"This is insanity."

I nodded. The thought of returning with so few defenses left me on edge; perhaps she was feeling the same way. I lowered my voice. "Are you scared?"

A pit in my stomach told me this was a terrible idea, but I had a habit of ignoring it. It came with the territory of being High Commander. Every decision was one that could lead to fatalities, including my own, so I'd learned to dismiss the foreboding signs and use my head instead.

"I... I'm terrified." She pointed a finger at my chest before I could tell her to stay behind. "But I *am* going."

"You don't have to. If it's too much, you can stay here."

"I'm not staying behind while you walk into enemy territory. I'm not letting you leave my sight."

I glanced around to see if anyone was watching before brushing a lock of hair behind her ear. I couldn't remember anyone ever being so concerned about my wellbeing, except maybe my mother. It was infinitely more adorable coming from Emilie. "I won't leave you behind."

"Is that a promise?" she asked, and the question in her eyes spoke far beyond this instance.

Promise never to leave me behind. Promise to always choose me. No matter the cost.

"I promise."

Our group was ready to go before dawn the next day. The world was eerily still while I waited at the border with Emilie, Marco, and three soldiers—Bianca, Aven and Mira. Our horses were resting, drinking from the narrow stream nearby. The stone bridge ahead of us was the only crossing for miles. It had once connected our two countries, but now it was crumbling and overgrown with weeds.

The journey would take two days, if I remembered correctly. I had been partially out of it after our escape from Reyna's clutches, but I recalled spending at least one night in the mountains before we crossed into Osavian territory.

"How much longer do you think it'll be?" Aven asked, picking at the dirt under his nails. To the untrained eye, he seemed bored, but he was one of my best intelligence soldiers. He had an average build, with some muscle, and he wasn't noticeably tall. His brown hair and brown eyes, with no distinguishing tattoos, scars, or other markers made him blessedly forgettable. He blended in perfectly wherever he went and had a habit of hearing conversations never meant for his ears. He was keen on picking up things others couldn't detect, which is why I had chosen him for this mission.

"We've only been here for fifteen minutes," Bianca replied.

I had to admit I didn't know Bianca well, but Emilie recalled her from the battle we'd fought, and she trusted her. It felt right to give Emilie one more person she could rely on while we both faced one of our worst fears—returning to Murvort.

"They didn't specify a time," I said. "We'll wait all day if we have to."

Thankfully, we didn't have to wait much longer. About half an hour later, leaves began to rustle on the other side of the stream, and we all went on high alert.

"There," Mira said, pointing to a spot straight in front of me.

Squinting, I did my best to find the source of the noise, but the shadows hid our newest visitors well. I shook my head and turned back to Mira. "I don't see anything."

Her hair, so dark blue that it was almost black, was tied into a knot at the nape of her neck, and I could just spot the tip of a tattoo peeking out of her jacket and curling around her ear. She was rough around the edges, but she was reliable and a valuable ally to our mission.

She was an earth wielder like me, and I wasn't too proud to admit that she was much more powerful than I was. Her ability to wield the elements was not limited to dirt and mud. I'd seen her morph stone into a dozen javelins and send them flying with ease.

Before Mira could help me spot the hidden figures, three individuals cloaked in black, masks covering half of their faces stepped out from behind the trees. Moments later, another set of three came out from the left, and three more ventured into view on the right.

They formed a menacing half-circle, and if I hadn't spent most of my life in the military, I might've been intimidated. Since I was the High Commander, I was confident we could take them if necessary.

The person in the center took a few steps forward and lowered their hood and mask, revealing a man with no hair and only gray stubble on his chin. Half his face was disfigured, as though it had been severely burned.

"Ladon Castelli?" His voice had a rasp to it, and I wondered if his esophagus also bore the scars of flame.

I raised my chin and met his gaze. "I am Ladon."

"It's a pleasure to meet you." His eyes moved over our group, counting to ensure I had obeyed Jesse's command for a limited entourage. "If you are ready, follow me."

Before he could fully turn around, I said, "Excuse me. You haven't given me your name."

His expression was blank when he said, "I am nameless."

I exchanged a look with Emilie, and she looked as wary as I did. She licked her lips and donned a brave face, grabbing her bag before moving toward her horse.

The nameless man held up a hand. "You won't be needing those."

"The horses?" Marco questioned.

"Yes. The path will not accommodate such beasts. You'll need to leave them behind."

I sighed. Every second that passed had me questioning this mission. I was only given five accomplices, and now we had to carry on without the horses. The animals would be sorely missed if we needed to flee.

"Fine," I said through gritted teeth. I patted my horse behind her ear and murmured, "Return home."

She may not have understood the words, but she understood my intent. She gave a high-pitched whinny before trotting off, the other horses travelling closely behind, while I crossed the stream with the others to follow the nameless.

It didn't take long to understand why we needed to leave the horses behind. The nameless took a path that was completely unknown to me. Rather than taking the old, abandoned road that connected with the bridge, we immediately veered off the path and into the woods. The pines here were dark, with almost black bark and leaves that ranged from navy to violet before disappearing altogether.

Once the dead trees thinned out, the mountains came into view. The ground turned to stone rapidly, a clear delineation of where the mountain range began.

The nameless trudged between two ridges, heading up at a rapid incline. While I missed my horse, her hooves would've been no match for this marble-like stone. Even I was having a hard time keeping my footing. At one point, Marco began to slip, but Mira quickly transformed the stone beneath him into a perfect step, allowing him to regain his balance. After that, perfect notches appeared in the mountainside that made it easier for us to climb, and I made a mental note to add a bonus to Mira's salary.

We climbed higher and higher, losing track of time. The clouds were heavy over Murvort and made telling time an impossible feat. My toes and fingers were like ice, and I was certain everyone else resented the bitter winds too, though no one complained.

Emilie stumbled in front of me, and I braced her back with my hand. "Are you all right?"

"I'm fine," she said, barely sparing me a glance. Her attention was devoted to the treacherous path ahead, but I kept close behind her.

"We're almost there," the nameless shouted from up ahead.

Almost there? It wasn't possible. Even if we hadn't taken the roads, it was inconceivable that we would be approaching the Lemaire estate.

While I was busy contemplating how we could've accomplished such speed, the ground beneath me evened out, and I stood face to face with a massive slate gray door carved into the mountain.

I moved past my companions until I approached the nameless, prepared to defend the people behind me. "What is this?"

"This is one of the many entrances to the tunnels. As I understand it, you are familiar with such underground routes."

"I am." Although I hadn't realized they extended so far. "How far out are we?"

"The tunnels are a shortcut, but it is still another day of travel until we meet Sir Holden."

My muscles stiffened. An entire day of travel beneath the mountains, wandering the dark caverns that had haunted my nightmares for months. This destination was inevitable, but I thought I had another day to mentally prepare.

Behind me, I felt something, or someone, shift. I knew without turning around that it was Emilie who now stood in my shadow. I could sense her, could feel the comfort of her hand even if she refrained from touching me in front of everyone.

Together. We would do this together.

Chapter Ten

Ladon

I DIDN'T EXPECT THE stone door to swing open—it looked immovable—but that was exactly what happened when two of the nameless threw their full weight against it. Half of the nameless entered first while the others waited for us.

I hated giving them my back, but they didn't give us much of a choice. Aven and Bianca led while Emilie and I trailed behind, Marco and Mira tucked between us.

Once everyone had entered the tunnel, they slowly pushed the door closed. Complete darkness, fell, and Emilie sucked in a sharp breath. While our sight was limited, everything else was heightened. I heard feet shuffling, smelled musty air, and felt a body press into mine. The texture of the hair tickling my chin told me it was Emilie, and I grabbed her upper arm to hold her steady.

A blue light appeared. And then another, and another. With nine mage lamps hanging from the hands of our escorts, I could finally see the space we were in—which wasn't much space at all. The tunnel was roughly five feet wide and less than seven feet tall. If I held my hand up, I could brush the stalactites above my head. I'd have to watch where I was walking since some of them hung low enough to hit my face.

It should've been a relief to get inside, away from the freezing wind, but an inescapable chill settled in my bones within these tunnels. It had only been a few minutes, and I was already desperate to leave.

"What are we waiting for?" I grumbled.

Emilie covered my hand on her arm with her own. Her touch brought a little comfort, but the walls still closed in on me. Thankfully, we moved forward.

The tunnel turned at random, and some sections were wider while others were even narrower. During the narrow parts, we had to file one by one until the tunnel opened up again. It was miserable, and I had to concentrate on my breathing so it wouldn't become obvious that I was suffocating inside these walls. I hadn't decided what to make of the nameless yet, but whether they were friend, foe, or somewhere in between, I wouldn't let them see my weakness.

Periodically, I checked in with Emilie. Knowing how much I was suffering, I had to assume she was too. She frequently reached back for my hand, especially in the sections where we had to walk single file, and I was all too happy to give it to her.

After the last time, I could feel how badly she was trembling, so I didn't let go.

"I've got you, princess," I told her quietly as we shuffled forward.

Eventually, we found ourselves in a cavern large enough for us to sleep for the night. The nameless hung their mage lights on posts that jutted out from the dark stone walls. It seemed this room had been used before, if not frequently.

"This is where we'll stop for the evening," the apparent leader of the nameless told us as he laid out a sleeping sack. My group began to settle into the opposite corner.

"We should take turns keeping watch," Aven said to me, low enough that the nameless couldn't hear. We were still skeptical of Jesse and his henchmen, even if they had agreed to meet with us.

"I'll take the first watch," I said, knowing how unlikely it was that I could ever fall asleep inside these tunnels with strangers by our side.

Despite the damp cold, we didn't light a fire since there was no proper ventilation for the smoke. Without heat to cook, we were forced to eat dried meat and room-temperature broth. My soldiers didn't complain; most were used to the less-than-ideal circumstances.

When it was time to tuck in for the night, I took a seat and rested my back against the wall, perfectly positioned to not only keep an eye on the nameless, but also on Emilie and the others.

Emilie was nestled between Mira and Bianca, her eyes still wide open and staring at the ceiling long after everyone else had fallen asleep.

"Emilie," I said softly, and her eyes flicked to me. "Sleep."

Her chest rose and fell in an effort to relax. She spoke so quietly I could hardly hear her words. "I can't."

It was silly of me to even suggest it, considering I couldn't sleep either. It was hard enough in my own bed, let alone under these conditions. "Try," I urged.

Her eyes fluttered closed, and I don't know how long it took before I heard her even breaths, assuring me that she had finally surrendered to sleep.

Time moved at an agonizing crawl while I tried to think of anything other than the cramped space. The dark depths that led back to our cage. The pieces of ourselves we had left behind...

Gods help us. I was more determined than ever to get inside, grab Vessina's venom, and get the hell out of Murvort before I lost my mind.

Someone stirred, and it shook me from my haunted thoughts. Mira sat up slowly, rubbing her eyes. "What time is it?"

I shook my head. "I'm not sure. If I had to guess, we still have a few hours left before morning. You should try to rest some more."

"Have you been awake this whole time?" she asked, voice laced with concern.

"Yes."

She pulled back the blanket and rose from her mat, approaching me while stretching her limbs. "Take my spot. I've had enough sleep, and I'm happy to relieve you."

"It's fine," I said. "I don't think I'm capable of sleeping right now."

She nodded like she understood, but then she said, "At least try. Tomorrow is an important day, and you need rest. We all do."

I glanced at the spot where she had previously been lying and noticed Emilie clutching the blanket closer to her chest. She was probably missing the warmth on her right side. If I couldn't sleep, at least I could keep her comfortable.

"Thanks," I told Mira. Then I lay down beside Emilie.

I couldn't be nearly as close to her as I wanted, but I slipped my arm under the blankets to hold her hand. Her fingers clenched before she relaxed again, interlacing her fingers with mine. Even though she was asleep, she still somehow knew whose touch she'd found.

It brought me a sense of peace, and I closed my eyes, brushing the back of her hand with my thumb until I, too, surrendered to sleep.

I woke to Emilie's hands gently shaking my shoulders. "Ladon, wake up."

My brows pinched together before I shot up to a sitting position. "What is it? What's wrong?"

"Nothing," she said softly. "We're going to start moving soon. Do you want something to eat?"

I nodded and rubbed the sleep from my eyes. Everyone else was already up and preparing to move. The nameless were standing like statues, and as I took a small bag of nuts and dried berries from Emilie, I wondered if they ever ate. Aside from the one who initially greeted us, I hadn't seen the others remove their masks at any point.

There was little time to consider it before they ushered us out of the cavern. I quickly rolled the mat and helped Mira place it back in her pack. "Thank you," I said as I tied it shut. "I appreciate it."

"Don't mention it."

The tunnel continued to slope downward into an endless abyss. The air seemed thinner down here—toxic, even. But as I looked around, I realized I was the only one having difficulty breathing.

It was just my anxiety taking over. My past coming to haunt me.

Get in. Get the cure. Get out.

I repeated the mantra over and over as we walked through the tunnels.

"How are you holding up?"

I nearly jumped out of my skin at the sound of Emilie's voice beside me. I hadn't noticed her approaching.

"Not great," I admitted.

"Do you need a break?"

"No. I want to get this over with as quickly as possible and get back to Osavian."

"Me too."

I turned to look at her. "And you? Are you doing all right? Are you regretting your decision to come yet?"

My attempt to tease her resulted in a half-smile. "I don't regret anything. I refuse to hide while life passes me by. If I let my fear get the best of me, then she wins. I want my life back."

"I admire your tenacity, Emilie."

She faked a gasp. "Was that a compliment? I didn't know you were capable."

"Only for you, princess. Only for you."

The ground beneath our feet began to slope up, and I stood tall, trying to see the path ahead. It seemed the rough walls were opening up into a larger chamber, and I breathed a sigh of relief. "We must be getting close."

No sooner had I said it than the nameless came to a stop at the front of the tunnel.

It was difficult to see over their heads, but I could just barely make out the top of an arched doorway carved into the stone cave. It was sealed with what appeared to be a massive stone block crudely wedged into the opening. I squinted to see more details, but the two mage lamps beside the door did little to illuminate the entryway.

I listened instead to the rustling ahead of us. The nameless were whispering amongst themselves until suddenly, the ground began to rumble beneath our feet.

Emilie grasped my forearm. "What's happening?"

Before I could answer, the door melted away. It started at the top, sinking lower and lower until I could no longer see it through the gathering of nameless. When the rumbling stopped, Emilie released my arm.

As we crossed the threshold and into the familiar hallways of Reyna's castle, my heart raced and my stomach clenched. I would know no peace for as long as we stayed in the underworld of Murvort.

It looked the same as I remembered—dark, damp, with a chill in the air that reached my bones. Although we were underground, a breeze tickled the hair at my nape and gave me the sense that someone was always watching. Perhaps the mountain itself was observing us, hoping it could tether us, angry that it had ever let us go in the first place.

Reyna no longer walked these halls, but I felt her looming presence regardless. Emilie let out an uneasy breath next to me, and I imagined she could feel it too.

If only I could reach out and take her hand, squeeze it to let her know everything would be all right. I wanted to wrap her in my arms and press her against my chest, kissing the top of her head until her anxiety eased, and mine along with it.

But we weren't alone. And I couldn't claim my heart's desire.

While we walked, a pair of passing figures made me halt in my tracks. The others didn't notice at first, except Emilie who was in tune with my every movement. "Did I see that correctly?"

Her question brought the attention of the rest of our group, but I sought out the leader of the nameless, glaring and pointing over my shoulder.

"Why are they here?" I hissed.

He looked around me to find the two women who had just passed—two maidens with vines covering their bodies. Only the tattoos on their necks were visible, but I'd seen enough of their skin in the pool to know they wrapped around their torsos and limbs too.

My hand crept toward my sword, but the nameless held up his hand. "It isn't what you think."

"Explain."

"We tried to release them. Actually, we practically forced them off the premises, but when we did, they screamed and their bones began to pop. I don't know what curse Reyna put them under, but they can't leave the estate without experiencing immense pain. We're still working on a solution, but for now, they must stay."

I looked back where the two maidens continued to walk, seemingly in peace. The sight of them made me ill, but if he was telling the truth, I couldn't hold it against the Holdens. "Where are they going?"

He shrugged. "I don't know. They're allowed to move freely on the premises. I'm telling you the truth—they are not prisoners here."

I glanced at Emilie, and although she seemed unsettled by the sight of them as well, she nodded. "I believe him. Let's keep going."

Turning back to the leader, I gestured for him to move forward. Eventually, the hallway opened into a large chamber adorned with black pillars carved crudely from the mountain and hanging mage lights from the thirty-foot-tall ceiling. I had never stepped foot in this room before, but I could tell it was a throne room. It was remarkably similar to the one we had in Renoa, although this was darker and had an air of abandonment to it. The lack of any natural light and the mosaic of bones covering the front wall did little to help combat my initial judgment.

At the head of the room, a young man with light olive skin, black hair, and thick brows sat upon a throne. If I had to guess, he was about Cyrus's age. His clothes were as neatly tailored as his facial hair was trimmed. My first thought was that he reminded me of Reyna with his dark hair and contrasting skin, but he had a gentle smile that Reyna could never achieve.

The only other person to accompany him was a woman standing to his left. She was closer to my age—late twenties, with matching black hair and a round face. A scar that slashed through her left brow added to her hardened demeanor. Unlike the man beside her, she wore no kind smile. In fact, she scowled as we approached.

They needed no introduction—Jesse Holden and his sister, Jade.

I stopped, and Emilie halted at my side. I could hear shuffling footsteps fading away as the rest of my company took their places behind me.

The nameless parted and moved to either side of the hall, watching and waiting for a command from their leader. They would observe from the shadows to ensure he remained safe.

I had no intention of hurting him. Not unless he refused to cooperate.

Jesse spoke first. "Welcome to Murvort, Ladon Castelli."

Chapter Eleven

Ladon

"It's actually not my first time," I reminded him, masking the bitterness in my tone.

Jesse frowned. "Ah, I forgot. I'm sorry for your misfortunes. Reyna is despised by many, so rest assured that you are in good company now. *The enemy of my enemy,* or something like that." He gave a small chuckle at his feeble attempt to recall some empty proverb, and it did little to earn my trust.

His sister forced a smile as if she owed him her amusement. It was short-lived, however, and her hawklike gaze returned to me and my companions.

"Well, you know that I am Jesse, and I know that you are Ladon, but please introduce the rest of your party. I would like to know who our guests are."

I cleared my throat and gestured to Emilie first. "This is Emilie, and behind me are Marco, Bianca, Aven, and Mira." As I spoke their names, they each bowed politely. It wasn't necessary, given that Jesse wasn't a king, but we were here to ask a favor. Respect and honor would be given freely until we got what we needed and returned home safely.

Jesse smiled, and it seemed sincere. Then he waved to the woman beside him. "This is my sister, Jade."

She didn't smile. Instead, she tilted her head up and peered at us down the length of her nose.

"She's a woman of few words," Jesse added.

As was I. "Forgive me, but we've come here for a time-sensitive matter, and while I appreciate the—"

"Ah, yes," he interrupted. "You mentioned in your letter that you were seeking Reyna's pet snake. Hideous thing with haunting eyes. A few of us attempted to kill her when we overtook the castle, but the slithery beast managed to escape."

"She's gone?"

Why the fuck were we here if Vessina was gone?

"I didn't say that," he replied. "She fled into the lower chambers of the mountain, and that is where we left her. Sealed away with the other heinous creatures that Reyna loved so dearly."

"Others?" I asked. Her hounds were dead. What other pets did she keep?

Jesse grimaced. "Yes. You didn't know? Reyna enjoyed experimenting with mutations. Her dungeons are full of unnatural beasts—rats with wings, snakes with two heads, that sort of thing. Even worse are the clearly failed experiments. The birds with no legs and felines with unseeing eyes. The cages are full of them."

I shouldn't have been surprised. Reyna was the cruelest person I had ever encountered. "And Vessina is locked away with them?"

He nodded once.

"Show us where," I said, motioning for my team to prepare.

"Not so fast," Jesse said, and for once his sister flashed a genuine smile. "Before we hand over the thing you so desperately desire, I'd like to discuss what's in it for us."

"What do you want?"

"I'm sure you know that most of Murvort lives in poverty. Osavian has cut off almost every trade route in and out of the country. You've threatened the other continents not to align with us. Your kingdom has been bleeding us dry for decades, if not centuries, and I am determined to bring a better future to my people."

"You still have Sage Harbor," I retorted. It was the only point of entry that wasn't heavily guarded by our naval forces, though it wasn't for Murvort's sake. It was only open because of negotiations with the western continent, Wyland, that predated my father's reign.

"You speak of a slow drip when I demand a rainstorm."

I ground my teeth, my patience wearing thin. "What *exactly* are you asking for?"

"I want the eastern and southern borders reopened. At least one into Osavian and Dreslen. And you'll remove your military ships from our shores. I want unrestricted travel for my people. And I want a new trade agreement. My people are starving, and I would see them well fed. Weekly shipments should suffice."

I huffed a laugh. "Is that all?"

"No." Jesse smiled. "I want a new peace treaty."

"Because the last one worked so well?"

There was a reason our trade routes had been decimated and left to crumble. There was a reason our ships were permanently stationed in the eastern sea. Murvort was not to be trusted; they would seize the first opportunity to betray us.

His smile faded. "I am not Reyna, nor am I her father or her father's father. We are entering a new era in Murvort, one that I am determined will bring peace and end the suffering of my people. As an outsider, you've seen very little, and you make snap judgments. You have prejudices against us in Murvort. Perhaps you even think that we deserve to live in such terrible conditions. But I have *lived* it. I didn't grow up in a castle like Reyna. I didn't reap the benefits of everything her family stole from those who live outside the castle walls. The Lemaires took what little we had to save themselves and didn't think once of their constituents. They sacrificed us for their own selfish gains, but that ends with me."

His intentions seemed honorable, but after a lifetime of fighting at the border, I had a hard time trusting them to be true.

"I'd like to believe you," I said. "But even if I wanted to give you everything you're asking for, I do not have that power."

Jesse leaned forward in his throne, hands gripping the armrests as he stared into my eyes. Not with malice, but with frustration, I guessed.

"Are you not the Regent? Acting King of Osavian? I was told King Cyrus inches closer to death every day."

I winced but quickly recovered before Jesse noticed the sting of his words.

"If you can't make these negotiations," he continued, "then perhaps I should visit his warm corpse."

This time, the snarl that escaped my lips was obvious. There was no hiding my distaste for his choice description of my brother's circumstances. "That won't be necessary."

He relaxed back into his seat. "Good. Now, I don't expect you to make a decision immediately. Think it over. Discuss with your advisors. Do what you must, and then we can reconvene at a later date."

My pulse quickened. "We don't have time for that."

Jesse's brow lifted. "You have an answer now?"

My shoulders slumped. I couldn't make such a decision without giving it more than five seconds of consideration. But Cyrus *was* inching closer to death, and we didn't have time to spare. I clenched my fists at my side, counted to five, and then released them. "Give me one day."

"Done." He turned his attention to his sister. "Jade, can you take our guests to their shelter for the evening?"

Emilie and I shared a quick glance as visions flashed in my mind. A brief recollection of the last time we'd been led to our lodging within these borders—a prison cell.

"We're not staying *here,* are we?" I asked, doing my best to hide my discomfort.

Jade was the one to answer me. "No, I'll be taking you to an inn just outside our walls."

Emilie breathed a sigh of relief, and a sense of calm washed over me too.

I tried not to pay too much attention to the rest of the castle as Jade led us out. The less I observed, the less I would recall about all the nights I'd spent tormented inside this mountain. Or at least that's what I hoped. My senses were still on high alert, and I didn't relax until I felt the fresh air on my face again.

"Gods," Emilie whispered once we were out in the open. "I don't remember it looking so..."

"Annihilated?" Bianca finished.

Emilie nodded. "Yes."

It could happen sometimes in the midst of battle. Memories became hazy, and details were quickly forgotten. Especially when the experience was as traumatic as what we had gone through. But she was right. It looked far worse than I could recall.

The exterior was hardly recognizable. I counted at least four piles of debris that smoldered, smoke rising in the cool, damp air. Occasionally, someone approached to toss more trash onto the mounds.

"We've been working as fast as we can to clean up, but as you can see, it is still ongoing," Jade said as we walked. "After your lot destroyed so much of the area, the outburst of civil feuds only contributed to the wreckage. Now that my brother has things under control, we've been dismantling all the rubble and clearing the way for new structures."

To the left, I could see what remained of a tall hedge wall. A few civilians were cutting into the dead branches and carrying the sticks to the fires to keep them ablaze.

The path was a mix of muddy sludge and slippery pebbles. Thankfully, my boots were meant for just this type of trek. I looked down beside me and was pleased to find that Emilie had equally sturdy footwear.

But as we passed an older woman, her feet sank into the milky brown puddles. When she took another step, her thin, flat slippers were completely drenched.

While everyone else was distracted, I pushed my magic outward, winding my way into the ground beneath the puddle and pushing it higher until the path leveled and the water moved aside.

An indiscernible noise came from beside me, and I turned to find Emilie hiding a smile.

"What?"

"I saw that," she whispered.

"You saw nothing."

Eventually, Jade led us to the smallest town center I'd ever seen. There were only three buildings. The first could hardly be called a building; it was more like a tent with a large opening in the front. From my vantage point, I could see people entering in a single-file line and exiting with bowls of steaming soup.

The second building was more structurally sound, though that wasn't saying much. It appeared to be made of scrap wood planks of various lengths and widths. Unlike the tent, the building had a proper door, so I couldn't see inside to assess its function.

The last building appeared to be our destination. It was also made of scrap materials, but the double doors were propped open and a small desk was stationed at the front.

Jade led us inside and stopped at the desk, thrumming her knuckles on the surface.

"How can I help you?" a young man, possibly even a teenager, asked.

"I need a room for our guests here," Jade said with a quick glance in our direction.

The young man opened a drawer and began to search.

"One room?" I asked. "There's six of us."

Jade kept her eyes fixed on the man. "One will be enough. We don't have extras to spare. Ever since word has spread that Jesse has taken over, people have flocked here to see for themselves, hoping they can be the first to plea for help. People with children. People who are sick. They're all desperate." Finally, she turned my way. "So you'll have to forgive us if we only allow you to take one of the very few rooms we have."

"It's plenty," Emilie said before I could respond. "Thank you for your generosity."

It was for the best that Emilie spoke on my behalf. I lacked the charisma and patience that came so naturally to her.

Despite that, Jade seemed unmoved. She still looked at us as though we were nothing more than pests to be exterminated.

Fine by me. We weren't here to make friends. We were here to retrieve what we needed and get out. Jesse's idea of a newly formed alliance was just a bump in the road.

The young man reached across the desk to hand me a key. "Room E. It's down that hall and to the right. We have a communal bathroom here, which you can find through that door over there."

"Thank you," I said, taking the key and turning to face my group. None of them looked eager to share a bathroom with dozens of other cohabitants, but I was grateful they had running water at all in this makeshift inn.

"I'll be back tomorrow at midday to collect you for your meeting with Jesse." Jade spun and left the inn before I could ask for anything else or even thank her.

"Let's check out our accommodations," I said with a sigh.

They weren't as bad as I expected. Although there were six of us crammed into one room, it had been designed to hold entire families. There were three sets of bunk beds—two along the left side and one on the right. The extra space on the right was filled with mismatched drawers for clothes and other belongings. Other than that, the room was bare. There were no decorations, and the only window was a thin slat at the top of the wall where it joined the roof. Actually, after staring a bit longer, I wasn't sure if the slat was intentional or just an accident resulting from cheap and quick construction of the inn. At least it provided fresh air.

"I call dibs on this one," Aven said, slinging his bag on the bottom bunk to our right.

Marco and Bianca quickly claimed the two on the bottom left.

I looked at them in disbelief, pointing at my chest. "I am your High Commander and Regent. I should get first choice."

Bianca made a noise that sounded like a horse impatient for its next meal. "You're an excellent Commander, Ladon, but you're mistaken if you thought your subordinates would ever roll over just because you asked us to. I trust and obey your battle commands. Your sleep arrangements? Well, that's a different story."

I glanced at each of my soldiers in turn. Aven quickly turned away while Mira raised her hands. "Hey, don't look at me. I didn't claim a bed yet."

But something told me she would've if she had gotten to the lower ones first.

Marco cleared his throat. "If you'd like, I'm willing to give up mine."

Of all the people in our envoy, Marco deserved the lower level the most. Being the eldest, he didn't need to climb up to get into bed.

I shook my head and pointed to the bed above him. "It's fine. I'll take this one."

Once Mira tossed her bag above Aven's bed, I took Emilie's pack and put it on the bunk next to mine.

"I'm starving," Bianca said, re-braiding her hair after it had come loose during our journey. "I wonder what they were serving in that tent."

"Probably nothing worth eating," Aven said. "It doesn't look like they have much to spare, but we already knew that."

Yes, it was common knowledge that Murvort was far from affluent. The fact that Reyna had been hoarding what little they had only made me hate her and her followers more.

The line for the dining tent had shrunk since we'd first walked past, but there were still a dozen people waiting before it would be our turn. While Mira and Bianca exchanged desires for what would be on the menu, my thoughts turned to Jesse's offer.

"If I make this agreement, will the conclave adhere to it?" I asked Marco—the only conclave member present.

"Possibly. You'll have to make the argument for why it was necessary. I don't think they will fight back too hard, though. They knew our purpose in coming here. And you are the regent until Cyrus can return to duty. The only options we have would be to save Cyrus and allow him to determine whether we abide by the agreement you made in his absence, or let Cyrus die. In which case, you'd be promoted from regent to king, and they would be obligated to obey your orders."

I massaged my temples. I *hated* being the one to make these decisions. The intention of ruling was not part of my upbringing. No one instilled in me the confidence to sign treaties that would affect everyone who depended on me. How did Cyrus do this? How did he rule with such faith in himself? All I had was doubt.

"Do you think we should agree to their terms, then?" I asked.

Marco licked his lips and stared off into the distance, contemplating before offering his advice. "I think it might be the only option. But if I were you, I would counter-offer. The first rule of negotiation is to never accept the first offer. See if there's anything he has to sweeten the pot."

I mulled it over. But what would Jesse have that I could possibly want? I supposed we'd have to wait and see.

Chapter Twelve

Emilie

Something startled me awake, although after listening quietly for a few moments, I was certain I'd imagined it. Maybe it was my own heart racing or the thoughts pounding against my skull. They were even louder than usual after being back inside Reyna's mountain.

I sighed and closed my eyes. It was still dark outside; I needed to sleep longer, or at least rest. Ladon had confirmed his intentions to come to an agreement with Jesse tomorrow, which meant we would hopefully make our way into Reyna's lair and find her beast in hiding. Who knew what other monstrosities we would discover in the process?

But these days, once I woke, it was nearly impossible to go back to sleep. I turned to my right and then to my left. Then I sighed again and nestled into my thin pillow. It was almost identical to the one Ladon and I had had while in captivity, which only made my thoughts whirl faster.

Suddenly, a hand wrapped around mine, and I stifled a gasp. Ladon's bunk was adjacent to mine, and we had chosen to lay with our heads at the same end. I should've known he was awake too.

His thumb rubbed soothing circles on the back of my hand, and I relaxed.

"Ladon?" I whispered.

"Yes, princess?"

I didn't even know what I intended to say. I just needed to hear his voice. We lay like that for a long time, hand in hand, while we listened to the wind whistle in through the crack near the roof. I would always appreciate Ladon's ability to set my mind and body at ease. Nothing else, neither drink nor meditation, gave me the same sense of peace he did. Eventually, I fell back asleep.

The next time I woke, I was refreshed, and although I was nervous, I was ready to get through the day—hopefully with Vessina's venom in hand and her head severed from her body.

Jade greeted us as promised shortly after we ate a hot breakfast of porridge and tea. It wasn't much, but it settled my stomach, and considering how little the people here had, I was thankful they spared any for us at all.

When we entered the castle, Jesse was already sitting on his throne waiting for us.

"Good morning," he said with a bright smile.

I couldn't quite figure him out—whether his joy was genuine or a façade. Perhaps if I'd met him a year or even a few months ago, I might've been less skeptical. But my brief experience of life outside my homeland had been enough to make me distrust even the most innocent people. It was an effort to give him a chance.

"Did you sleep well?" he asked.

A chorus of unenthusiastic approval was enough to please him.

Jade, however, was unmoved. She stood by her brother's side, looking down upon us. Her piercing eyes rattled me, but most chance gazes did these days. Every glance that swept my way made my skin crawl, but hers even more so.

I wasn't sure why, but before I could give it any more thought, Jesse spoke again.

"Have you come to a decision?" he asked, placing his elbow on the armrest of his throne and resting his chin on a closed fist. If I didn't know better, I would've thought he did not care about the outcome of this meeting.

But he did. So much was riding on it for his people. He'd made a lot of promises that he would have difficulty fulfilling without Osavian on his side.

"I have," Ladon said. He stood at the front of our group, so I couldn't see his face as he spoke. His shoulders were pulled back, and he stood tall, regal even, in front of our hosts. His confidence was so natural and enthralling. "We will reopen the border crossings, but there will be guard posts. And we must discuss necessary travel documentation."

Jesse nodded and motioned for Ladon to continue.

"I won't remove our presence entirely from the western sea, but I will cut the number of ships in half."

Jesse's eyes narrowed for the first time. "Twenty percent."

"Forty," Ladon countered.

"Thirty."

Ladon paused for a moment but ultimately nodded his agreement. "Lastly, the issue of trade."

Jesse sat up straighter in his seat, and Jade seemed more attentive as well.

"We will send one caravan per month."

Jade scoffed and turned around impatiently. Her brother showed more restraint. "I asked for weekly shipments."

"And I'm offering monthly."

I watched Jesse's jaw ripple with frustration. "Biweekly."

Ladon didn't budge. Surely, he didn't mean to walk away from these negotiations? His brother's life was on the line—a fact that we all, even Jesse and Jade, knew very well.

The silent moment grew longer and longer while we all waited for his response. It was a standoff to see who had the most patience and fortitude, and Ladon won.

Jesse sighed. "What would it take to make it biweekly? There must be something else you'd like."

"What do you have to offer?"

Jesse turned to his sister, who leaned down so he could whisper in her ear. Her brows pinched together, and she mulled over whatever he had said.

I rocked back and forth on my feet, eager to hear what else they could barter with.

They exchanged a few more whispered words and stilted expressions before Jesse faced us again and Jade slipped out of the room. "There's one thing I could offer that I think might interest you. Though it's a bit unconventional. Under normal circumstances, I never would've entertained the thought, but Murvort direly needs those resources; there's no use pretending we don't."

My curiosity was piqued. The way he squirmed in his seat made me impatient as well. Was it something dangerous? Or some scarce resource? Possibly something that was antique or unusual that wouldn't be practical for Murvort but could be of some interest to the richer folk in Osavian?

We waited on edge until Jade returned. Four guards followed her, and between them, two prisoners in chains dragged along.

I sucked in a sharp breath. The first thing I noticed was their tattered clothes covered in dirt. Their hair and skin were also a mess, and I almost felt sorry for them. Almost... because when the first prisoner raised his head, I recognized him immediately.

I'd seen him many times inside this very estate. Even in his current state, I couldn't miss his crooked nose and invasive gaze. His hands had been all over my body. I vividly recalled the way he had laughed at my discomfort and the imprint of his heavy limbs wrapped around me.

I turned quickly and clutched my stomach. "I think I'm going to be sick."

Ladon grabbed my arm at the same time Bianca placed a hand on my back. "I've got her," she said, urging Ladon to handle business. But he didn't loosen his grip.

I attempted to reassure him even though my legs were shaky, and my heart was racing. "It's okay. I'll be okay."

He nodded and released me, allowing Bianca to wrap an arm around my waist and keep me steady. I couldn't express my gratitude for her support and the fact that she didn't pry or question my reaction. She simply held me until my legs found their strength again.

Returning my attention to the prisoners, I gave the second one a good look. She was familiar too, though I wasn't her chosen plaything. She favored Ladon.

My first instinct was to reach for his hand, to check that he was all right, but he appeared to be handling it all much better than I was. Memories flooded my vision faster than I could fight them, and I couldn't understand how he masked his pain while I struggled to breathe.

I needed to get myself together. I didn't want the two prisoners to know how deeply they affected me. If they looked our way, I couldn't be crumbling into nothing. It took far too much effort to straighten my posture and lift my chin, but I did it anyway. Bianca still had a supporting arm around me, but she gave me some space upon seeing my resolve return.

"Are you familiar with Zayn and Clarise?" Jesse asked.

The woman's name sounded familiar, but I couldn't recall if I'd ever heard the man's name. Learning them had never mattered to me.

Ladon shook his head.

It was unclear how much Jesse knew about our time in captivity. He studied the two of us with a neutral expression. If Ladon had been on his own, he might've convinced Jesse that we didn't recognize the two prisoners.

But my unease must've been written all over my face. I was still trembling, despite my best efforts to remain stoic. Jesse appraised me for another excruciating moment before cutting the silence.

"Interesting. I thought you might've been, considering they were two of Reyna's closest *friends.* Are you sure you haven't seen them before?" Rather than waiting for Ladon's response, he fixed his eyes on me.

And I felt the weight of the world crushing me. Breathing was nearly impossible, and I was afraid that if I didn't get out of this cave, I would soon begin to hyperventilate.

I broke first, looking down at my feet. The stone was black and jagged. If I fainted now, I would earn some cuts and bruises. Maybe Ladon or Bianca would catch me first.

"Hmm. It seems one of you might recall their faces," Jesse said.

Ladon turned around for the first time since Zayn and Clarise had entered the hall, and his face drained of color upon seeing mine.

"Emilie." His voice was thick with concern—did I somehow look worse than I felt?—and his eyes snapped to Bianca. "Take her back to the inn. Get her out of here."

"No," I said, resisting Bianca's pull on my waist. "No, I want to stay."

Ladon sighed and tilted his head. I could tell he wanted to argue. Driving each other mad was one of our favorite pastimes, but he wouldn't win this quarrel. If vital decisions were to be made, I wanted to be present. No matter what it cost me.

I spoke softer, just for him to hear. "I'm not going anywhere, Ladon. I have every right to be here. I'll be fine."

He looked taken aback for a moment. "I didn't... Of course you have a right to stay. I'm only worried about your wellbeing."

I took a deep breath. "I'm okay."

I sounded more confident than I felt, and perhaps he sensed that too. But he turned his attention toward Jesse once more, standing noticeably closer to me than he had been a few minutes before.

"Fine. You are correct. Our paths did cross on occasion while Emilie and I were kept hostage here in Murvort. What does it have to do with our agreement?"

Jesse remained calm and maybe even uninterested. Again, I couldn't discern how much he knew of our time in Murvort. If he knew the things Reyna put us through—the *parties* that these two prisoners had attended—he didn't say so. He didn't seem to care *how* we knew the prisoners, and he didn't ask.

"Zayn and Clarise are the only two of Reyna's supporters that we could find. At least alive." Jesse and Jade exchanged a grin at that. "I'll admit I had my own uses for them, but I'm willing to hand them over for the sake of our treaty and trade agreement."

"Hand them over? And what am I to do with them?" Ladon asked.

Jesse shrugged. "Whatever pleases you. I haven't been able to get any useful information out of them, but maybe you'll have more success. Or you could just kill them. They would be yours to decide which purpose they serve."

My throat was so dry, I could hardly swallow.

Zayn glared at Jesse, and Clarise shuffled back and forth, the chains around her ankles and wrists clanking with each movement. My eyes were drawn to my own wrists, where white scars still covered my skin in the shape of pale vines. I would live with them for the rest of my life.

Could I also live with myself if we took the two of them back to Renoa and… did what exactly? Torture them? Humiliate them the way they did us? Kill them?

As it turned out, I could. The anger coursing through my veins was enough to calm my unsettled stomach. I didn't know if it would make me feel better or not, but I was certain that I *could* live with myself. It was what they deserved.

My eyes met Ladon's, and I knew before he said a word—he could too.

Chapter Thirteen

Ladon

"Are you sure about this?" Mira asked, a little apprehensive.

We were standing at the base of a massive pile of rubble where the tunnel leading to the lower chambers had caved in. It was dark; the only light we had to rely on was the single mage lamp that Bianca held.

I was ready, excited even, to venture beyond the rubble wall and find Vessina. For the first time since I found my brother unconscious in Emilie's arms, I felt hope. We were so close to getting him the help he needed.

"Let's go," I said. While Emilie, Aven, Bianca and Marco took turns grabbing rocks and tossing them to the side, Mira and I used magic to remove the larger boulders. Magic flowed from my fingertips and through the air, dipping beneath the heaviest stones and lifting them with ease.

Marco grumbled as he went to pick up another rock. It wasn't my problem that he wasn't an earth wielder. Marco was like my brother—a fire wielder. I supposed he could've melted down some of the stone, but it would've taken longer than removing it through manual labor. He'd get over it.

We cleared the path faster than I could've hoped for, and Bianca picked up the lantern and stepped forward, leading the way. Beside me, Emilie carried a small piece of paper—a hand-drawn map that Jesse had been kind enough to give us after we signed our agreement. Neither he nor Jade were willing to venture into the lower chambers with us.

"Good luck," had been his parting words before he chuckled and walked away.

I didn't need luck on my side. I had hatred. And fury. And retribution. Luck would merely be a bonus to the drive I had within me.

Emilie studied the map in the low light of the mage lamp. "We should take the first right and then go straight until the tunnel slopes down."

Everyone nodded, trusting her completely.

There was no way to know for certain where Vessina would be since she was free to roam after being trapped in the caves. But Jesse felt confident that Reyna's lab was her likely hiding spot.

The map was far from perfect, as Jesse and his supporters hadn't spent much time in the lower levels before sealing them away. But Jesse had started his cartography project before they abandoned the tunnels, using his memory to fill in some of the blanks afterward.

We took the first right turn as Emilie had suggested, and it didn't take long for the ground to begin to slope. It was gradual at first, but then it became a challenge not to slip on the loose gravel beneath our shoes.

"Here," Emilie said, pointing to her left.

We continued to make our way deeper into the mountain with Emilie and Bianca leading the way. I didn't think it was possible for the tunnels to get even darker or for the air to feel even thinner. It was an eeriness I'd never known.

"What's that?" Aven asked.

I looked ahead to where he gestured. A small yellow-orange light infiltrated the darkness, flickering occasionally.

"A fire?" Bianca asked. "They wouldn't leave a fire burning in an abandoned tunnel, would they?"

It would've been incredibly foolish if they had. Imagine making such an effort to take control of Murvort, only to turn the prime estate to cinders. The Holdens were too ambitious and too smart to let that happen.

We cautiously approached the light, Bianca peeking around a corner once we were close enough to see what was causing such a sight. She quickly whipped her head back, her eyes wide with alarm.

"What did you see?" Emilie asked.

Bianca licked her lips and spoke softly, like she was afraid to disturb whatever was in the next vault. "Dragons."

"Have you fucking lost your mind?" Aven hissed.

Dragons existed in our world, but they hadn't been spotted in Lourova in centuries. The only ones I knew of kept to Moridia—the wild continent full of magical beasts and barren of humanity, save for a few research outposts. But I wouldn't put it past Reyna to somehow bring a dragon back to Murvort.

"Are you certain?" Mira asked.

"Well, I've never seen one before, but are they black and breathe fire?"

I could tell Mira and Aven were holding back their laughter despite the inappropriate timing.

"There's no way," I said. "These caves are too small for a dragon to fit."

"Maybe it's an infant," Mira said.

"It's not very big," Bianca admitted. "Smaller than a foal."

I shook my head. I was no expert on beasts, but surely even a baby dragon was larger than a foal. I pushed forward and took Bianca's place, edging to the corner so I could see for myself.

When I craned my neck to see into the next chamber, I immediately caught sight of what Bianca had seen. But it wasn't a dragon. In fact, it was three—no, four—small flying creatures that I did not recognize. I pulled back and frowned.

"Well? Do you believe me now?" she asked.

"No."

Bianca snorted.

"That's not a dragon. I'm not sure *what* they are. They looked... They looked like bats. Overgrown bats that happen to breathe fire."

"They did say Reyna liked to experiment on animals, did they not?" Marco asked.

"That's horrific," Emilie said, her features pinched together in anger.

"What should we do?" Mira asked.

Aven answered quickly. "Kill them."

"No!" Emilie and Marco exclaimed at the same time. An echo rang through the tunnel, and I hoped we hadn't disturbed the tiny creatures. Were they aggressive? Or would they flee if they sensed a threat?

"They're innocent," Emilie added. "We can't kill them."

"Personally, I'd love to take one back to Renoa to study," Marco said.

Emilie glared at him, and I smiled. Indignation looked good on her. I loved it when she got riled up. That was probably why I teased her for so long, and continued to do so today.

I snapped out of it and turned to Marco. "We will not be bringing back any extra passengers on our way home. The two prisoners are more than enough."

It was difficult to tell in the low lighting, but I could've sworn his shoulders slumped at my disapproval. He'd get over it.

"I could freeze them," Bianca said. "It wouldn't kill them. Just enough to ground them and keep them from flying away. And keep them from shooting flames in our direction."

"You can do that?" I asked.

"I can try."

It would have to be good enough. I didn't see many other options—at least none that kept them alive and appeased Emilie's righteousness.

I looked to her for approval, and she nodded.

"Do it," I told Bianca.

We traded positions so she was closest to the chamber once more. She slowly crept around the corner and extended her arms, palms facing up. The temperature rapidly began to decline, and I watched her fingers turn an icy blue.

The fire-breathing bats didn't notice what was happening at first, but as soon as they did, they let out an ear-splitting screech. Flames lit the chamber, though I could only see the light as it crept into our hiding space.

Bianca's magic pulsed and hummed. I shivered but kept close watch in case they attacked her.

Slowly, their cries subsided, and their flames with them. There was a chorus of thuds, and I assumed that the creatures had fallen to the ground.

Bianca lowered her hands and waved us forward. "It's safe now."

We passed through several more chambers and tunnels of various lengths. I lost track of the number of turns we made, but Bianca and Emilie consulted the map frequently.

"We're almost there," Emilie said.

Right after she spoke, a disturbance came from up ahead. It was a hellish combination of hissing, roaring and squawking. Like every beast imaginable was fighting till the death. And maybe they were. They'd been trapped down here, and food was scarce. Perhaps they'd turned on each other to survive.

Marco began to retreat, his eyes as wide as saucers. I grabbed his arm and tilted my head. "Don't you dare."

He blinked a few times, glancing back and forth between the source of the noise and me. "I... I don't... I should've..."

"You're right where you're supposed to be. We need you. And there's no safer place than with us."

I was used to calming nervous soldiers—young warriors who stepped onto a battlefield for the first time. It didn't matter how much a person prepared—the first experience with real combat was enough to make the strongest person's knees wobble.

"Bianca and Mira, lead the way. Aven, I want you at the rear with me. We'll proceed carefully and be prepared to strike."

Marco found a comfortable spot between the strongest of us, and Emilie fell back, closer to me.

"You know I can handle myself, too," she said.

I grinned. "I know you can, princess." She had learned a lot in a short period of time, but she still wasn't as good as Bianca or Mira. Not that I would tell her that. I liked this version of her—self-assured and prepared for the worst. It was much better than beaten-down and defeated. "Maybe I just want to keep you close."

To prove my point, I reached for her and trailed my hand up her spine. I felt her shiver, and she shot me a look of surprise. She whispered, "Someone will see."

They wouldn't. It was too dark, and she was too close for anyone to notice anything suspicious. Aven was the only one with a view, and he was focused on the tunnel ahead, straining to see any surprise attacks. I dragged my finger down her spine for good measure and felt her relax.

"Ready?" Bianca asked from the front.

I responded, "Ready."

We turned the corner, and the dark tunnel opened into a massive cave. The walls were lined with cages upon cages of various sizes. A monstrous enclosure sat in the center of the room, and above it, the ceiling was cracked open and letting a pale blue light inside from far, far above our heads. Like a chimney that reached the sky.

Inside the center cage was a beast that was half eagle, half jaguar. Its body was feline, but it had wings that beat against the cage and a beak that bit into the bars that trapped it. When it noticed us, it flapped its wings in our direction and rammed its massive body against the metal bars. Marco jumped, but even if it could escape its cage, there were two shackles around its hind legs.

I slowly spun in a circle, realizing that all the creatures were safely tucked in cages. Terrifying as they may be, none of them could attack us. The only harm was the damage to my eardrums as they carried on with their wailing.

"What has she done?" Emilie asked, on the verge of tears. "What has she done to them?"

I grabbed her hand when she tried to approach one of the cages. "Don't get too close."

Emilie shook me off. "They're terrified. Look at them." She came to a stop in front of a cage that held what appeared to be a small critter—a chipmunk or gerbil. It was hard to tell because its head was misshapen. It turned to the side, and we both gasped. It had a third eyeball, but it was completely white, and I didn't think it could see out of the extra one.

"What the fuck?"

"She's a monster," Emilie said, shaking with anger. "How can someone be so cruel?"

I grabbed her wrist as she tried to reach for the latch. "You can't."

"Why not?" she cried. "We can't leave them here to starve to death. I won't leave them locked away for the rest of their short lives."

She had more compassion than I could begin to understand. Reyna's experiments would be better off dead, in my opinion. They were unnatural and more deserving of a swift death than freedom. "That's not what we came here for."

She ceased fighting me long enough to look at me with hurt in her eyes. "They're innocent. They're victims too."

I understood the reason for her unshed tears. She looked at those creatures and saw herself—saw us. Objects that existed only for Reyna's amusement.

She was right; it wasn't fair.

But what the hell did she expect us to do? I looked around the chamber and the dozens if not hundreds of experiments. "So we free them, and then what? How are we supposed to help them?"

I loosened my grip when she no longer seemed likely to go on a liberation spree. Wiping her teary eyes, she looked up at the sky. After a second of thought, she pointed. "There. We let them fly away."

"They can't all fly." Most did not have wings, and those that did—well, were they even strong enough after being caged for so long?

"Then I'll help them." She lifted her hands, and a small breeze encircled us.

She could lift them with her magic. Once they were out of the mountain, they'd be on their own. But at least they'd be free. At least they'd stand a chance.

"All right. But let's do it quickly."

The others must've been eavesdropping because when I turned to give them instructions, Bianca and Mira were already moving toward the cages, and Aven had taken up the lantern so they could see clearly.

"What if they're dangerous? You don't know if they're poisonous. Or if they are aggressive. They could kill each other or *us*," Marco said.

I didn't have the time or the patience to argue with him. "Let's free those with wings first. Bianca, be ready to freeze any that seem on the verge of attacking. Mira, can you use your shadows to calm the others until we get to them? The fewer distractions, the better. Aven…"

"I'll just keep holding this lantern," he said. "Unless there are any fish that need to be rescued."

Aven was a water wielder, and he was right. His magic wasn't of much use in this situation, but he could still help by unlatching the cages.

Marco stood aside and didn't bother to offer his help. I wasn't expecting him to, since he wasn't keen on the idea to begin with.

Once everyone was ready, we began to unlatch the cages. Most of the animals were freed smoothly. There was a large hog-like creature that wasn't thrilled to be lifted into the air by Emilie's wind and tried multiple times to flee through the tunnels. Another that reminded me of a rabbit with long talons refused to let go of the bars of its cage. One by one, we set them free and into the sky above.

We were almost done when Marco shouted, "She's here! She's fucking here!"

Everyone's heads turned in unison. For a fleeting second, I thought he meant Reyna, and my stomach dropped. Heat flared in my chest at the same time as the urge to take my time killing her rose like a tidal wave. I would savor every second of her pain and pleading for mercy.

But it wasn't Reyna.

It was Vessina.

Perhaps she had heard the ruckus and came to see for herself what was going on. Or maybe she scented us. Either way, she knew that her lair had been invaded by outsiders, and she wasn't happy about it.

The giant snake hissed and flicked her tongue, tasting our fear and anticipation in the air. She was as big as I remembered her, maybe even bigger. Her black scales glistened as if they were wet, but it was just the metallic texture that reflected like water.

Her beady eyes danced around the chamber, unable to focus on so many things at once—the creatures who had resumed their screeching, the humans who had disturbed her sanctuary, the flickering light from the lantern casting shadows on the walls. She flicked her tongue again and slithered around the far side of the room.

"What do we do?" Marco asked, inching toward the rest of us from where he stood near the center of the room.

The half-eagle, half-jaguar flapped its wings furiously as Vessina came closer. She lifted her head and swayed before striking the cage that held the mutated beast. Her fangs hit metal on the first attack, but she recovered before striking again. The second time, her fangs sank into the beast's right wing, and it cried out in pain. Its uninjured wing flapped even harder as it tried to escape Vessina's grasp.

"No!" Emilie cried.

Before I could stop her, she darted toward the cage in the middle of the room, hands outstretched for the latch a few feet ahead.

Vessina was quick to notice the unexpected movement, and she reared back, readying to strike again. This time her eyes were set on Emilie.

I grabbed the set of daggers at my side and launched the first one at the snake. It lodged itself between two scales, but Vessina simply hissed and continued to track Emilie's movements.

My second dagger hit one of Vessina's shiny scales and bounced off. I needed to aim for her underbelly if I wanted to do any actual damage.

"Don't kill her," Marco cried.

Fuck that. He could still get her venom even if she was dead. And I wasn't about to let her sink her fangs into Emilie a second time. The memory of the first occasion made me hurl my third dagger toward her delicate underside, but it barely grazed her skin.

Vessina lashed out toward Emilie, who was fiddling with the cage's latch.

"Emilie, move," I yelled.

She looked up and dodged out of the way at the last second. The door to the cage swung open, and the creature scrambled out, almost trampling Emilie in the process. She rolled onto the floor, avoiding the heavy jaguar's sharp claws, then spun to her left to avoid another strike from Vessina.

For a moment, Vessina was distracted by the freed creature. The tormented thing roared and sprang forward, latching onto Vessina's body. The snake's length began to wind its way around the creature's body, and together they rolled to the side. Emilie sprang to her feet before they could crush her, bolting and falling into my arms.

She looked back and pushed the hair out of her face. "She's strangling her!" she cried.

She struggled against my hold, but I refused to let her go. "That beast isn't worth your life, Emilie."

"That's. Not. For. You. To. Decide." She writhed and jerked, fighting me every second.

Meanwhile, Vessina latched onto the beast's other wing, creating a matching set of puncture marks. It thrashed and beat its wings wildly until they seemed to drop like dead weight.

"The poison is spreading," I said. "We need to act now!"

Bianca was the first to move. She raised her hands and a chill spread through the room. Ice formed at the base of the cages, slowly spreading upward until they were all covered in glistening white.

But Vessina remained black as night. Perhaps her scales protected her from the frost. One thing was certain, however—she remembered we were still here. Her head swiveled, finding the source of magic. Then she abandoned the pitiful creature with useless wings and made for Bianca.

"Watch out!" Aven shouted as Vessina pulled back, ready to launch at Bianca. He threw out a wave of water, and Bianca froze it like a shield in front of her.

Vessina crashed into it with an angry hiss.

Aven sent another wave. This time, he wrapped it around Vessina, drowning her on dry land. She thrashed her head back and forth, trying to shake it away, but his water held strong, circling her like a hurricane.

The snake released one wild flail, and her head collided with Aven, sending him flying. He crashed into the empty cages. The water fell to the floor and splashed before settling into puddles.

I looked around, hoping to see a boulder I could use to attack since my daggers had been so ineffective. Before I could find something of use, Emilie ran across the room, diving and dodging Vessina's attacks with ease. I started after her on instinct—the urge to protect her was more overwhelming than my need to slay the viper.

Emilie raised her hands, and the cages we'd cleared so far began to rattle as her wind ripped them from the walls. She threw them at Vessina while Bianca, Mira, and Marco ran for cover.

The cages slammed against Vessina's steel scales and the ground, breaking to pieces.

Another surge of magic erupted from Emilie, and just as Vessina reared to strike again, a dozen jagged bars shot up from the ground like spears, piercing Vessina's belly in multiple places.

She hissed violently, but her body slammed to the ground with her massive weight, and the bars only drove deeper into her flesh. She made multiple attempts to slither forward, but the bars made it impossible for her to move without causing further injury and pain.

As the life slowly drained from her, I approached with caution, just in case she got one last surge of energy before death ultimately claimed her. Once I was close enough, I drew my sword and drove it deep into her eye. Deep enough that I was certain it had pierced her brain. When I pulled it out, she ceased all movement.

"Damn it," Marco shouted, the sound echoing in the now quiet chamber. "Move."

He barely waited for me to step aside before he was at Vessina's mouth, forcing it open so he could milk her fangs while her venom was still fresh. Black liquid seeped from her sharpest teeth, and he collected it into multiple vials, stowing away as much as he could.

"Will that be enough?" I asked. I didn't know the first thing about brewing antidotes.

But he nodded confidently. "Yes; this is good. We can go now."

"Not yet," Emilie said, and we all turned to her. She still looked a bit rattled after taking down Vessina. Her eyes were wide, her pupils blown. I could tell it hadn't fully settled in yet that she had killed her. She should be celebrating. We both should be celebrating. But the blood of one beast wasn't enough to quench my thirst for retribution. "We have to free the rest of the creatures."

When the last of the mutations was set free, we began our ascent back through the tunnels. We were met at the entry to the tunnels by a disgruntled-looking Jade.

"Did you get what you needed?" she asked, eyes narrowed as she took in our dirty and bloodied clothing. Her nose crinkled like she could smell the filth on us.

"Yes," I replied. "Thank you for your hospitality. Unfortunately, we can't stay much longer. It's important that we get back to Renoa to work on the antidote. We'll be out of your hair before nightfall."

"Excellent. My bags are already packed."

I frowned and studied her expression with unease. "What do you mean?"

She forced a smile. "My brother has demanded that I go with you to Renoa. To make sure you uphold your end of the bargain."

Chapter Fourteen

Emilie

"Are you sad to be leaving your brother behind?"

Jade turned to me with a questioning look, as if annoyed that I was trying to engage in conversation with her. I wouldn't call her intimidating per se, but she did give off a combative aura.

Still, I didn't have many friends, and she looked to be about my age. We shared a mutual loathing of Reyna—surely we could be friends if she would be staying in Renoa.

After a few moments of silence, she responded, "Not really. I'm looking forward to his absence. I won't have to listen to his barking out orders every morning and afternoon."

I thought I caught a glimpse of a smile, but she quickly hid it, returning to her cool, detached demeanor.

"The two of you seemed to get along fairly well. I have a brother too, you know. I wish I got to see him more often. He was—"

"Does it look like I care?" she asked rudely, interrupting my feeble attempt at bonding. "I am here for one purpose—to make sure Ladon stays true to his word. And if Cyrus resurrects to reclaim his title, then I will make sure he upholds our bargain, too."

I didn't ask how she intended to do that. First, because I was certain she would snap at me again; and second, because I figured her means of persuasion were of the deadly variety. Instead, I made a mental note to ensure both Ladon and Cyrus had extra security once we got back.

Jade sped up to walk behind Bianca and Aven, leaving me behind to bask in my failure.

"Don't worry about her," Ladon said, coming up beside me. "I think she hates everyone."

"Were you eavesdropping?"

He shrugged. "You weren't exactly quiet."

"I suppose not," I grumbled.

"Don't look so upset. You did just kill Vessina and saved Cyrus in the process. Who taught you to be so deadly?"

I turned to see him grinning in a way that made my heart stutter. Heat rose to my cheeks, and I faced forward again, hoping he wouldn't notice.

But of course he did.

He spoke quietly so that only I could hear. "Gods, Emilie. I can't even begin to explain how much I love seeing you flush for me. It makes me want to kiss every inch of you just so I can feel your warmth against my lips."

I had to resist the urge to clench my thighs together. Somehow he still noticed my unease, because he chuckled in a deep, throaty way that brought the flush right back to my cheeks.

"Ladon," I admonished. "You can't speak to me like that. At least not while we can't act on it."

"Hmm, soon, we will be able to act on it. Very soon, princess."

The thought cheered me up. Yes—soon, Cyrus would be awake, and I could break off our engagement. It wasn't a conversation I was looking forward to, but the sooner I got it over with, the sooner I could move on with my life. Then I could show my affection toward Ladon out in the open.

I couldn't wait for the day that our love was no longer a secret. When I could lie next to him without feeling guilty. It seemed like a dream—freedom from my parents' expectations and freedom to love Ladon unapologetically. Once Cyrus was awake, nothing could stop us from living happily ever after like the stories in children's books.

A knot formed in my stomach, and it only took a second to recognize the discomfort.

Reyna.

Her hounds and her snake were long gone, but her ghost still haunted me every night. She interrupted every moment of peace I'd found since leaving her prison. How could I move on with my life while she still breathed?

My eyes were drawn to the two hostages we'd been given in exchange for helping Jesse. They staggered behind Mira while Bianca and Aven ushered them forward. Their wrists were bound behind their backs, and chains circled their ankles with just enough space for them to shuffle, which made for a slow journey home. It was uncomfortable to see people being treated this way, but then I recalled how they'd treated Ladon and me, and my sympathy for them faded. At least they hadn't been given permanent scars around their wrists and ankles like we had.

They didn't speak at all even when offered food or drink. It was a miracle they walked without being forced. Either they were hopeful we'd be merciful to them, or they were quietly plotting their own escape and praying we'd let our guards down if they behaved.

They were foolish if they believed that to be the case.

"What do you intend to do with them?" I asked Ladon.

He followed my gaze. "They'll get what they deserve."

"What *exactly* does that mean, Ladon?"

He swallowed, taking his time while he considered whether I could handle the truth. I knew it would be sinister, but I hoped he knew I'd prefer his honesty over blissful ignorance.

He settled somewhere in between, rubbing the back of his neck. "You don't have to be involved in this. We'll get answers from them one way or another, but it won't be civil."

"Answers about Reyna's whereabouts?"

He nodded.

"Then I want to be involved."

Chapter Fifteen

Ladon

AFTER ANOTHER DAY OF travel, we made it back to Fort Malek, where Bianca, Aven, and Mira took their leave. We devoured a quick meal before setting off again, this time on our way back to Renoa. Thankfully, we had our horses again, so our two prisoners didn't slow us down with their shuffling.

I'd half-expected them to make some sort of plea by now, but they still hadn't made a peep. I didn't think they'd be stupid enough to try anything while surrounded by enemies, but just in case, I kept them separated and on a short leash.

The weather was unkind to us, as it rained the entire trip from Fort Malek to Renoa. By the time we made it home, we were all miserable and tired.

Nighttime had fallen over the city, but a string of lamps lit the entrance to the castle where two figures waited for us. Though I could only make out their silhouettes, it wasn't hard to guess who they were. The larger one was Hudson, and the smaller frame belonged to my mother.

She stood quietly as I climbed the handful of steps that led to the front door, and I could tell she was still unhappy with me for traveling to Murvort against her wishes. But I'd made it in and out safely, and I was home again.

"Mother, I'm—"

I was interrupted as she threw her arms around me and hugged me tightly. She shuddered, and it only took a moment to realize she was sobbing.

I gently grabbed her shoulders and pulled back. "Why are you crying? I'm fine, Mother. Look—I'm safe."

She sniffed and wiped away her tears, but the agony on her face still broke me into a million tiny pieces. I pulled her in for another hug, and she slumped against me.

I craned my neck to peek over my shoulder, silently encouraging the others to disperse. Aside from those handling the two prisoners, the rest were no longer needed and could enjoy a nice break and a handsome reward for their service on this mission, even if most of them hadn't ventured past Fort Malek.

The only two that remained were Emilie and Jade, who had the decency to look around at the gardens surrounding the castle rather than my mother and me.

"Hudson, can you find Jade a room? She will be staying with us for a while."

He nodded and offered to take Jade's belongings, but she declined, hugging them closer instead. They disappeared through the door, and my mother finally pulled herself together. Then she caught Emilie off guard, giving her a hug as well.

Emilie blinked a few times before embracing my mother. "Sophia, it's all right." She looked at me, baffled at my mother's meltdown. I didn't know what to say either. I'd never seen my mother behave in such a way. Even when my father died, she kept it together for my sake and Cyrus's.

My mother finally released Emilie and blew her nose into a handkerchief. "I'm sorry. I know I'm a mess."

She wasn't slurring her words, so I knew she hadn't been drinking. At least not enough for it to be the cause of her meltdown.

I suddenly became anxious. "Is everything okay? What happened while we were gone? Is Cyrus—"

"No, no," she said. "He's fine... or he's the same, I guess. I was just so scared that you wouldn't come back. It took me back to that day when they broke the news that you'd been taken, and then I didn't see you for *months*. Do you know what that was like?"

Tears filled her eyes again, and I felt horrible for putting her through this.

She shook her head. "I'm sorry. I'm rambling on about how awful it was for me, and I know it was even worse for the two of you." My eyes found Emilie at the casual mention of our trauma, but she kept a calm composure, listening attentively to my mother. "I'm just so..."

"Scared?" I suggested, and she nodded her confirmation, tears spilling over again.

I sighed and reached for her hands. "You can't live like this—in fear of the worst that could happen. Emilie and I won't live like that, and you don't need to either. And we brought good news."

She perked up a little, and her eyes bounced back and forth between Emilie and me.

"We've got the venom we need to revive Cyrus. We're going to get him back. Marco has orders not to rest until he's discovered the exact recipe for the antidote."

My mother didn't immediately rejoice, and I didn't expect her to. It wasn't in her nature to celebrate prematurely. She had every reason to be cautiously optimistic, and she had just shown how much this had all been affecting her on the inside. It was okay, though. She didn't need to have blind faith. I would prove it to her.

"Let's get to bed," I said, waving to the door. "It's been a long day, and we're all tired. Now that you've seen me, you can sleep in peace."

She allowed me to guide her inside, and Emilie followed. Before she headed off toward her bedroom, she turned to me one more time and kissed my cheek. "I'm so glad you're safe, sweetheart. And you too, Emilie. This home wouldn't be the same without you."

Emilie's brows rose, and she managed to squeak out a "thanks."

Once my mother was out of earshot, she murmured, "I thought she hated me."

"She doesn't hate you. My mother is incapable of hating anyone."

"But she was so upset about us. And Cyrus and me."

I clenched my jaw at the use of her and Cyrus in the same sentence. It was a natural reflex at this point, always followed by a wave of guilt that I was so agitated by his engagement to her when he didn't even have a clue about our feelings for each other.

"She's protective of my brother, as am I. But she knows you're not in love with him. And she knows that I'm in love with you. It's complicated, Emilie. Try not to worry about it. Everything will work itself out once Cyrus is awake."

She stopped outside her door and turned to me with a beaming, flirtatious smile.

"What?" I asked.

"You're in love with me."

I huffed a laugh. "That's not a secret, princess."

"I know. But I like hearing you say it anyway."

"If I say it again, can I kiss you goodnight?"

She bit her bottom lip, eyes flicking to either end of the hall. We were completely alone. "Perhaps."

"Emilie Duval, I'm inescapably in love with you. You're in my veins." I moved closer until her back was pressed against the wall and a tiny gasp escaped her lips. "My heart beats only for you."

Her hands roamed over my chest and found their resting place near my hips. I meant every word I said. Without her, I was certain my life would cease to exist. Even pretending not to be in love with her was slowly killing me.

"How about it, princess? Can I get that kiss?"

I cupped her cheeks and tilted her head up, closing in on her lips until there was just a paper-thin space between us. We teetered on the edge, waiting to see who would cave first. Who would give in to temptation first.

But we were playing by Emilie's rules. She was the one who created this boundary between us, and she would be the one to cross it. I might tease and taunt my way along the line, but she had to be the one to step over it.

When she did... Fuck, it was ecstasy. Like I'd been going through withdrawal and didn't realize it until I got another dose. It hadn't been that long, but I couldn't get enough of the way her soft lips melted into mine. The way she tasted like sin and salvation. I craved her.

I pressed harder against her, my hips rolling as I hitched one of her legs up to my side. She moaned, and I devoured that too. My fingers wandered across her body and cupped her breast over her clothes.

That seemed to snap her out of it. She separated her lips from mine, breathing heavily. Her eyes were filled with desire and an unquenchable longing. I don't know how she managed to stay in control while I was unravelling right before her. How could she resist when I had never felt weaker?

I dropped her leg and reluctantly allowed her to slip from my grasp. Before she closed the door to her room, she smiled and said, "Goodnight, Ladon. I'll see you in the morning."

That night, my reason for being unable to sleep was much different than the typical one. Instead of being plagued by nightmares, I was too fixated on the coming days—being able to hold Emilie, to touch her and kiss her freely. I was too excited to sleep.

But tomorrow was a big day. There were two prisoners being held in the dungeons, and I needed to have a word with them.

I still wasn't sold on bringing Emilie into the interrogation. Even if she had survived Reyna's torture, it hadn't been her choice. There were some things that no one should ever have to see or do in their lifetime, and that included violent methods of extracting information. I wanted to keep her out of it as much as possible.

I went for my morning jog and skipped breakfast. It was better to head into the dungeons on an empty stomach, just in case things got grisly. Nausea wasn't very intimidating.

The corridor leading to the dungeons wasn't used much since it only led to one destination. It was dimly lit and smelled faintly of rain and rust the further I went. At the end of the hall, two guards stood on either side of a weathered iron door. Once they noticed my approach, the one on the right pulled out a key and unlocked the dungeon door.

"Thank you," I said, slipping inside.

The mage lights inside the dungeons were few and far between. I was sure it had something to do with sensory deprivation, but I hated that I had to pause for my eyes to adjust. It left me feeling vulnerable; the prisoners down here could see me while I couldn't see them, even if just for a moment.

Once the room materialized, I spotted Clarise and Zayn. It wasn't difficult since the other cells had been emptied of the war prisoners while I was gone. Xavier had been quick to dispose of them, as he'd promised. I hoped these two would have more answers than the others. They certainly were closer to Reyna—close enough to know her whereabouts.

Clarise and Zayn shared a cell, though they were both in shackles on opposite ends. Far enough that they couldn't reach one another but close enough for me to question them both at once.

As I approached their cell and opened the door, Clarise looked up. The right side of her mouth curved into a mocking grin, and I was immediately taken back to those *parties* where she had handled my body as if it belonged to her. I suppressed the shiver that ran up my spine as her eyes drank in my figure. She would not be smiling soon.

"Did you come to see me?"

"Where is Reyna?"

"Tsk, tsk. That's not a very kind way to greet me."

My magic rattled the ground underneath her feet, and she shook violently. When the rumbling stopped, she tugged against her shackles, looking agitated by my unspoken threat.

"It's not so fun, is it?" I asked. "When you're the one who's powerless, at the mercy of another?"

"This is—"

"Shut up," Zayn interrupted. "Don't say another word."

I tilted my head and appraised him. Unlike his companion, he couldn't even look me in the eye. He stared at the metal shackles around his ankles, barely moving an inch. I moved closer, grabbing his chin and forcing it up so he had no choice but to meet my stare.

"And what about you, hmm? Do you know where your bitch tyrant is hiding?"

"Fuck you," he spat.

Clearly, neither of them understood the lengths I was willing to go to find Reyna and see her head severed from her body.

I sighed, pulling out a lethal carving knife. It was time to get messy.

Before Zayn had time to react, I grabbed his hand and sawed through his pinky finger. It only took a few passes back and forth before his digit fell to the floor, and his screams followed shortly after.

Clarise let out a horrified noise that sounded like she was choking on her own vomit. Perhaps she was beginning to understand what kind of vengeance would be coming her way too.

I pulled a handkerchief out of my pocket and wiped the blood off my knife. "Let's try this again," I said calmly. "Where is Reyna?"

Zayn trembled with rage and pain. "I'm not telling you anything. You'll have to do much worse than that."

Honestly, I'd expected nothing less. If Reyna found out that anyone in her inner circle had betrayed her, she'd kill them slowly and cruelly. But Zayn and Clarise didn't seem to realize I would do the same if they didn't talk.

I rubbed my jaw and pretended to be impressed with his valiant display of loyalty and bravery. He barely noticed as I slowly sent dust and dirt to fill his throat, blocking his airway until he began to cough and sputter uncontrollably. I sent it into his eyes too, and he blinked and thrashed his head back and forth, desperately shaking it out.

Once I let up, I removed his second finger effortlessly, and he screamed again. His cheeks turned red as he fought hard to keep his secrets to himself.

While I let Zayn's pain simmer, I moved on to Clarise. It would be easier to break them if I kept them on their toes. Never knowing what stunt I would pull next.

"And you," I said, pointing my knife at Clarise. Her face drained of color as I approached. Perhaps she would be easier to break.

She tried to retreat as I stepped closer, but the chains held her in place. "Wait," she pleaded. "I don't know anything. I don't know where she is."

"I don't believe you," I said. Then I grabbed her arm, squeezing harshly while I took the edge of my blade and sliced a thin layer of skin away from her flesh. She screamed, and the gash in her arm began to fill with blood. It wasn't deep enough to gush, just enough to expose the delicate, sensitive layer of skin underneath.

I took the tip of the knife and trailed it along her exposed flesh, and she cried out again.

"Please, I swear I know nothing!"

"You know, every time I felt your hands on me, it felt like I was being burned alive. It felt like my body was being ripped apart—tainted and poisoned by some flesh-eating disease. I couldn't scrub it off, no matter how hard I tried. You and your friends did that to me. Reyna did that to me."

Tears streamed down her face, and I caught them with the knife, scraping the tip against her cheek. She jolted back but could only move an inch before hitting the wall.

I dragged the knife through her open wound again, and she gritted her teeth. "I'm going to need you to tell me something useful. Before I take more of your skin like you did mine."

"Ladon?"

I spun around to find Emilie staring at me. She didn't seem frightened, despite the bloody knife in my hand and the crazed expression I was certain I wore.

"What are you doing here?" I asked, reaching for her and nudging her out of the cell. I closed it behind me and locked it. We walked far enough that we could speak in hushed tones but close enough I could keep my eye on our two prisoners. They weren't going anywhere, but I also didn't want to give them a chance to talk. It would be better for us if they didn't have a moment to come up with lies to feed us.

"You said I could be a part of this," Emilie said. Her brows pinched together like she was hurt that I'd excluded her. Not at all concerned about what I'd just been doing to Clarise.

"I know, but..."

"But what?"

"The things that I will have to do in order to get information are not going to be pretty, Emilie. I don't want you to see this. To think less of me, or view me as a monster."

I didn't feel like the bad guy in this situation. In fact, I felt righteous about the pain and suffering I wanted to inflict, and I thought that might be worse. Emilie would never be impressed with this version of me. The one who sought revenge.

"Ladon, I would never think less of you for retaliating." She pointed to Zayn and Clarise. "Those people are the real monsters, not you. How many times do I have to tell you we are in this together? I want to see them pay just as much as you do."

My gaze darted between her and the two prisoners. I still wasn't sold on the idea, but I couldn't deny her the opportunity when she was so adamant. And maybe I was being too protective of her. She was smart enough to understand what she was asking for. "Okay. But if it's too much, say the word and we can stop."

She nodded. There was no fear in her eyes—only determination. "I understand."

Together we re-entered the cell, and Emilie stayed near the door.

"Now, where were we? I think it's your turn again," I said, moving closer to Zayn. The blood loss and trauma to his hand had him hanging limply from his shackles, but he focused his attention on me. "I don't want to take another finger, Zayn. I would much rather hear whatever info you have on Reyna. Tell me and we can be done with this."

He grumbled, his eyes wandering the room. It took a second before I realized they'd landed on Emilie. I grabbed his face again, demanding he look back at me. "No, no, Zayn. She is not yours to behold."

He chuckled. "I still see the memory of her cunt every time I close my eyes."

He barely had time to finish his sentence before my fist connected with his mouth. I reached for his hand with my knife ready to sever the next finger when Emilie spoke.

"Wait."

She grabbed my arm, and it would've been easy to shake her off, but I let her restrain me.

I gave her a questioning look. "Emilie, this man—"

"I know what he's done." She eyed him with a level of hatred and disdain that I'd only ever seen her display toward one other individual. And he deserved every bit of it. When she spoke again, it was hardly more than a whisper. "I still feel their eyes on me. I hate being in a crowded room of people because it brings me back to those nights. I'm suspicious of anyone who looks at me for more than a few seconds. It makes me shake. It makes me nauseous."

I nodded. It was the same for me. When someone bumped into me, I grew aggravated. A simple handshake or hug from my own mother made me want to scrub a layer of my skin off. Every day was a reminder that although we were safe, we would never be the same.

Emilie held my gaze for a few more seconds, eyes filled with angry tears. Then she turned back to Zayn. "I don't want his fingers. I want his eyes."

She turned to face Clarise and sneered down at her. There was something fiercely protective and possessive in the way she spat, "And I want her hands and tongue."

The parts that had been all over me without my permission.

Clarise made a panicked noise and pleaded once again. "I don't know anything. I swear I don't."

But I was still watching Emilie with admiration. She looked at me with a nod of reassurance. I smiled in return.

I'd give her whatever she wanted.

Chapter Sixteen

Ladon

Breathe in. Breathe out.

My legs were heavy against the sandy shore, but it wore my muscles down in the best way. Getting back into the habit of training was doing wonders for my sleep and mental health. I'd asked Emilie a few times if she'd like to come with me to see if it would help her too, but so far, she hadn't taken me up on it.

Instead, she had spent most of the past week with Marco and Selene working on that gods-damned antidote. I wasn't an expert in alchemy, but I had expected a solution by now.

My arms pumped harder, and cool air brushed through my hair. It was impossible to know whether my accelerated heart rate was because of my frustration or the intensity at which I ran. Perhaps a mixture of both.

The only thing more frustrating than Cyrus's unchanged status was the fact that Zayn and Clarise still hadn't shared anything of use. I was confident that Clarise was telling the truth—that is, before I cut out her tongue. She was weaker than her partner, but even so, she never broke. She didn't even offer false information just to get me to stop.

Zayn, on the other hand, was holding onto something of worth. I could sense it. He was trying *too* hard to prove he could handle the torture. Like he was taunting me. But he had passed out after I carved out his eyes, so I had to take a break. I'd check in on them both after I met with a few advisors later today. On top of everything else, I was still juggling my duties as regent.

I turned around at my usual halfway point—Treye's Grove. There was an entire horde of religious fanatics worshipping and begging the gods to save my brother. I used to get annoyed seeing them all out here so early in the morning, but today I took comfort in it. Maybe their mythical higher beings would give us a solution soon.

As the castle came into view, I slowed to a walk and headed to the water. I pulled off my shoes and rolled up my pants before stepping in and letting my feet sink into the sand. It was as calming as it was cooling—something I desperately needed after my run.

The waves rolled in and out, and I closed my eyes, getting lost in the sound and basking in the sun on my face. I'd never take the sunlight for granted again after spending so many months without.

A faint voice called to me, and my eyes shot open. I turned around, unable to tell if that was alarm in her voice or something else.

Emilie waved her arms in the air, shouting, "Come here. Come here!"

My legs found their strength again, and I bolted toward her. I ran up the stairs from the beach to the gardens two at a time until I stood before her. "What's wrong? What's happened?"

She grabbed my hands and squeezed, and I realized that she wasn't worried or frantic—she was beaming. "Nothing is wrong. It's happening. They've figured it out. Marco and Selene, they've come up with the antidote. They're going to administer it any second now, and Sophia wanted me to come find you. Let's go. Hurry!"

She didn't have to tell me twice. Together, we raced through the castle corridors and into the healer's ward. The guards stepped aside when they saw us coming, and we barged into my brother's room, interrupting the silence.

"Ladon," my mother admonished. "No running in the castle."

I could've laughed at the way she spoke to me like I was still seven years old, but I was too focused on Cyrus. Marco was standing over him with a syringe just inches away from his arm, a blue vein prepped and ready to be jabbed.

"Well... what are you waiting for?" I asked.

Marco blinked in annoyance. The answer was obvious—they were waiting for *me*. But I was here now, so there was no more time to waste. This was it. I was going to have my brother back.

Emilie's hand touched my arm, and she slowly rubbed her thumb over my skin. The movement lured my mother's gaze, but her eyes quickly returned to Cyrus. Still, I moved in front of Emilie. I didn't want her to stop touching me—soothing me—but I also didn't want it to be the first thing Cyrus saw when he woke up.

Marco slid the needle into my brother's vein, and the liquid in the syringe slowly seeped into his body. Afterward, Marco placed a bandage over the puncture.

"How long does it take?" My mother asked.

"It's hard to say," Marco answered. "We've never done this before. The serum won't take long to circulate, but we will have to wait and see how his body reacts."

It dawned on me how dangerous this was. I trusted Marco's abilities, but we were experimenting on my brother. I had every hope that this would work, but it was still possible that it wouldn't.

My mother sat on the bed next to Cyrus and held his hand, slowly stroking his face and whispering his name.

I took one of the open chairs that was pressed up against the wall and leaned forward with my chin resting on my clenched fists.

We waited… and waited…

An hour later, we were still waiting. Cyrus hadn't shown much improvement. I thought I could see more color in his cheeks, but that might've been my brain playing tricks on me.

My mother alternated between sitting by Cyrus's side, encouraging him to wake up, and standing so she could pace about the room with her hands pulling at her scalp. Meanwhile, Emilie bounced back and forth between the two of us, hoping she could instill some peace.

"Why don't you go get something to eat?" I finally told her after she got my mother to sit down for the tenth time. "You don't have to stay."

"Of course I'm staying," she said. Then, with a little more sympathy, she added, "But if you or Sophia are hungry, I will go get something from the kitchens."

"I'm not hungry," my mother said.

I wasn't either.

I leaned my head back against the wall and closed my eyes. This waiting was going to kill me.

After another hour passed, I stood up. "I need to go for a walk."

I had just put my hand on the doorknob when a gasp came from behind me. I turned on my heel to see what had shocked my mother.

"Cyrus," she cried. "Oh, gods, Cyrus!"

She threw her arms around him, and he winced, looking around the room in confusion.

His eyes were open. He was awake!

My legs nearly gave out, but I forced them to carry me forward until I sat on the bed opposite my mother. "Brother," I said softly.

"What happened?" he asked, his voice hoarse from weeks of nonuse. "Am I in the healer's ward?"

Emilie appeared with a glass of water in hand, and I took it from her, pressing it to my brother's lips and slowly tipping it. "Here. And yes, you are. What's the last thing you remember?"

He swallowed and licked his lips, eyes bouncing around the room. "I remember going to Murvort and rescuing the two of you. There was a battle. That part is fuzzy. I don't remember blacking out, but I must've. Gods, I must've given you all a fright. You look like you've seen a ghost."

I exchanged a look with Emilie and knew she was sharing the same thought as me—Cyrus had no idea how long he'd been out nor the severity of his situation.

I cleared my throat. "That's right. There was a battle in Murvort, which we won. But you were struck by a poisoned blade. You passed out on the field, and we had to bring you back to Renoa. It took some time to find the cure. Cyrus," I said, gaining his full attention. "You've been in the healer's ward for a month now."

His face twisted in confusion. "A month? How is that possible?"

He started to sit up, but our mother pushed him back down. "You will rest until a healer has given you a full checkup."

"Mother—"

"Don't 'mother' me. Do you know what I have been through? How many times I've had to watch my sons face death?"

I grinned at my brother. "I'd listen to her if I were you."

He relented, settling back into bed. After a moment, he spoke again. "What else have I missed? I presume you've been filling in for me?"

He looked hurt at the idea, but I took no offense. I understood how much he loved being king, and it was a role I could confidently say that I never wanted.

"I've hated every second of it, Brother. I'm sure the conclave will be pleased to have you back as well." I bit my tongue, determining how much information he needed to know right this second. "As for what you've missed, not much. Mostly business as usual. There is one item we should go over, but we can do that once you're feeling better."

I didn't mention that the one item was a momentous agreement with Murvort where we agreed to give them crops, open travel routes, and diminish our naval presence. I wouldn't give him a heart attack after we'd just revived him.

"I'm feeling fine," he said. "Though I am hungry, I guess. And could I get something stronger than water?"

We all laughed.

Mother kissed his forehead and stood up. "I'll go get the healer and find you something to eat. I doubt they'll approve of giving you wine, but I'll see what I can manage."

I couldn't tell if she was kidding, but she left the room without another word.

"Emilie. It's good to see you, too," Cyrus said. She had been so quiet, standing in the corner of the room, that I'd almost forgotten she was here.

She came closer and offered a timid smile. "How are you feeling?"

It was uncomfortable, watching the two of them exchange subdued pleasantries and surface-level remarks. Part of me felt like I should leave the room; right now, she was still his betrothed. He had no idea what had happened in his absence. It felt as though *I* was the intruder rather than my brother.

Suddenly, it became very real, this thing between Emilie and me. The conversation that was inevitable.

My palms began to sweat. How would I break the news to Cyrus? Where would I even begin?

We'd spent so much time focused on getting him back that I hadn't considered what this would mean for our family. I could picture my mother's face clear as day, wagging her finger and saying, 'I told you so.'

I needed more time to thoroughly plan how to break the news.

My brother laughed at something Emilie said, and I was ripped from my thoughts. I should be present with my brother, not thinking about tomorrow's problems. This moment was worth celebrating, not dwelling on how I would break his heart. Gods, I was a selfish asshole.

A knock on the door saved me from my self-loathing.

"That was fast," Cyrus said. "I didn't expect Mother to be back so quickly."

But as the door opened, it wasn't our mother who entered the room. It was Jade.

"Sorry to interrupt the reunion. I was told King Cyrus was awake and couldn't wait to introduce myself." Her smile was forced, her words full of shit. How had she even found out my brother was awake? And who had let her in? The guards and I would have to share a few words.

"And who are you?" Cyrus asked.

"We can do this another time," I said before Jade could speak. "This isn't appropriate."

She was unfazed by my contempt. "I'm surprised your brother hasn't told you."

"Jade," I growled.

"I'm Jade Holden, emissary from Murvort. I'm here to make sure you hold up your end of our deal."

"Murvort?" Cyrus said with a mixture of confusion and disgust. "What deal? Ladon? Explain, please."

I released a heavy sigh and then began to tell him everything he'd missed.

Chapter Seventeen

Emilie

I watched Selene work in utter fascination. She was so sure of herself, so confident. She reached for vials and measured by sight alone, stirring until her brew thickened to the right consistency.

"What is this one for?" I asked. I enjoyed joining her during my spare time and had seen her craft several healing concoctions, but this one was new to me. It was a deep shade of red that shimmered in the light.

Selene pulled out her notebook and turned to a page near the middle, handing it to me so I could read. It was clear this was the remedy she had been working on, though she hadn't needed the recipe. She knew it from memory alone. I read over the ingredients and the instructions and at the bottom saw a handwritten note: *For blood replenishment.*

I nodded in understanding. We had used most of our stores after the battle with Murvort, so it made sense Selene would be working to restock them.

She had fallen right into place in Renoa. The other healers loved her and her vast knowledge of potions and magical remedies. She seemed happy, and it was a splendid sight. It was well-deserved after everything she'd been through.

She still couldn't tell me much about her life before becoming Reyna's prisoner. Who knew whether her memories would ever come back or if they were lost to trauma? But at least she had a future now.

There was a knock on the door, and we both turned to find a castle guard. "Sorry to interrupt. Miss Emilie, the king is looking for you."

My brows rose. It had been three days since he had awoken and three days since we had spoken. I hoped it wasn't too obvious that I was avoiding him. I carefully chose times to visit when I knew he would be surrounded by others and found a reason to leave before we could be alone together. But I could only put off the inevitable for so long.

"He's in his room, my lady," the guard said, then turned to leave.

I closed the notebook and tapped my fingers on the spine nervously. If he was waiting for me in his room, then surely he was alone. There would be no way to avoid him now. Was I ready for this?

Selene grabbed my hands, and I looked up at her as she squeezed. She placed one hand over her heart and then cupped my cheek. It was a comforting gesture, and though she spoke no words, I knew what she was saying.

Everything will be all right.

I handed her notebook back and steeled myself. "I will see you later."

She nodded, and I waved goodbye, forcing my feet to make their way to Cyrus's chambers.

When I arrived, his door was slightly ajar. I knocked before letting myself inside. "Cyrus?"

His room was tidy—almost too tidy. But of course, it hadn't been lived in for a month.

I walked farther inside, and my mind was flooded with memories of the last time I had stepped foot in his room. I had been so young and naïve then. Convinced that I could force myself to fall in love before the world so cruelly reminded me that nothing was ever that easy.

Rain pattered against the windows, and I moved closer to the fireplace, studying the trinkets on the mantle. Miniature carvings and a jewelry box that was old enough that it had to have been passed down through generations.

"Emilie," Cyrus said from behind me, and I nearly jumped out of my skin. He chuckled. "I'm sorry. I didn't mean to startle you."

I spun and watched as he folded an article of clothing and placed it on the arm of his chaise. He was casually handsome in a loose pair of slacks and an untucked shirt. His hair was wet, like he'd just stepped out of the shower, and his beard was freshly trimmed. He looked much healthier than he had when he first woke up.

He came closer, and I instinctively took a step back, almost knocking over a small pile of firewood. He hesitated. "It feels like it's been so long. First with Murvort and then my poisoning. It's almost like we're starting over, isn't it?"

A smile took over his face, and he offered his hand to me.

Tears stung my eyes. I hadn't expected everything to fall apart so quickly. I thought I could at least entertain whatever conversation he had planned for us. Maybe help him get settled back into his room. I thought I could pretend that everything was fine for more than fifteen minutes, but I was wrong. My guilt came crashing down on me, and I couldn't keep it together.

"Hey, hey," he said, pulling me to sit beside him on one of his plush couches. Gods, he was fucking comforting me when I had betrayed him. The fact that he was such a gentleman with a big heart made this harder than I ever could've imagined.

"Stop," I cried. "I don't deserve your kindness."

He looked at me with complete bewilderment. "Why would you say that?"

I bit my bottom lip to keep it from trembling. My eyes wandered the room, looking anywhere but him. There was no better time than the present, but I didn't think I could be brave unless I avoided his gaze. So I looked down at my hands twisting in my lap and took a deep breath, getting control over my emotions.

"I can't marry you," I said quietly.

Silence fell over the room, and for a moment I wondered if he had heard me. I dared to look up at him, and he looked even more confused than before. He started to speak and stopped on multiple occasions, searching for his response.

I saved him the effort. "A lot has happened in the past few months. I think... I think I need time to heal. I'm still..." I trailed off. Dealing with nightmares? Relying on his brother to fight them off? I couldn't say any of that, of course. "My life hasn't been my own, and although I haven't been happy about it, I've also never pushed back. I think my time in captivity made me realize that I deserve to have a say in my future. I'm so sorry, Cyrus."

"Are you certain? If you want to slow things down... I know we hardly got to know one another before everything happened, but I meant what I said about trying to make you happy if you'll give me the chance." He gave me a half-hearted smile. "You could do worse than me, you know?"

"I know," I said with a crack in my voice. "That's what makes this so hard. You are a good man. I may not know you that well, but I know that much. Any woman would be lucky to have you."

He nodded slowly. "You might change your mind..."

Those words, and the hope in his eyes, crushed whatever bit of strength I had left.

I shook my head. My heart only yearned for one Castelli, and he wasn't the one sitting before me. "I'm so sorry," I said again. It didn't feel like there was anything else I *could* say.

Ladon wanted to be the one to tell Cyrus about us, and I wouldn't take that from him. It would be better for him to hear it from Ladon anyway. I was a fleeting moment in Cyrus's lifetime, but his brother...

Family meant everything to them, and if the news came from anyone else, it would cause irreparable damage.

My tears spilled over, and before I knew it, Cyrus was leaning in to wrap me in his arms. It wasn't the embrace I yearned for, but I allowed it anyway. It was the least I could do.

When he let go, I wiped my cheeks with the back of my hand. "I should go."

Cyrus stood and led me to the door. Before I slipped out of his room, he grabbed my hand. He dropped it quickly, then cleared his throat. "Everything will be okay, Emilie. I can't imagine what you and Ladon have been through, but I can see how strong you are. You're going to make it. And if you ever need someone to talk to, just know that I'm here."

I did my best to mask the involuntary effect that hearing Ladon's name had on my body. The flush that spread across my chest and the chills that ran down my spine. I held my breath, wondering if he had noticed.

Once the door closed, I finally exhaled. My feet moved before my brain could catch up. I had to get out of the castle, to breathe and leave it all behind.

I walked briskly through the corridors and out into the gardens. Rain was still falling, but I didn't care. It soaked my hair and my pale purple dress, and then I was running. I made it down to the beach and kicked my shoes off. Bundling the hem of my dress in one hand and gripping my flats in the other, I sprinted across the sand.

When I passed a fishing boat, the sailors shot me curious glances. I couldn't imagine how I must look... the king's betrothed—*former* betrothed, although they didn't know that—running through the rain in an elegant summer dress. They probably thought I'd gone mad. Maybe I had.

Their stares only drove me to run faster.

When my lungs and feet could go no farther, I collapsed in the sand. Shallow waves washed over my lower half as I pulled my knees up to my chest and wrapped my arms around them, burying my head as I sobbed.

There was nowhere I could run where my demons wouldn't catch me. They were always with me—in the eyes of strangers, the lingering glances from Sophia and Selene, and the dark memories that infiltrated my dreams.

I was lost, and I didn't know how to pull myself out of this misery. Maybe I could drift away with the waves. Would they bring me peace, or just pull me under?

The rain was coming down so hard that I didn't hear the approaching footsteps. I only noticed a pair of feet through the gap between my elbow and knee.

Reluctantly, I raised my head to see Ladon towering above me, two vertical lines prominent between his brows.

"What are you doing here, Emilie?"

"How did you know I was here?"

"I saw you scurrying through the gardens from my window. You're a mess." It wasn't judgmental. Merely a fact. My hair was plastered to my head, and my dress was stained with sand and salt water.

My head dropped back to my knees. "I know."

"Get up."

"I don't think I can."

Couldn't he see I was completely drained? I had nothing left to give. My will to keep going had dissipated, washed away with the rain.

Ladon ignored me, bending down to scoop me up in his arms.

"What are you doing?" I demanded, throwing my hands around his neck.

He said nothing as he waded deeper into the water. The turbulent waves rushed over my belly and up to my chest, and I scrambled, attempting to climb out of his arms. He held me tighter while I fought to catch my breath. The water was much colder than I had expected, and I shivered.

Mercifully, he rearranged our bodies so my chest was pressed to his. I wrapped my legs around his waist, my skirt riding up under the water. He rubbed my back, and my teeth slowly stopped chattering.

"Why did you do that?" I asked. There was no space left between us, but I tried to inch closer. I was so cold, but his body was so warm.

"For a minute, it looked like you were giving up." Anger flickered in Ladon's eyes. "After everything we've been through, you're not allowed to give up."

My body slumped, and I let my forehead rest against his. "I'm so tired."

"I know, princess. But I can't live without you. So, I need you to keep going. If not for yourself, then do it for me."

Rivulets of water streamed down his face, and I couldn't tell if it was rain or tears. His eyes were a mesmerizing shade of silver in the storm, and they drew me in until our lips collided. I could taste the saltwater on his lips, and when his tongue slid past mine, I squeezed him tighter.

"I will. For you, I will."

Chapter Eighteen

Emilie

Light filtered into my bedroom too early, and I stretched, feeling the empty space next to me. The blankets were cool, so Ladon must've left my bed long ago while I slept peacefully. He had likely gone for his morning jog, slipping out long before Cyrus woke. Gods, I could only imagine the chaos that would follow if Cyrus caught his brother sneaking out of my room only days after I broke off our engagement.

Ladon hadn't had a chance to tell him the full truth, but it was coming soon. It wouldn't be much longer until Ladon could keep me company every night and ward off the nightmares.

My stomach tightened. I had grown to rely on him so much. That moment when he came to my rescue on the beach... I should have been ashamed of my display of weakness. It wasn't like me. Or at least it wasn't like the person I hoped to be. But Ladon knew me, flaws and all. He knew what I needed even when I didn't have a clue.

It was pathetic. The old me would've been appalled by how dependent I'd become. But the current me, the one who had been tormented in ways I never could've imagined, was overwhelmed by how much I cared about him and how lucky I was to have him.

When my parents traded my hand in marriage for political motives, I had accepted that I would never find love. Somehow it had found me anyway. Moving forward wasn't easy, but Ladon made it bearable.

I smiled and pushed myself up into a seated position, stretching my arms high above my head. Slipping out of bed, I headed toward the balcony door, unlocked it, and stepped outside.

It was going to be a beautiful day. The sun was already bright enough to warm my skin, and clouds were scarce. If I could stomach the crowds, it would be a great day to spend on the training field. The last time hadn't gone so well, but now I knew what to expect. Perhaps I could strengthen my mental fortitude just as much as my physical.

I couldn't spend the rest of my life avoiding crowded rooms. It aggravated me that, whenever I felt too many sets of eyes on me, I was transported right back to Reyna's parties. I could feel everyone staring and waiting for me to break. In some ways, I hadn't escaped at all. I was still in a glass cage surrounded by insidious gawkers.

I couldn't live like that anymore. At some point, I needed to learn how to cope with the trauma. To find a way to heal...

I dressed in a sleeveless top and black denim pants, then tamed my bedhead into an unkempt braid. Finally, I slipped on my boots and sheathed my daggers, leaving my bedroom behind.

Before I headed to the field, I stopped by the kitchen to grab an orange. I would've been happy with just a piece of fruit, but the chef saw my attire and insisted I take a cinnamon roll too. I obliged; I needed the extra energy, and it smelled too heavenly to turn down.

Armed with a spare water canteen, I was finally ready to train.

I stretched and did a few warm-up exercises, thankful there were only two others on the field this morning. More would come soon, but I could mentally prepare for that. In fact, I decided right then to add meditation to my training regimen before I started hurling any daggers or wielding my magic.

I took a seat near the wall and closed my eyes, conjuring a calm scene. Images flashed before me—the sea, the stars at night, silver eyes with a touch of blue. I settled on the waves, breathing in and out with each crest.

A sense of peace washed over me, and I felt more relaxed than I had in quite some time. My skin was warm from the sun, and I dreaded opening my eyes. What if all of this serenity fell apart the second I did?

The clash of swords and laughter from the others sounded in the distance, and I knew that more soldiers were filtering in. Maybe if I kept my eyes closed long enough, I could tune them out.

Unfortunately, a shadow crossed my face and the warmth disappeared. I sighed, knowing I needed to finish my meditation and get to work, even if I wasn't certain I could face the stares from everyone else on the field.

"Am I interrupting something?"

I jumped. My eyes shot open and up to Ladon, who towered over me. "I didn't hear you sneak up on me."

"I'd hardly call it sneaking. You were completely zoned out. Everything all right?" he asked, extending his hand to help me up. I took it, and he easily pulled me to my feet.

"I'm okay," I said, brushing the dirt off my pants. "I didn't expect to see you here. Don't you have important meetings today? Contracts to sign or people to pester?"

"I'm officially retired from my kingly duties," he said with a grin. His carefree smile was genuine and beautiful. It suited him.

Without thinking, I reached up and traced his smile line. His eyes fell to my hand before he licked his lips. A burst of jeering snapped us out of it, and he took a step back.

Although we were isolated from the others, I still spoke quietly. "Have you talked to Cyrus yet? About us?"

Ladon shook his head. "Not yet. Every time I try to bring it up, something or someone interrupts us. I have a feeling it's only going to get worse now that he's thrown himself into his responsibilities again. The one time I even mentioned your name, he quickly found an excuse to leave the room."

He rubbed the back of his neck, looking frustrated, and I shared the sentiment. Though I had to admit, as much as I wanted to be tangled up in bed with him and feel his hot skin against mine, there was something to be said about taking it slow, using this time to get acquainted while we weren't under mortal threat and isolated from the rest of the world. I'd be lying if I said I didn't enjoy it at least a little bit. Once the obstacles were removed, the wait would've been worth it.

I loved him so deeply, I would wait an eternity if I had to.

"I'll try again this evening," Ladon said. "Mind if I keep you company while you train?"

"Is that your way of imposing and taking charge of my training?" I teased.

He shrugged. "Some would say I'm highly qualified for the job."

"Mm-hmm. I guess I could use your guidance. I was going to work with daggers and magic wielding today."

He made a face that told me he wasn't sold on that plan.

"What?"

"I had something else in mind. I was thinking we could work on your hand-to-hand combat. Your precision with the daggers is lethal, and you have an excellent grip on your magic, but it means little if someone is in close range."

I grinned. "I think you just want an excuse to put your hands on me."

His eyes sparkled, and his tongue crossed his bottom lip. He lowered his voice. "I don't need an excuse to lay my hands on you, princess."

Heat rose in my cheeks, and I turned away so he couldn't see. Judging by his chuckle, I wasn't fast enough.

"Come on," he said, pulling me out into the open.

We sparred for what felt like hours, but I knew by the sun's position it wasn't even noon yet. Time just moved slowly when Ladon trained me. Every moment he took to correct my stance, placing his hands on my hips or my shoulders... my arms... my neck... the world came to a standstill.

And when he removed his shirt and his skin glistened in the sun—gods, I was a simple woman with simple desires. He caught me staring and shook his head, smiling like he was pleased with himself. As if this was what he'd hoped for all along.

"Think you can focus for a bit longer?" he asked, eyes sliding down my body as if he could envision my naked figure. My chest burned, and I resented that my shirt didn't cover more of my skin. He opened up his palm and motioned me toward him. "Come on. Show me what you've learned."

I took a deep breath and moved into a fighting stance. He waited for me to attack first, and I took my time searching for a weak spot. It was hardly fair, though. He had the confidence of a man who'd trained all his life.

I moved to the right, forcing him to move too. If I kept moving, perhaps I'd eventually catch him off guard and he'd leave something vulnerable. I wasn't picky—a leg, a rib, his chest. I'd hit any target he made available.

When I shifted to the left, he mimicked my steps, still keeping his guard up. "Don't be shy, Emilie. We're fighting, not dancing."

"I thought you were supposed to be training me, not taunting me. You should know better than anyone not to take unnecessary risks. It's why you're hoping I'll take the first shot."

He grinned, proud of how much I'd learned. As a reward for my competence, he stepped forward, taking a swing that I easily dodged. It left an opening on his right side, and I aimed a hook into his ribs.

He didn't even grunt. Instead, he brought his arm down, trapping my wrist, and twisted until my back was against his chest and his other arm was wrapped around my neck. I couldn't move unless I wanted to lose all access to oxygen.

"Ladon," I whined.

His lips brushed my ear, and his hot breath tickled my neck. "I know you can do better than that, princess."

I squirmed, but his hold on my neck was too tight. He loosened his grip ever so slightly, not wanting to do any real damage, and I almost laughed. Would it be cheating to use *this* weakness against him? His love and affection for me? It wouldn't work on a battlefield, but I couldn't resist the temptation.

I backed into him and circled my hips, pushing my ass against his groin.

He sucked in a sharp breath, and his chest inflated. Then he rumbled an amused laugh. "Once a cheater, always a cheater."

"I don't know what you mean." I bit my lip, trying to hold back my laughter.

"Play nicely, or you won't like my punishment for you."

My cheeks flushed, and so did the place between my thighs. A shudder rolled through my body, and his hold on me tightened.

His voice was practically a whimper. "Fuck, Emilie. I didn't realize you were into that."

I hadn't either, but my mind spun with the image of him having his way with me. What *would* he do? Where would he start?

His hand skimmed across my stomach, setting my skin ablaze. My chest felt heavy when I tried to catch my breath.

"Ladon," I sighed, my head rolling to the side and coming to a stop on his shoulder. I craned my neck to find him, and he stared down at me with a lust-filled gaze that was sure to send me over the edge. My head emptied of all thoughts except one—I wanted him to take me to bed. I wanted to strip off our clothes and remember what it was like to feel him inside me. "I—"

"Your brother is looking for you."

Ladon released me, and I hastily created space between us. We were training. It was innocent. Or at least that was what I told myself as I met Jade's eyes.

Her glare told me she didn't buy it.

Ladon cleared his throat. "Did he say why?"

Jade grinned, her gaze bouncing back and forth between the two of us. I didn't care for the way she studied Ladon. I suddenly wanted to step between them just to block her view. He was mine, and her lingering stare was unwelcome.

I took a deep breath and scolded myself for being a hormonal, territorial wretch. I might've been confused about where my life was headed and the person I was becoming, but I was certain about one thing—Ladon would be by my side. Sensing a threat to that security had me acting out of character.

Once I had gotten my jealousy under control, I rejoined the conversation. Thankfully, I hadn't missed much in my momentary insanity. Jade was rattling on about Murvort and scouts that were scattered throughout the countryside.

"We have them everywhere, you know," she said, like we were supposed to be impressed by the allies she and her brother had gained.

I wasn't an expert in politics, but it seemed like the bare minimum. Looking to my right, I could tell Ladon agreed. He crossed his arms and waited for her to explain why she'd interrupted our training.

Jade picked at her nails like it was a contest to see who could be more disinterested in this conversation. Nodding, she added, "A couple of them were in Sage Harbor when they saw a certain malevolent monarch sneaking onto a merchant ship."

Ladon and I exchanged a look, and I could see it in his eyes—desperation to fly across the continent and catch the bitch who had made our lives hell. To ruin her the way she had ruined us. I felt that desperation in my soul too. I wanted revenge.

We gathered our belongings, and Jade was on our heels as we left the field, muttering something I couldn't make out. I didn't care. She didn't matter right now. All that mattered was that Reyna had been spotted.

Chapter Nineteen

Ladon

I MADE QUICK WORK of the maze of halls that led to my brother's office—the office I had occupied for the past few weeks. I was thankful to no longer claim it as my own, but my legs carried me there as if it were second nature. Like I'd never left at all.

It was unnerving and a reminder that I should've left for Fort Malek as soon as my brother resumed his position. I would've, too, if it hadn't been for Emilie. As long as she stayed in Renoa, so would I.

Plus, I still needed to divulge my big secret.

I opened the door without asking permission, and Cyrus looked up, clearly startled by the intrusion. When he realized it was me, his face softened, and he gestured for me to come inside. Jade and Emilie followed. He seemed to expect the former, but the latter... He gave Emilie an odd look before he composed himself.

"Reyna has been found?" I asked, not bothering with pleasantries. Patience had never been my strong suit.

Jade snorted. She'd already told us as much, but I needed to hear it from my brother's mouth. I wouldn't believe it until someone I trusted told me it was the truth.

Cyrus nodded.

My fists clenched at my sides. Anger coursed through my veins. Up until now, I hadn't had anywhere to place it. But now... now I had a clear target.

"When do we leave?"

There was nothing worthy enough to keep my feet planted in Renoa while Reyna stood on the other side of the continent. I was restless and hungry for vengeance.

Cyrus raised his eyebrows. "Hold on a minute. We can't just go barging into Murvort."

"Actually, we can," Jade interrupted. We all turned to stare at her, and she shook her head. "It's one advantage of our treaty. Murvort no longer belongs to Reyna. You don't need her permission to enter, nor do you need my brother's. I am here to act on his behalf, and I'm telling you it's okay to go after her."

Maybe she wasn't so terrible after all.

Emilie looked like she could've hugged her but thought better of it when Jade scowled at her.

Okay, she was still awful.

"Perfect. I can be packed and ready to go by dawn." I glanced at Jade. "It won't take long to reach Sage Harbor now that the old travel routes are open, right?"

She shook her head. "I wouldn't recommend it. They're open, yes, but they haven't been maintained for years. There are looters and violent criminals who patrol many of our roads."

"Why would you allow that?"

Jade pulled back. "*We* haven't allowed anything. You can thank Reyna for that. It'll take some time before my brother can clean up all the delinquents."

I might've felt a little remorse for my outburst, but her negative attitude made it so easy to lash out.

Emilie stepped forward, positioning herself between us. "What do you suggest, then?"

Jade turned to Cyrus. "Do you have a map of Murvort?"

"I do." He stood from behind his desk and rifled through the center cabinet on the left wall. It took a minute before he found what he was searching for, but he pulled out a few large sheets of paper that curled at the edges. Placing them on the desk, he used some thick books to hold the corners down. "This is the most recent I have. I'm afraid it's at least a couple decades old, so I'm not sure how much has changed."

Jade scanned the map, rubbing her chin. She pointed to the northern part of the continent, dragging her finger through what appeared to be wilderness. It was covered in forests, and I couldn't spot a single landmark or distinguishable path. "This is the best route."

"What route?" I asked. "There's nothing there."

"Well, it's old," Cyrus said. "Perhaps there's a road now."

Jade shook her head. "No. There's no road. The northern forests are mostly abandoned. Some recluses have made homes in the wilds, but there aren't any settlements."

Cyrus frowned. "Then why would we go that way?"

"This is the best way if you don't want to alert Reyna that you're on to her. She still has loyalists who would report any sightings. This way you'll avoid the vigilantes and remain unseen. I know my way well enough."

"Who said you were coming?" I growled. "Emilie and I can do this on our own."

"Emilie?" Cyrus asked. I wasn't sure why he was caught off guard. Of course she would be coming with me. But maybe he didn't know her like I did. There was no way she would stay in Renoa. This retribution was as much hers as it was mine.

"Is that a problem?" she asked. It was subtle, but I noticed she took a step closer to me. Like some kind of magnetic pull of destiny that refused to see us divided. When threatened, the draw became stronger.

"I don't know," Cyrus said, still trying to assess the situation. To assess her. His eyes softened. "I assumed you'd rather be safe here in Renoa, protected from danger."

"I will never feel safe until Reyna is dead." Emilie's words both sent chills down my spine and warmed my heart. She said it with such determination, and I knew she wanted to be the one to take Reyna's last breath. And I would happily give it to her, even if I wanted it for myself too. Perhaps we could share it.

Cyrus looked at me, silently asking whether I thought this was a good idea.

"Emilie has been training with me for weeks. She's more than capable of joining this mission."

A small laugh left my brother's lips. "I'm surprised. Not that long ago, you were demanding I leave her behind in Renoa while we visited Fort Malek. I had hoped the two of you would get along eventually."

Jade snickered, and I shot her a look to shut the fuck up. I didn't know how much she'd seen on the training field or what she had made of it, but now was not the time.

Cyrus didn't seem to notice any of this. He sighed. "Maybe if I'd listened to you then, we'd be living in an entirely different reality. I trust your judgment, though."

Taking his seat once again, I couldn't help but notice he looked older and more exhausted than I had ever seen him. Was it because of his prolonged illness or the effect of resuming his ruling position? On top of that, his fiancée had just broken off their engagement, and I would make that wound double in size when I told him the truth.

I couldn't bear to think of it any longer, so I focused on the task at hand. "It's settled then. Emilie and I will track Reyna down and take care of her."

"And me," Jade added. I rolled my eyes, but she carried on. "I'm the one who knows how to navigate the northern woods."

"How hard could it be?" I mumbled under my breath.

She shot me a look that said she'd heard it. "*And* if you encounter any trouble, having the new monarch's sister at your side will offer some protection."

I couldn't deny that. If we came across a small group of vigilantes, we could handle them ourselves, but it would be nice to settle things with words rather than violence. It didn't make it any easier to accept her choice to come along.

"Fine," Emilie agreed, removing my chance to argue further. "The three of us—"

"Four," Cyrus said. "The four of us will travel to Sage Harbor."

Now I'd really had enough of this strategy session. "Cyrus, you've *just* recovered. You need to be here, resting and reassuring the people that you are well and fit to rule. Not to mention, Mother will be furious if we both leave her again. You don't know what it did to her last time..."

"I know perfectly well what losing a son did to her," my brother said quietly. "And I'm going to make sure she doesn't lose him again."

I paused my rant to take in his haunted expression. Was this what had aged him so quickly? The months I was gone, when for all he knew I was dead... how deeply had it hurt him? I knew my mother had mourned my loss, still did in some ways, but I hadn't considered that my strong and resilient brother had mourned too.

There was sadness in the air. An indescribable agony for the innocence and naivety stolen from all of us. Like shattered glass—the pieces had all been accounted for, but they'd never fit together the same.

Jade was the first to disrupt the silent suffering, clicking her tongue. "The four of us, then? I'm looking forward to it."

Without another word, she spun and left the room.

I sent my brother an apologetic look. After all, it was my fault Jade had entered our lives.

He shook his head. "Have you ever met someone so self-centered and oblivious to her surroundings? Gods, you'd think she was living in her own world and we were all of zero consequence."

Emilie chuckled reservedly, and I let the corner of my mouth turn up into a hesitant smile. "She is quite a character," Emilie said.

Cyrus gave her a nod, and my stomach twisted in knots. I hated this. How would I travel with them when guilt and jealousy exploded inside me every time they looked at each other?

"We should go," I said. "If we're going to leave at dawn, we need to pack and get a good night's rest."

"Of course," Cyrus said, waving to the door.

I let Emilie leave first, and just as I was about to exit, Cyrus stopped me.

"Ladon," he called.

"Yes," I asked, looking over my shoulder rather than turning around completely.

"Can you do me a favor?"

"Anything, brother."

"Will you keep an eye on Emilie? While we're on this mission, I mean. I know I'm still weak from being bedridden for so long, and you've always been a better warrior than me. Will you protect her?"

My mouth felt dry, and I struggled for words. "I meant what I said before. She is strong and has exceeded even my expectations with her training."

He huffed a laugh, and I turned fully to face him. He was grinning widely.

"What's so funny?"

"I was just remembering the day I told you to train her to fight." He leaned back in his chair and gave another shoulder-shaking chuckle. "You were so angry with me. It's nice to see that you've changed your mind."

My throat closed. I could barely manage a single word. "Hmm."

"I'm thrilled to hear that she's a natural fighter, but I'd still feel better knowing that you were looking out for her. If we are attacked and it comes down to it, I'd prefer you defend her rather than me."

I finally managed to wet my tongue. "Don't be ridiculous. You're the king. My duty is first and foremost to you."

Cyrus shook his head. "Then listen when I command you."

I hated when his requests as my brother turned into commands as my king. There was no arguing with him now. Still, I didn't understand why he would make this choice. Why would he put Emilie's safety above his own? Unless...

"You care about her?" I asked. "Even though she ended your engagement?"

He shrugged. "It's hard not to. I know it's difficult to understand, but when you're one half of an arranged marriage, it's easier to live with the situation when you choose to go all in. I thought she was going to be my wife. I forced myself to envision a life with her—what our kids would look like, how we would spend our free time, our shared interests. It's not easy to move on from that."

The gods were punishing me. There was no other explanation. They'd seen the way I'd fallen for Emilie, and this was their reminder that in doing so, I'd betrayed my flesh and blood. He didn't deserve this.

And yet... I knew I was doing the right thing. If my actions and my feelings were wrong, then why did every fiber of my being demand to be tied to hers?

Cyrus would understand. He had to.

My head spun and my palms began to sweat, but this seemed like the best opportunity I could hope for. If we were leaving in the morning, I wouldn't get another chance to speak to him alone for gods knew how long.

I cleared my throat and made a feeble attempt to swallow. "Cyrus, I—"

A light knock sounded on the door, and a low voice came from behind me. "Pardon the intrusion. I was told you needed me, King Cyrus?"

"Yes, Hudson. Please come inside. I wanted to go over a few things for you to handle while I'm away."

Our mother. He meant for Hudson to handle our mother. He'd been employed by our family for my entire life, and if anyone could keep her calm while we were away, and keep her from following us, it would be Hudson.

"Ladon, I will see you in the morning," Cyrus said, and then began listing the responsibilities he expected Hudson to cover during his absence.

My chance to tell him the truth disappeared yet again.

Chapter Twenty

Emilie

JADE WASN'T KIDDING ABOUT the lack of civilization in the north. It took three days to reach an abandoned border crossing in the mountains. Hidden between two snow-capped peaks, the tiny trail wound down one side and deep into a canyon hidden by fog. It was the kind of place you could only find if you knew what to look for, and thankfully, Jade did.

From the look that Cyrus and Ladon exchanged, I wasn't the only one wondering how or why she knew. But as I stared up at the menacing mountain on the opposite side of the chasm, it became clear why the post had been abandoned in the first place. The trip across the border was miserable—some might even say impossible. Anyone brave enough to cross here deserved to reach their destination.

"How are we supposed to get up that?" I asked, praying my nerves weren't obvious. Had I taken on more than I could handle?

"Climb," Jade said matter-of-factly.

I waited expectantly, thinking there had to be more to it than a one-word directive. Ladon and Cyrus both looked apprehensive as well. Our group wasn't prepared to scale a mountainside.

Just as Ladon was about to say something, a frown on his face, Jade extended her arm and flexed her fingers. A bluish hue danced around her fingertips like mist, and I watched as it glided toward the base of the mountain. Slowly, a rectangular prism formed. The top was flat and a little more than shoulder-width. It raised about a foot off the ground before it solidified. Another formed, and then another. Soon, a dozen steps jutted from the side of the mountain, completely made of ice.

I'd never bothered to ask what Jade's magic was, but here was the answer. She was an ice wielder like Bianca, and in this case, it had come in handy.

"Does that work for you?" she asked once her stairs had climbed farther than I could see.

I nodded, and so did Ladon and Cyrus.

Jade went first, strengthening and creating more stairs as she went. I followed her, while Ladon and Cyrus climbed behind me. The ascent was still dangerous even with her magic. It was ice, after all, and one slip would be deadly. I didn't even chance a look over the edge of the ice block under my feet, because I knew it would make me dizzy and nauseous. Instead, I focused on my breathing and counted my steps until we reached the top. I lost track more than once and started again at zero each time.

Who knew how many stairs it actually took before we reached the peak again, this time in Murvort territory. I released a heavy breath. We had visited this place more often than I would've liked, but it was for a good reason.

"How do you know your way through these lands?" Cyrus asked as we headed west. The mountains turned into hills and eventually melted into flat ground and a sea of trees. The trunks were dark, almost black, the canopies so thick that they blocked out all sunlight. It was as if we were traveling at night, even though I knew it to be mid-afternoon.

Jade pushed through tree branches, not bothering to check if we made it through before she sent them flying back toward us. Thankfully, Cyrus switched places with me after I caught one too many stray branches with my bare hands. Thorns had sliced through my skin, but I'd live.

"I was born in the wilds," she said.

For some reason, I expected her to share more than that, but I should've known better. She was a woman of few words, and she'd likely never detail her life story for us. Still, I tried to break her icy exterior a little further.

"At what point did you move?" I asked. At some point, her family had to have rejoined society if they'd been part of an early rebellion. It was one of the few details Ladon had shared with me about Jade and her brother—that their parents had been slaughtered in a public square for their criticism of the Lemaires.

Jade sighed with annoyance. "I don't know. When I was fifteen or so."

"What was it like?"

I second-guessed my curiosity when she turned around and squinted. The combination of her dark green eyes and the jagged scar through her brow was unsettling. There wasn't anger or hatred in her expression, but skepticism. An innate distrust of the unknown. Had spending half of her life in the wilds instilled that in her? She certainly wouldn't have had much opportunity, if any, to socialize during her formative years. Or had someone or something else made her so wary after she'd reentered society?

I tried again. "It must've been difficult living out here. Without easy access to food, water, and supplies. What did you do for fun?"

She faced forward again and pushed another branch out of her way. "We lived close enough to a spring for fresh water. We had an abundant garden, and everyone in the family knew how to hunt."

When she stopped speaking, I assumed she wouldn't answer my last question. Perhaps I'd pressed her enough for one day.

But then she added in a hushed tone, "We didn't have fun. Every day is work when survival isn't guaranteed."

"It must've been hard," Cyrus said.

"Yeah."

Quiet fell around us as we carried onward. My arms began to ache from holding back tree branches, and my feet dragged on the forest floor. No one else showed any signs of fatigue, so I pushed myself to keep moving. We likely still had hours ahead of us, though it was difficult to tell the time when the sun couldn't pierce the trees above.

Finally, Jade came to a stop. "We can set up camp here tonight."

It was the largest space we'd come across all day long, and that wasn't saying much. It was still less than ten feet in diameter and surrounded by thickets and tree trunks wider than a horse.

Ladon pulled off his backpack and dug out a separate bag of food while Cyrus cleared a space to build a fire. There wasn't enough room to set up either of our tents, so we'd be sleeping on the ground tonight.

I grabbed a few sticks without leaves to use as skewers for our peppers and potatoes and then took a seat on top of my sleeping roll.

Somehow, the sky grew darker, and I knew that night had fallen. The fire flickered long after we'd finished our meal, and it warded off the chill that lingered in the air.

"Do you remember the last time we went camping?" Cyrus asked.

Ladon grinned. "That wasn't camping, Cyrus."

"What would you call it, then?"

Ladon smiled, toying with his stick in the fire. "Two spoiled kids whose parents made a campsite in the middle of the gardens because they wouldn't shut up about sleeping in a tent."

I listened while the two brothers recounted stories of their childhood. They were as devious as they were adorable.

"I wish my brother and I had half the childhood you two did," I said. "My parents never would've made the effort to see us so happy. They were far too concerned with their own pursuits. I sometimes wonder why they even had children, but then I remember it was to keep their legacy alive. To use us for their gain. Like selling off a daughter for financial gain…"

I trailed off and felt everyone's stares on me. My cheeks heated, but miraculously, there was no wave of nausea and panic that usually accompanied uncomfortable attention.

"Well," Jade said. "This has been a blast, but I think I've had enough chit-chat for one evening."

I felt for her. My parents weren't the greatest, but at least they were still alive.

I stood, grabbing a mage lantern and making my way to the exterior of our campsite.

"Where are you going?" Ladon asked.

Turning back to him, I crossed my arms. "I need to relieve myself. Is that okay with you?"

He glared at me before nodding.

I rolled my eyes and tramped through the weeds and overgrowth until I found a spot far enough away that they wouldn't hear or see me. It was amusing to watch Ladon act so territorial over me. Did he even realize how he sounded? Hopefully Cyrus and Jade hadn't seen the protectiveness in his eyes.

When as I finished my business, I pulled my pants up and buttoned them.

A branch snapped nearby.

My heart sped up. Even with the mage light, it was difficult to make out the figure hidden between the trees.

"Hello?" I whispered.

There was no answer.

Fuck. I felt around my waist, checking for my daggers and pulling one free.

"Who's there?" I demanded, bringing the dagger back and ready to throw if I needed to. "Show yourself."

Ladon stepped into the light. "Were you going to kill me?"

I released the breath I'd been holding and sheathed my dagger. "What are you doing? Have you been there the whole time?"

"You were gone for too long. I had to make sure you were all right."

"I've been gone for five minutes," I said, shaking my head at him. "You shouldn't have followed. What if Cyrus suspects something?"

Ladon moved closer, and I found it hard to resist his allure. "Cyrus is already asleep. Jade too. They were both out the second their heads hit their mats."

He took another step toward me, placing his hands on my hips.

"Ladon?"

He gently pushed me backward until my foot hit a tree root. I stepped over it clumsily and found my back against the thick trunk.

Ladon kept approaching until there was no space left between us.

I sighed. His body against mine just felt right. My legs separated naturally so he could fit between them, and then his hands were crawling up my sides, teasing the underside of my breasts.

With one hand, he massaged my breast over top of my shirt while the other traveled down to pull my shirt out of where it was tucked into my pants. His fingers slid across my stomach with the gentlest touch until they came to a stop, splayed out over my abdomen.

"Do you want me to stop?" he asked in a husky tone.

"What?" I was delirious. My eyes rolled back in my head, and it was my turn to yank his shirt out of his pants. I pulled on his belt and heard him chuckle.

He leaned close, whispering against my neck, "Do." He kissed the spot under my ear. "You." Another kiss, lower this time. "Want." His mouth traveled along my neck until it reached my collarbone. "Me." His hands were under my shirt, gently lifting the fabric. "To." Oh, gods. "Stop?"

"Don't stop," I said, horrified by how pathetic I sounded. But I lost all control when it came to Ladon. Sure, I'd said we should wait until I'd broken off my engagement and he'd confessed the truth to Cyrus, but we'd crossed off half of those requirements. Wasn't that enough?

Ladon grabbed the backs of my thighs, pulling me up in a swift motion. I locked my legs behind him, bringing him close until I felt his hardening cock press into my aching core.

My head fell back, and I shivered with delight. It didn't seem possible that this kind of pleasure could exist. In the afterlife, maybe, but here and now? I needed him to grind harder, to prove that it wasn't fleeting.

As if he could read my mind, his hand sank past my underwear, sliding through my folds and the slickness at my entrance. He made a hungry sound that rumbled in his chest and made me tremble with anticipation. He used two fingers to circle my clit, and I swore I was going to come undone.

"Gods, Emilie. You're my greatest addiction. I fucking love the way you respond to my touch. Like a secret weapon that only I can wield. Tell me, princess. Has anyone ever made you feel this way?"

"No," I panted as he massaged my clit. I could feel the wetness soaking into my panties. I needed more, needed him to fill me—with his fingers or his cock, I didn't care which. I was clenching around nothing but emptiness, and he knew it.

"And will anyone ever make you feel like this?"

"No. Please, Ladon."

"Promise me. Promise me that you are completely mine."

"I could never be anyone else's."

He growled against my chest before biting my shoulder. His fingers worked their magic on my clit, still teasing me and avoiding the one place I needed them most. It was unfair.

I reached for the buttons on his pants and quickly undid them, pushing my hand down his front. When my fingers wrapped around his thick erection, he gasped.

All movement ceased. I hadn't thought this far ahead. I'd never seduced him before, hadn't had to learn the things that turned him on and what drove him to the edge, because he was usually in control.

As if he sensed my hesitation, he shoved his hand down his pants and closed it over mine. He squeezed, clenching his jaw as he did so. Together, our hands glided up his cock and back down to the base. A shudder ripped through his body on the second stroke, like he could hardly contain himself.

The feeling was mutual.

I ground my hips against him as we both ran our hands over his length. I couldn't get enough of him, no matter how desperately I tried. "Ladon..."

"Tell me, princess. Tell me what you want."

Fuck, it was more than a want. It was a *need.* I had to feel him inside me, or I might die. Had to be as close to him as I possibly could.

"You," I said. "I want you."

I released my hold on his cock and pushed his pants down farther. I pouted when he set my feet on the ground, but it was just long enough to remove my pants and underwear. Then his hands were on my thighs again, and he pinned me to the tree, rubbing his head against my hyper-sensitive clit.

I threaded my fingers through his soft white hair and found his lips, biting the lower one when he didn't immediately give me what I wanted.

As I whimpered, his lips curved against mine. How dare he find amusement in my suffering?

My remaining restraint fizzled, and I reached between us, taking his cock and lining it up with my entrance. I forced my hips down, and felt him slide into my pussy with ease. Ladon's arms braced on either side of my head while I sighed in relief.

"Gods, Emilie. You're fucking perfect. I wish you could feel what I feel—how tightly you squeeze my cock. It's fucking ecstasy."

He didn't have to explain it to me. The way he stretched and filled me was unlike anything I'd ever experienced. It was more than just the pleasure that burst inside me—it was the way we coexisted. There was no me without Ladon and no Ladon without me.

He pulled out a fraction and eased back inside at an impossibly slow pace.

And I. Felt. Everything.

I clawed at his back and rocked my hips, but he grabbed them, re-straining me against the tree.

Leaning back, he let his forehead fall to mine, leaving enough space to see where our bodies joined. I could see every inch of him as he sank into me again.

He took slow and controlled breaths while he drove into me over and over again. My toes curled, and my walls clenched around him. He was pushing me to the edge and holding me there when all I wanted to do was fall over.

"Look at you," he said with a rasp. "Look at how well you take me."

"Ladon, please," I cried. My body was vibrating, full of electricity that would burn me alive if I didn't find a release soon.

"Mm. Say my name again," he growled, digging his fingers into my hips.

Between two erratic breaths, I obliged. "Ladon..."

He slammed inside me harder. Faster. His hold on my hips tightened to the point of pain and I squeezed my eyes shut, focusing all my senses on the delightful friction between my legs. Every thrust had me gasping for breath.

"Open your eyes, princess. Watch my cock disappearing inside you. Look at how wet you've made me. How your arousal covers me."

It was true. His vein-covered length was glistening in the mage light, and I flushed at the sight. I'd done that to him. I'd claimed him and left my essence on him.

My walls tightened again, eliciting a moan from Ladon. Now he was driving inside me without restraint. Two wrinkles formed between his brows while he devoted all his attention to our mutual pleasure. I was so close, and when he brought his fingers to my clit, it was the release I'd been starved for.

I panted as my pussy fluttered around him, spasming every time I thought my orgasm was winding down. It seemed endless, and Ladon kept driving inside me all the while. When he finally came too, my body was spent—my limbs heavy and my torso still trembling in his arms.

Ladon fell against me, covering me in his warmth. He leaned his head on my shoulder while he slowly recovered, and I rubbed circles on his back. I didn't want to move. I would've been content to stay like this all night, safely nestled in his arms with his cock still inside me. Every time he moved an inch, I shivered and squeezed him tighter.

I don't know how long we stayed like that. At some point, my eyelids grew heavy, and I wondered how Ladon had the strength to hold himself up, let alone my weight too.

"We should go back," I said, stroking his hair.

He murmured, but it was hard to tell if it was in agreement or simply approval at the way I massaged his scalp.

"Ladon," I said softly when he didn't move.

He lifted his head and met my gaze. I loved the pink on his cheeks and the drowsiness in his eyes.

I ran my thumb over his bottom lip and gently kissed him. "I love you."

"I love you too, Emilie."

Those words were a comfort that I hadn't realized I was seeking. I kissed him again, pleading for him to understand just how consumed by him I was. His tongue slid into my mouth, and I sucked on it, earning a moan from him. If we didn't stop now, we'd be chasing another orgasm.

A snap made me pull back, scanning the woods for the source of the noise. "Did you hear that?"

Ladon slowly lowered me to my feet, finally pulling out of me. I immediately missed his presence. He looked around the woods before bending over to grab my discarded clothes and prompting me to step into my underwear.

"We should go back now."

Chapter Twenty-One

Ladon

I WAS THE FIRST to wake the next morning. Years of getting up early to train had made it a habit that was hard to break. I tried to stay still and rest a while longer since I knew we had a long day of travel ahead of us.

To my right, Emilie slept soundly, snuggled up in her sleeping roll. Down towards my feet, my brother twitched like he was fighting off a nightmare. I contemplated waking him, but then he smiled, and I figured it wasn't too serious. Jade was on his other side, stiff as a board and facing away from us.

It was possible she was awake and pretending to be asleep, like me. I didn't trust her. I'd heard the same noise as Emilie last night, and I was certain it was the sound of another person in the woods, watching us. If it had been my brother, he would've shown himself and had it out right then and there.

But Jade...

What was she up to? Had she followed us out of malicious curiosity, or had she simply needed to use the bathroom too?

And how much had she seen, exactly? Emilie had to have been blocked by my body, but was it obvious that I was buried deep inside her?

My cock twitched at the thought, and I tried to think of something else. It was difficult, though. After staying away from her for so long, even the smallest, stolen intimate moment was hard to forget.

Who was I kidding? There was nothing forgettable about Emilie.

I looked back toward her, watching her curls dance in the light breeze. Her chest rose and fell with each breath, and I desperately wanted to hug her close to my side. It was my own fault I couldn't do so this very second. I should've had the courage to tell my brother everything before we began this journey.

If I told him now... Well, it could get very messy. As much as I hated to admit it, the matter would have to wait until we returned home.

Finally, Cyrus stirred. He sat up slowly, stretching his arms over his head. He cracked his neck before looking around our campsite. Jade and Emilie were still asleep, but he saw my open eyes and grinned. "Good morning."

"Morning," I said, yawning as if I'd also just woken up. "How did you sleep?"

"Like garbage," he said with a wince. "These pads need more cushioning, if you ask me."

I huffed a laugh. "Are you saying they're unfit for a pampered king?"

"They're unfit for a prisoner."

I frowned. I knew he'd said it without thinking, but these sleeping arrangements were far better than what we had in Murvort. I'd take a clean, thin pad over the dirty mattress with a sheer blanket any day.

"Definitely," I agreed. I slipped out from under my covers and stood up. My muscles ached a little from our travels and the hard ground, but it was nothing I hadn't dealt with before. "Do you want to start a fire? I thought I heard some fowl chirping this morning. Might be nice to have some fresh protein for breakfast."

He nodded while I fastened the belt around my waist and made sure my weapons were all accounted for. Not that I needed them. It'd be easier to hunt with my magic—setting up a trap to catch the small animals.

I set out, and it didn't take long to come across a couple birds perched on a low-hanging branch. With some well-placed magic, I nudged them from their resting spot and into a container I made from the clay soil, leaving just enough space to reach in and snap their necks.

By the time I made it back to our campsite, a fire was burning and everything was packed. Everyone sat around the flames in silence, and when my brother noticed me, he gave me a pleading look.

"What did I miss?" I asked, dropping the dead birds next to the fire. They'd need to be plucked before we could cook them, and my stomach was growling already.

"Nothing," Cyrus said. "You haven't missed a thing."

Emilie looked anxious, but Jade almost smiled. She glanced at me before grabbing one of the birds and starting to prepare it. She spoke in a hushed tone, but I still made out her words. "Can't imagine why there would be such uncomfortable silence."

Emilie shot me a look, but Cyrus stoked the fire without a sign that he'd heard or questioned what Jade had said. Maybe he'd just chalked it up to his and Emilie's dissolved engagement and Jade's unapproachable persona. Regardless, he seemed delighted that I had returned and chattered away while we prepared breakfast.

Once we finished eating, Cyrus put out the fire, and we ventured into the wild, tangled woods once again.

"It won't be much longer before the trees begin to thin out," Jade said after we pushed through the overgrowth for a few hours. Good thing, because I was tired of stomping over tall weeds and through thick bushes.

We came across a shallow stream with crystal-clear water running over an array of gray stones and refilled our canteens.

"You were right," Cyrus said, pointing to the opposite side with a pleasant smile. "I can already see through the trees over there. Patches of light and clearings. I can't wait."

"We could cross here." Emilie pointed to a section of the stream where three stones rose high enough out of the water that their tops were dry.

She headed there first, and I quickly followed. Once we landed on the other side, we started for the tree line, but Jade suddenly yelled, "Stop!"

I drew my sword without a moment's hesitation.

The panic in her voice was a warning, and if she had given it a second sooner, I would've been able to block the arrow that sped toward me. But she hadn't.

It slammed into my shoulder even as I attempted to dodge.

Before I could attempt to fight back, Emilie had flung a dagger in the direction of the archer. I had no idea if it struck the target because my attention was stolen by a second arrow flying from a different direction.

"Behind you," I shouted.

She spun just in time and hurled another dagger into the woods.

Jade and Cyrus crossed the river, taking up arms and readying for a fight. Our assailants hid in the trees, giving them the advantage. Jade charged ahead, disappearing behind a tree. There was a grunt, and then it sounded as though a body hit the ground. When she reappeared, two more attackers were running away from her.

They tried to cross the river back in the direction we'd come from, but I thrust out my hand and a burst of magic threw up a wall of clay blocking their escape.

The first person ran into it, smacking his head so hard that he collapsed to the ground. The second man skidded to a halt and spun only to find that they were surrounded.

I scanned the tree line, but there didn't appear to be any other movement.

"Don't kill me." The man's voice shook. Bold request from a man who'd tried to do just that to us.

I approached him, keeping one hand on my shoulder where an arrow still protruded from my body. Someone would have to pull it out for me, but that could wait for a few minutes. "Who are you?"

"I'm no one. I'm just a merchant." His eyes bounced around, never stopping on one of us for more than a few seconds. Like he was trying to discern the most sympathetic of us to latch onto but realizing he was out of luck.

"A merchant?" Jade repeated, pressing her sword to his throat. "I doubt it."

"I am. I swear!"

"What is it you sell?"

The man gulped, and the tip of Jade's sword made a small nick in his skin.

"What do you sell?" she asked again, more forcefully this time.

"P... please..."

"Answer the question or I will take my time flaying the skin from your body."

Tears welled in his eyes, and his hands were shaking as he raised them in surrender. "All right. All right. I... I sell *entertainment.*"

"What does that mean?" Emilie asked, frowning.

Piercing the man with her gaze, Jade asked, "Do you know who I am?"

He attempted to nod, forgetting about the sword at his neck and wincing when it punctured his skin again. "You're Jade Holden, sister of Jesse Holden."

"That's right. Now why would a bunch of armed vagrants be pursuing me and even trying to assassinate me?"

"N-No, it wasn't like that. I'm a good person. I didn't choose to be part of this. I... I had to. They wouldn't let me out of it."

They? Who was he referring to?

"You are not a good person," Jade said, sliding the tip of her sword along his jaw. He froze, only his eyes moving as he tracked her sword's path. "You are a spineless coward. After all, only a pathetic lackey would be stupid enough to think they'd be better off under Reyna's rule than my brother's."

Jade's silver blade flashed in the light, and the man's head fell to the ground.

"What the hell?" Cyrus shouted. "How are we going to know who sent them?"

Jade cleaned her sword and sheathed it. "I already know who sent them. Reyna did."

"You can't know that for certain," I said. "How could she possibly have any followers left at this point? I was under the impression that most of Murvort was in poverty while she held the throne. Why would they fight for her?"

Jade sighed. "You are right; most people are barely surviving. But she had her circle, and within that circle of wealthy individuals, there's an entire network of *merchants* just like this guy." She gave his head a little kick, and it rolled toward the stream. "My brother made their business illegal, so of course they'd want Reyna back. They are easy targets to become hired arms or bounty hunters. I have no doubt Reyna or one of her devotees sent them."

"He said he sold 'entertainment,'" Emilie said. "What did he mean by that?"

With a look of pity, Jade responded, "Bodies. He sold bodies."

Chapter Twenty-Two

Emilie

"Hold still," Cyrus said. He had one hand planted on Ladon's back and the other wrapped around the arrow protruding from his shoulder. Cyrus's face was paler than Ladon's, and if one of them were to pass out, I'd bet money on the former.

"I didn't expect you to be squeamish, Cyrus," I said. As king, he didn't spend as much time as Ladon on a battlefield, but he wasn't completely shielded from it.

"I'm normally not. It's different, though, when it's a family member. There's a hole... in his flesh," he said with a shudder.

"Just pull it out," Ladon hissed. They'd been going back and forth like this for the past fifteen minutes. Ladon obviously wanted to get the ordeal over with, but Cyrus wasn't sure how to do it without causing more damage.

Initially, I had volunteered to do it, but they both agreed that I didn't have the strength needed to pull it through. I watched with dread; I didn't know how much more I could stand.

Meanwhile, Jade leaned against a tree, twirling half an arrow in her hand—the half that had been snapped off in preparation to pull the rest through. She noticed my glare and ceased her idle activity.

Ladon growled, and my attention snapped back to them. "Gods, Cyrus, if you can't do it—"

"I can do it. I can. Okay, now breathe... On the count of three?"

"Whatever."

Cyrus sighed and seemed uncertain still. He wasted a few more seconds, and I could tell Ladon had lost all patience. The silver in his eyes reminded me of a sharp blade, and his lip curled up in a snarl.

"Gods, you are pathetic," Jade said, stepping forward. She walked around Ladon and pushed Cyrus out of the way. In one swift motion, she ripped the arrow from his shoulder.

Ladon gasped, throwing his hand over his wound and applying pressure. He huffed a laugh. "*Fuck*. Thank you."

"You're welcome," she said, throwing the arrow aside. "Can you take it from here?"

"Yes," Cyrus grunted, reclaiming his spot behind Ladon. "Can you remove your shirt, or do you want me to cut it off?"

Ladon responded by using his good arm to pull his shirt over his head awkwardly and down his injured arm. I inhaled a sharp breath when I saw the blood on his skin. Somehow it was equally as awful as seeing the arrow sticking out of his shoulder. Blood had seeped from the wound and dried halfway down his torso.

Cyrus touched Ladon's back, and Ladon twitched. He quickly masked his discomfort, and Cyrus carried on as if he hadn't noticed. It saddened me that even his brother's touch was difficult to endure. I'd hoped that his journey toward mental healing had been going better than mine, but apparently not.

Light emanated from Cyrus's hand, and the smell of burning flesh filled my nostrils. I looked away and covered my mouth, afraid I might gag. Ladon handled it exactly how I would've expected—with gritted teeth and a string of curse words.

After a few seconds, I heard the shuffling of feet. I looked over my shoulder to find Cyrus standing in front of Ladon and braced to cauterize the other end of his wound. I spun away again just in time to hear Ladon hiss.

"All done," Cyrus said. "How does it feel?"

When I turned around, Ladon was carefully lifting his arm and winding it in a circle. "It's sore, but I'll live."

"Do you need a minute before we continue on?"

Jade answered before Ladon could. "We don't have time to waste. There's a good chance Reyna sent more loyalists after us. We shouldn't stay in one place for too long."

"I'll be fine. Give me a minute to wash up, and then we can keep going."

Ladon's answer seemed good enough for Jade. She walked away and began to monitor the tree line.

I found Ladon's pack and threw it open, grabbing a clean shirt and a spare. Approaching the stream, I knelt down and wet the spare before returning to him.

He reached out for the wet cloth, but I pushed his hand aside. "Let me."

Carefully, I rinsed the dried blood that lingered near his wound. The flesh there was angry and red, no doubt a result of Cyrus's magical healing. This method would have to do while we were out here in the wild, but it would leave a grisly scar.

Ladon's back muscles rippled under my touch, and I dared to let a finger trail over his skin. Goosebumps spread down his arms, and I smiled.

"Turn around," I said once I finished with his back.

He spun around, and I wasn't prepared for how close he was. His face was mere inches from mine, and I withdrew a step. Ladon grinned, seemingly enjoying the way he could so easily rattle me. He spread his legs so I could reach his torso without bumping into his knees, and I hesitated before inching closer.

"Why are you smiling?" I asked him. Whatever the reason, I didn't want him to stop.

He just shook his head.

I gently patted the area around his burnt skin, and he sucked in a breath through his teeth. His knees squeezed my sides, and I wasn't sure if he did it intentionally or if it was merely a reaction to the pain I was inflicting.

"Sorry," I said.

"Don't be."

I studied his face again, and the way he was looking at me made my skin flush. Like we were the only two in the world. Like his brother wasn't standing feet away...

I cleared my throat and finished cleaning his shoulder. Softly, I said, "All done."

Before I could stand, he grabbed my wrist. "Princess..."

"Yes?"

He smirked, and I immediately regretted responding to his pet name for me. But I'd given up fighting it some time ago.

"Tell me what you're thinking. Tell me something honest."

What was I thinking? Everything had happened so fast, I didn't feel like my brain had had a chance to catch up to my adrenaline. It had been awful watching an arrow pierce his body, but it could've been much worse if he hadn't jumped out of the way.

I was thinking about how those awful attackers were in the business of trading *people.*

My face must've shown my disgust, because Ladon grabbed my chin and lifted it. "Now I'm even more curious."

I chuckled. "I'm glad you're alive."

He waited for me to say more, but I didn't have the energy this time. Honestly, I wanted to return to the woods where we could pretend like it was just the two of us and then sleep for a week.

Finally, he said, "I'm glad we're both alive."

"Are you all finished?"

Ladon and I both jumped and hastily stepped apart. I wasn't sure when Jade had snuck up on us, but she seemed to have a habit of popping up at the least opportune time. It was starting to get on my nerves.

Ladon took the clean shirt from my hands and pulled it over his head. "Yes, we can carry on now."

I stood up and went to rinse out his bloodied shirt. I wasn't sure if it was salvageable, but I didn't want to toss it back in a bag without attempting to clean it.

While we finished packing up, Cyrus addressed both of us. "I've got to be honest, I never expected the two of you to get so close."

My heart started to race, and I looked toward Ladon for support. He quietly pulled his pack over one shoulder, the good one, and stared at his brother.

Cyrus continued, "It's surprising. That's all."

"We've been through a lot together," I said, hoping my voice was as steady as I aimed for it to be. "I don't think anyone expected this."

His eyes darted to me on the last word, and I wondered if he was reading into it.

What exactly was *this*?

If I were asked to define it, I would've called it fate. Or destiny. An undeniable and unbreakable tether to one another. Ladon's answer might be more grounded—it was love. It was affection and maybe even a little obsession.

But Cyrus... Cyrus would call it betrayal.

Was that the word running through his mind now? Was it on the tip of his tongue?

"I'm happy," he said. "That you've become friends. Gods, my brother needed one."

Ladon rolled his eyes, but his shoulders relaxed, so mine did too. "When did you become such a sap?"

Cyrus ruffled Ladon's hair, and Ladon pushed his hand away. "I've always been looking out for you. You just never noticed. Come on. We should get moving before Jade leaves without us."

Jade gave him a blank stare, unamused. But then she took her place as leader of the pack again and guided us through the forest.

"Have you ever been to Sage Harbor?" I asked while we walked on. It had been quiet too long, and I was growing tired of counting trees as a means of entertainment.

"No," Cyrus said first.

Ladon shook his head. "No one from Osavian has ventured this far. Our borders have always been locked down."

"Oh, that's right," I said, feeling foolish. I had read that in a history book somewhere. "What about you, Jade?"

Jade glared at me with disinterest before answering. "Yes."

Okay then. If it weren't for the fact that she treated everyone so curtly, I would've been offended. But she rejected all of us equally, so I brushed it off.

"What is it like?"

She scoffed and walked on, and I wondered if boredom would've been a better alternative than trying to engage in conversation with her.

I pursed my lips and started counting trees again. Maybe I could switch it up and count rabbit holes instead.

"You don't need to be so rude," Cyrus said.

I shook my head. "Cyrus, it's okay."

"No, it's not. In case you've forgotten, we didn't ask you to come on this trip. We didn't ask you to come to Osavian either. You forced yourself into our lives, and we're all more miserable for it. The least you could do is to be polite."

Jade turned to look at him, and I swore she was fighting a grin. The two of them squared off and engaged in a war of glares. I'd never seen Cyrus angry before, and I was thankful not to be on the other end of his irritation.

When Jade finally spoke, it was with an air of tediousness. Like it was the hardest task she'd done all week. "It's a harbor. It's exactly what you'd imagine. There are a few shops and taverns and a lot of boats."

"Was that so hard?" Cyrus snapped.

"It's fine, really," I said, attempting to ease the mounting tension. "I just thought some conversation would help pass the time. We don't have to, though."

Jade faced forward again and moved between the trees. I waited a moment, and when Cyrus began to follow, I did as well.

Ladon came up behind me, and his hand grazed my arm. "Maybe next time you can ask something less personal. Like what color is the sky?"

I snorted. "Then she'd think I'm stupid *and* too inquisitive."

"Hey, Emilie," Jade called from the front of our group. "What do you intend to do now that you're no longer engaged to Cyrus? Don't you think it's a little weird to stay in Renoa with your ex-fiancé?"

My face turned bright red, and I was grateful she hadn't even bothered to look back at me. Cyrus did, though, his eyes bouncing between me and Ladon, who was almost attached to my hip. Ladon sensed it too and fell back a step.

Cyrus was polite enough to answer on my behalf. "I've told Emilie she is free to stay. She's a guest in our home for as long as she wants to be."

Jade chuckled.

"What's so funny?" he asked.

"Oh, nothing. It's very benevolent of you to let her live in your home. You don't get anything in return?"

"I wouldn't dream of asking for anything. She has been through enough. It costs me nothing to give her a place to stay while she heals."

"Ah," Jade said, toying with a tree branch as she moved ahead. "Is that it? You're hoping once she gets over her trauma, she'll come back to you?"

"For fuck's sake," Ladon grumbled beside me.

"Could you stop?" I snapped. "We all get it. You have no interest whatsoever in making friends or even being cordial. You've made your point."

Finally, she peeked behind her over her shoulder, eyes locking with mine. "I'm not certain I have, Emilie. There's so much more to talk about. Don't you think?"

Chapter Twenty-Three

Emilie

We traveled the rest of the day in silence. Even our last night camping in the woods was stilted and uncomfortable. We hiked as long as possible before turning in for the evening, and no one made an effort to engage in small talk.

When the sun rose the next morning, we were all ready to reach Sage Harbor and have a task to distract us from the unending tension.

Early in the afternoon, there were finally signs of life ahead. Smoke billowed out of a couple of chimneys, and I could hear the sounds of civilization—laundry whipping in the breeze on the clothesline, a cart with creaky wheels, and a bell ringing over a building where children poured out into the street.

As we drew closer, I was surprised to see so many welcoming faces. My experience in Murvort had painted a picture in my mind that all their villages would be harsh and unkind, both in their physical appearance and in the spirits of their residents. But the people in Sage Harbor seemed happy, and while I'd expected our group to stick out as strangers, most townsfolk didn't give us a second look.

"Do you think they get a lot of outsiders here? With the harbor?" I asked Ladon. Jade probably knew the answer best, but I wasn't about to ask her another question.

"I would assume so. Before we opened our border crossings, this was the only place to get in or out of Murvort."

"They don't have any other coastal towns?"

"There are a few, but they were all guarded by our naval fleet."

"Why?" I asked. Murvort was far from paradise, but it seemed odd to blockade them almost entirely.

Ladon shrugged. "It's been that way for generations. It started because of a war between our nations, and it has carried on because every time there was an attempt to form a treaty, Murvort broke it. I don't recall the last time there was an alliance between Murvort and Osavian."

"Until now," I said, eyes tracking Jade as she led us through town.

"Until now," he agreed. After a moment of consideration, he added, "I hope it sticks this time, but I won't hold my breath."

I wished for the same. I had hoped that Murvort might be more reliable without Reyna at the helm, but so far, Jade hadn't set my mind at ease. How long would it take for her and her brother to betray us?

Slowly, businesses began to pop up between the cream-colored houses with timber frames. Awnings in shades of reds, greens, and blues—all faded and muted—caught the light drizzle, keeping the shopkeepers and their outdoor displays dry.

I found myself searching faces as if Reyna might pop out any second. But she was smarter than that. She'd been spotted boarding a ship and was probably destined for Wyland, the continent to the west. Even if she hadn't set sail yet, she would likely be hiding somewhere, not out in the open. But I couldn't help but feel her haunting presence.

The street crested a hill and then began to descend. I inhaled sharply as a breeze caressed my cheeks and the sea appeared ahead.

All along the coast, there were ships docked with workers loading and unloading freight. Sails could be seen in the distance as more boats came in or departed. A lighthouse stood atop a cliff to the right, shining brightly through the gray sky.

"The inn is closer to the docks," Jade said, and her voice sounded unnatural after more than a day of silence.

We walked down the street and the magnificent skyline disappeared as the buildings grew two and even three stories high. But there was still a small sliver of sea that could be spotted straight down the street.

We approached the water's edge, and just before we reached the docks, Jade turned down a narrow street to the right. It was less crowded than the main strip, but there were still clusters of loitering merchants and tradespeople exchanging coins and nondescript packages. For the first time, folks stared at us, and I wondered if they were dealing in illegal substances.

We passed a few unassuming doors and some dodgy alleyways before Jade pushed one open without even knocking.

She knew exactly where she was leading us, though, because as I stepped inside, I found myself in a cozy waiting room. There was a lit fireplace with bookshelves on either side. A dozen or so mismatched chairs were arranged around two coffee tables; only two of the seats were taken. A large bay window displayed the docks outside, though the rain distorted the image.

On the opposite side of the room, there was a semicircular desk where a young woman stood waiting to greet us. "How can I help you?" she asked as we came closer.

"We'll take two rooms," Cyrus said.

"We'll take three rooms," Jade corrected.

I pursed my lips, but I was glad she had said something. Assuming Cyrus and Ladon were sharing a room, that would've left the second for Jade and me to split, and I wasn't sure I could handle another night of her judgement. I would be fine sleeping alone even in a strange town.

The woman behind the counter frowned. "I only have one room, I'm afraid." Seeing our unhappy faces, she quickly added, "It has two full beds and a couch that can be used as a bed. I'm sorry, but with the storms coming in, the town is packed with travelers who've extended their stay."

So other inns were likely to be full too. Fantastic.

Jade scowled and looked around the waiting room, as if hoping she could bully someone into giving up their room.

Before she took any drastic measures, Cyrus told the receptionist, "That'll be fine. Thank you."

The receptionist handed over a key and pointed us in the direction of the staircase leading to our room.

"I don't know about the rest of you, but I'd like to clean up before we do anything else," Cyrus said.

We agreed and followed him up two flights of stairs and down a hall that led to our room. As promised, there were two beds and a couch tucked into a cramped space. There was just enough room for a dresser with a mirror hanging above it and a single nightstand nestled between the two beds.

The floors creaked as we entered, and rain pelted the small circle window that let in minimal light.

Cyrus dropped his bag on the first bed and lit the two lanterns hanging on either side of the room. "Ladon and I can take this bed," he said, unfazed at the prospect of sharing a bed with his brother. Although he was a king, he was more generous and altruistic than most people I knew.

"I'll take the couch," Jade said.

The couch was short and looked uncomfortable even for someone of her height. She wasn't very tall, but there was no way she'd be able to stretch out completely.

"Are you sure?" I asked. "I don't mind sharing the bed."

"I'm positive." She dropped her sack on the floor and pulled a cloak from inside. She threw it on and tied it under her chin.

"Where are you going?" I asked.

Her hand was already on the doorknob before she responded, "Out."

Once the door closed, Ladon scoffed. "I don't trust her."

"Me neither," Cyrus said.

I was still undecided. I wanted to trust her, but she made it so difficult. "Is anyone else hungry?"

We hadn't eaten a proper meal in days, and the scent of food had trailed us through town.

"Definitely. Cyrus, do you want to take your turn in the shower while Emilie and I grab something to bring back?"

Cyrus looked between the two of us and nodded. "Yeah, that sounds like a plan."

Back outside, the rain was coming down even harder. Ladon looked both ways down the alley, and I followed his gaze.

"Did you have something in mind?" I asked.

He grabbed my hand, and the breath caught in my chest. If anyone saw us... Wait. No one knew us here, aside from Cyrus, who was occupied upstairs, and Jade, who had run off to who knew where.

He smiled as he watched the realization sink in.

I intertwined my fingers with his and squeezed.

"Come on," he said, pulling me behind him.

I followed closely in his footsteps, my eyes falling to our connected hands every so often. I liked the way his warm hand felt against my icy one. The rain had soaked into my skin already, and I could've kept my hand dry by sliding it into a pocket, but I refused to let go of this cherished moment.

We walked past a dozen food stands along the docks before we settled on one. We huddled close underneath the awning while waiting for our turn to order. Holding his hand made my heart skip a beat, but snuggling against his chest in the middle of the market kicked my heart into overdrive.

When the cook turned to us, we ordered four plates with a variety of seafood and veggies over rice. He had a handful of different sauces, so we decided to try one of each and waited while he grilled everything in front of us.

"Should we stop there next?" Ladon asked, pointing over my shoulder.

The stand next to us had a pyramid of barrels stacked ten feet tall, each of them with a small tap jutting out.

"Wine?" I guessed.

Ladon nodded. "Looks like it."

The cook finished preparing our meals and wrapped them up, placing them in a fabric tote so we could carry them easily.

It turned out that each of the barrels at the next stop held a different fruit wine. Ladon let me choose, and I decided on the black currant.

As we started our walk back to the inn, I sighed.

"What's wrong?" Ladon asked. He carried the food while I had the wine bottle, our free hands still melded together.

I lifted them. "I wish we didn't have to go back. I wish we could spend a little more time together, just the two of us."

Ladon brought my hand to his lips and gave the back a gentle kiss. "Soon, princess. When we're finally free to be together, I'm going to take you on a date and show you off to everyone in Renoa. They should all know that you are mine."

I liked the sound of that, but they needed to know that he was mine too.

We entered the inn far too soon and headed back upstairs to our room. Ladon knocked twice and Cyrus opened the door, looking rejuvenated with clean skin and wet hair.

He smiled and backed up so we could enter. Inhaling deeply through his nose, he asked, "What did you get? It smells incredible."

Ladon laid out the trays of food and told Cyrus the difference between them. "You can choose which you'd like first."

Cyrus waved to me instead. "No, ladies first, of course. Emilie, which one would you like?"

I grabbed one of the meals and went to sit on the bed since there were no chairs or tables inside our tiny room. "Jade's still gone?"

Cyrus nodded and took a seat next to me with his meal in his lap. "Yep. Between you and me, I'm grateful for her absence. She brings the mood down, don't you think? Would it kill her to smile occasionally?"

I gave him a half-hearted smile. I could admit that the atmosphere lightened while she was gone, but I also was curious about where she had run off to. When would she be back? Did her little outing have something to do with Reyna? I'd be irritated if that were the case. She should've allowed us to come with her.

Jade might've had her own reasons to hate Reyna, but her dying breath belonged to Ladon and me. I wanted to see the light fade from her devious eyes.

Once we had eaten, Ladon opened the bottle of wine and poured it into three cups. We drank while I listened to them tell more stories of their childhood. It was clear that Ladon had always looked up to Cyrus, and Cyrus had always protected Ladon.

From the day their father died, Cyrus stepped into the position of not only leader of a country, but leader of their family.

"Do you know how hard it was to keep this one out of trouble?" Cyrus laughed, nudging Ladon with his elbow. "He was always sneaking out of the castle to meet up with friends or girls." Ladon scowled, but Cyrus carried on. "You know I'm right. Gods, it was like you had a different girlfriend every other week for a while."

Ladon's eyes met mine, and I tried to give him a sympathetic look. Of course I knew he wasn't celibate before we met.

"You're exaggerating," Ladon grumbled.

Cyrus took another sip from his cup and then frowned, realizing he'd drunk every drop. His cheeks were pink, and his eyelids seemed too heavy to keep open. Normally I was the lightweight in any given group, but maybe the wine had been too much, especially after being in a coma for weeks.

"I'm only teasing," Cyrus said. "I do sometimes wonder, though..." he trailed off, his body sliding down until his head rested on a pillow.

"Wonder what?" Ladon asked.

Cyrus yawned and closed his eyes. "What happened? You were such a ladies' man. And then you just...weren't."

I watched Ladon with curiosity, but he only tucked his brother in before clearing our cups.

"So," I said after a moment. "What *was* the reason?"

He placed his hands on his hips and stared at the wall.

"You don't have to tell me," I said quickly. If he wasn't ready to talk about it, I wasn't going to pressure him.

He turned to face me. "Do you want to get out of here?"

I spared one glance at Cyrus, who was already breathing evenly in sleep, before nodding. I wasn't tired at all, and after the afternoon I'd had with Ladon, I was eager for more time together.

He grabbed my cloak and threw it around my shoulders. Then he opened the door, and we scurried out. Once outside, he took my hand and led me down the street. I didn't bother asking where we were going. I'd follow him anywhere.

We turned left down an alley and weaved through a busy side street. Night had settled upon us, but the streets were well lit with lanterns hanging over most doors we passed.

The rain was still coming down steadily, and it didn't take long to feel the water in my boots. I held on to the hood of my cloak so it wouldn't fall and jogged to keep up with Ladon.

When he turned another corner, I couldn't help but laugh. "Do you know where you're going?"

He paused to smile back at me. Then he tugged my hand, and I launched forward, falling into his chest. We stumbled a few steps until we collided with a stone wall. He spun and suddenly he was towering over me, water dripping down his face and across his parted lips.

I didn't hesitate for a second to reach up and lick the droplets from his lips. They curved into a soft smile before connecting with mine. He kissed me slowly and sensually, making every inch of my skin sizzle with heat in the cool rain. Alternating between gentle and a more commanding pressure, he knew exactly how to make me melt.

I wrapped a leg around his hip and tried to pull him closer, but his laugh interrupted my carnal desires. He tucked a piece of hair behind my ear and kissed my forehead.

"Come on," he said, pulling me inside the door to the left.

Inside, music filled the air, and a sea of patrons all faced a small stage where a band played their song and a man and woman sang a lively duet. I looked around the crowded tavern, unable to find a single open table.

Ladon must've noticed the same thing. He took my hand again and said, "Let's go to the bar."

There was only one stool available, and he pulled it out for me to sit, standing behind me with one arm around my waist. He signaled for the bartender and ordered us a couple pints of mead. I leaned back into his chest and sipped from my mug.

"It was my mother," Ladon said, and I twisted in my seat to look at him. He swallowed a drink and licked his lips before looking down to meet my gaze. "The reason I became... less social."

"Oh," I replied, though I was uncertain how Sophia played a part in his changed behavior.

"After my father died, I went through a really tough time. You know that. Eventually, it got easier—living without him. I started to get used to my new normal. And while Cyrus was busy becoming a king, I made new friends. And yes, many of them were girls my age."

He rolled his eyes, though I hadn't given him a hard time about it.

"I came back one night after sneaking out of the castle. I thought for sure that either Cyrus or my mother would catch me as I tried to make my way back to my bedroom. Instead, the halls were abnormally still. It was silent except for the sound of someone crying. I followed the noise until I was standing outside my mother's bedroom. She moved into a different, smaller room after my father died. Because of our bloodline magic, I was able to open her door without knocking."

He looked tired, as if reliving this memory drained him physically and emotionally. I almost told him he didn't need to finish the story, but then he spoke again.

"She didn't hear me come in. I remember seeing her lying in bed, curled with her legs tucked against her chest and squeezing her pillow tight. She sobbed and pleaded with the gods to bring back my father. It was killing her. All that time, I was so focused on my own sorrow that I didn't notice hers, or Cyrus's for that matter. But my father's death was literally killing her."

Ladon paused and swirled the mead in his mug, looking around for the bartender so he could order another.

"So you wanted to be a better son? Make life easier for her and stop sneaking out?" I asked, trying to fill in the blanks.

I felt his chest rise and fall against my back as he sighed heavily. "I love that you think so highly of me, but no. I wanted to make sure I never felt that kind of pain. To lose the one you love—your soulmate... I didn't think I could survive what my mother was going through. So I stopped giving my attention to the girls in town. That I became a better son and a better brother was an accidental side effect. I devoted myself to my family and training to become a better warrior and never went back to my less honorable habits."

I squeezed him, and he leaned down to kiss me, cupping my face. His lips brushed mine as he spoke. "You have all of my attention now, Emilie."

The words left unspoken were louder than the music and singing on stage.

Don't leave me, Emilie. Don't die. Don't be the reason I can't go on.

Chapter Twenty-Four

Ladon

As TIME MOVED ON, guests slowly filtered out of the tavern, either too drunk or too tired to carry on. I, on the other hand, was full of energy and never wanted to leave. To leave this dusty, smoke-filled bar would mean my time with Emilie would come to an end, and I was enjoying it too much.

Soon.

It was what I'd been telling myself for weeks, but every day that passed where we had to hide our feelings was like our dream was getting further away. I knew it was selfish to sneak out of the inn with her, especially while my brother slept, but I didn't care. There was a chance we'd get caught—Jade was still wandering around town somewhere, and she already had her suspicions—but I didn't care about that either. It was none of her business.

I lowered my head and nuzzled Emilie's neck. Her skin was hot, and it made me want to strip the clothes from her body so I could see where else she was flushed. I kissed the spot beneath her ear before running my tongue along the shell of it. She giggled and tried to pull away, but my arm was wrapped firmly around her waist.

She raised her arm and hooked it around my neck, bringing me down to kiss my lips. I teased her, only surrendering small pecks until she was practically whimpering for something more. When I could tell her frustration had reached a breaking point, I kissed her, gripping her chin and holding her right where I wanted her.

Her body stiffened as my tongue slid between her lips and met hers. Then she relaxed with a moan, and my cock twitched. If only there were a place we could hide out and I could properly satisfy her. I'd make her come over and over again until her body trembled and she was too spent to speak properly.

My hand traveled down her neck and came to a stop at her breast, gently squeezing before continuing to rest on her hip. She shivered, and I wondered if I should stop. If this was too much for her or if she was worried about wandering eyes. She didn't like to feel as though she were on display or the object of people's entertainment, but when her hand traveled south and came to a stop over my cock, I knew she was all right. Maybe she just felt safe with me.

That thought had me grinding against her palm.

While we were busy getting lost in each other's touch, a man sitting on the other side of Emilie began to shout expletives at the bartender. I tried to ignore it, but when he knocked over a half-full tankard, I pulled away from Emilie with disappointment.

Emilie turned around to see what the ruckus was.

"You can't leave without paying," the bartender said, frowning at the spilled drink on his counter. "If you can't pay, you'll need to work it off."

The man, who had clearly drunk too much, slurred his words. "I don't fuckin' have it." He opened a coin purse, which lacked the typical jingle of coins inside. "My boss ripped me off. The fucker hired me to do his dirty work and then disappeared without paying me."

I perked up and listened more closely.

The bartender waved to another man on the opposite side of the tavern—a big guy who probably handled drunkards and other patrons who'd overstayed their welcome. He began to move closer, which only made the drunk guy more irritated.

He flung his hand around, trying to wave off the tavern guard. "This is unnecessary. You'll get your money."

But the bartender and guard had already stopped listening. The guard pulled him off his stool.

"Fucking ridiculous," he shouted. "Do you know who I am? I know people. You can't treat me like this. I'll tell Reyna about this, and she'll burn your tavern to the ground!"

I stood at the same time as Emilie, taking a handful of coins and tossing them on the counter to pay for our drinks. We followed the guard and the drunk through the tavern, and when the inebriated man was tossed on his ass out in the dark, rainy street, we were right behind him.

I pulled Emilie to the side and kissed her, pretending that we weren't here to follow the man. He got to his feet slowly and stumbled a few steps. Then he hobbled down the street with his head hung low.

Emilie pulled away and stared after him. "You heard that, right? I didn't imagine it?"

"I heard it, princess. I don't know if he was serious or just spewing nonsense, but it's worth investigating."

She nodded, and I pulled the hood of her cloak up over her head and tucked her brown hair inside. "Let's go."

We followed our target down three different side streets and up a cobblestone set of stairs, staying in the shadows as much as possible and keeping enough distance that he didn't hear our footsteps. Thankfully, the rain helped hide any noise we made.

Finally, he stopped and climbed a small set of stairs leading to what I could only assume was someone's home. There was a single door and a small rectangular window next to it that revealed only darkness inside. The man knocked once, then twice. He cupped his hands around his mouth and shouted for someone's attention, but no one came to answer. Whoever lived there was either not home or not interested in entertaining our prey.

The man stumbled down the steps and began to walk again, this time toward Emilie and me.

"Quick," I said, pulling her behind a stack of crates and out of sight. There were gaps between them, and if the man looked hard enough, I was certain he would spot us. I held my breath while Emilie hid behind me, waiting for him to pass. Only after he had made it several feet away did I breathe again.

"Where is he going now?" Emilie asked.

"I don't know."

"Should we follow him or see who he was trying to visit?"

I looked toward the seemingly empty home. "Let's see where he's headed. We can always come back if he leads us to a dead end."

Through empty streets and down narrow paths, the man led us all the way back to the sea and onto the docks. They were far less busy than earlier in the day. Most crews had gone to bed for the evening or were still out at one of the taverns.

The man slowed, and I thought he might be looking for his ship—that in his drunken stupor he had lost the boat for which he was a crew member. But then he collapsed on the dock and curled into a ball, using a sack for a pillow.

"What the hell?" I said softly, moving to approach him.

Emilie grabbed my arm. "What if he's dangerous?"

"I am dangerous."

Her grip loosened. She must've been satisfied with my response because she released me, and when I moved closer to the man, she wasn't far behind.

I tapped his foot with my shoe. Was he even alive, or had he drunk himself into oblivion? I pushed harder, and he rolled over, mumbling a string of curse words.

"Hey," I barked. "Wake up."

He grumbled again and situated himself so I was staring at his back. It was hard to understand what he said, but it sounded something like, "Get lost."

My patience wore thin, and I bent down, grabbing him by the collar of his jacket. I lifted him and threw him against a nearby barrel. His head slammed against the faded oak.

"What the fuck? Are you fucking mental?"

His vocabulary wasn't particularly impressive.

"Who are you?" I snarled.

"Let go of me, you—"

I punched him, cutting off his latest unintelligent insult.

"Who are you?" I asked again.

He reached up to hold his bleeding nose and pinched his brows in pain. "I'm Devyn. Who the fuck are you?"

"The man who is going to end your life," I said, pinning him down with my eyes.

He stopped moving, and I watched as his gaze scanned my face. Then he laughed and pointed at me. "You're joking, right? Boss sent you to fuck with me?"

I tilted my head to the side. "Who is your boss, Devyn?"

His smile faded, and he looked over my shoulder to where I knew Emilie was standing and watching. "No... I don't have anything to tell you."

I could sense fear taking over. He was beginning to understand that we weren't his friends. We weren't here to play pranks or rough him up a bit for some distant *boss*. I was here for information, and I would do whatever it took to get it out of him.

"How do you know Reyna?" I growled.

"I... I don't."

"Don't lie to me," I said, wrapping a hand around his throat.

His hands flew to mine, but he was too weak to fight me. His eyes went wide as he struggled for breath. His efforts were futile, and his face turned a vivid shade of crimson while his lips turned blue.

Then he did something I hadn't expected—he laughed. The drunk piece of shit chuckled, or something similar to it, since my hand was cutting off his oxygen. His mouth moved, and I could faintly hear him say, "I've got nothing to say to you. You can kill me now, or she can kill me later."

I released his throat, and he choked as air filled his lungs once again. He coughed and clawed at his neck as if my hand were still wrapped around it.

Emilie appeared at my side and placed her hand in mine. I turned to look at her, and she said, "Let me try."

I didn't particularly like the idea of Emilie questioning the man. Who knew what he was capable of? But if I couldn't get anywhere with him, then perhaps she could.

"Go ahead," I told her, taking a step back against my instincts. I clenched my jaw as she stepped closer to Devyn, and he looked up at her, his face a mess with blood dripping down his mouth and onto his short beard.

His eyes scanned her from head to toe, and I didn't care for the way they bounced back to her chest. Truth be told, I wouldn't have liked them lingering anywhere on her for too long. If he had any connection to Reyna, he didn't have the right to look at Emilie. He didn't have the right to live another day.

"Back in the tavern," Emilie started. "You said you were hired to do a job. What was it?"

Devyn smiled. "If I tell you, what will you give me in return?"

My feet moved faster than my brain, and my fist collided with his face a second time.

"Ladon," Emilie said softly. Not a reprimand, but an assurance that she could handle whatever slimy comments he threw her way.

I took a deep breath and returned to my spot behind her.

"The only reward you'll be getting for your cooperation is the ability to live another day," she told him matter-of-factly. The way she said it surprised me... and thrilled me. So self-assured and confident. I didn't expect to be so attracted to this wicked side of her.

Devyn scoffed. "Do it, then. I've already told you; I'm a dead man either way."

Emilie looked back at me, and I gave her a small nod, putting my faith entirely in her.

"You know what I think, Devyn? I think that you were hired to track down Reyna's adversaries and either kill them or sell them off to the highest bidder. Is that what you were paid to do?"

Devyn grumbled, "I wasn't *paid* to do any—"

"Is that what you were paid to do?" Emilie shouted. Her hand sped through the night air, and I caught a glimpse of light reflecting from a blade before it pierced Devyn's thigh.

He roared in pain, and I acted quickly, grabbing him and pinning his arms behind his back so he couldn't retaliate. He struggled against my hold, but he wasn't as strong as me. The copious amount of alcohol wasn't doing him any favors.

I held him against my chest and watched Emilie over his shoulder. She was sizing him up and determining the next spot to land another strike. "Did you even think twice about what you were doing? Did you care if they were raped or abused? Or did you only care about your payout?"

The answer was obvious, but I snarled at him anyway. "Answer her."

"I... I needed the money."

Emilie dragged her knife down his cheek and across his neck. I felt him wince and knew she'd made a line of blood across his skin. Then her blade came to a stop with the tip pointed at his chest. "You sold your soul."

Devyn fought against my hold, trying to get away from Emilie's weapon. In doing so, he met the prick of her dagger numerous times, wailing each time it punctured his skin.

"If you'd hold still, you wouldn't get pricked," I growled. It wasn't entirely true. Emilie was definitely going to stab him again, but she should have the honor of doing so. And his scrambling was taking that choice away from her.

When he didn't listen, my grip tightened. "What should we do with him, princess?"

Her eyes caught mine, and I was mesmerized by the mixture of anger, tenacity, and perseverance I saw in them. There were so many layers to Emilie, and I wanted to uncover them all.

She placed her dagger back in its sheath and, for a second, I thought she'd reconsidered. That she'd chosen forgiveness over retribution.

But then I felt it.

The wind picked up, circling around us in a cyclone. The water became turbulent, splashing against the dock as Emilie's magic disturbed the surface. A few waves even crashed over the side, spilling at our feet before draining between the wooden planks.

Devyn thrashed more violently than before, and I let go, watching him drop to the ground with his hands around his neck. He was searching for something to pry away from his throat, the source that had stolen his oxygen. But I had been on the receiving end of Emilie's tricks once before.

He was completely at her mercy, and judging by the look in her eyes, there was none to be found.

Chapter Twenty-Five

Emilie

My mind raced as we walked the streets back to the inn. The world was quiet—the rain had finally stopped and everyone else in the small city was fast asleep in their beds, where we should've been all along.

Did I regret sneaking out with Ladon? Or the events that followed? I didn't think so.

I had killed a man.

I'd done it before, but unlike those times, I couldn't claim this was self-defense. Devyn hadn't attacked us. In fact, we'd followed him out of the tavern and into the night, had tracked him like prey in his vulnerable state, drunk and disjointed. It wasn't even a fair fight.

Did I regret it?

I should. And maybe in another life, I would. But after everything I'd been through and knowing that Devyn was involved in hunting and selling humans... I felt no remorse.

I was tired and a little numb, but I felt vindicated. It was a small reparation for what had been done to Ladon and me. I didn't even care if Devyn had never seen or spoken to Reyna directly. He was associated with her, at the bottom of a long line of command in which she sat at the top, and that was enough for me.

I enjoyed watching the light fade from his eyes while he gasped for breath. A sense of accomplishment had filled me, watching his body roll off the dock and into the water. He'd be devoured by sea serpents before the sun rose in the morning, and I had a hunch that no one would miss him.

The only downside was that we hadn't been able to get any information out of him.

"We should go back to the townhouse," I said, my voice piercing the quiet that had fallen upon us.

Ladon glanced at me. "In the morning. It's late, and we need to get back to the inn. You should wash up too."

His gaze flicked to my hands, which were speckled with blood. I had avoided making a mess for the most part, but carving into his skin and stabbing his leg had sullied my right hand.

I searched Ladon's face for something. Disappointment, perhaps? That I had let my fury get the best of me. That I hadn't been able to control my emotions, and I'd killed a man without a second thought. Had I ruined the image he had of me, whatever that was?

But I didn't see any of that. He was looking at me with admiration and maybe even a little pride.

I smiled. "Okay. In the morning then."

We strolled through the inn's entrance. The fire in the entry hall had burned down to embers, and the night clerk was asleep at his desk. He didn't even wake when the stairs creaked beneath our feet.

Upstairs, Ladon quietly opened the door to our room, and I sighed in relief. Cyrus was still passed out in bed, snoring with one arm thrown over his face and the other clutching the patchwork quilt.

Ladon kicked off his boots, and I did the same, hanging my cloak on a hook by the door. Then I grabbed my bag so I could change into my sleep clothes after I washed up.

I started for the bathroom, but a noise made me jump and almost trip over my own feet. I grabbed the wall to steady myself. "Fuck," I said, placing a hand over my racing heart. "What is wrong with you?"

Jade, who had appeared out of nowhere in the dark bathroom, slid onto the couch that was to be her bed for the evening. "I don't know what you mean by that. I just woke up and needed to use the toilet."

Ladon sighed behind me. Why was Jade always in the most inconvenient of places at the worst times? Whatever relief I had at seeing Cyrus sleeping so peacefully had dissolved.

"Where were you two?" Jade asked, not bothering to keep her voice down.

I looked back at Cyrus to make sure he hadn't stirred. Quietly, I answered, "That's none of your concern. You haven't told us where you slipped off to."

"Well, I can tell you one thing for certain—I was not out for a romantic stroll."

My heart hammered so hard it was almost painful. I wanted to strip the air from her lungs too. Thankfully, the room was dimly lit, so she likely couldn't see how red my cheeks had turned. The gods had cursed me with that particular trait.

"Neither were we," I said.

Jade just laughed.

"Shh," I snapped. "You'll wake Cyrus."

"Oh, we wouldn't want that, would we? What would you tell him, I wonder?"

"This isn't any of your business," Ladon said, stepping closer to me.

"It is, though. I'm here for one purpose—to ensure that my people get what they deserve. You made a promise, a binding agreement, to provide Murvort with the aid we need. I won't see it undone because you can't keep your dick out of your brother's wife."

"I'm not his wife," I spat. "I don't belong to him or anyone else."

Jade threw her hands up in feigned surrender. "No, of course not. You're a perfect little princess who could never do anything wrong. You take whatever you want, consequences be damned."

"Knock it off," Ladon snapped. "You have no idea what you're talking about."

As much as I appreciated Ladon's support, I held up my hand to stop him. I could handle Jade myself.

"You don't know me," I said. "I have never gotten a single thing that I wanted for myself. My parents made every decision in my life, down to the dresses I wore and the man I was supposed to marry. I don't expect you to understand what that's like, but I won't listen to you judge my character when you don't know the first thing about me."

I stepped inside the bathroom and closed the door before she could respond. Putting my back against it, I closed my eyes and counted to ten.

Jade had no idea what she was talking about. She spoke about me as if I were a selfish, spoiled brat, but Ladon was the first thing I'd wanted in this life enough to go for it. Enough to ignore my parents' demands and stand up for myself. Jade couldn't take that from me.

I approached the sink, grabbed the bar of soap, and scrubbed my hands clean. My reflection in the clouded mirror looked back at me with anger and hurt.

I was a good person, wasn't I? Was I truly that awful for following my heart?

It took only a moment of reflection before I decided I was doing the right thing. All I had to do was picture a life chained to Cyrus in a loveless marriage to know that I never could've lived like that. Not after I'd discovered what it was like to love and be loved in return.

I dried my hands on the towel hanging on the wall and did my best to brush my hair back into a ponytail. My cheeks were still rosy, but at least my heart had returned to a normal rhythm. A few more minutes and I might be able to face Jade and Ladon again.

Or I could sleep in the bathroom. But avoiding all my problems came at the cost of a rough tile floor for a bed, and I quickly concluded that I couldn't handle an entire night sleeping on the cold, hard floor.

So I changed out of my clothes and into a cotton set of pajamas. I reached for the bathroom door and carefully opened it, expecting to be greeted with the continuation of our argument. Instead, Jade was lying on the couch, her back to the room. I couldn't see her face, but I assumed she was still awake. No one could fall asleep that quickly, or at least, I certainly couldn't.

I tiptoed over to my bed and slid under the blanket. It was surprisingly comfortable for an old inn. My body sank into the mattress, and even though my mind was racing to process everything that had happened tonight, I found myself drifting into a lethargic state.

The shuffling of a blanket to my right made me roll to my side. I watched as Ladon extinguished the lamp on the table between us.

When my eyes adjusted to the darkness, I could just make out the outline of his body. Even without the light, I was so familiar with the features of his face that I could still envision them in the dark.

A flicker of moonlight reflected off his eyes, but it faded just as quickly as it had appeared.

I wanted to reach across the gap between our beds and find his hand. Or call his name to have him move over and snuggle in beside me. It was always so much easier to sleep when he was holding me.

He sighed, and I was certain he was thinking the same thing.

Chapter Twenty-Six

Emilie

I woke the next morning to the sound of the door slamming shut.

"What the hell was that?" Cyrus asked in a sleep-distorted mumble.

I didn't have to look over at the couch to know that Jade had left the room. "Glad to see she's as pleasant as ever this morning," I said, pulling up the blanket to shield my eyes from the light shining through the window.

Ladon huffed a laugh. "What time is it?"

His voice was low and husky, and it was enough to pry my eyes open to search for him. I found him in the same position I'd stared at in the dark while drifting to sleep last night. But now I could see that he was shirtless, lying on his stomach with one arm wrapped around a pillow, his muscular back and biceps on display.

Before I could get too lost admiring his body, Cyrus sat up and interrupted my thoughts. He got out of bed and looked out the window, yawning as he turned back around. "Just a little before sunrise. Gods, I slept like a rock last night. I don't think I woke up once."

Out of the corner of my eye, I noticed Ladon's body go rigid. I hoped that my cheeks wouldn't betray me by turning pink. It was hard to tell if Cyrus was serious or if he had secretly woken during our quarrel and was challenging us now. But when he didn't press further, I released a breath.

He walked to the bathroom and closed the door behind him.

Ladon pressed up onto his forearms and craned his neck to stare at the bathroom door. "That was weird."

I nodded. "Do you think he heard anything last night?"

Ladon mulled it over before shaking his head. "No. I know my brother. If he overheard anything, he would've been direct about it. He's not the type to eavesdrop anyway. If he was awake, he would've joined in the conversation while it was happening."

He dragged himself out of bed, and then he was hovering beside mine. He placed his hands on either side of my shoulders, bending down to give me a kiss. "Good morning, princess."

He retreated, and I sat up, stretching my arms over my head until my joints popped.

Before I could get out of bed, Cyrus returned from the bathroom. "So, what is the plan for today?" he asked, buttoning the shirt he had just put on.

Ladon and I exchanged a look. I hadn't even considered how we would convince Cyrus and Jade to join us on an outing to the townhome. How could we tell them about our new lead without giving away our adventure together?

"I have a confession," Ladon said, and I froze. "Last night after the two of you went to sleep, I went for a walk."

My jaw went slack, and I blinked rapidly, surprised that Ladon would flat out *lie* to his brother. I supposed he was doing it to protect me, but it still caught me off guard. I snapped my mouth shut and did my best to act as if this was news to me.

"I came across a rogue bounty hunter—drunk and carrying on about the Lemaire family. Seems he was expecting a payment, but it never came."

Cyrus looked confused. "And you didn't come back to tell us? What else did you find out?"

"I considered returning to the inn, but he started walking away. I followed him on my own and watched him enter a townhome a few blocks away. I think we should start there."

Ladon looked at me—a silent plea to go along with his story and a request to back him up.

I shook off my surprise. "I think that's a smart idea. Very lucky of you to run into him."

"I agree," Cyrus said. "Although I don't approve of your wandering off on your own. What if something had happened?"

Something *had* happened. Just not to Ladon.

My eyes fell to my hands, and although the blood was gone, I could still feel Devyn's death on my hands. I would never be able to forget the sound of his lifeless body falling into the sea.

"I was fine, Cyrus. I am more than capable of defending myself. Don't forget that I am the High Commander."

Cyrus shook his head. "I know you are a skilled warrior. But you could've been outnumbered. You're not invincible—a fact that we are all too aware of."

Ladon couldn't argue with that. "You're right. I'm sorry for going off by myself without telling you. It won't happen again."

"Thank you. Now, about this townhome. What else can you tell me?"

"Not much," Ladon admitted. "I didn't stick around long enough to investigate further. It was late, and I didn't want to barge into a room full of enemies."

"At least you had that much sense."

Ladon's jaw clenched, but he accepted Cyrus's remark without comment.

"The two of you should get ready," Cyrus continued. "I'll go find something for breakfast."

Ladon nodded, and so did I.

But before Cyrus could make it to the door, it opened and Jade came in carrying a brown paper bag that smelled like sausage and herbs.

"Jade," Cyrus said. "I was just about to go get breakfast, but I see you've done it for me. Unless you only brought enough for yourself."

Jade snarled, but it was exactly the type of thing I would've expected from her—to go out for breakfast without considering the rest of us. She placed the bag on one of the end tables and opened it, pulling out three different trays.

I stretched to see what was inside. The first held sausage like I'd guessed while the other two had potatoes and eggs. My stomach growled.

"I brought enough for everyone," Jade said in an oddly polite tone. It was a stark contrast to the way she'd spoken to us yesterday. Did she regret the way she'd behaved? Probably not. She didn't seem like the type to live with regrets.

I dressed quickly and then helped myself to some food and water. Cyrus filled Jade in on our plans for the day, but he missed the way she looked between Ladon and me when Cyrus recounted the fictional story of Ladon's excursion. I held my breath and waited for her to correct him, but she didn't.

As soon as the food was cleared, we headed into town. Ladon led the way while I pretended like I didn't know where we were going—which was half true since it had been late and I hadn't thought to memorize the steps we'd taken to get to the townhouse.

When we arrived, Cyrus looked up at the residence with squinted eyes. I followed his gaze and took in the building for the first time. In the daylight, I could see that it was three stories tall, with windows spaced evenly and framed with burgundy shutters. Planters hung outside of each window and vines covered part of the façade.

"Should we knock?" Cyrus asked.

Truthfully, I didn't expect anyone to answer since no one had last night. But neither Ladon nor I could say that without exposing his lie.

Ladon cleared his throat and climbed the small set of stairs leading to the front door. He knocked a short melody and then waited. When no one came, he knocked again and took a step back.

"Maybe they aren't home," Cyrus suggested.

"Or maybe they're dead," Jade countered.

I nearly choked at her bluntness, but she was likely closer to the truth than Cyrus. Something shady was going on in this home, and we already knew that Devyn wouldn't be returning anytime soon.

Ladon didn't respond to either of them. He wrapped his hand around the doorknob and twisted, but the door didn't budge.

Jade moved over to the window on the left and peered inside through a small crack between the curtains.

"Do you see anything?" I asked.

"Nothing. Just an entry parlor with empty seats and a junk-filled table."

The front door swung open, and we all turned our heads. Ladon was standing with a key in his hand, crafted out of clay that matched the color of the dirt beneath my feet.

"Did you just..."

"Door's open," he said, taking a step inside.

Jade followed him without a second thought while Cyrus looked at me with a dumbfounded expression.

Inside, the entry hall and adjoining parlor smelled like dust and wet carpet. The house was old and hadn't been well-maintained. There was a fireplace where charred logs sat and ashes had spilled out onto the floor. The table Jade had mentioned was overflowing with books, pamphlets, and letters—she wasn't kidding about the junk.

"Hello?" Cyrus called out. "Is anyone here?"

I moved through a doorway that led into a long hall. Both ends were dark, so I had to guess which way to investigate first. I chose the right. The floors creaked beneath my feet, but otherwise I didn't hear a sound. The walls were covered with peeling paint and a random assortment of hangings. I stopped to study one and discovered it was a map of the sea between Lourova and Wyland, with tiny ships drawn on blue waters.

As I kept moving, there were multiple iterations of the same map, and I had to study them for a few moments to find the differences. Then I saw it—the ships were drawn in different patterns, seemingly pointing toward various routes that could be taken from continent to continent, keeping in mind the currents and shallow or treacherous waters.

At the first door I came to, I knocked before gently pushing it open. The room was dark, but I noticed a window nearby, and I pulled the drapes open to allow sunlight to roll in. Dust billowed from the draft of the curtains, and I began to wonder if this home had been vacant for longer than I'd first imagined. No one had been here last night, but when was the last time someone had occupied this residence?

The room I'd discovered appeared to be some type of meeting spot. A large oval table occupied the center of the room with half a dozen matching dark wooden chairs. Cabinets lined the wall to my left, and I walked toward them, hoping I'd find something useful. Unfortunately, they were empty except for a box of old linens and a few chipped coffee cups. Maybe this was simply a storage room for abandoned odds and ends?

The parlor was empty when I returned. I called out, "Ladon? Cyrus?"

Looking down the hall, I ventured to the left this time and found a winding staircase. Perhaps everyone had gone upstairs.

I reached the first landing and called, "Jade? Are you guys up here?"

Cyrus's head popped out of a doorway, and Jade was right behind him. "Did you find anything?"

I shook my head. "You?"

"No," Cyrus said. "There are two bedrooms and a bathroom on this level. All of them look like they haven't been used in weeks. Let's go to the third floor and see if Ladon's found anything useful."

Jade walked past me and climbed the stairs.

I turned back to Cyrus. "Are the two of you friends yet?"

"The day we become friends is the day I will have to step down from the throne because my mental capacity will be questionable."

I laughed.

Cyrus pointed to the stairs. "Shall we?"

I made my way to the third floor with Cyrus at my back. Hopefully there was something of use upstairs, or this would all be for nothing. We'd be right back where we started without a hint of where Reyna had gone or if she was still in the harbor somewhere.

I was so distracted that I didn't notice the warped wooden step. It fell out from under my feet the moment I stepped on it. My heart dropped, but Cyrus had his arms around me before I could fully comprehend what had happened.

I looked up at him, and his face was close enough to see the golden specks in his green eyes. His lips curved into a grin, and I felt a wave of heat—not like the searing desire I felt for Ladon, but like a burning allergic reaction. My skin felt too tight, and it was suddenly hard to breathe.

His embrace was too soft. I knew he only meant to save me from falling down a flight of stairs, but the way he held me felt romantic. It felt intimate. And if Ladon saw us right now, I feared what this would look like.

Reaching for the handrail, I pulled myself up and out of his arms, steadying myself on the next step, which was sturdy and reliable.

Cyrus sucked in a sharp breath. "I'm sorry."

"For what?" I asked, unable to face him.

"I don't know. This is all so... weird. I've never had an ex-fiancée before. I don't know the proper protocol." He laughed, and it did little to settle my discomfort. "I've also never had to court a woman before."

Finally, I turned to see him still standing a few steps lower than me, so our eyes were level. "What do you mean?"

He put his hands on his hips, and his brows pinched together. "I, uh... I'm trying to give you your space, you know."

I nodded and swallowed the lump in my throat. Everything about this situation was making my skin itch.

"I'm just hoping that if we take things slowly—if you have more time to heal and work through your trauma—maybe we could figure out a way to move forward. You already get along with my family so well, and I couldn't ask for a brighter, smarter woman..."

Cyrus began to ramble while I tried to process what he was saying.

He hadn't given up hope for us. But there was no *us*.

There never would be.

I stood in shock, trying to find the right words, but thankfully I was saved from my struggle.

"We've found something," Ladon said from above us.

I looked up the stairs, relief flooding me.

Ladon studied me, tilting his head, and I could see the question on his face.

Is everything okay?

No. It absolutely wasn't.

Chapter Twenty-Seven

Ladon

Emilie and Cyrus joined us upstairs, and I tried not to think too hard about the look on her face when I ran to tell them the news. She looked like she'd seen a ghost, but she quickly brushed it off. I'd ask her about it later when we had a moment alone. It was clear that, whatever it was, she didn't want to talk about it in front of our group.

"What did you find?" my brother asked as he followed me into the upstairs office.

Jade was sitting in a cushioned velvet chair behind a large desk looking quite comfortable. Like she'd made herself at home. She tossed a journal onto the desk, and I picked it up, passing it to Cyrus.

He opened it and read a few pages, trying to make sense of what he was seeing. I saw the moment it clicked. He flipped forward several pages until he found what I had.

"What is it?" Emilie asked, trying to read the journal from Cyrus's side.

He shifted a little so she could see it too. "It's a captain's log. It contains the history of a ship called the Green Tide—everything from its course to its cargo and—"

"Its passengers," Emilie said, her eyes going wide. She pointed at the journal, to a page dated two days ago, and said, "Reyna was on this ship."

She looked up, and our eyes met. I smiled wide and nodded.

"So, we just missed her," Cyrus said, sounding a little deflated. I understood. I was hoping we'd find her in Sage Harbor too, but at least her trail hadn't gone cold. We could work with this.

Jade stood and headed toward the doorway.

"Where are you going?" Emilie asked.

"I know someone who owes me a favor. They also happen to have a ship. Meet me at the docks around dusk."

She left without another word, her braided hair whipping behind her.

We made it back to the inn in record time to pack our belongings and check out. It didn't take long, since we'd hardly had time to unpack. We still had hours to kill before dusk, so we walked through town to take care of a few errands while we waited.

There was a blacksmith where we had our weapons sharpened and a textile shop where Emilie talked a woman into washing our clothes, but only if we bought a few items. Then we visited a bakery and stocked up on a few goods to take with us on the ship.

Cyrus also requested we visit the apothecary for some herbs that helped with seasickness. He had never been a fan of sea travel.

After a bite to eat, it was finally time to make our way to the docks. The setting sun glistened off the waves, nearly blinding us while we tried to search for Jade.

There were so many ships lining the walkway, and Jade hadn't been very descriptive. We walked along the water, and I searched for her face in the crowds. Emilie moved closer when we walked past the spot where we'd discarded Devyn. In the daylight, I could see that the rain had already washed away the blood from our scuffle.

I glanced at her and offered a warm smile. There wasn't a body floating around to condemn us for our crimes. She had no need to worry.

A few minutes later, I caught sight of Jade leaning against a post with her arms crossed. A man stood next to her, chatting nonstop while she stared straight ahead. I didn't know what he was saying, but she wasn't interested in a word of it.

"You made it," she said, interrupting him.

He looked at us and looked back at her. "Is this them?"

"It is," she said, turning and walking across the bridge to the ship before us.

The man watched her, confused by her abrupt departure, but we were used to it by now. He suddenly remembered that we were still standing here, and he held out a hand. "My name is Drip; I'm the chief mate. You must be Jade's friends."

"What kind of name is Drip?" I asked. It was rude, but I didn't care.

He laughed. "Well, technically my name is Samuel, but I go by Drip."

I raised a brow. Surely there was a story there, but I wasn't particularly interested in it.

Drip began to tell it anyway. "When I first started working on ships, I was a clumsy kid—twelve or thirteen and still growing into my lanky limbs. Anyway, I had a habit of tripping over things, and I fell overboard more times than I could count."

He laughed while the rest of us exchanged concerned glances. Was this really the best Jade could find?

Drip caught our questioning stares and waved his hands. "Nothing to worry about now, of course. I grew out of it, and I've been working on ships for decades now. You don't get to my position without being highly qualified. But my crew back then thought it was hilarious. Each time they pulled me out of the water, I'd walk around for hours, dripping everywhere I went. So, they called me Drip, and the rest is history."

I nodded like I understood, but I still had my reservations about him. I pointed toward the ship. "Should we just—"

"Oh yes, of course! Here, let me grab your bag, Miss…?"

"You can call me Emilie," she said, letting her backpack slide off her shoulder and handing it over to Drip. "Thank you."

"So, Drip," Cyrus said. "What happened for you to be in Jade's debt?"

Drip shrugged. "That's a long story. We'll save it for another time. And what did you say your name was?"

"I'm Cyrus and this is my brother Ladon."

If Drip knew anything about Osavian's royal family, he didn't let on. He simply stated, "It's nice to meet you both. Watch your step here."

The bridge from the dock to the ship was several feet wide and plenty sturdy, but I understood how someone with the name 'Drip' might struggle with it.

"The captain has some business in town, but he will be back soon. I'm supposed to show you to your cabins."

Drip led us across the ship's deck and into the hull. I'd been on enough boats to know they weren't spacious, but even I wasn't prepared for my shoulders to barely fit as I walked.

"This first one is for the ladies," Drip told us. "And this one next to it will be where the men can sleep."

I peered into the room assigned to Cyrus and me. It was everything I imagined it would be—a small rectangle box that hardly had room to stand and a set of bunk beds I wouldn't be able to stretch out in. "Thank you. When do we set sail?"

"Captain wants to get moving as soon as he comes back. We should be on our way before dinnertime. Make yourselves at home, and if you need anything, don't hesitate to ask. I have to make sure the rest of the crew is ready."

Drip left us, and I tossed my bag on the top bunk. Cyrus squeezed by to throw his on the bottom bed, and I was instantly overwhelmed by the lack of space we'd been given. It only seemed to heighten the anxiety I felt over keeping secrets from my brother.

I checked the room next to us to see how the women were doing. Jade had already settled into the bottom bunk, reading from a tattered journal, and Emilie was climbing into hers, giving me an excellent view of her ass in her tight pants.

I quickly wiped the grin off my face and cleared my throat. They both turned to face me.

"I'm going to go for a walk around the deck if anyone would care to join me."

Jade turned back to her book without giving a response, but Emilie nodded.

"Give me one second," she said, searching through her bag. She found the hair tie she was looking for and quickly braided her hair. Then she climbed back down and followed me back into the fresh air.

We found a spot to lean against the railing and watch as the sun descended into the sea.

"Are you going to tell me what happened back at the townhouse?" I asked, moving close enough to Emilie that our arms brushed.

"Hmm?" she said, distracted by the beauty of the rainbow of colors—from the pinks and oranges that feathered out in the sky to the blue and purple waves that rocked against the boat. It was exactly the kind of scenery I would've loved to paint once upon a time.

"You looked rattled back there. Did something happen?"

"Oh," she said, her cheeks flushing like they always did when she was nervous or she'd attracted too much attention. "It was nothing."

"Come on, Emilie. It's me you're talking to. You don't have to hide anything from me."

She turned to face me, biting her lip, and I resisted the urge to pull it free from her teeth and caress it with my own. "There was a moment..." she started and then frowned. "I don't know how to explain it."

"Try," I encouraged.

She sighed. "I think... I think Cyrus might believe there is still a chance for him and me."

I wasn't sure what I was expecting, but it certainly wasn't that. I thought we had put this specific issue behind us. "What do you mean?"

"He said something about *courting* me and how he wanted to try again after I'd had enough time to heal." She chuckled darkly. "As if I'll ever be healed enough to play the role of his adoring wife."

"You'll heal, Emilie. We both will. I don't know how long it'll take, but we won't carry this with us for the rest of our lives. I refuse to. And I know you're too stubborn to carry it too."

She nodded half-heartedly. "You're probably right about that."

"I am."

Rolling her eyes, she looked like she might smack me. Good. Then I'd know she was returning to normal.

"So, what did you say to him?"

"I didn't say anything. You appeared, and that was the end of it."

I clicked my tongue and stared back out at the sea. The sound of the waves put my mind at ease, even in our predicament. I should've been more concerned about my brother's words and intentions, but all I could think about was how much I wanted to wrap Emilie in my arms and hold her while we watched the sliver of sunlight disappear.

It would be okay. I had to believe that.

It wasn't long before the captain came back. He briefly introduced himself as Bronson before heading off to his cabin. He was determined to set sail as soon as possible, and after hearing that it would take five days to cross the sea, I couldn't blame him. I was equally eager to reach Wyland.

In the lounge area, a few crew members set out some sandwiches for us to eat and a pitcher of ale. I took a seat at a table near the kitchenette, and Emilie slid in next to me. It wasn't long before Jade showed up too.

"Where's my brother?" I asked. The last time I'd seen either of them, they were both in their respective rooms while Emilie and I had gone for a walk.

"I don't know. He's not my responsibility."

"Isn't he, though? That's why you came to Renoa and why you're with us now. To keep an eye on us."

She glared at me, but I didn't back down.

"Can we just have a nice, peaceful evening for once?" Emilie sighed. "Jade found us an entire ship and crew to sail to Wyland. She might not be the most charismatic companion, but she has been useful."

"Thank you," Jade said, taking us all by surprise.

"You're welcome," Emilie said, gracefully picking up her sandwich to take a bite.

I supposed I could be nice for five minutes. I grabbed the pitcher and poured myself a glass of ale. "Would either of you like some?"

Jade nodded, but Emilie shook her head. I poured another glass and handed it to her. She immediately brought it to her lips, setting it down again after she swallowed. "I actually wanted to apologize for my behavior last night."

I nearly spat out my drink, my eyes bouncing between Emilie and Jade. Were my ears working properly? It wasn't possible that this hardheaded woman, who'd been following us around like a grumpy watchdog, knew how to admit she'd been unkind.

Jade continued, "I said some things that I'm not proud of. You're right, Emilie. I don't know you that well, and that's mostly my doing."

I narrowed my eyes at her.

"Well... it's all my doing."

Much better.

"I shouldn't have assumed anything about you or your relationship with Cyrus... or Ladon."

"Why the change of heart?" I asked.

"I can admit that I don't know either of you very well, but you don't know me either. I may have an affinity for pushing boundaries, but I know when I've crossed a line. I'm not stupid."

No, it was much more likely that she was conniving and calculated.

"Plus, I know the best way to serve Murvort and ensure this alliance sticks is by making sure that your little affair remains a secret."

"Is that so?" I asked. "And if we decide it's time for everyone to know the truth about our feelings?"

"Frankly, I hope that never comes. No offense to either of you, but we all know that will cause turbulence within the royal family. And turbulence is not good for my family and our needs."

I scoffed. At least she was honest. "Well, Jade, I am very sorry to disappoint you. I will do everything I can to keep my promises to Murvort and make sure our treaty holds. But there is going to be a day in the very near future when Cyrus knows the truth about Emilie and me."

"And what truth might that be?"

I felt as though I'd just been dumped into the icy water that rocked the ship. I spun in my seat. "Cyrus."

My brother met my gaze, hurt and resentment clear in his expression. "What secrets are you keeping from me, brother?"

Chapter Twenty-Eight

Emilie

Shit.

Shit. Shit. *Shit.*

"Cyrus," Ladon said, his voice much steadier than I felt. "I was—"

"Don't lie to me," Cyrus interrupted. "I can see it in your face. You're more transparent than you think. You forget that I've known you all your life. It's the same face you make when you're strategizing your next battle plan. What is it, brother? Tell me the truth."

Jade stood up and deserted her plate and glass of ale. She looked terrified, and I couldn't blame her. I'd never seen Cyrus so upset. "I think I should go."

Unfortunately, things were about to get much worse.

"Cyrus, please calm down," I tried, but he put a hand up to stop me.

"Please understand that I didn't ask for this," Ladon said, his voice rough. "How could I have known this would happen? We were kidnapped, and Emilie was all I had. And she... she became all I needed."

Cyrus pinched his eyes closed, and I felt the first tear stream down my face. "I don't want to hear this."

My hand reached for Ladon's, and Cyrus's eyes opened just in time to catch the movement. He glared at our combined hands and then his eyes locked with mine. "You said you needed *time*. That you weren't in the right headspace for a relationship."

I bit my tongue because there was nothing else I could do.

"Please don't take your anger out on her," Ladon said.

I jumped when Cyrus shouted, "I have enough anger for both of you!"

Ladon hopped out of his seat and stood with his chest inches from Cyrus's. "Do not speak to her that way."

I scrambled to my feet and wrapped a hand around his arm, attempting to pull him back, but he was fixed to the ground like a statue. "Ladon, please."

"At what point did you decide to take my wife?" Cyrus demanded. "Tell me when you decided to betray your family."

Ladon shook his head, and I could feel the anger and hurt radiating from him. Ladon adored his family and would do anything to protect them, including threatening me once upon a time. Back when he thought I was a harlot and a leech. He would never betray his family.

"Cyrus, stop," I yelled, but his gaze remained fixed on Ladon.

"I didn't take anything," Ladon snapped. "And she was never your wife."

"Oh, so that makes it okay? Since we didn't make it to our wedding day, it's okay for you to ruin a royal engagement and our kingdom's alliance with Dreslen?"

"No." His voice turned hard. "None of this is okay. Spending months in captivity wasn't okay. Being forced to rape her wasn't okay."

I flinched, but neither brother paid me any attention.

"Watching her get assaulted and brutalized wasn't okay. None of it was okay. You don't know half of what we went through, and if you did, you wouldn't be demanding explanations right now."

Cyrus stammered, searching for words but coming up empty.

Ladon's voice was softer when he said, "I love her. I love her with everything in me, and I won't apologize for it."

Silence stifled the room, and my heart thundered in my chest. It felt like it was on the verge of exploding. My whole body trembled while I waited for either of them to say something. I was terrified of what would come next.

Cyrus's jaw clenched, and he straightened his jacket. "When we return to Renoa, I want you to collect your things and leave. You can stay at Fort Malek. I know how much you love it there. I never want to see your face in my castle again. Emilie, you're free to follow him or return to Dreslen. I don't really care what you do."

He walked away, taking all the oxygen in the room with him.

Ladon fell back a few steps, and I hugged him, whispering, "He didn't mean it. He's upset and needs some time to cool down. Your family means everything to you, and he knows that."

Ladon shook his head. "I've never seen him like that."

This wasn't fair. Cyrus had no right to treat Ladon this way. He hadn't even known me when we were betrothed; it was an arranged marriage that my parents had brokered. I meant nothing to him. Couldn't he see that I meant everything to Ladon? I hated that his loyalty was being questioned when he was the most devoted person I knew.

I let go of Ladon, and he sat back down on the bench seat. He stared down at his hands, his bangs shielding his eyes from me. He looked so broken. It reminded me of the first time I'd found him in the shower after Reyna had assaulted him.

That thought stiffened my spine.

No. I wouldn't let the conversation end like this.

I gritted my teeth and stormed after Cyrus.

"Hey," I shouted once I found him on the bow of the ship. He didn't turn to face me, and that only pissed me off more. "What is wrong with you?"

I gained the attention of a few crew hands, but they quickly turned away, focusing on their work as if realizing this was a confrontation they didn't want to get involved in.

Cyrus hung his head, but he didn't say a word.

"You're a coward," I said. "And you're being selfish. Your brother loves you, and you have no idea how hard this has been for him. You'll never understand what we went through. What it means to be completely broken, the pieces of your shattered heart and soul lying on the ground. Ladon knows that feeling. I know it too. And the fucked-up part is that all our pieces are scrambled together now. Neither of us can live without the other."

Cyrus's knuckles turned white on the rail, and I wondered if I'd struck a nerve or if he was simply tuning me out.

"How dare you stand there and act as though you have some claim on me? And to turn on him when he needs you, after everything he has done for you. He would give up his *life* for yours, but you can't grant him this one happiness?"

Cyrus refused to face me.

I sighed. "I thought you were a better man than this, Cyrus."

Accepting that he wasn't ready to admit he was wrong, I turned around and headed back to the kitchen space, except Ladon wasn't there anymore. He must've headed back to the bunk room. He hadn't finished his sandwich or his ale.

I grabbed our food and retraced our steps from before until I found the narrow hall that connected our rooms. The ship was swaying now, and I ricocheted from side to side.

Up ahead, Jade stumbled out of our room with her bag in her hands. She caught sight of me and said, "I offered to switch bunks with Ladon. Figured the last thing either of them wanted was to be locked in a tiny room together for the next five nights. I'd prefer if we all made it to Wyland in one piece."

She forced the world's most unnatural smile, but I appreciated the effort. I doubted Cyrus would be thrilled to find Ladon sleeping in my room, but given the options, this seemed to be the best arrangement.

"You're probably right. Thank you."

Her smile faded. "I really am sorry. I know I haven't been the best travel companion, but I didn't mean to cause all this chaos. We may not be friends, but we are supposed to be allies, and I haven't been acting like one."

I blinked in surprise. "It's okay. It wasn't your fault. This has been coming for a while now. I'm only sorry it happened on a boat where none of us can escape."

We shared a soft laugh before the air grew thick with discomfort again. I reached for the door to my room and hesitated for a second before adding, "Have a good night, Jade."

"You too," she replied, and disappeared into the room next to mine.

I eased the door open. "Ladon?"

He sighed, rolling onto his side on the bottom bunk. Grief was apparent in every facet of his face, from his dark eyes to the slight pout on his lips.

"Well, that could've gone better," I said, attempting to ease some of the tension.

He scooted over, making room for me to join him in bed.

"I brought the rest of your sandwich." Wrapped in a napkin, I handed the half-eaten food to him.

Ladon groaned and sat up, resting his back against the wall. He bent his knees, his forearms lying across them while he stared at the sandwich. "I'm not hungry."

"I know," I said, sliding across the small bed to mimic his seated position. I nuzzled against his shoulder, inhaling the scent of salt water and baked bread. "But you should still eat."

He forced himself to take a bite, and a disgusted expression crossed his face.

"You look like a child who is being forced to eat their vegetables."

"I'm not a fan of turkey."

I held back a laugh. "Switch me. Mine is chicken."

We traded and finished our meals in heavy silence. Now that the adrenaline had worn off, I was feeling the impact harder than when it had happened. And I was pretty sure Ladon was too. He was unusually quiet.

"Ladon."

"Hmm?"

"Tell me something honest."

He turned to face me, his eyes sparkling like precious silver. "I'm content. I'm at peace."

I tilted my head. That seemed impossible right now.

As if he could read my mind, he continued, "Don't get me wrong—this is awful. I don't know what's going to happen... if Cyrus will forgive me or I really will be banned from my home. I like Fort Malek, but I don't want to be exiled and separated from my family. I couldn't have imagined a worse way for things to play out."

He reached up and brushed a loose strand of hair behind my ear. "But I truly feel content. You're here, right next to me in this bed, and we don't have to hide it anymore. I can touch you."

He set his sandwich on the small nightstand protruding from the wall and took mine too, placing it next to his.

"I can kiss you."

He grabbed my waist and pulled me into his lap, running his hands over my sides before finding the hem of my shirt. I lifted my arms, and he pulled it off, tossing it to the side. I inhaled sharply when his lips gently caressed the place between my breasts. My fingers tangled in his hair, and I ran a finger down his spine.

He grabbed my ass and pressed my body into his, making me melt against him.

"I can have you."

"Yes, yes," I panted. It wasn't even a question, but I answered anyway. I wanted him to know just how badly I wanted to have him too.

I cupped his face, running my thumbs over his cheeks, and he stared into my eyes, searing me with an unfathomable amount of lust and want and need.

Our lips met in a frenzy of desire, his tongue seeking entrance, which I eagerly gave him.

He moaned, and—gods, the things it did to me. My stomach did flips, and I felt an aching desire for him to touch me. To tease me and indulge me. To feel his cock inside me.

I gasped as he bit my lip playfully.

"I fucking love you, Emilie. I will love you all my life and even in the next."

I shuddered and reached for his shirt, tugging it off so I could feel his skin. He wrapped an arm around my back and held me close, the heat of his chest sinking into me and fueling my burning desire for him.

Suddenly, his hot tongue was coursing over my neck, and he sprinkled kisses in a trail from my ear to the top of my breast. My eyes rolled back in my head when he pulled my bra down and covered my nipple with his mouth.

"Ladon," I said, breathy and desperate.

"Shh. We have to be quiet."

Gods curse these thin walls. I wanted to cry out his name, not hold back.

Ladon gently tossed me on the bed, sitting back on his heels and making quick work of my pants. He stopped to take in my body, and the familiar rush of pink spread across my cheeks and chest.

"Take off your bra," he commanded. "I want to see you."

I pressed up onto one elbow and used the other arm to reach behind me, undoing the clasp and pulling the bland piece of fabric off. I tossed it, and it landed somewhere on the ground next to me.

"Lay back down."

My pussy clenched with each order he gave me. I fell back and watched him, running my legs up his thighs. He grabbed hold of them, yanking me toward him, and I yelped.

"What did I say about being quiet?" He dragged his hands along my stomach.

How was I supposed to be quiet when he was making my body sing? I wasn't in control anymore.

I reached for his face, and he grabbed my hand, kissing the inside of my palm. Then he peppered kisses along my arm and across my shoulder. I swallowed as he continued his trail down the center of my chest, to my stomach, and then the hem of my panties.

I whimpered at the sensation of his mouth hovering above my clit.

"Emilie..." He looked up at me from between my legs and smirked. "Do you need to stick your face into a pillow?"

I gasped and then clamped my mouth shut. Maybe that wasn't such a bad idea. My imagination ran wild—images of my face buried in a pillow while he held my hips and eased his cock inside me. We hadn't had sex in that position before, but the idea of him pounding into me from behind left my panties soaked.

I nodded eagerly, and he made space for me to flip over. Before I could get too comfortable, his hands grazed my hips. His fingers slipped into my underwear, and he slid the fabric down. I lifted my legs so he could finish removing them and then I bent forward, grabbing the closest pillow and preparing to press my face into it.

My hips tilted up, eager for him to touch me.

"You're fucking glistening for me, princess."

My cheeks grew hot—not out of embarrassment, but because my hunger for him had reached its peak. I buried my face in the soft pillow and let out a moan.

I jumped when Ladon's fingers trailed along my inner thigh. He moved them up and down and up again, coming closer to my center but never pressing inside me. I struggled for breath and lifted my head just enough to inhale and dropped it again.

"Oh, gods," I mumbled into the pillow. My legs were trembling, and I wasn't sure if I could even continue to hold myself up.

"That's right. You're such a good girl with your face buried and your pretty pussy displayed for me."

My walls clenched, and I wished he would *do* something. Anything. I didn't think my grip on the pillow could be any tighter.

The lightest touch brushed against my clit, and I bucked my hips. Ladon chuckled, and I wanted to reach back and smack him. Then a finger pushed into my pussy and I lost all coherence.

I hummed my approval as he moved in and out. Eventually, he added a second finger and I rocked my hips to match his pace.

"Gods, I wish I could slap your ass right now, but that would make too much noise." Instead, he gripped my left cheek and squeezed hard.

My pleasure was building and expanding, reaching the edge of ecstasy but never quite tipping over. A little bit more and I'd be coming apart for him.

But then he removed his fingers, and I smothered a whimper. I looked back to see why he had stopped, but he was only changing positions. Seconds later, his tongue was lapping at my entrance, tracing my folds and sucking on my clit.

He gripped my waist tightly, and I was forced to stay still while he had his way with me—eating me like I was his favorite meal. It was everything I wanted, but I still needed more.

Lifting my head, I took a deep breath and spoke in little more than a whisper. "Ladon. Please fuck me."

He kissed the back of my thigh and then the curve of my ass. "Well, since you asked so nicely."

He moved, and the bed shifted as he stripped out of his pants and underwear. Before I could miss him too much, he was right back behind me with one hand on my back and the other wrapped around his shaft.

I tried to watch, but it was difficult from my vantage point. His arm moved, his muscles flexing as he stroked himself. The head of his cock press against my folds, dragging through my arousal and his saliva.

I was so fucking wet and frantic.

But Ladon took his time, his eyes directed to where he was carefully pressing inside me. His mouth dropped open as he moved further inside me.

When he finally grabbed my hips and sheathed himself entirely, I had to bite the pillow to stifle a whimper. He pulled out and thrust inside again, his thighs hitting mine.

My sense of touch was at its limit. We'd never had sex where I wasn't facing him, and now that I couldn't see him, I felt everything at a greater magnitude—his cock sliding in and out of me, his fingers digging into my hips and ass, his balls bumping against my clit. My fingers were going numb from how tightly I held the pillow.

I let out a whimper as the first orgasm washed over me, leaving my entire body limp and spent. My arms fell loosely to my sides, and I lifted my head to breathe in short, choppy breaths while Ladon continued to drive into me. Thank the gods the bunks were bolted to the wall, so they weren't making too much noise. I didn't want him to stop.

He thrust into me over and over, and my legs began to tremble once again. I loved the way he stretched me and filled me, my pussy clamping around him until he moaned.

Without warning, Ladon leaned over and wrapped an arm around my waist, the other hand pulling on my shoulder. He lifted me up and into his lap, my legs straddling his thighs and my back propped against his chest.

I pinched my lips together, silencing a moan—a difficult task without the pillow.

Ladon's fingers circled my clit, and I didn't think it was possible to become even more desperate. I bounced on his lap, taking him deep and rough. A small whine escaped my lips, and Ladon squashed it with a hand over my mouth.

His heavy breaths tickled my back, and my own breathing became attuned to his. His fingers continued to rub my clit, faster and faster until I was fluttering around him a second time.

This time I wasn't alone. He grunted, biting down on my shoulder to silence his pleasure. We stayed like that for a few moments, catching our breath. Ladon's hand fell from my mouth, and he wrapped his arms around my stomach.

I leaned my head back on his shoulder, finally making eye contact. I curled one arm around his head, fingers tangled in his hair, and pulled him closer until our lips met in a slow and passionate kiss.

Ladon cradled me in his arms and lowered us both onto the mattress. Pulling the blanket up to my chest, I tangled my legs with his and trailed my finger along his collarbone.

The silence was comforting. Just being near him was enough to soothe my fears and worries. But I hadn't forgotten everything that awaited us outside of our room. We would deal with it in the morning, though.

Tonight, I wanted to linger in euphoria with him.

Chapter Twenty-Nine

Ladon

THREE DAYS.

It had been three days since my brother had spoken to me. We were more than halfway through our trip across the sea, and things between us hadn't gotten any better.

A small part of me had believed he might go to bed and wake up with a clear head and an open mind, but he had avoided me since that night.

The sun was beating down on the deck, and the crew was hard at work dealing with the ever-changing winds. The boat rocked more than normal, and I wondered how Cyrus was managing his seasickness. Had the herbs helped? I was in no position to ask about his well-being.

"What are you looking at?" Emilie asked, sitting next to me on a stack of crates.

I hadn't been looking at anything. I was staring at the sea while contemplating our predicament. The waves were a soothing lullaby to my tumultuous thoughts.

"Nothing," I told her, leaning back and placing an arm behind her.

Instinctively, I scanned the deck and didn't see Cyrus. Not that it mattered. He couldn't possibly get any angrier with me. If I wanted to touch Emilie in public, I could, now that our secret was out.

Emilie shielded her eyes from the bright sun. "The captain says we're on track to arrive in two days. I told Jade we should have a chat about our next steps when we get there. I couldn't find Cyrus…"

My chest felt heavy as I inhaled. Was this how it was going to be? He couldn't check out completely while we were in a foreign land chasing down our enemy. He needed to keep it together, even if he was pissed at me.

"Leave him to me," I said. "Find Jade and meet me in the lounge. I'll bring Cyrus."

It didn't take long to find him. After one lap of the deck, I moved down into the hull where our cabins were. The door to his and Jade's room was shut, so I knocked, listening for the sound of movement or snoring. Without much to do on the ship, it wouldn't surprise me if he were taking a nap.

No noise came from inside, but I wasn't entirely convinced the cabin was empty. He was pissed at everyone aboard, so why would he respond?

"Cyrus," I shouted. "We're going to have a meeting in ten minutes in the lounge. If you still consider yourself part of this mission, you should be there."

I waited, but the silence lingered.

Sighing, I walked away and headed to the lounge alone.

When I entered, I found Emilie and Jade already waiting for me. They seemed to be in the middle of a conversation, which was strange but nice to see. My opinion of Jade had changed slightly after she'd offered to trade cabins with me a few days ago. She still had work to do before I could trust her or even tolerate her, but it was a sign she wasn't completely irredeemable.

"Where's your brother?" she asked when she saw that I was on my own.

I shrugged and shook my head. "I think he's locked in his room. I told him we were having an important meeting to discuss our plan of action, so we'll see if he shows up."

I took a seat opposite the ladies and pulled out the captain's log we'd taken from the townhouse. "According to this, they'll be landing in Baumheim, so we should start there. But it won't be easy. We'll need to set up a meeting with King Marsden before we do anything else. He's a strict ruler and won't appreciate us coming into his lands and causing havoc."

Emilie nodded. "We can explain Reyna's crimes, and Jade can back us up. Can we have her extradited back to Murvort?"

"Will he help us?" Jade asked. "What if he's just as awful as Reyna was?"

"He's not," Cyrus said, and all our heads snapped to the doorway. "He's an honorable man and an old friend of mine. I don't think we'll have any trouble with him."

It was the first time I'd heard him speak in days. And the first time I'd seen him other than in passing. He avoided making eye contact with me, focusing on Jade and the table between us instead. I forced down the ache in my chest. At least he had shown up.

"Will he have an idea of Reyna's whereabouts?" I asked.

Cyrus crossed his arms and turned his head toward the kitchen, uninterested in answering my question. The rest of us at the table exchanged confused glances.

Jade cleared her throat. "Does King Marsden keep tabs on foreign visitors?" she asked, rephrasing my question.

Cyrus grunted. "Not extensively. But he might know where she is if she's within the city's limits."

My leg bounced under the table with irritation. So this was how it was going to be? It was childish, and I couldn't pretend otherwise. I mumbled under my breath, "Fucking ridiculous."

Emilie shot me a look that clearly said to be nice. And she was right. I shouldn't make things worse by picking another fight right now, but my brother was making it difficult.

"Then it's settled," Emilie said. "We'll meet with King Marsden first and then go from there. Hopefully Reyna hasn't gotten far. Cyrus, can you arrange a meeting with him?"

Once again, Cyrus looked away, but not before I caught him rolling his eyes.

My jaw dropped open, and I looked at Emilie, as if she might give me permission to *not* be nice. She bit her lip in disappointment and nodded to Jade, silently asking her to relay the question.

Absolutely not.

"Don't be rude," I scolded my brother. "You don't have to be kind to me—I can take it. But I won't let you treat Emilie like shit because of me. Answer her."

Jade and Emilie both tensed, looking like they wanted to flee the room so Cyrus and I could have it out.

Clenching his jaw, he responded, "Yes, I will set up a meeting."

Then he turned and left the lounge. We all sighed as the hostility left the room with him, but I was stunned by his behavior.

"Well, that went well," Jade said once Cyrus was out of earshot.

I grunted my irritation. "We won't get any messenger hawks this far out to sea. We'll need to wait until we're closer to shore before he can send a message. That being said, I have no doubt that he'll be able to get an audience with King Marsden."

"Perfect," Jade said. "Then we'll just waltz in and ask if we can murder a psychopath that's hiding in his territory."

Emilie smiled, and I almost laughed, thankful for the break in tension.

"The real question is, who gets to kill Reyna?" Jade asked, and the conversation grew serious again.

"Emilie and me," I said flatly. "I don't care what quarrel you have with her. It's nothing compared to what Emilie and I went through."

"She's the reason my parents are dead."

"She assaulted us and stole Emilie's innocence. She abused us and tormented us in ways you can't even imagine. Humiliated and terrorized us. She scarred us for life." I held up my wrist where white vines still marred my skin. The scars there could not tan and, as such, were more prominent now that I'd been in the sun again for a few weeks. "It would have been kinder to kill us."

Jade's dark eyes scanned my face, and then Emilie's, contemplating my words. I waited for her to make a snide remark—something that would make me take back the grace I'd given her earlier. Gods forbid she say something about Emilie because I would tear her limb from limb.

But she just tapped her fingers on the rugged table. "Guess we'll see who gets to her first."

Chapter Thirty

Emilie

I'D BEEN AWAKE FOR at least an hour, drawing patterns on Ladon's chest as it rose and fell in his sleep. Not because I couldn't sleep—quite the opposite, actually. I hadn't slept this well since before I'd left Dreslen.

Despite being crammed into a small bunk bed, I had Ladon next to me, and we no longer bore the weight of our secret. My life was beginning to feel like it belonged to me once again, with just one exception.

Reyna.

My stomach turned. She'd evaded us so far, but it ended here. It ended in Wyland. She wouldn't escape this time. We wouldn't let her.

Today was the day we made landfall in Wyland, and we were all ready to disembark and leave this cramped space behind. But it was still early, and for now, I was content to stay in bed with Ladon.

Eventually, his eyes fluttered open, and he smiled when he realized I was watching him. "Good morning, princess."

I didn't think I'd ever tire of hearing his sleepy inflection when he woke up in the morning. It was sexy and intimate in a way that was all mine. This piece of him was something only I got to witness, and it woke a possessive side of me I didn't know existed.

"Good morning," I replied.

Ladon grabbed my hand that had been grazing his chest for several minutes and slithered his fingers between mine. Then he brought it to his lips and kissed my knuckles. "Are you ready for today?"

I nodded. "I'm ready to put this behind us. It's weird, though."

"What is?"

"I expected to be angrier than I am right now. Don't get me wrong—I still want to see Reyna's head roll. And I will do whatever it takes to make that happen. But the feeling isn't as intense as I anticipated."

"What do you feel instead?"

I smiled. "Hopeful. Calm. Eager to move on."

Ladon processed this. "I feel hopeful too. Like I can feel Reyna's end coming closer. And we will finally have a future."

There was a knock on the cabin door.

Ladon groaned, squeezing me tight against his chest. "Go away."

I smiled, wrapping my arms around him.

A muffled voice came through the door. It sounded like Drip. "We'll be docking in about thirty minutes. You should gather your things and head to the deck."

Ladon sighed. "Guess that means we'll have to get out of bed."

"Guess so," I said, pressing a quick kiss to his lips. He grunted as I rolled over top of him and scrambled to my feet.

It didn't take long to pack our things. Together, Ladon and I said goodbye to our tiny cabin and made our way upstairs. Jade and Cyrus were already waiting on the bow, engaged in conversation. It was nice that he was talking to someone, even if he still couldn't look at Ladon or me. I hadn't given up hope that he would change his mind, though. I couldn't imagine cutting my own brother out of my life.

Past them, I saw land in the distance. It was foggy, but the sun was trying its hardest to break through. The shore was mostly made up of cliffs and rolling hills, but I could see an opening straight ahead with docks similar to the ones in Sage Harbor. Light reflected off the peak of the tallest hill, and I squinted my eyes.

"What's that?"

"I believe it's the Gem of Baumheim—the grandest castle in all of Wyland."

"That's where King Marsden lives? Gods, the view must be stunning from up there."

As our ship approached, I could make out houses lining the hillside along with paths that snaked from the ground to the sky. There were several stunning hills, but none as majestic as the one that boasted the Gem.

Jade offered a welcoming grin when she spotted us. She jutted her chin toward the land. "I can see why Reyna would choose to come here. The mountains feel like home."

I stared at them, but I didn't see the resemblance. Murvort's mountains were harsh and unforgiving. These hills were full of green and vibrant yellow flowers scattered throughout. They rolled with gentle inclines while Murvort's cut with jagged edges.

Minutes later, we were close enough to make out the faces of those working the docks. Our crew exchanged shouted words with a team on land, and lines were thrown to reel us in and secure the ship. After that, it didn't take long for us to cross the bridge and return to dry land. My legs felt a little unstable, but the feeling wore off after a few minutes.

Unlike the bustling docks of Sage Harbor, Baumheim was serene and methodical. There were a few ships docked and a dozen or so men and women roaming the marina, but it was missing the markets and music and conversations. The bulk of activity in Baumheim appeared to be centered around the castle on top of the hill.

"Lead the way," Jade said to Cyrus. He was the only one of us who had ever been to Wyland, and I wasn't sure how long it had been since his last trip here. Had he even been here in adulthood?

He adjusted his backpack and set off toward the towering castle peeking out over the tree-covered hill. The rest of us followed in his footsteps.

The path that led to King Marsden's castle was made of red dirt that popped against dark green foliage. Tiny, fluffy critters scurried up the trees and peered down at us with curiosity. From my previous studies, I identified them as squirrels. They weren't native to Lourova, but after seeing them up close, I wished they were. One stared at me, and I smiled; how badly I wanted to hold and pet it!

But we kept moving forward, and soon enough, houses began to appear. Most of them were quiet in the early hours of the day, the families inside preparing breakfast or still sleeping in.

The first civilian we came across was a young mother hanging clothes on a line while her toddler hugged her legs. She waved politely and carried on with her chores.

As we climbed higher, more houses lined the path, and it was clear we were growing closer to the center of town. If the congestion hadn't made it obvious, then the shadows from the castle would have.

Finally, we reached a tall exterior wall that appeared to wrap around the entire hill like a defensive border. It was a swirl of greens and browns like marble, but the surface was rough. I'd never seen anything like it, but perhaps it had been magically crafted.

As we approached the gate, two guards stood at attention. They waited for one of us to make an introduction and state our business. Cyrus stepped forward and announced, "I am King Cyrus Castelli of Osavian.

I'm here for a meeting with King Marsden. These three are with me, and I can vouch for them."

I quietly thanked the gods that he had put his anger aside long enough to bring us through the gate with him.

The guard turned around, and I noticed a lever behind him. He pulled it, and the metal barricade began to slide to the right. Then he waved us through.

Inside the wall, more homes and shops filled the streets, made from the same marble material that mystified me. There was something elegant about the architecture that distinguished it from its countryside counterparts.

A short time later, we ascended a grand set of stairs leading to the castle's entrance—complete with columns three stories high that held up a cluster of balconies. Nothing was uniform here; it was all haphazard, like the castle itself had sprouted and grown limbs like a tree. And in some places, there appeared to be actual tree limbs growing and weaving with the ornate pillars, bannisters, and window dressings. It was all stunningly beautiful.

We walked through a tall archway and into a massive entry hall. Our steps echoed and caught the attention of a tall, thin man with a bushy beard and mustache. "How can I help you?" he asked, striding toward us.

"I am King Cyrus. I have a meeting with King Marsden."

The man pulled a small notebook from his front pocket and flipped through it, pausing to read a page. He shut it abruptly after finding confirmation and smiled. "He's busy presently, but he will speak with you shortly. While you wait, would you like some tea? Coffee? Have you had breakfast?"

"That would be greatly appreciated. Thank you."

"There's a waiting room this way if you'll follow me," he said, leading us under another smaller archway decorated with tree limbs.

As I walked underneath, I looked up and discovered that it wasn't truly a tree. It was gemstones—emeralds and rubies crafted intricately into the design to give it the appearance of foliage. I blinked rapidly, admiring the creativity and attention to detail.

So that was how they'd gotten tree branches to grow intertwined with the castle. They weren't trees at all.

Inside the waiting room, the man took our bags and placed them in a closet near the entry. "I'll be right back with your breakfast and beverages."

He left, and that gave us a chance to explore the room. Portraits adorned every available inch of the walls, except where rose-colored lanterns hung instead. The faces within each were so similar to one another, I was certain they must be related and most likely part of the royal family. With as many as there were, I supposed a good portion of them were probably also deceased.

I slowly strolled while we waited for our host to return, admiring the little girl with wild blonde hair and the couple standing behind her with one hand each on her shoulders. The next portrait was of a young man in a military uniform. His hair was slightly darker, but his eyes matched her shade of amber. Were they cousins? Or perhaps he was an uncle? There was no way to tell.

I moved on, observing the many portraits until I found Ladon stopped in front of the largest one in the gallery. Two young children, around six or seven, who were almost identical. The boy was slightly taller than his sister, with rounder cheeks and a wider smile. The girl was scrawnier, and her long blonde hair was braided down to her stomach, with tendrils tucked behind her ears. The boy had one arm around his sister's shoulders while her hands were clasped in front of her.

I'd been subjected to similar sessions with Adrien—long hours where we were forced to sit still while someone painted our faces to be hung one day in a room where no one would ever see them. At least this gallery was being used.

"Are you thinking about your brother?" I asked Ladon quietly. Cyrus was on the other side of the room, intentionally avoiding us.

"What?"

"Your brother," I said again, nodding to the portrait. "Did the two of you have to do these growing up? I always hated them. My mother would get so mad if we moved even a little. She had to bribe us with dessert just to get us to sit down. I was usually too scared to disobey, but Adrien..." I chuckled. "He loved seeing how far he could push her boundaries."

I smiled, thinking of the one occasion when he'd run to play outside and dirtied his clothing and Mother had to find a different outfit for him at the last minute. She was furious, but his smile had never been more genuine.

"No. I mean, yes, we had to sit for portraits, but that wasn't what I was thinking about."

"Oh?"

Just then, our host returned and pressed a cup of tea into my hands.

"It's magnificent, isn't it? The artist did such an amazing job of bringing them to life. It's such a shame what happened to them," he said, the light in his eyes dimming as he viewed the portrait with a sense of loss.

"What happened?" I asked.

The lump in his throat bobbed as he swallowed. "They disappeared almost ten years ago. No one knows what happened to them, or if they're still alive. The King spent years searching for them, but there was no trace, no trail to follow. He nearly drained the family's savings in his search and eventually had to call it off before the realm fell into catastrophe."

"That's awful," I said. They were so young. They must've been terrified. And the families didn't have closure after all this time. I looked at Ladon, knowing that could've been our families if we hadn't escaped. Never knowing what happened to us...

My eyes fell to his hand. He was toying with a ring I had never seen him wear. His thumb rubbed the face of the piece of jewelry while he stared at the portrait with a pensive expression.

Ladon turned down the host when he asked whether he wanted sugar or milk in his tea. Once the host was out of earshot, Ladon turned to me. "What are the odds that these two children are the ones I saw in Murvort?"

The question stole my breath away. I looked between him and the portrait. "Is that what you think?"

His gaze returned to the portrait, and he nodded. "They look a lot like the kids I ran into—if you add six years."

"Are you sure? I mean, you only saw them once. You could be mistaken."

"I will never be able to forget their faces, Emilie."

I believed him. I hadn't been there when Reyna killed those kids, but he had told me enough details. Actually, the look on his face when he returned to our room that night was enough for me to understand the horrors he'd witnessed that day.

He held out his palm, and I picked up the ring he'd been playing with. I spun it around until I could see the crest on the front—a bold 'M', but the lines of the letter were made of tree branches like those that embellished the castle.

I knew in my gut that he wasn't mistaken. These twins were the same ones he'd met in Reyna's castle. The same ones she'd murdered brutally and left nothing behind but ash. They would never come home, but maybe we could give their family some closure.

The large door to our left swung open and another castle servant, dressed similarly to our host, stepped out. "The King is ready to see you now."

Chapter Thirty-One

Ladon

THE MARSDEN FAMILY RING weighed heavy in my pocket as we stepped
inside the King's throne room. I couldn't even take a moment to admire
the sparkling emerald windows that made it seem as though we were high
in the trees and sunlight was filtering through the leaves. The image of
the twins' faces and their final moments was impossible to shake.

Looking at King Marsden only made it worse. His children resembled
him so much, particularly in the nose and high cheekbones. His eyes were
nothing like theirs, though. Theirs had been big and bold, filled with
desperation. Looking into his eyes, I saw only weariness.

We walked the carpet-laden path until we were at the foot of his
throne, and Cyrus bowed his head. King Marsden did the same, though
he remained seated.

"Thank you for taking this meeting, King Marsden," Cyrus said.

King Marsden stood and took the two steps down to our level, stopping in front of Cyrus. "Please call me Vincent."

"As long as you call me Cyrus."

The two kings smiled and shook hands before colliding in a friendly embrace. Vincent sighed before pulling back and placing his hands on my brother's shoulders. "It's been too long, Cyrus. What has it been? Fifteen years?"

Fifteen years... when my father had died. Shortly after Cyrus had been crowned as the new king, rulers from all around the world had visited Renoa to pay their respects and establish a connection with my brother. They were about the same age—although Vincent had more gray sprinkled throughout his hair and beard—so I imagined they'd hit it off all those years ago. I'd been in too much distress and had spent the entire month holed up, avoiding the parade of regal guests that ventured into our kingdom.

"It's good to see you again," Cyrus said. Then he waved his hand behind him, to the rest of us. "This is my brother, Ladon, my... uh... Emilie of Dreslen, and Jade of Murvort."

Vincent didn't notice the way he stumbled over Emilie's name or the stilted tone he used to say mine. But I did. It hurt more than it should have.

"Murvort," Vincent repeated. His eyes flickered over to Jade, appraising her with a stern face. The friendly greeting he'd given my brother was long gone. "Never thought I'd see the day when a representative of Murvort would step on my soil."

Jade opened her mouth to respond—no doubt, with an insult or something that would embarrass us all and complicate our mission—but Cyrus cut her off. "It's quite a surprise, isn't it? I never expected to host an emissary either, but sometimes life blindsides us in ways you'd never imagine."

I could've sworn I saw him glance between Emilie and me, but his attention returned to Vincent. "Actually, that's why we're here. I'm sure you've heard that Reyna Lemaire is on the run and the Holdens have claimed power over Murvort. We believe Reyna is hiding here in Baumheim. We followed her here because we have some unfinished business to attend to."

"I know the business you speak of," Vincent said, looking past my brother to me and Emilie. "I've heard what happened to you, and I am very sorry for what you've been through."

My stomach tightened, but I remained stoic. From the corner of my eye, I saw Emilie turn rigid. I stepped closer to her instinctively, knowing how much she loathed unwanted attention. Cyrus noticed my protective stance before his eyes fell to his feet.

Somehow, our trauma had made it all the way to Baumheim. If only we had been given the choice of whether we were ready to share what had happened to us. But someone—Reyna or any number of her surviving loyalists—had spread the word, and now it was beyond our control.

I tried to keep my anger at bay. It wasn't Vincent's fault, after all. "If you know, then you'll help? Have you heard anything about her whereabouts?"

Vincent grimaced. "I have not. Nor do I wish to. As much as I sympathize with your situation, I can't get involved. I can't put my country in the middle of this. If a war is brewing between Murvort and Osavian, Wyland cannot afford to get caught up in it."

Next to me, Jade scoffed, and I shared her irritation. What kind of person refuses to stand on the right side of a war? Not that it would come to that. Reyna had already been chased off, and there was no way we'd let her or her supporters return to power.

"It won't come to that," I said. "Reyna's grip on Murvort is completely severed. There is no war to be fought."

"I can't take that risk."

"There's no risk to be taken," Cyrus argued. "In fact, you don't even need to help us. We'll find her on our own. We simply request your assurance that we'll be able to leave the continent with her imprisoned. Will you at least allow us to extradite her?"

Vincent paused to consider. "I don't like this, Cyrus. I know we've been friends for a long time, but you have to understand—I want to keep my kingdom safe. I can't put a target on us."

"Your kingdom isn't safe as long as Reyna stays here," I growled. "She's a bigger threat to you than we are."

Nothing we said seemed to matter. It was clear that Vincent had made up his mind before we'd ever landed in Baumheim. There was only one thing now that might sway him.

I pulled the ring out of my pocket—the one with his family crest. Reaching out to him, I unfurled my clenched fist, the ring displayed in my palm.

It took him a second before he noticed. Then his eyes narrowed as he stepped closer. Taking the ring from my hand, he held it up to the light. "Where did you get this?"

My suspicions were confirmed, and even though it improved our circumstances, my shoulders slumped, knowing that I was the last one to see his two precious children alive.

"While we were held captive in Murvort, we witnessed many other atrocities under that mountain—slaves incapable of speaking, animals that had been experimented on, soulless vultures who delighted in our pain—but one of the most horrendous scenes I had to witness involved two young adults. A boy and a girl, around sixteen or seventeen. They had your blond hair."

A mixture of sorrow and shock washed over his face. In his eyes, I saw his conflicting emotion—longing to know what happened to his children, yet terrified to hear of their gruesome end. Regardless, he wouldn't be able to rest until his children had been found, and I was the only one who could give him that.

"I didn't know there were other captives," I said softly. "I thought we were the only ones. By the time I ran into them, they were already doomed. It seems that one or both of them killed one of Reyna's pets—a hound. As you can imagine, she didn't take that well. She…"

I trailed off, unsure how much detail I should provide. Was it worth tormenting him just to get him to help us?

"What did she do?" he asked, stepping closer to me. The color had drained from his face, and he grabbed my shoulders like he could shake the response from me.

"The boy—"

"Vincent. Vincent the Third."

I nodded. "Vincent was killed first. Reyna burned him alive with her lightning."

A sob escaped the King, and he released his hold on me. He turned and started pacing, pushing his hair back with shaky palms. When his attention returned to me, his eyes were full of tears. "And my daughter? Violet?"

"Reyna set her snake on Violet. It attacked, and the poison—"

Vincent fell to the floor, his knees slamming into the red-flecked marble.

"The poison spread pretty quickly, and then she was gone too," I finished softly.

I felt awful watching Vincent break in front of me. Perhaps I should've kept the information to myself. He didn't deserve to hurt like this.

My brother kneeled beside him and wrapped one arm around his shoulders, comforting him while he trembled. I heard a sniffling noise and discovered Emilie was crying too. I reached for her hand and laced our fingers together, which only made her sob harder.

"Give us a minute," Cyrus said.

Jade left the room first, and I pulled Emilie behind me, returning to the portrait gallery. The door closed behind us with an echoing thud.

For several long minutes, we stood speechless. The only sound was Emilie's stifled sobs. Eventually, those subsided too.

Jade sat on a bench and crossed her legs and arms, inhaling a deep breath. "You did the right thing."

"Did I?"

She nodded and stared at the dirt beneath her fingernails, doing her best to pretend she wasn't fazed. She was, though. We all were. "He would've spent the rest of his life wondering what happened to his children. It hurts now, but he'll survive. And when he's done falling apart in there, he's going to appreciate what you did for him."

"She's right," Emilie said through a choked sob. Red splotches covered the skin beneath her eyes, and her nose was pink.

I pushed her hair back behind her ear and wiped away a stray tear. Then I sighed. "It doesn't make it any easier."

Emilie nodded and then her arms were wrapped around my torso, her face buried against my chest. I smoothed her hair and kissed the top of her head.

I heard Jade moving behind me, and then she spoke. "I'm going to find that host. Maybe he can give us another round of tea or sandwiches. Food always helps with sorrow."

Then she disappeared, giving Emilie and me a moment alone.

"Are you all right?" I asked.

"Yes. I don't know what came over me. I didn't even know them. I didn't see them die. I have no idea why I'm crying like this."

I huffed a laugh. "Because you care, princess. You know what it's like to suffer, and it hurts to see others doing the same."

"It's more than that. I don't know how to explain it, though."

"Try."

"It's like... this feeling in my soul, deep inside me, ripping me from reality and taking me back to that drawing room. It felt like I was there, being tortured all over again. It was a reminder of everything she is capable of and everything she put us through. I can feel their hands and their eyes—" Her voice broke.

"Shh," I said softly. "It's not real. You're here with me. You're safe."

She pulled back far enough to look me in the eye. "She has to pay for what she has done."

"She will. I promise."

Moments later, Jade came back with the host at her side. He left a tray of mini sandwiches on a stand along with a pitcher of water and some glasses. Then he pointed at the appetizers. "These are the King's favorite. Jade filled me in on what happened, and I think he'll want some when he's ready to see you again. They were the Queen's favorite too."

"What happened to her?" Emilie asked.

The host hung his head. "After the twins' disappearance, she was bedridden with grief for nearly a year. King Vincent did everything in his power to find them and bring them home, but as you know, it was never enough. In the end, when he couldn't bring home her beloved children, she decided that they must've already passed on to the next life. And so she chose to go with them."

Instantly, my mother's face flashed before me. How she'd broken down before me. How hard was it for her while I'd been held captive? Was there ever a point when she was ready to give up? I doubted it. Cyrus never would've let her.

I glanced toward the door that separated me from my brother, wishing it was the only thing keeping us apart. Would he have fought so hard for my life if he knew what I had done?

Probably. He was noble in that way.

The door suddenly opened, and Cyrus appeared, eyes fixed on me.

I took a step forward, but Cyrus closed the door behind him and stood in front of it like a guard.

"What happened?" I asked.

Cyrus sighed. "He doesn't wish to speak to us any longer."

"That's it, then? He wants us to just leave without Reyna? Let me in. I don't care if he doesn't want to talk. He has to—"

"Stop," Cyrus said. "I didn't say he wasn't going to help. Just not in the way we hoped."

I took a deep breath and waited for Cyrus to explain. How was he going to help if he wasn't willing to hand over Reyna?

"Vincent said we can search for Reyna on our own. He was telling the truth when he said he didn't know where she was. But he's willing to look the other way if we track her down on our own and force her out of Baumheim. He also said that if we happen to commit any crimes during our hunt, we will be pardoned."

My brows rose. "Crimes?"

Cyrus cleared his throat. "Yes. Any acts of violence or espionage, etcetera, will be forgiven as long as we do not harm any innocent civilians."

"That's great news," Emilie said.

Jade was quick to ruin it. "We don't know where she is, though. How are we supposed to search an entire foreign city with no leads? And what if she's left for the countryside?"

Cyrus held up a hand. "Vincent doesn't know her exact location, but he has a guess as to where she might be. He said we need to check the

Stygian Market. It's where the dregs of society spend their time, and if Reyna is still in Baumheim, she's likely in that area."

"All right then," I said. "Let's go to the Stygian Market."

Chapter Thirty-Two

Emilie

KING VINCENT WAS KIND enough to offer lodging while we remained in Baumheim. Since our other option was to sleep in the bunks aboard the Aria, we immediately took him up on his offer.

We were each given a room—although I would've been happy to share with Ladon. I had a feeling he would sneak into my room later, but neither of us wanted to make a scene in front of Cyrus.

My room was the perfect size for a short-term guest. Large enough to fit a bed and a sitting area, but comfortable too. White linens covered the soft mattress and hung above the window, pushed to the side so I could see the forest around us and the sea in the distance.

While the room wasn't grand in size, it made up for it with ornate details. The same green and red gems we'd seen in the portrait hall and entrance were also encrusted in the floor and walls of my bedroom. The bed frame was carved like a tree trunk with a headboard of branches crawling up toward the ceiling. Even the chairs in my sitting area looked like the perfect place for a bird to perch, though they were cushioned with plump green pillows.

I didn't have much time to clean up, so I quickly undressed and hopped in the shower. I scrubbed my body and hair in record time, anxious to get to the Stygian Market. Our host had also provided clean clothes, which I found lying on the bed.

I held up a forest green blouse and a pair of black leather pants. They were both a little big on me, but it was better than wearing any of the dirty clothes in my bag. Tossing my towel aside, I dressed and stepped into my boots once again. Then I grabbed my cloak and went to find the others.

Jade was already waiting in the hall.

"Where are Ladon and Cyrus?"

She shrugged. "Still cleaning up, I guess."

I rolled my eyes. "I thought women were supposed to be the ones who took a long time getting ready?"

To my delight, Jade smiled. "That's horseshit. Men are equally vain, if not more so, than we are." Our laughter was short-lived, though.

Ladon stepped out of his room. "What's so funny?"

"Nothing," Jade said. "Can you tell your brother to hurry up?"

Ladon ran a hand through his damp hair, looking down the hall toward the door to Cyrus's bedroom. "I'm not sure I'm the best person for that job. Why don't you go instead?"

I knew he was only joking, but Jade took his suggestion seriously, stalking down the hall to bang on Cyrus's door. She shouted, "Let's go, Your Royal Highness. We've got things to do. You've primped enough. It's not like you have anyone to impress."

She looked back at us and winked. Ladon groaned, and I cringed. We were doing our best to diffuse the situation, but of course Jade would light a match and watch it explode.

Jade cupped her hands around her mouth and sucked in a sharp breath, ready to yell something else, but the door opened and Cyrus towered over her. He frowned and forced his way forward, knocking Jade back a step.

Her look of surprise was something I'd yet to see.

"Let's go," he grumbled.

Cyrus led the way again, since the rest of us were unfamiliar with the streets of Baumheim. We treaded down the hill on the opposite side of the bay, deeper into the wooded region. Cyrus hardly said a word the entire time.

There was a section of the route that was surrounded by nothing but trees. The houses disappeared, and so did the sunlight. Other than birds chirping and leaves blowing, I heard no signs of life.

It wasn't long before voices filled the air again, growing as we approached a black archway. Unlike the gate around the castle, it was unguarded. In fact, no one even gave us a second look as we walked through. We were all wearing cloaks with hoods pulled over our heads that cast shadows on our faces. It would've looked suspicious if it weren't the standard appearance for everyone around us.

The Stygian Market was shaped like a wheel—a glistening lagoon in the center with a small channel, lined with rowboats, leading away to the sea. From the lagoon, multiple stone-paved spokes fanned out in all directions. Unlike most markets, the buildings here were run down and covered in dust. The merchants didn't set up inside them, but outside in carts and blankets strewn across the ground.

We passed the first few, including a woman selling bottles of substances I was certain were banned. Another woman was missing an eye and selling trinkets and antiques, which she described as 'one of a kind'.

A man with a bald head and tattooed face inched closer to me, and I grabbed Ladon's hand. Ladon gave the man a sharp glare, and he backed off, but I tried not to make eye contact with anyone after that.

A bell chimed four times to signal the top of the hour, startling me and causing my hood to fall. I quickly pulled it back up, making sure it was properly hiding my face. If we did come across Reyna, I wanted to see her before she saw us.

"Where should we start?" Jade asked in a hushed tone. Despite the crowds, Stygian Market was still eerily quiet except for the bell. Everyone was whispering their business, as if they feared the trees might eavesdrop and spill their sins to the gods.

"We should split up," Cyrus answered. "I'll take the northern side of the lagoon."

"I'll go with you," Jade said, squinting her eyes when he showed the first sign of dispute. She effectively shut his objections down before he ever had a chance to express them.

Ladon nodded. "You can take the top half of the market. Emilie and I will take the lower half."

We all agreed to meet back in an hour with any findings.

Ladon and I took our time wandering through the crowds, keeping our heads low and sneaking glances whenever we could. Some had face coverings or hoods, like we did. Others didn't care if they were seen, openly showing their faces while bartering with customers. I tried not to look at any of them for too long, lest they realize and stare back.

"Which way do you want to go first?" Ladon asked when we made it to a fork in the road.

"Left," I said, side-stepping a man on a horse who otherwise would've trampled me.

"Careful," Ladon said, and I could hear the grin in his voice even if I couldn't see his face.

In reality, we were being anything but careful. We were stepping into the pit of danger and throwing ourselves to the gods' mercy.

"Is this a crazy idea?" I asked as we walked by a man with a bloodied face and clothes that were torn to shreds. Wherever he had been, I didn't want to go.

"Yes. That doesn't mean it isn't necessary."

We made it to the end of our first spoke with nothing to show for it. Walking around the outer rim, we headed toward the next street in our allotted area.

The second street was equally disappointing, as was the third. It wasn't until we got to our fourth spoke of the wheel that Ladon and I saw anything of interest.

"Do you see that man over there? With the gray coat and cigar?" Ladon asked, pulling me aside and pretending to observe a woman who was bending into all sorts of unnatural positions. It was as if her bones were missing.

I let my eyes leave her long enough to look where he had suggested. There was a table on the other side of the street where three people were playing a card game, one of them in a gray coat just like Ladon had described.

I looked back at the contortionist, afraid to stare for too long. But something made me look back once more. I got a clearer look at the man's face this time, and when I did, I abruptly faced forward with a gasp.

"Is that...?"

"I believe so."

Luther, Reyna's right-hand man, was only feet away from us.

My heart pounded, and blood rushed to my head. If he was here, Reyna couldn't be far. After all, it was his magic as a traveler that had kept her alive when Ladon tried to kill her. He had taken her from us. Taken our chance at revenge.

But we'd been given a second one.

I grinned as excitement coursed through my veins. Our chase was nearing its end.

My hand reached for the blade sheathed at my waist.

"Don't," Ladon said.

My smile disappeared. "Why not?"

"He's not our target. Let's wait. See where he takes us."

I sighed, but Ladon was right. As good as it would feel to gut Luther, he wasn't the one I wanted most. I wanted Reyna's blood on my hands, and I would settle for nothing less.

Thankfully, the contortionist continued her performance, giving us the perfect excuse to linger nearby. We took turns glancing back to see if Luther had left, but the only movement he made was to purchase another tankard of ale from the stand a few feet away.

Good. Let him drink himself into a stupor. It would make getting information out of him easier.

We stayed until the bell rang five times to signal the hour was up.

"Shit," I whispered.

Ladon shifted restlessly. "We can't go back now."

"They're going to wonder what happened to us. What if they get worried?"

"Then they worry," Ladon replied. "This is more important."

I hated it, but he was right about this too. We couldn't leave now. This was the closest we'd gotten to Reyna in over a month.

So we waited. And waited. And waited.

After what felt like forever, Luther finally got up from the table and stumbled away.

Without a word, Ladon tossed a coin into our contortionist's cup and we turned to follow him.

We kept a few feet between us and Luther, just in case he turned around. Not that he would likely recognize us in his current state. He stumbled into several people as he walked away, and they grew increasingly aggravated with him. I only hoped none of them tried to beat him up before we got the chance.

Luther wandered into the inner ring around the lagoon and continued to the right.

"Where do you think he's going?" I asked. "Somewhere in the market? Or a hiding place outside of here?"

Ladon rolled his shoulders. "I hope he stays in the market for now. I don't want to get too far without letting Cyrus and Jade know where we are."

We didn't have to wait much longer before discovering his intended destination. He strolled up to a dilapidated building, which, surprisingly, had a guard at the door. An odd sight to see, since I couldn't fathom why anyone would want to enter such a run-down building. It looked as though it could collapse at any second, killing anyone who dared to venture inside. Why on earth would it require a guard?

Unless something valuable was tucked inside. Or someone.

Ladon and I hid behind a pile of rubble and waited to see what happened next. We couldn't hear the words they exchanged from our position, but we watched as the guard opened the door and Luther stumbled inside.

"Do we follow him?" I asked.

"Do you know how to get back to our meeting place?"

"Yes," I replied cautiously. "Why?"

"I need you to go back."

I scoffed. "I'm not leaving you, Ladon. It could be dangerous in there. Besides, this is as much my fight as it is yours."

He turned to me with a smirk. "I'm not going in there on my own. I need you to go get the others while I wait and make sure he doesn't come back out."

"Oh."

Ladon leaned closer until his lips were on mine, gently sucking my bottom lip. His arm wrapped around my waist, pulling until I was pressed against him. His hand slid down to my ass, and he squeezed before giving me a quick slap.

I broke our kiss with a gasp and found him grinning wide.

"Go. Quick."

It took a second to remember what he was even talking about. But when I did, I reluctantly turned away and rushed back to our designated meeting place.

When I got to the plaza with the bell next to the lagoon, it didn't take long to find Jade and Cyrus. They were bickering in hushed tones. I didn't need to eavesdrop to know what their argument was about. They were obviously trying to decide what to do about the fact that Ladon and I hadn't returned.

"Hey," I called, coming to a stop in front of them.

They both turned to me—Cyrus with a look of bewilderment and Jade with one of annoyance. Before either could begin interrogating me, I urged them to come with me.

"Ladon is waiting," I said quickly. "I can fill you in while we walk."

Thankfully, neither of them wasted precious time resisting or requiring clarification. I walked as fast as my legs could carry me while telling them what we'd seen—Luther, Reyna's closest companion, and where he had taken up shelter.

"Ladon is there by himself?" Cyrus asked.

The worry in his voice wasn't lost on me. He might be mad at his brother, but he still cared. That gave me hope for their future.

"He's fine. He won't do anything stupid. I'm only in a rush in case Luther leaves and Ladon decides to follow him. Then we will have lost both of them."

My concerns were unnecessary, though. When we arrived back at the crumbling building, Ladon was still waiting patiently where I'd left him, eyes glued to the door and the guard that stood in front of it. He glanced over his shoulder just in time to see us approaching, and his shoulders visibly relaxed.

"Any change?" I asked.

"Luther hasn't left the building," he said. Then he took a second to glance at his brother before adding, "But many more have entered. They've been filing in regularly since you left. I don't know what we should expect inside, but I can guarantee it won't be good."

Chapter Thirty-Three

Ladon

DOING OUR BEST TO look inconspicuous, we approached the door to the run-down building. If we looked as though we were certain of our destination and that we belonged, we were less likely to be turned away.

Cyrus allowed me to take the lead—a good thing since boasting the title of King wouldn't do us any favors in a place like this. The guard met my gaze as we stepped closer, and I gave him my most condescending glare. Whatever this place was, he was working the door, and anyone worthy of stepping inside outranked him. I acted accordingly.

"What are you here for?" he asked bluntly.

He was a large man, and he was probably used to intimidating people with a simple squint of his eyes.

"I'm here on business." I said vaguely. It was believable enough in a variety of settings. Even if it was a casual setting, which I doubted it was, I could play it off as a meeting with someone to discuss discreet matters.

The guard looked down to my feet and back up to my face with a suspicious snarl. "What kind of business?"

I opened my mouth to reply, but before I could speak, two men stumbled into our space. One appeared to have drunk too much and had his arm across the other's shoulders. The sober man greeted the guard like a friend. "We lost track of time. Have the fights begun yet?"

"Not yet. The first one should start in a few minutes, though. You should get inside and find a spot, or you'll be watching the back of people's heads instead of the matches."

The guard opened the door, and the man dragged his friend inside. Then the guard's attention was back on me. He raised an eyebrow, waiting for my response.

"I have some bets to settle." It was a gut feeling, but if there were fights happening tonight, it seemed obvious to me that there would be gambling going on as well. I left it at that, just in case I said too much and gave away that I had no clue what was really happening inside.

The guard nodded and opened the door again.

I strained to keep the smile off my face until we were through and standing in a small entry space.

"That was some quick thinking," Emilie said.

"You're not the only one with brains, princess." I grinned wide and grabbed her hand, leading the way into the building.

The first room we entered was dark, and it took a moment for my eyes to adjust. It looked like an old warehouse—a massive open space with plain stone walls and a dirty floor. It was less crowded than I expected, but it didn't take long to realize the reason.

In the center of the room, a massive pit opened up to a basement below, and that was where all the action was.

We walked around the pit until we came to a rickety staircase, so rusted that I was impressed it was still standing. Carefully, I descended the steps while surveilling the room below.

The basement stretched beyond my line of sight. There were two square roped-off areas to my right where I assumed the fights took place. Between them, the word 'Underground' was written on the wall in black paint. Must've been the name they'd given this place... Very creative.

On the opposite side, there were tables spaced out where people were playing cards and dice games. Trays of alcohol wound through them on a phantom breeze, hovering without a server in sight.

Past the tables, there was a glass wall with a bluish hue. I squinted, noticing movement beyond it. "Is that the lake?"

Beside me, Emilie shivered. "I hate the idea of being beneath the water. What if that glass were to burst?"

I looked back at the wall—no, *tank*. The entire place was so run down... "If it hasn't burst yet, I don't think it will."

I didn't know if I believed that myself, but she didn't need to know that.

"Which side should we start with?" Cyrus asked. "Or do you two want to split up again and leave us?"

Resisting the urge to roll my eyes, I said, "Let's stick together this time. Luther was playing cards before. Maybe he's come here to continue. Let's take a look around the tables."

I briefly gave them a description of Luther—a tall, stocky man with a buzz cut and the long dark gray cloak we'd seen him wearing. Other than that, there weren't many defining features I could share, except he looked like a man you wouldn't want to cross in an alley...which also happened to be ninety percent of the people in the dodgy underground.

There had to be at least fifty tables to check, all of them full of gamblers who didn't bother to look up as we passed by. They were so enamored with their games that they didn't care if we stopped to stare or get a good look at everyone seated. Some kept their faces half hidden, but others didn't bother.

Since my description hadn't been much help to Jade or Cyrus, they walked behind us and watched for any suspicious activity, like someone staring too long or running in the opposite direction.

The place was so packed; I had to squeeze and push my way through, grimacing every time I felt a stranger's body fall into mine. I tried to think about anything other than the way my skin crawled as I brushed against other attendees. My mission was more important than my discomfort.

We made it all the way to the tank with no sign of Luther.

"He's absolutely inside here somewhere," I said. I could feel it in my bones. Every piece of me was more alert than usual. Even the hair on the back of my neck stood at attention.

"Maybe one of us should go back to the staircase. In case he tries to leave," Emilie suggested.

"No," I replied. I didn't want her leaving my sight. Plus, Luther was a traveler. If he really wanted to escape, he could do so without using the exit.

A few fish swam near the glass, and I watched them scatter when a tipsy woman pointed in amusement.

"Let's check the other side then," Cyrus said.

We crossed the room, and even though we'd already painstakingly checked every table, I still scanned each of them just to make sure we hadn't missed him somehow. When we made it to the other side, I was confident Luther wasn't hiding in the games section.

The two square pits were starting to draw a crowd. The first fights had to be about to start. Before I weaved my way through, I reached back to grab Emilie's hand so we wouldn't get separated. I focused on her touch rather than the swarm of bodies around me.

It was much more difficult searching the faces around the pit. The people here were more alert, their attention fixed straight ahead. Annoyance splashed across their faces whenever we got in their way or bumped someone's shoulder. We had to be careful and move slowly.

Screams erupted, and my head whipped toward the pit. People were cheering as the first two fighters entered the roped area, their faces painted—one blue and one orange. Along the opposite side of the pit, I spotted a few more fighters in various shades of face paint.

A man's voice broke through the shouting long enough to introduce the fighters. I stopped listening when neither of them was named Luther or Reyna.

I pulled Emilie forward. We needed to keep looking.

The crowd slowly thinned as we made our way toward the second pit. For the first time, I noticed this one had a red light hanging above it, casting a sinister glow on the pit below. Immediately, I sensed a difference in the atmosphere. Was it magic somehow?

The people gathered around the second pit were calm. For all I knew, they could've been drugged. One thing was similar though—they were all giving the pit their undivided attention.

For a moment, I forgot what I was supposed to be looking for. I pushed forward until I could see who was fighting, coming to an abrupt halt when the pit came into view.

It wasn't a fighting pit.

I turned around and tried to push Emilie back. Her eyes met mine with confusion and curiosity. "What? What is it?"

Despite my best efforts, she looked over my shoulder, and I watched the color drain from her freckled skin.

I knew she had seen it... seen *them*.

Two men and a woman were featured in the middle of the pit—completely nude and tangled together in a passionate position. The crowd was watching while they kissed and groped each other. If I had to guess, this was just the warmup.

"Emilie," I said, grabbing her chin and pulling her face back to me. "Let's go."

Her eyes were wide and unseeing. Or maybe she was seeing too much. She was remembering everything that had happened under Reyna's roof. The parties we'd been forced to attend, bare and vulnerable while everyone watched with excitement. This was too much for her.

I pulled her frozen body against me, purposefully keeping myself between her and the pit. I didn't want her to see anything more than what she'd already witnessed. It didn't matter if they were here voluntarily or if they'd been coerced into the pit against their will, bound to bare it all like we had. All that mattered was that in those few seconds, Emilie saw herself, and she was about to have a panic attack because of it. I had to get her out of here.

Cyrus and Jade stepped aside as I pushed back through the crowd. Cyrus grabbed my arm. "What's wrong? What happened?"

I didn't answer. My thoughts were focused only on Emilie, who was beginning to tremble in my arms.

After what felt like a lifetime, I broke through the crowd and made my way to the stairs, but Emilie was in no shape to climb them. I scanned the room for a quiet space away from the sea of strangers, but everywhere I looked was overrun.

Pulling her behind the stairs, I sat her down in the corner and dropped to my knees in front of her.

"Emilie," I said, cupping her face. "Emilie, look at me."

Her chest was heaving, and I could tell breathing was hard for her.

"What's wrong?" Cyrus asked again. I felt him hovering behind me, and Jade's shadow cast over us too.

"Is she okay?" Jade asked.

Emilie nodded, but her eyes were still unblinking.

"That's right," I said. "You're okay. You're safe. Can you look at me, princess?"

Her vision slowly focused until she looked up at me. I rubbed my thumb over her cheek.

"There she is," I said with a soft smile. "You're going to be all right. I won't let anything bad happen to you."

She nodded again and grappled to get control of her rapid breaths.

Leaning in, I pressed my forehead to hers and closed my eyes. "*You* won't let anything bad happen. Ever again."

She needed to know that she was strong. That she was cunning and skilled now with her knives too. That she was in control. I was just her support.

I felt her nod again, and at last she spoke. "I can do this."

Her voice was raspy, and I pulled away to get a good look at her. Her eyes were misty but clearing with each blink. She pressed her lips into a thin, determined line, letting me know she was recovered enough to carry on.

A part of me wanted to take her back to the Gem, but I knew that wouldn't help. She wouldn't want to wait or avoid her triggers knowing Reyna was within our reach. This was where she needed to be—in the middle of the action and in control of her own life.

I stood and helped her to her feet. Then I pulled up her hood, which had fallen off in the commotion, observing her carefully in case she showed any signs of fracturing.

"Are you okay? Do you need water or something?" Jade asked hesitantly. The cautious tone didn't suit her.

Emilie shook her head. "I'm fine. Let's keep searching."

When I turned around, I found Cyrus staring at the two of us with a strange expression on his face. Like he was beginning to understand the connection Emilie and I shared but still couldn't grasp how it had happened. There was a certain codependency that we shared that couldn't make sense to anyone but us, no matter how hard he tried.

"Cyrus," I started, but he turned away.

I sighed. Now wasn't the time anyway. We had bigger tasks at hand. I'd try to speak to him again once we'd captured Reyna.

"We should go back to the pit," Emilie said from behind me.

I spun on my heel. "No."

But Emilie wouldn't hear it. "It's where Reyna would be, and you know it. That is exactly the kind of *entertainment* that would appeal to her."

Fuck. I hated that she was right.

"Fine," I said. "But stay close to me."

She rolled her eyes. "Like I would be anywhere else."

The four of us traveled back to the pit where the threesome was taking place, but we were no more successful than our last attempt. After three laps around the pit, disappointment set in. Maybe we'd gotten it wrong. What if Luther had snuck out through a hidden entrance? Were we wrong to assume that Reyna had been here at all?

I put my hands behind my head and looked up at the ceiling, cursing the gods who never seemed to favor me.

But as I looked up, I saw half a dozen balconies. Private viewing areas hidden in darkness. I looked through each of them, my heart racing as I tried to spot a familiar face.

The first was completely empty, with a closed red curtain. The second held a pair of men, the taller one standing behind the other with his arms wrapped around his partner and nuzzling his neck.

I moved onto the third and blinked rapidly, not sure whether to trust my eyes. Was I hallucinating or had the gods finally shown me mercy?

There, standing on the balcony with two unknown companions, were Reyna and Luther.

A strange mixture of elation and agony washed over me at the sight of her. I'd spent all my time thinking of how much I wanted to kill her, and not enough time processing what it would be like to see her face to face again. It was a pain that would only be dulled once I drove my sword into her heart.

Reyna and Luther were too focused on the pit to see my face, but I wasn't taking any chances. I looked back at the ground, secured my hood, and turned to the others. "They're here."

"What? Where?" Emilie asked, searching frantically.

I grabbed her face and held her steady. "There are private rooms above the pit. We need to find a way up to them without drawing attention. Stay calm and follow me."

Chapter Thirty-Four

Ladon

It didn't take long to find the hidden staircase that led to the balcony rooms. It was less hidden and more so lackluster, nestled in the corner of the room and withdrawn from the action. Luck was finally on our side because it was surprisingly not guarded, and we snuck up the stairs without being seen.

At the top of the landing, a narrow hall stretched to what I could only assume was the other side of the Underground. If I had counted correctly, Reyna was behind the third door.

I turned around and held a finger to my mouth. Then I moved stealthily down the hall, coming to a stop in front of a black metal door with rusted hinges. It looked weak enough that I could probably kick it down, but just in case I couldn't, I pulled Emilie closer.

"Can you unlock it?"

She frowned, looking at the door. "I've never tried."

I gave her a nod of encouragement anyway. Of all the powers we possessed, Emilie was best suited for the job. If there had been some loose soil or a spill around, perhaps Jade or I could've crafted a key, but Emilie could manipulate the air itself and twist the lock where we could not.

She held up her hand, and although I couldn't see what was happening, I pictured her magic sliding into the keyhole and applying the perfect amount of pressure to turn the lock.

With a small clicking noise, I knew she'd done it. She turned back to me and flashed a smile.

My princess—wickedly stunning.

Slowly, I turned the doorknob and peeked inside. I spotted Reyna and Luther instantly, their attention still lowered to the pit below. Their two companions—a redheaded woman and a man with a black bun—were also too focused to notice the door opening. I scanned the room, happy to note that it was only the four of them.

I moved inside as quietly as possible, and Emilie, Jade, and Cyrus followed. Emilie's hand was already on her dagger, ready to lodge it into Reyna's head as soon as I gave a sign. If we each took on a single individual, it would be over before it even started.

I gave everyone a silent signal to arm themselves, raising my hand to start a countdown. I held up three fingers and used the other hand to pull out my sword. After finding everyone ready to attack, I dropped down to two. Then one.

Right before I dropped the last finger, the door opened, and a tray crashed to the ground. My head whipped around to find a server with wide eyes and drinks splattered around their feet. They held their hands up in surrender, but they weren't of any consequence.

Our true targets were suddenly very aware of our presence.

There was a moment when everything seemed to stand still. I faced forward again to find Reyna on her feet, eyes blazing with hatred and alarm. Her eyes met mine, and I narrowed them, a pit forming in my stomach.

I was overwhelmed with anger and the need to seek revenge. All the time I'd spent attempting to move on with my life felt like a waste because, in this moment, I couldn't remember life outside of Murvort. I could only see black stone walls, could only feel foreign fingerprints on my skin, could only taste bile and hunger for freedom.

Just like that, I was diminished to the tortured soul Reyna had created. I existed only to fulfill one goal—to kill the monster in front of me.

Reyna stared at me, and her eyes flicked down my body and back to my face. She smirked, and I knew she was picturing everything she'd done to me. Every way she'd taken advantage of me. I was picturing it too. My rage reached an uncontrollable level. She licked her lips, and I saw red.

Then chaos broke out.

With a furious roar, I swung my blade at her head. A crack of lightning hit the tip of my sword and sizzled down to the handle. I gasped at the heat underneath my hand, but I didn't drop it. I relished the pain as it burned my flesh and raised the blade to swing again.

I repeatedly lashed and lurched, but I only managed to make a small mark across her upper arm. She was faster than I remembered.

She taunted me. "Ladon, my darling. I can see you're upset. Why don't we find somewhere private to talk about it? I've missed you so much."

A dagger flew through the air, landing deep in her shoulder, and she screamed. Blood began to soak through her gray top, but she knew better than to pull it out.

When she looked up, Emilie was ready with a second dagger in her hand.

"You little bitch," Reyna spat. She held out a hand, and the room crackled. Emilie dropped to her knees and covered her head with her hands, the lightning zapping her skin in random spurts.

"Enough," I shouted, swinging my sword again. But a body came out of nowhere and I was tackled from the side. Luther slammed us both to the ground. My breath escaped me, and seconds later, he was hurling his fists at my face. My sword was pinned beneath me, and I struggled to throw him off.

A blast of flames created a halo around him, and he roared in pain. In that moment of distraction, I shoved him to the side and rolled away. As I regained my breath, I watched the shirt on his back burn to ashes, and the fire extinguished just as fast as it'd come to life.

Something cold dripped on my head, and I looked up to see a broken pipe. The droplets of water flew through the air and expanded into a miniature hurricane, whipping around the room and searching for the perfect target. It settled on Jade and rushed toward her like a howling storm.

I searched for Reyna, but she wasn't controlling it. She was, however, watching her redheaded friend with an eager expression. This was all just entertainment for her. She didn't care about anyone's life, including those who defended her.

"Jade," I shouted, pointing at the water-wielding mage. Jade let her eyes leave the hurricane for a fraction of a second, glimpsing the mastermind behind the unnatural phenomenon. She threw out her arm and twisted her hand, siphoning water from the center of the funnel and turning it into a sheet of ice.

She raised it high above the water-wielder's head, and it came crashing down, knocking the woman to the ground. A second sheet of ice formed, and Jade forced it through the woman's neck, severing her head completely.

It rolled toward Jade, and she kicked it aside with a snarl. I had to admit I was happy to have her on our team and not as an enemy.

The man with the bun shouted with anger and leaped toward Jade. He pushed his hands out like he was about to shove her, but he wasn't within arm's reach yet. Instead, a blast of air knocked Jade off her feet.

The man stood over her and grabbed her by the collar, shaking her like a madman. But then my brother was behind him, wrapping one arm around his throat and putting him in a chokehold.

I didn't pay attention to what happened next. It was clear the two of them had it under control. My energy was best spent on Reyna.

Speaking of... I spun around to see where she had gotten off to, my eyes widening when I found her raining strikes of lightning down upon Emilie. Emilie was doing her best to ward them off, and she was doing a remarkable job forcing each blow off target with the use of her air magic. But it was exhausting more of her energy than Reyna's. I could tell by the way each strike came closer to hitting her.

I lunged forward, driving my fist into Reyna's jaw, and it cracked with the impact—a sound that I absolutely delighted in. Even my sore knuckles couldn't keep the smile off my face. She tumbled to the ground, and I didn't hesitate to wrap my hands around her neck, squeezing until her eyes bulged.

When she tried to send her lightning my way, I just grinned ferociously.

"You have nothing," I snarled. Her magic was filtering into my hands. I wanted to siphon the life from her, but I would settle for her powers. "Any last words?"

Her lips moved, but without oxygen, her speech was inaudible. Her face started to turn purple, and I laughed. I *shook* with deranged excitement to see the life fading from her eyes.

I felt like I held the world in my hands. Nothing could stop me.

Except...

A high-pitched cry rang out, and I recognized it immediately as Emilie's. I looked to my left where Luther had a fist in Emilie's hair, dragging her across the floor.

Jumping up, I crossed the room in a matter of seconds, reaching for my sword at the same time. He never saw me coming, and I drove it into his back with ease.

He released Emilie with a gasp, and I watched as she massaged her scalp. She scrambled to her feet, eyes widening as she realized what I'd done. I gave her a questioning look, asking if she was all right.

She gave one nod in response.

There was another crashing noise in the distance, and I turned to find Cyrus and Jade leaning over the balcony, the other man nowhere to be seen.

It didn't take long to put the pieces together. Somehow in the fight, the man had toppled over, and the screams below were growing louder as people discovered a dead body.

"Shit."

There was just one more life we needed to claim before the underground became a scene of mayhem. Looking back to where I'd last strangled Reyna, I saw nothing but an empty floor.

I looked around the room. Emilie was still watching me with appreciation. Cyrus was checking on a head wound Jade had suffered, wiping the blood away with his sleeve. And Luther was lying on the ground, blood seeping out into a puddle beneath him.

"Where'd she go?" I demanded, sinking to my knees beside him. "Where did she go?"

I shook him, and he coughed up blood. "You're not allowed to die, you fucking piece of shit. Cyrus!" I shouted for my brother.

He appeared at my side without question.

"Keep him alive. Cauterize his wound. Whatever you have to do. Do *not* let him die."

I rushed toward the balcony, looking at the madness below. I spotted the body of Reyna's man easily. A circle had formed around him—no one wanted to be the first to touch his broken and mangled form.

At least half of the crowd was rushing toward the staircase, fearful that there was an assassin in the building. In a place like the Underground, everyone had enemies. Everyone had a reason to be scared that someone was after them, and they ran toward the exit, toward safety.

In the sea of people, I couldn't see a damn thing. If Reyna was down there, she blended in seamlessly. I couldn't spot her black hair or the gray outfit she'd been wearing. I didn't even know if she was still inside or if she had been one of the first to escape.

"Damn it," I yelled, slamming my palms against the railing.

I turned around, and Cyrus was working with Emilie to save Luther's life. I wasn't sure what could be done for him, but we needed to keep him alive long enough to tell us—or better yet, show us—where Reyna had run. Where was she hiding?

I took three deep breaths before returning to Luther. His face was scrunched in pain, but he was still alive. His eyes were still open, and he glared at me with pursed lips.

"Where have you been staying? Where can we find Reyna?"

Luther grunted and rolled his head to the side, uninterested in my demands.

I kicked his foot, and he groaned through gritted teeth.

Kneeling, I spoke softly. Calmly. "Luther, we can do this the easy way—where I ask you a question and you answer me without pause and without attitude. Or..."

I spotted one of Emilie's daggers on the floor and picked it up, twirling it in my hand.

Luther straightened, but other than that, he did a great job pretending he wasn't nervous.

"Hold him down," I said in a low tone that left the room in unsettling silence. No one moved except Emilie, who grabbed the arm next to her and pinned it to the ground.

Luther tried to tug his arm out of her grasp, but he'd lost a lot of blood and wasn't as strong as he otherwise would be.

I looked at my brother, who was on the opposite side of Emilie. "Hold him down," I said again.

Cyrus blinked, looking as though he wanted to stop and question me but thought better of it. Carefully, he grabbed Luther's other arm and held him still.

I scooted forward and sat on his legs. His shirt was barely hanging on between the fire and the hole they'd made to patch up his wound. They'd used some of the fabric as a wrapping, but I reached forward and ripped it back open.

He sucked in a sharp breath when I pointed Emilie's dagger at his freshly scarred skin. Slowly, I pushed it forward until a dot of red appeared. I watched with fascination as it swelled and began to drip.

"I think there are a lot of ways I could make you suffer, Luther. But it doesn't have to be that way."

I pressed the dagger flush against his skin, snapping my wrist so a thin layer of flesh was severed from his chest. He bit back a roar, and I wondered how long it would take to break him.

"Fuck you," he snapped.

I eyed him with disdain. "I'm glad you didn't bleed out, Luther. You deserve to have a much more painful death after everything you've put us through. Everything you've done at Reyna's side."

I jabbed the dagger into his upper thigh and twisted.

And twisted.

And twisted.

I turned the dagger until tears streamed down his face.

My brother made a gagging noise, and I snapped at him, "If you can't handle this, then let Jade take over."

She was watching from the corner, completely unfazed.

Cyrus looked from me to Emilie to Jade. And then he stood and made space for Jade to step in. He never could handle the tough shit. While he was sitting safe on his throne, I was the one tasked with punishing our worst enemies. Maybe he was weak, or maybe I was desensitized.

I checked on Emilie, but she showed no signs of revulsion. She wanted to see him punished as badly as I did.

"Hold his shoulder," I told Jade, and she switched her grip from his arm to his right shoulder.

I grabbed his wrist and, without warning, sliced through his pinky finger.

He was unable to contain his scream this time.

"You can stop this, you know. We only need a location."

"I don't know where she is," he said.

I flayed the thin, delicate skin on his palm, and he cried.

"Do not lie to me."

"I swear. I haven't—"

Another scream was ripped from him as I removed a second finger.

"I can do this all evening, Luther."

And I meant it. As long as he stayed conscious, I would continue to slice away at him, piece by piece, layer by layer. I'd peel back his skin until only bone remained. Whatever it took to get an answer out of him.

I would bleed him dry.

Chapter Thirty-Five

Emilie

I WASHED MY HANDS with a rag and some water from the busted pipe, but it did little good. There was so much blood; it was impossible to get rid of it. Ladon was in even worse shape. His shirt was drenched with it. I didn't know a body contained so much blood.

Cyrus was the cleanest of us all, having avoided most of the questioning. He crossed his arms while Ladon wiped the blood from his face.

"Don't look at me like that," Ladon said.

"Like what?" Cyrus replied.

"Like I've committed some unforgivable sin."

"You skinned that man alive," he said, his voice full of repulsion.

"And I got the answer I needed."

Jade spoke up before they could continue. "Aren't you two a little old to be bickering like this? Cyrus, get over it. You're sensitive, we get it, but it had to be done."

"I'm not sensitive," he mumbled under his breath.

I almost smiled. Cyrus was an honorable king, and I could understand why he hadn't enjoyed watching Ladon mutilate Luther.

But I had. I wanted to rip that bloody shirt off him in a way that made me question my sanity.

"Fine. You did what you had to do." Cyrus turned away. "We should get moving."

We all agreed. The commotion in the underground had settled, but we could still hear a few lingering voices. I wasn't sure why anyone would still be hanging around—perhaps they were hoping to steal from the gambling tables. Whatever they were up to, we didn't need to draw any more attention to ourselves. Getting out of this place covered in blood would be suspicious enough.

"All right," Ladon said. "I don't think I'm going to get any more of this out." He looked down at his shirt, which was stained a deep shade of red.

"Stay behind me," Cyrus said. "I can lead the way and hide you from view."

We took his word for it, letting him head out of the room and down the stairs. No one noticed us at first; they were too busy searching through the bodies.

Bodies.

Reyna's comrade wasn't the only dead body lying on the floor. There were dozens. Either vigilantes had taken advantage of the commotion or people had been trampled to death as they rushed toward the exit.

I tried to remind myself that none of these people were innocent. They weren't our targets, but they all had vices worthy of damnation. It didn't bring me any joy to see them killed, though.

What did bring me a sigh of relief was the sight of a clear path to the stairs. It would take less than ten seconds for us to sprint across if we needed to.

Cyrus started walking toward the exit. We followed him around the pit where the trio of adults had been fucking for the audience. I shuddered and pushed the thought from my mind, but I didn't get much of a break before the image was forced in front of me again.

As we rounded the corner, I spotted a woman curled in a ball with a slash across her neck.

"Stop," I said softly.

"What are you doing?" Cyrus asked.

I bent down and ripped a jacket from another lifeless body, then tossed it over the woman's naked body before returning to my place in line.

Ladon's eyes met mine.

"I couldn't leave her like that."

He nodded. "I know."

We were halfway up the stairs when a voice rang out from above. "All of you, get out! Enough!"

Leaning around Cyrus, I tried to find the owner of the commanding voice. I quickly whipped back into line when I noticed a proper uniform, flanked on either side by a dozen more. Word must've reached King Vincent, and he had sent his guards to break up the disruption.

Cyrus looked back, appraising all of us covered in blood, before he carried on.

Once we reached the top of the steps, the primary guard stopped us. "Spread out," he demanded.

I looked down at the blood all over my hands and clothing. They'd take one look at us and arrest us on the spot.

Cyrus didn't move aside, but he raised his hands slowly in surrender. "I am King Cyrus, a guest of King Marsden. We have immunity."

"Show me."

Slowly, Cyrus reached into his pocket and produced what looked like a coin. He handed it to the guard, who flipped it over once, then twice, before handing it back to Cyrus.

"You're free to go."

I filled my lungs with air, not realizing that I'd stopped breathing during the exchange. We practically sprinted toward the exit after receiving clearance.

Night had fallen outside, but the moon illuminated the market, and we fled to the north end.

Luther's instructions had been clear enough—along the shoreline, at the bottom of the tallest cliff, lay a cave entrance that was only visible during low tide. If his description was accurate, we had less than an hour to find it and get inside before the water began to surge back in.

We took the quickest, most direct path to the water's edge, and from there, it wasn't hard to spot the cliff we needed.

"What if it's a trap?" Cyrus asked.

No one responded because the answer was unsettling—we would drown and die. I swallowed the lump in my throat; we couldn't let fear stop us now.

"I don't believe it is," I said.

"The real concern is how many are inside," Ladon added.

Luther had finally succumbed to his injuries before Ladon could extract that particular piece of information. For all we knew, we could be about to battle an entire army, though I doubted Reyna had that many supporters left. She likely couldn't afford many hired hands either, especially if she already wasn't paying her bounty hunters back in Murvort. Purchased loyalty was easily broken.

We made our way down to the beach and approached the cliff; its bottom was surrounded by rocks and trapped water pools. Carefully, we climbed across, searching for the hidden entrance Luther had described.

"There," Jade said, jumping down from a jagged boulder. She landed in a puddle of water that was only a couple inches deep, then trudged forward, bending in half to enter the narrow opening at the base of the cliff.

We followed her.

Inside, Cyrus raised his palm, and a ball of fire appeared, casting the cave in an orange glow. It wasn't large, but it was spacious enough for us all to fit comfortably. There was only one opening to continue moving forward, so Cyrus led the way, followed by Jade, me, and Ladon at the end.

Almost immediately, the tunnel took a turn upward. There were steep, rough ledges that we needed to climb. Ladon moved to the front of the line and helped by forging footholds and grips for us to use.

We'd been climbing for all of ten minutes when I heard water trickling below.

"Do you hear that?" I asked.

Jade looked down, searching around me for the source of the noise. Cyrus's flame was just bright enough that I could see her squinting before her eyes went wide. "I think the tide is rising. We need to keep climbing."

I looked down again, trying to see the bottom of the tunnel, but it was too dark.

Then Cyrus's flame reflected off the surface below. Waves were rushing in at an alarming rate.

"Go," I cried.

Our group moved as rapidly as they could. Ladon's craftsmanship became sloppy as he worked with half as much time to form ledges worthy of climbing. We didn't need perfection, though. We only needed efficiency.

The water approached, filling the tunnel below us faster than we could climb. I didn't dare look down, knowing it would only cause panic. The water level couldn't continue rising at this pace. The pressure would eventually be stifled by gravity. We just had to make it past that point.

Cold water lapped around my ankles, and I shuddered. "Oh, gods."

Ladon glanced back. "Fuck."

"Keep going!" I shouted. I could see in his eyes the desire to be my savior, but there was nothing he could do except press on.

He abandoned his efforts to make our climb easier. Speed became our only focus, and we were running out of time.

"I see an opening ahead," he finally called out.

I didn't have time to thank the gods. The water was already at my calves, and I was moving as quickly as I could.

It's going to be okay, I told myself.

The water made my climb extra challenging. My feet slipped without Ladon's proper footholds, and every push upward took twice as much effort. Sweat dripped down my temples despite the cold water soaking through my boots.

"We're almost there," Ladon said, and I tried to calm the terror taking over my mind. I couldn't see ahead of him and had no idea how far we truly were from safety, but water was starting to overcome me. I didn't know how much longer I could stay ahead of it.

Suddenly, Ladon disappeared from view. He must've reached the top of our climb and rolled onto a platform of sorts. Sure enough, Cyrus disappeared shortly after him.

The water was up to my hips now, but I could see the end of the tunnel. I just needed to climb a few more steps...

My boot slipped, and I lost hold of the wall, dropping into the frigid water. It took a second to reemerge, coughing and spitting out the water that had poured into my mouth and nostrils. I gasped for breath.

"Emilie!" Ladon yelled.

I blinked away the water and reached for the wall, but my fingers found nothing but wet, slippery rock. There was nothing to grip.

My back bumped into the opposite side of the tunnel as the surge tossed me about. It knocked the air out of me, and I swallowed more water as I tried to refill my lungs.

I was losing the battle against the tide.

Just when I was certain that the tumultuous water would overcome me, a hand wrapped firmly around my wrist and pulled me up. I rolled onto dry ground, coming to a stop on my back. I turned to my side and spat up water, wiping the remaining drops from my eyes. Finally, I could see again.

It wasn't Ladon that had pulled me up, as I had suspected, but Jade. She smiled but said, "Get up. The water is still rising."

I jumped to my feet, and before I could properly take in my surroundings, I was running toward a mountain of rocks leading to the next tunnel. I stumbled up them, but it didn't take long to reach the top.

I turned around, expecting to see water flooding this cavern too, but a gentle wave spilled over the ledge we'd climbed over and gradually came to a stop.

I collapsed to the ground with an unsteady chuckle.

Ladon appeared above me, staring like I had lost my mind. And maybe I had. "Are you okay?"

"Yes." I was wet and still full of adrenaline, but I could breathe perfectly fine and had no lingering injuries. My back might bruise from the hit I took, but I would survive.

He held his hand out and helped me to my feet.

"Are we good to keep moving?" Jade asked.

We all nodded.

"Thank you, by the way," I added.

She smiled. "Don't worry about it. It's not like I could let you drown. I'm not that terrible."

By now, I didn't think she was terrible at all. Just misunderstood and a little slow to open up to people.

The path ahead was much easier to travel than the tunnel before it. We no longer had to climb vertically, and the caves opened up rather than closing in on us. At some point, the walls expanded so far that I couldn't even see them anymore, which led to an unsettling feeling. The space was vast and unknown, and it felt as though someone or something was lurking in the shadows.

It would've been easy to get lost in the expansive cavern if it weren't for the pattern etched into the ground, leading us deeper inside the cliff.

The air was freezing cold, and my breath puffed in a cloud in front of me. My wet pants turned rigid and uncomfortable against my skin. I moved closer to Cyrus and his flame so I wouldn't freeze to death.

After what felt like hours, we finally came to the end of the infinite cavern. A large archway opened up, but none of us were prepared for what awaited in the next chamber.

We walked right into the heart of it all—Reyna's hideout.

Chapter Thirty-Six

Emilie

"Get down," I snapped, and we all dropped to our stomachs.

We had exited the cavern onto a platform several stories above an occupied campsite. Scooting toward the edge, we peered below.

"Do you see her?" Jade asked.

"Not yet."

"How many do you count?" Cyrus asked.

"At least two dozen," Jade answered.

The site below was made up of eight canvas-covered tents, including a mess tent with a table sticking halfway out of the opening. Another tent was twice the size of the rest with a unique web-like pattern on the closed flap. That had to be Reyna's.

Which left six for her loyalists to share. Two dozen enemies seemed like a reasonable estimate, but we couldn't be certain there weren't more resting inside the tents or lingering outside the caverns and waiting to return when the tide allowed.

"I wish we knew what powers they possessed," I said quietly. "It would make an ambush less risky."

"I think we should go for the element of surprise," Jade said, turning to look at Cyrus. "Send the whole place up in flames."

Ladon shook his head. "They won't be the only ones to suffer from breathing in the smoke. In case you've forgotten, our path back to the beach is blocked until the tide moves out again."

"Ice them out," I suggested.

Jade contemplated. "I can't send one massive blast—I'm not that strong. But I can target one at a time."

"That'll have to do," Ladon said. "Take out as many as you can before anyone notices. Thin their ranks as much as possible before they realize we're here."

"Will do," Jade said. She sat up and pushed her shoulders back. I watched as droplets of water began to seep from the cave's walls and gather in her hands, freezing in the shape of a slender lance. She carefully maneuvered it, and I helped to keep it lifted high in the sky and out of sight until she was ready to drop it on an unsuspecting camper.

"Okay," she said, and I pulled back my magic.

The lance fell to the ground and pierced straight through a man's head. He crumpled to the side.

Now we just needed to do the same thing twenty-three more times... without being noticed.

The next six targets went down without a hitch. But after the seventh, someone found one of the dead followers and shouted for help. Jade took him out quickly, but it was too late. He had alerted the camp that there was a threat in their midst.

"Time to go," Jade said.

While Jade had been taking out followers, Ladon had been quietly crafting a slide down into the campsite. We flew down, and Reyna's loyalists didn't notice us until we were already attacking.

I threw my daggers left and right, taking out as many as I could. I only took breaks to retrieve my daggers from bodies, slicing throats if any of them remained alive.

I took out four people before I met anyone worthy of a challenge.

I had barely pulled back the opening of a tent when a woman shot out and tackled me, sending us both tumbling. She got in one good jab before I collected myself and punched her in the gut. She doubled over, giving me the perfect opportunity to throw her off.

Keeping my eyes on her, I reached for a dagger but came up empty. I had lost track of how many I'd thrown and how many I should've been collecting.

She noticed me scrambling and sent a blast of fire my way. Instinctively, I threw up my hands, and a wall of air encircled me, protecting me from her flames. The unfortunate side effect was a cyclone that burned through the two tents closest to me. So much for *not* inhaling smoke.

I threw out my hands and blasted the air away from me, singeing everything within an arm's reach. The woman couldn't control the fire inside the gale, and it slammed into her with such force that she was knocked off her feet. Her clothing instantly caught fire, and she screamed.

Out of the corner of my eye, I spotted another enemy sprinting in our direction. His wide eyes were locked on me. With one arm, he threw out a cascade of water to his burning friend and with the other, a wave came crashing directly toward me.

I dodged out of the way seconds before his magic could collide with me, rolling on my side until I came to a stop. Disoriented, I looked around the cave to see where he had gone, but something silver caught my eye—one of my missing daggers.

I snatched it from the ground and leaped to my feet, running back to the enemies who had evaded me. The man was kneeling beside his friend, checking her vitals.

He never saw me coming.

I grabbed his hair and pulled his neck back, sliding my dagger over his throat and watching blood spray the ground, and his friend, in front of him.

Stepping around his body, I moved to attack the woman too, but she was already burnt to a crisp, and very, very, dead.

Panting, I took a moment to assess the cavern. Cyrus was dueling someone who was already missing a limb. Jade was wrestling another, and Ladon was using his sword to fight two more. There couldn't be many enemies left.

I began searching the tents for anyone who may be hiding, including Reyna. Every tent flap I pulled back led to disappointment, but she couldn't hide forever.

Grinding my teeth, I stomped toward the next tent, whipping back the fabric just in time to see a woman with black hair escaping out the back.

"Bitch," I screamed, running after her with a dagger clenched tight in my fist.

I flew through the opposite side and was met with a bolt of lightning. Dodging out of the way, I sent a low sweep of wind to knock her off her feet. She stumbled but didn't fall, like I'd hoped.

Reyna ran, and I had no choice but to follow.

This game would end tonight.

Reyna sent strikes my way as she ran, but none of them hit their mark. She looked back, and I could see the fear on her face. Her time was running out, and she had no more places to hide.

I grinned as she ran toward the cave's exterior, knowing she would have to stop and face me soon. But she surprised me, sliding and slipping into a small crack in the stone.

I almost skidded to a stop, but a blast came out of nowhere and the rock tumbled away. Glancing behind me, I found Ladon only feet away. Knowing that he was close gave me the confidence I needed to sprint into the hole he'd created, blindly chasing after Reyna.

I heard her before I saw her. Her maniacal laughter echoed in the next chamber, and I whipped my head around, trying to find her in the darkness.

Another bolt of lightning illuminated the room for a brief moment. She hadn't aimed at me, but at the wall of the cave. The opening behind me collapsed, and I had to charge forward to avoid being buried.

"Ladon," I yelled, but I couldn't hear anything aside from the mountain rumbling and rocks free-falling. I scurried forward with my hands outstretched, not knowing where I was headed.

When the dust finally settled, the cave went eerily quiet. My own breathing felt loud, though I tried to suppress it. I inched forward, hoping my eyes would adjust.

A whisper came from the darkness.

"Emilie."

I spun around, but I couldn't discern where her voice had come from. The hair on the back of my neck rose, and a shiver slid down my spine.

"Emilie..."

Reyna's voice was lyrical, singing my name like a tune and a taunt. She sounded like she was on the opposite side now.

"What did you think would happen if you followed me in here, Emilie?"

I growled, "I will kill you, you filthy, heinous bitch."

"Tsk, tsk. That's such unsuitable language for a future queen. Perhaps you should come back to my estate to be my maiden for a little while longer. Just until you've had enough time to learn a lesson or two in manners."

"You're one to talk. And last I checked, you don't have an estate. You have nothing. You've lost everything except your life. And you're about to lose that, too."

Lightning flashed and, for a brief moment, I saw her standing in the center of the room.

Was this how we were going to play the game, then?

I knew if I went in her direction, she would be ready for my assault. So I did the opposite. I moved to the right and listened for her footsteps, waiting to see if she attacked the spot where I'd been standing.

She moved equally quietly, though.

I needed a strategy if I wanted to gain the upper hand.

I felt around my belt, confirming what I'd thought—the dagger in my hand was the only one I had left.

If goading her had brought out the lightning, then I would just need to do it again and again, until she ultimately snapped.

"Why are you hiding?" I asked softly, using my magic to let my voice flow throughout the cavern, disguising my true location. "Is the big, bad Reyna too afraid to defend herself? You're not very brave without your guards or your followers."

I kept my eyes peeled in case she lit up the cave again, but that wasn't enough. I'd have to try harder.

"You said something earlier... about being the future queen. I'm surprised you didn't hear that I'm no longer engaged to Cyrus."

She chuckled. "He didn't deem you worthy?"

"No, I broke off our engagement. Do you want to know why?"

My question was met with silence, but I thought I heard footsteps to my left, so I circled the spot, preparing to strike.

"It's because I'm in love with Ladon. And he is in love with me. I know how badly you wanted him to yourself, but you disgust him. It's important to me that you know that before I kill you."

She screamed, and a ball of electricity circled her. The blue light burned my eyes. I couldn't do much with the barrier surrounding her, so I dodged to the right and tried to hide from the light.

Eventually, the lightning sizzled out.

I came out of hiding with a smile on my face. "No one will ever love you, Reyna."

A streak of light lashed out, but I had already leaped a few steps to the right. I lunged toward her and thrust my dagger into whatever flesh I could find.

Reyna screamed, but I didn't stop there. I pulled the dagger out and kept one hand wrapped around shirt so I could swipe a second time. My dagger landed, and her flesh gave way easily. I had no idea what body part I was maiming, but I didn't care.

When I pulled it out again, I tried to aim with more accuracy. I thought I had hold of a sleeve, so if I plunged the dagger a bit higher and...

Reyna's tortured shriek pierced the air, ringing in my ears.

If I had hit where I wanted, and I believed I had, she had just lost one of her eyes.

I laughed. I'd never felt so crazed in my life, but knowing I had taken one of her nightmarish yellow-orange eyes filled me with joy. I'd take the other, too, if she would hold still.

A blast of lightning caught me off guard and hit me square in the chest. I flew off her, landing on my back and clutching my burning chest. It felt as though electricity was coursing through my veins and scorching me from the inside out. I couldn't breathe, and I was certain I was about to burst into ash.

My smile was long gone, and tears rolled down my face. The muscles in my neck strained as I bit down. I felt around for my dagger, but then I remembered it was still lodged in Reyna's face.

Fuck.

The burning sensation slowly faded, or maybe I was just growing accustomed to it. I turned on my side and pressed up onto all fours, shaking and nauseous. I crawled away from Reyna, but she sent another strike at me, and I collapsed onto my stomach.

I screamed as the lightning seemed to ricochet through my bones and settle in my brain, throbbing like the worst migraine I'd ever had. If it lasted any longer, I thought my head might explode.

She finally let up, and my body went limp. I was desperate to drive another dagger into Reyna's skull, but my mind and body were failing me. Tears of pain and frustration filled my eyes.

Lightning lit up the room and crackled across the ceiling. It continued long after she lowered her hand, and it would've been beautiful if it weren't so terrifying. At least I could see her now as she approached me. She'd already tossed my dagger aside, and blood was gushing out of her left eye.

"Sweet, sweet Emilie. You should've known better than to chase after me on your own. What will Ladon think when he comes to save you and finds nothing but ashes?"

"Emilie," a distant voice called. "Emilie!"

Was that Ladon? Perhaps I was further gone than I'd realized.

"Should I take your eyes like you've taken mine? Or maybe I'll take those pretty lips so he can never kiss them again."

I whimpered and clawed at the ground, but I had no energy to prop myself up.

Reyna's spindly fingers wrapped around my ankle and dragged me toward her.

"Enjoy your last breath, Emilie. I know I will."

The ground rumbled, and rocks began to fall all around us. I tried to raise my head, but I could barely muster the strength. I did see Ladon climbing over the pile of rocks, having just blown a hole through the rockslide from earlier.

I was so grateful he was alive and hadn't been crushed in the cave-in that I almost forgot the fatal condition I was in. He was here; he wouldn't let Reyna get away.

Ladon's eyes narrowed on Reyna, and he pointed his sword at her.

"Do not touch her."

Chapter Thirty-Seven

Ladon

THE SECOND I SAW Emilie lying on the ground on her stomach, the light in her eyes fading, I almost lost my mind. Reyna let go of Emilie and glared at me, and I grinned when I noticed one of those cat-like eyes was missing.

That's my girl.

Reyna cocked her head and bared her teeth. "And what are you so happy about? Thrilled to see your lover one last time before she incinerates?"

"Touch her again and I'll—"

"You'll what? Tell me what you'll do to me, my sweet Ladon."

A metallic taste filled my mouth, and I realized I was biting my cheek. It didn't matter that she'd interrupted me, though. I was done with threats. I was here to act.

Without another word, I darted toward her and swung my sword.

Reyna pivoted. Even with a missing eye, she moved with agility and precision. It fueled my rage even further.

I sliced my sword through the air and struck her in the back. She cried out, but it wasn't good enough. I needed more, needed to see her blood entirely spilt on the ground. To watch it drain from her body.

She tried to attack me with her lightning, but I created a shield of rock, tossing dirt in her face for good measure. She howled in frustration.

Bringing my blade down again, I aimed for her neck. To my dismay, she dodged it, but not fast enough. My sword cut deep into the back of her leg. Blood sprayed from the wound, some of it landing on my hand. I looked at it with fascination and a desire for more.

"This is hardly a fair fight," she said. "Shouldn't I have a blade too?"

"What was fair about keeping Emilie and me imprisoned and using us for your sick fantasies? Hmm?"

She chuckled, and I swung my sword at her again, aiming for her chest. When she evaded it, I struck again and again and again. Over and over, I lashed out, striking less than half the time. My movements were erratic, but I couldn't control my anger.

Just as my energy was almost spent, I connected with her left arm, slicing all the way to the bone. Before I could celebrate, though, lightning struck directly in the center of my back, sucking the air from my lungs.

I dropped my sword and clutched at my chest, watching as Reyna cradled her arm with anger in her remaining eye. Blood poured freely from the wound.

I laughed, earning myself another blast of energy. Although pain radiated through my body, I pushed forward, stumbling in her direction. She sent another lightning strike at the same time I blasted the ground beneath her feet.

She wouldn't get the best of me. Not today.

We volleyed back and forth, each sending damage toward the other. Blinding light flashed before my eyes, and I wondered how much more my body could handle. If I had to die to take her down, I would. My drive to see her dead was unparalleled.

Somehow, she found her footing, and I cursed under my breath. By now, the bolts of lightning were raging through my system, and all I could do was crawl to reach her.

"Pathetic," she snarled.

I didn't respond.

"You're going to die in this cave with your precious darling Emilie. Is she worth it?"

Of course she was. She was more precious than any gem in Baumheim. Nothing in this world meant more to me than Emilie did.

"Will your brother even come to save you? After you stole his bride?"

She unknowingly struck a nerve with that one, but I was close enough to reach her now. My sword had fallen out of my grip a while ago, so I lunged for her ankle and wrapped my hand around it.

Reyna laughed. "Are you going to beg me for your life? Say the magic words and I might let you be my pet again. You were the best I ever had."

I tightened my grip, and she showed the first sign of alarm as she realized what I was doing. She tried to kick me away, but my hold was too strong for her bloody, injured leg.

"Stop it," she cried.

Her magic was rapidly leaving her body and siphoning into mine. I spat at her and dug my nails in. "How does it feel, Reyna? To be completely powerless? To be at someone else's mercy?"

She shook her head and fixed her hair with her good hand, like she needed to appear proper before meeting the ruthless gods. "You think too highly of yourself, Ladon. I could stomp the life out of you right now if I wanted to. I don't need magic to—"

Her words were abruptly cut off, and I stared up at her, wondering why she hadn't finished her threat. Her face dropped to the center of her torso, where a blade was protruding from her abdomen.

My blade.

The tip was covered in her blood, and a drop fell, landing on my arm. I craned my neck to see Emilie standing behind Reyna, her hand on the hilt of my sword, her expression wickedly victorious.

Reyna choked, and blood spilled out of her mouth. Her good eye flicked from her fatal injury to her blood-soaked hands. Then she stared at me again, confusion blanketing her face.

Emilie pulled the sword out, and Reyna fell forward. I moved out of the way just in time to avoid being trapped under her weight. With effort, I pushed myself up to my knees to find Emilie hovering over Reyna.

Reyna raised her hands—as if she could surrender. She blinked and said, "You don't need to do this."

Emilie smirked. "I know. I *want* to do this."

Then she plunged the sword into Reyna's chest, pulling it out and driving it back in repeatedly, carving her like a beast for consumption. Reyna screamed, but eventually her cries faded into shallow breathing, and then nothing at all.

Once Emilie was satisfied, she bent down and pressed her hand to Reyna's disfigured chest. I couldn't quite see what she was doing, so I sat up straighter and watched, mesmerized, as she pulled Reyna's carved heart out and held it in her palm.

Gods, what a magnificent woman.

She squeezed the heart, her nails digging into the malleable organ. But then her cold expression cracked. Her eyebrows pinched together and her mouth fell open. She opened her fist, and Reyna's heart fell to the ground.

"Emilie," I said softly.

She briefly looked at me. "It's done. She's finally fucking gone."

"Yes, princess. She's gone for good, and we never have to think about her existence ever again. We don't have to spend another second of our lives worrying about her whereabouts. We are finally *free* of her."

"We're free?" she repeated.

"Yes."

I moved to my feet and embraced her, kissing the top of her head. She tilted her head back, and I sought her lips, melting into her when her tongue flicked over mine.

Her body shook, and I wasn't sure if she was laughing or crying. Maybe a little of both. For months we'd been tormented, haunted in our nightmares, and it had felt like this moment would never come. Reyna escaped our grasp on too many occasions, and I had started to think I would spend the rest of my life chasing her.

But it was over.

Emilie grabbed my shirt, yanking me closer to her, and I winced.

She immediately released me and pulled back, her eyes roaming my body. "Are you all right? Are you hurt?"

"I'm fine."

"You're not. I saw what she did to you. She could've killed you. You're going to need rest and—"

"Emilie," I whispered, tucking her hair behind her ear. "I will live. And what about you? She did much more damage to you." I shook my head. "I should've gotten through sooner. You shouldn't have had to fight her all alone. I never would've forgiven myself if I'd... if..."

I couldn't bring myself to speak the words.

Emilie cupped my cheeks. "You weren't too late. Nothing she did will leave permanent damage." She smiled then and licked her lips. "Nothing she has ever done will leave permanent damage."

It sounded idealistic, but I loved her optimism. One day, I hoped, we wouldn't carry these scars with us. Everything that had happened—physical, emotional, and mental—would be left in the past.

The future was something to look forward to, and I was elated that I would get to share it with her. This dark chapter of our lives was finally over, and we had an entire story yet to be written.

Wrapping my arms around her waist, I gently pressed my forehead to hers. "Do you have any idea how much I love you?"

She huffed a laugh. "I think I do. But I will never say no to hearing it again."

"I'm going to spend the rest of my life confessing my love for you, Emilie Duval." I kissed her cheek, and then her neck, then gently nipped at her ear.

Her hands slid around my neck, massaging my shoulders and the back of my head, driving my hunger for her. I wanted to stay here and get lost in her, savor her in every way imaginable, but my brother and Jade would likely show up soon. There hadn't been many surviving followers when I'd left them. Surely they were all defeated by now.

Grudgingly, I took a step back and pried her fingers from my body. I held both of her hands and laced our fingers together, giving her one last kiss on the lips. "Are you ready to head back?"

Emilie took one more look at Reyna's lifeless body on the ground. At the blood-soaked area surrounding her. Her mangled heart was a foot away, and the way her body had fallen, it looked as though she was reaching for it—an exquisite vision of justice and reckoning.

I wished I could paint a picture, but on second thought, it was best for her to remain here in the dark—alone and forgotten.

"What the hell happened?" Cyrus demanded when Emilie and I stepped out of the cavern and walked back into the campsite. "You two look like you've survived a fire."

He was right. Emilie and I both had burn marks on our skin, some of which had even blistered, though they didn't hurt much. The adrenaline and bliss must've concealed the pain. We'd probably feel them later.

"Where's Reyna?" Jade asked.

Emilie and I exchanged a look, smiling.

"She's dead," Emilie said, her eyes still fixed on me.

Jade gave a frustrated huff. "Are you sure? How do you know? She's fucking cunning, so if—"

"I removed her heart," Emilie said, whipping her head toward Jade. "She is absolutely, definitively, and irreversibly dead."

Jade considered her for a moment and then nodded with a wicked smile. "Perfect."

"What happened?" Cyrus asked again. "I was so caught up in the fight, I didn't notice you disappear."

He sounded *scared*, but that didn't make much sense. I was a trained warrior, and he had no reason to doubt my abilities. But he also didn't need to know how close we'd both come to defeat.

I scanned the campsite before I spoke. "We can fill you in, but first, has everyone here been taken care of?"

"Yes," Jade replied.

"Are you certain? Did you do a sweep of the tents?"

"Twice," Cyrus responded, crossing his arms. "Now, could you please tell us what happened?"

His temper was beginning to show, and I didn't want to see what would happen if we made him wait any longer. Emilie recounted chasing Reyna through the cavern, and I had to listen to each horrific moment that occurred before I had reached her. I clenched my jaw and swore that I'd do better—be better—in the future.

While she told us how she fought Reyna, she caught my distressed gaze and paused long enough to whisper, "I'm fine."

I brought my hand to my forehead and massaged the stress lines I'd developed over the past couple months.

Once she made it to the point in the tale where I'd entered, I took over. Cyrus and Jade listened with rapt attention and, thankfully, did not interrupt. I wasn't sure how to tell them about Emilie carving Reyna's heart out—it was violent and messy, and I didn't think they needed to hear that bit. But Emilie happily provided the information.

"I took Ladon's sword and stabbed her. Repeatedly. Her heart came out pretty easily after I cut a square into her chest."

She said it with zero emotion. Cold and confident. I almost crushed my lips to hers again because of how attractive I found her in that moment.

Jade looked equally impressed. "Well done. I suppose we should climb out of this place. Although I'm not sure the tide has rolled out yet."

"Probably not," I said. "We likely have a few hours left."

She looked around, and her eyes fell on the mess tent. "I bet they have a bottle of something to celebrate our victory."

Cyrus rolled his eyes, looking like the last place he wanted to be was drinking in a cave with the rest of us. It hurt, but there wasn't much I could do about it. He needed more time, not an evening of drinking and merriment.

Or maybe a night of drinking was exactly what he needed.

Jade disappeared into the tent and came back holding three dark bottles and a basket. Looking inside, I found two whole loaves of bread.

"To soak up the alcohol," she explained. "I can't imagine the trek will be very safe if we're all sloshed."

I grinned, and so did Emilie. We looked at Cyrus expectantly, hoping he would join us and put everything aside, at least for the night.

He waited, forcing me to hold my breath, until he finally grabbed a bottle from Jade's hands and uncorked it. He held the bottle up and said flatly, "Cheers."

He took a long swig and passed the bottle to me.

Before I took a sip, I echoed his sentiment. "Cheers, brother."

Chapter Thirty-Eight

Ladon

THE SUN WAS CLIMBING the sky by the time we reached the Gem of Baumheim. After successfully finishing all three bottles of wine, we had caught a few hours of sleep before climbing out of the cave in the early hours of the morning.

Now we were headed back to King Marsden's castle so we could gather our belongings and return home. I couldn't get over how amazing it felt, knowing that Reyna was gone. I could finally breathe easy.

But every time I thought about it, I remembered I wasn't allowed to remain in Renoa. I could go home to pack my things, but after that, I needed to head out of the city and back to Fort Malek. Once, I had craved returning to Fort Malek so I wouldn't have to deal with Emilie or childish demands from Cyrus and my mother.

But so much had changed. I wanted to be close to my family and close to Emilie. I had no doubt she would follow me to Fort Malek if that was what it would take to be together, but she shouldn't have to.

A guard opened the gate as we approached the Gem. He obviously recognized us from our previous visit. I wondered what he thought of our tattered and bloody clothes.

Inside the castle, the host from the first day greeted us—first with a smile and then a look of horror when he took in our appearance. "Oh, you should get cleaned up. I will send up extra towels and let King Marsden know that you're back. I believe he had expected you at breakfast, but I'll let him know it's going to be a minute."

I chuckled as I imagined King Marsden's reaction if we had shown up to breakfast in our current state. I was covered in sand and blood and sweat and looked forward to washing up and stepping into clean clothes. My muscles ached and the burn marks on my skin were screaming at me, just as I'd suspected they would.

I showered as quickly as possible, gently washing my inflamed skin and patting it dry. I was thankful I'd packed at least one loose shirt and pants that didn't rub my blistered skin. Perhaps there was a healer in the castle who could provide some burn cream. That likely wouldn't work on my insides, though. It felt like I'd swallowed lava and injected it into my veins. The wine probably hadn't helped, but consequences had been far from my mind at that time.

I just needed to drink water and suck it up until my body healed. Hopefully Emilie wasn't suffering too much either.

By the time I made it downstairs to the dining room, Vincent, Jade and Emilie were already seated and filling their plates with fruit and some type of breakfast casserole that smelled heavenly. My stomach growled, and my mouth immediately began to water.

"Good morning, Ladon," Vincent said after spotting me. "I was just telling the ladies here that this is our traditional breakfast here in Baumheim. Thought it would be nice to share it with you all before you left."

"Thank you," I said, taking a seat next to Emilie. Vincent began to fill a plate for me. "What's in it?"

"This and that. It's a mash-up of whatever we have on hand—potatoes, egg, cheese, mushrooms. You get the gist."

"Sounds perfect."

Before he handed me the plate, he added, "Grab some toast and fruit too. A balanced meal is the best way to start the day."

I smiled and took his advice, glad that he was in better spirits than when we'd left him.

Cyrus entered a few minutes later, and we finished our meal in near silence, aside from hums of approval and gratitude for the delicious food.

"I have to admit, I thought when you came back that you'd have Reyna with you. Do I want to know what happened to her?" We all nervously looked around the table, but Vincent chuckled. "You don't need to answer that. At least tell me this—is there going to be a body for my citizens to stumble upon in the near future?"

Cyrus shook his head. "No. You won't find a body."

"That's good." Vincent turned to me. "I also want to thank you for bringing back my son's ring and sharing what happened. I might've gone the rest of my life not knowing, and I don't think I could've handled that."

I cleared my throat. "You're welcome. I'm sorry it happened, and that I didn't come bearing better news."

The king's eyes turned misty, but he dragged a hand over his face and put on a smile. "Well, then. Is there anything else I can do for you before you go?"

"No," Cyrus said. "You've been a gracious host. We couldn't ask anything else of you."

"Excellent. I hope you have a safe trip back to Lourova, and let's not let so much time pass before we see each other again, Cyrus."

"I agree, friend."

Jade rounded up her crew in record time. Thankfully, since it was still early in the day, most of them had not started drinking yet and were ready to set sail immediately.

Cyrus shared a few words with the captain, and before we knew it, the ship was drifting away from the harbor. The sun was now high in the sky, and there were few clouds in sight. I hoped it would stay that way and we would have smooth water as we traversed the sea.

Jade immediately went below deck, and Cyrus followed her, leaving Emile and me on the deck. I took her hand and led her to the stern, finding a place to sit and watch Baumheim shrink in the distance.

"How are your burns?" I asked, turning her arm to get a good look. She had a few angry welts that matched my own, but it looked as though they were already healing. I frowned. "Do you have ointment?"

"I do."

"And you didn't think to share with me?"

She rolled her eyes. "Of course I did. I brought it with me to breakfast, but it slipped my mind once we started eating."

"Do you have it with you now?"

She nodded and stood up. "Give me one second."

Emilie went below deck and returned a few minutes later carrying her backpack. She opened it and pulled out the burn salve. "Would you like me to...?"

"Rub me down? Yes, princess."

"Don't think I won't smack you, Ladon. Even with those blisters."

I chuckled, taking my shirt off so she could lather all my burns. She scooped some onto her fingers and began to gently cover my chest. I watched her carefully, enjoying the way her fingers brushed my skin. Then she grazed a particularly painful welt, and I hissed.

"Sorry," she said.

"Don't be. I really enjoy having your hands on me. We should do it again sometime when I'm not charred."

Emilie smiled and bit her lip. "You're insufferable."

"You like it," I teased.

She didn't respond but kept applying the ointment with tender hands. Sinful thoughts entered my head when her fingers got dangerously close to the trail of hair that stuck out of my pants.

"Emilie," I said in a low, husky groan. "As much as I'd love to see where this is headed and watch you explore my body, I don't think this deck is the place to do it."

Her cheeks turned pink, and she pulled her hand back, but I could tell by the look on her face that her mind was still full of delicious thoughts.

I grabbed the back of her neck and lifted her face to me. "Hey. Tell me something honest."

Emilie's eyes met mine. "I can't believe you're real, and that life led me to you. I want to always keep you with me, keep my hands on you, just so I know you're not a figment of my imagination. I need to know I didn't die inside that mountain."

Keeping my right hand on her neck, I used my left to hold her hand and bring it to my lips, kissing the inside of her wrist. "You're alive, and I'm very real, princess."

"Promise?"

"I promise."

There was only one day left of our voyage, and I hadn't talked to my brother almost the entire time. It was like he forgot I existed once again. Now that our mission was finished, he seemed content to ignore me.

I wanted to wrap my hands around his throat and strangle him... in a friendly, brotherly sort of way. The kind of way that makes a person realize they're being an idiot.

Emilie had just stepped out of the room to grab something to eat when I decided I couldn't take it anymore. I got out of bed and knocked on the door next to ours.

"Cyrus," I shouted. "Cyrus, we need to talk."

When he didn't respond, I pounded on the door some more. He had to be inside. I'd been listening for the sound of doors opening or closing and footsteps in the hall all morning.

I was about to give up, but then the door opened. Jade squinted at me. Her hair was a mess, as if she'd just rolled out of bed. "What do you want?"

"My brother. Is he in there?"

She let the door swing open wider, and I could see him inside, still in bed. His shirt was missing, and his beard was unkempt. He had dark circles under his eyes and overall looked like a mess.

The wind left my sails, and I sounded pathetic when I asked, "Can we talk?"

His chest lifted with a heavy breath, and he dropped his head. "Yeah. I guess so."

"I'll meet you in the crew lounge?"

"Sure. Give me fifteen."

I let the door close and dashed to the lounge space, taking a seat at the empty table. Thank the gods the crew woke up and ate so early. I would've yelled for them to get lost if any of them had been hanging around.

I waited nervously, tapping the tabletop while my eyes flicked toward the staircase every few seconds, expecting to see Cyrus. Every sound made me jerk my head up, then sink with disappointment.

Finally, Cyrus appeared, taking his time to slip into the seat across from me. He stared at me with a blank expression, making me question whether I was pressing him too soon.

Shifting uneasily in my seat, I cleared my throat. "How are you?"

Cyrus merely raised a brow.

Okay, that was a stupid way to start the conversation. But I'd never been in this position before.

I wiped my hand down my face, feeling sweat coat my palm. "Listen, I know that I've broken your trust, and I'm going to work really hard to earn that back. Please believe me when I say that I did not do any of this intentionally."

"Any of what?" he demanded. "If we're going to do this, we should be completely honest. Right? So, say it. What did you do?"

I swallowed the lump in my throat. "I didn't intentionally fall in love with Emilie."

He blinked, and I watched as his jaw rippled with irritation.

"I didn't know how much I would come to care for her. And I didn't intend to come between the two of you or break up your engagement. You're my brother, Cyrus. I love you, and I would never hurt you on purpose."

He tilted his head back, staring at the ceiling. "And lying to me? Was that intentional?"

I hung my head and numbly drew circles on the table. "Yeah, I guess that was a choice I made. For what it's worth, I planned to tell you. I was just waiting for the right moment."

"Because you couldn't be with her if you didn't tell the truth."

How could he be so callous about all of this? I didn't deserve his sympathy, but I had never seen him act so heartless.

After a long pause, I said, "Because it was the right thing to do."

Cyrus turned his head, clearly growing tired of this conversation.

I didn't know what else I could say or do to make this better.

Shaking my head, I sighed. "I really am sorry, Cyrus. Not for loving her, but for hurting you. All my life, I've looked up to you. I admire you so much and would do anything for you. I just hope one day you'll believe me."

Cyrus didn't bother to look at me, and I knew it was time to give up. I wouldn't get anywhere with him like this. Standing, I opened my mouth to say something else but realized there was nothing left to say. So I turned my back on my brother one last time and started for the stairs.

"Wait," he said hoarsely.

My head snapped around so fast, I thought I heard a crack.

"I... I can forgive you."

I waited, hope building in my chest.

"I don't know how long it'll take," my brother said quietly, "or how. But I think I can."

"I understand."

He raised his eyes and finally looked at me, saying simply, "I don't want you to leave Renoa."

"I don't want to leave either."

"You can stay. Emilie too. Though I'd appreciate it if you didn't flaunt your relationship in front of me. Can you do that?"

"Absolutely." I could keep the public displays of affection to a minimum when he was around. And if it would make him happy and improve our relationship, then I couldn't say no. It was a small request in exchange for coming home.

Home. I was coming home.

Chapter Thirty-Nine

Emilie

RENOA WAS A SIGHT for sore eyes. I could've fallen to my knees and kissed the ground outside the castle gardens if my legs weren't so stiff. I just had to make it up one more set of stairs...

"Oh, gods," Sophia shouted from ahead. She ran out of the castle doors, straight for us, her skirts flowing wildly behind her. Her arms were outstretched as if she were ready to catch us all in a large group hug.

Which is exactly what she did. First her sons, and then me and Jade. She cried tears of joy and behaved like her usual theatrical self, but I was so happy to see her that I cried too.

She stood back for a moment, her hands covering her mouth, eyes wide and unblinking. "Did... did you succeed?"

Ladon's lips curved upward. "Yes."

Sophia burst into another round of tears, using her sleeve to wipe them up. I didn't even think she'd been drinking; she was just that happy to have her family back.

"Sophia," I said softly. The urge to comfort her was overwhelming.

Her glistening eyes met mine, and her tears faded. "Welcome home," she said, embracing me a second time. I barely caught a breath before she was squeezing me and grabbing me by the shoulders.

I tried not to flinch too much—my arms were still blistered, though they were fading quickly—but of course she caught it. "What's wrong? Are you hurt?"

"I'm fine," I assured her. "Better than fine, actually."

She watched me for a moment before deciding I was telling the truth. "It's so good to have you back. And my boys."

She released me so she could hold them again, and I laughed at the faces they made. Their mother was prone to excessive worrying, but after everything her sons had been through, perhaps it wasn't excessive at all.

Ladon softened and squeezed her back while Cyrus did his best to break free.

"You two are not allowed to leave me again for at least fifty years."

I laughed. There was no way she could keep them locked away, but she would try her damnedest.

"And you, darling," she said, wrapping Jade up in her arms again. Revulsion was written all over Jade's face, but she didn't dare tell Sophia to let go. Even she understood that Sophia was the true leader of Osavian. As Cyrus's mother, she held just as much power as he did, if not more. Her words influenced him, and Jade would be an idiot to cross her. "You're all skin and bones. Let's get some food in you. Are you hungry? Have you eaten?"

"You don't have to do that, Mother," Cyrus said, his face sagging. I wasn't sure if it was the fatigue from traveling or the sadness from the betrayal finally catching up with him. I knew he and Ladon had had a conversation before we landed in Sage Harbor, but Ladon had made it clear that Cyrus wasn't ready to move on just yet. He was still holding on to his anger and disappointment, and it showed.

Sophia must've noticed something similar because she quirked her head to the side, and her eyes narrowed as she assessed her eldest. "Something is wrong."

No one spoke, because none of us wanted to be the one to bring up the situation at hand. Sophia already knew about Ladon and me, but revealing that now would be tricky. Cyrus would find out he was the last to know, and I couldn't imagine that would improve his mood.

She looked back and forth between her sons, and when Ladon looked at me, it finally clicked for Sophia. All she had to do was give me one quick glance, and she understood. "Oh."

That one word was Cyrus's unraveling. He shook his head in disbelief. "You knew?"

Sophia swallowed, her eyes falling to the ground. "I did."

"And you didn't tell me either."

Her sympathetic tone turned to one of parental scolding. "It wasn't my place. And I was a little busy praying to the gods that you would wake up, only to say goodbye when the lot of you left me once again."

Cyrus scoffed, and Sophia's eyes narrowed into slits.

Before she could further berate him, Jade suddenly moved aside, grabbing her bag. "This isn't a conversation that I need to be part of. Thank you for the dinner offer, Sophia, but I will pass this evening."

Ladon placed a hand on my back. "Emilie, you should go too. Get some rest or catch up with Selene. I'll find you before it's time to eat."

As much as I wanted to see Selene, I didn't think I could do anything at all until I slept. I began to walk away, but Cyrus snapped, "You should go with her. I don't have anything else to say to you."

"Cyrus!" Sophia reprimanded. "Don't talk to your brother like that."

"It's fine, Mother," Ladon said. "He can take all the time he needs."

"Taking the time to process everything doesn't mean he can treat you that way. Go on. I have a few more words to say to your brother."

Ladon looked as though he'd rather stay to defend Cyrus, but when Cyrus refused to acknowledge him, he conceded. He turned to me and said dully, "Let's go."

We walked in near silence as he led the way back to my room. Once we arrived, I stood in the doorway. "I don't think I can stay here."

"What do you mean?" Ladon asked, nudging me aside to look into the room. There was nothing wrong that he could see, and he turned to me with confusion. "You don't want to stay in Renoa?"

"No," I said quickly. "It's not that. It's just... Cyrus's room is right across the hall. And this bedroom was given to me when it was assumed I would be his wife. It feels wrong to stay here now. Not to mention I don't want to run into him unexpectedly. At least not for some time while he sorts through his feelings."

Ladon sucked in a breath through his teeth and thrummed his fingers on the doorframe. "I see. There's an empty bedroom on my side of the living quarters. I'd be more than happy to run into you unexpectedly."

He smirked, and I couldn't resist his charm. It wasn't like I was in any position to turn him down. Where else would I go without a job or a coin to my name? Another aspect of my life that I'd need to figure out, now that my life was my own.

"Sounds good to me," I told him. I looked around the room, deflating at the idea of packing everything up and moving it to the other side of the castle. "What if I stay in your room tonight?"

It wouldn't be the first time. We'd spent most of our nights together even while we were supposed to be keeping things platonic, although those times had been because I needed him to comfort me and help me feel safe. Now I only wanted to feel him next to me. To see the way his face relaxed when he was fast asleep.

"You want to stay the night with me while we are unwed? Scandalous, Emilie."

I rolled my eyes. "Is that a yes?"

He chuckled. "Of course."

I snaked an arm around his waist and buried my face in his chest, listening to the beat of his heart. "I'm so glad to be home."

"Me too, princess. Me too."

We slept straight through dinner and well into the following morning. Ladon's drapes were pulled closed, so I had no idea what time it was when I opened my eyes. His arm was wrapped tightly around my waist, and I had no desire to move, but my bladder begged me otherwise.

Gently moving his arm, I slipped out of bed and entered his bathroom. A few of my things were already moved—my toothbrush and toothpaste, a comb, and some lotion. A smile crossed my lips, thinking about how I'd already staked my claim. Did I even want to have my own room? Would it really be that obscene if we lived together?

Probably. He wasn't a king, but he was still a prince. We'd have to get used to sneaking into each other's rooms for the foreseeable future. It wouldn't be so bad, though. There was a thrill that came with doing something we weren't supposed to be doing, and I hoped that excitement never faded.

I freshened up and returned to bed, where Ladon was still snoozing peacefully. He was shirtless, and I could see that his burns were healing nicely. They likely wouldn't scar, thank the gods. We had enough of those already.

My eyes fell to the vines that scarred my wrists and the matching ones on his. Some days, I forgot they were there. Other days, they reminded me of my unbreakable connection to Ladon. In the immediate aftermath of our escape, they'd felt like an eternal curse, but I hadn't felt that way recently. Not since Reyna died.

Since I'd killed her.

I smiled and took a deep breath.

"What are you thinking about?"

I startled and glanced over at Ladon.

He moved closer, his hand slipping beneath the blanket and finding its way to my thigh. The satin nightgown I wore slid up to my hip.

"Did I wake you?"

His voice was muffled as he spoke half into the pillow and half into my hair. "No."

"Mm-hmm," I murmured, unconvinced. I nestled into his warm chest. Heat radiated from his body, and I took a moment to kiss his collarbone.

Ladon's legs tangled with mine, one of them shifting higher until his thigh was pressed to my naked core. He moaned when he found my hot, slick skin and not a pair of panties.

"Fuck," he groaned, twisting so he could see my face properly. He felt his way up my thigh and around to my ass, squeezing until I gasped. "Do you know what you fucking do to me?"

I smirked and bit my lip. "No. Do you think you could tell me?"

His hips pressed against mine, and I could feel his hard cock pressing against my pussy through his briefs. I whimpered as his shaft slid along my cunt until he reached my clit. His cock strained against his underwear, and I was all too happy to release it.

Ladon leaned forward to kiss me, pulling my bottom lip between his teeth. His chest rumbled with pleasure as my hand glided over his stomach and into his briefs, carefully fondling his balls.

Passion and *need* built in my belly, and I sucked on his lip, grabbing his other hand and moving it to my chest. He massaged my breast over top of my gown, my nipples visible through the thin fabric.

With one palm still gripping my ass, he rolled me onto my back and slid between my legs, grinding and rolling his hips and sucking a trail down my neck.

My breathing was choppy, and I struggled to push off his underwear while he was pressed against me so tightly. I whimpered, "Ladon. I want to *feel* you."

"You will, princess. But I want to take my time with you."

He skillfully shimmied my nightgown up and over my head, throwing it aside and returning his lips to the hollow of my neck. Taking his time, he meticulously moved his mouth down my body, sucking and biting and licking. His tongue flicked my nipple before he took it into his mouth and hummed.

Slamming my head against the pillow, I bit my lip and tried to hold back a cry of ecstasy. I couldn't reach his cock, so I threaded my fingers in his hair instead. He hadn't even made it past my belly button yet, and I was already struggling to maintain my sanity.

I tried to push his head farther south, but he chuckled against my sensitive skin.

"Patience, Emilie."

What was patience? I was sure I'd heard the word before, but I couldn't recall what it meant. I could only think of taste and touch and the pulsing between my legs.

"Please," I said, hoping he would take pity on me and give my cunt the attention it deserved.

He ignored my request and continued making his way down my body, leaving a trail of kisses over my stomach and then my lower abdomen. He was so close to my pussy that I could feel his hot breath bringing every nerve in my body to life. I vibrated with a longing that only Ladon could satisfy.

But he avoided my clit, choosing to leave bite marks on my inner thigh instead. He had to see how soaking wet I was, ready for him to drive inside me and fill me with his cum. I clenched at the thought but whined when I had nothing to clamp down on.

Since he was stringing me along and turning me into a puddle of desperation, I tried to reach down and circle my clit myself. My fingers were almost to my sensitive bud when he snatched my wrist and pinned it to my side.

With a wicked smirk, he looked up from his merciless task. "I should punish you for that."

I writhed beneath him. "Don't."

"Okay. This time I'll be kind. Next time, I'll leave you panting and squirming and won't let you come until I say so."

Wasn't that what he was already doing? If I didn't come soon, I would combust.

"Spread your legs for me, princess. I want to see that pretty pussy."

My knees were already open, but I pushed them wider, letting him see every bit of me. It didn't matter that I was exposed and vulnerable; my fears and discomfort were nonexistent with him.

Then his lips pressed against my clit, and he sucked, alternating between flicking his tongue over my bud and pulling my lips into his mouth. He swirled his tongue, eliciting a breathy moan from my throat.

When he slid a finger inside me, my back arched off the mattress.

A single finger was a tease, and he knew it.

I gripped the sheets until my knuckles turned white.

He continued to toy with me. How could he possibly have this much composure when I was a pitiful mess? My entire body began to tremble, and my eyes rolled back in my head.

By the time he added another finger, I was seconds from falling apart.

Ladon pushed inside me, caressing my inner walls. He gently moved his fingers in and out, pressing up at the same time and hitting a spot that made my vision tunnel. With a few more thrusts, I was pulsing around his fingers and shaking uncontrollably.

My thighs squeezed his head, and I was singularly focused on the unending euphoria zipping up my spine and the endless spasms between my legs.

When my tremors subsided, I let my legs fall to see Ladon licking his lips and sucking his fingers. My pussy clenched again at the sight.

He kneeled between my legs, and my eyes were drawn to the erection in his briefs. It was my turn to lick my lips; I wanted to taste his arousal and watch as he experienced the same amount of pleasure I just had.

I propped myself up on my elbows and stared at his cock rather obviously, biting my bottom lip. He didn't miss a beat and jumped off the end of the bed, grabbing me by the ankle and pulling me down.

I squealed and wrapped my legs around his torso as he picked me up from the bed. "What are you doing?"

His hands gripped my thighs, and my arms circled his shoulders, pressing my breasts against his chest. I was slick with sweat, but I would never deny the chance to be close to him.

He carried me across the room and into his bathroom, setting me down on the edge of his giant bathtub. Reaching past me, he turned the knobs until warm water began to fill the basin.

"Get in the water," he commanded.

"What about you?"

He tilted his head in disappointment. "It's almost like you want to be punished."

Heat covered my chest, and I spun around, dipping my toes into the water. Lowering into the tub, my muscles slowly relaxed. I hadn't realized just how sore they were from all the fighting and traveling. I found a seat and laid my head back on the side of the tub.

Between the post-orgasm high and the comfort of the bath, I almost closed my eyes and fell asleep. But right before my lids shut, I saw Ladon reach for his briefs. My eyes popped back open.

Ladon chuckled as he pulled them down, keeping his eyes glued to mine the entire time. It was almost like he was daring me to look down and take in his cock. He was testing me to see if I could keep my eyes on his.

I did my best, but when I heard his underwear hit the floor, my eyes fell and my thighs clenched at the sight of him. Hard and the perfect length with a vein that was easily visible on his pale skin. He gripped his shaft and pumped himself a few times before he walked over to the tub and climbed inside.

Ladon sank until the water reached his shoulders, and his arms wrapped around my waist and pulled me on top of him. He leaned back against the tub's edge, staring at me with his beautiful silver-blue eyes. His hands came to rest on my thighs underneath the water, and I waited patiently for another command.

His eyes flicked down and back up at me in silent encouragement.

Water dripped from my hands as I ran them down his chest and back into the water, finding his cock hard and waiting for me.

His head rolled back and his eyes fluttered closed as I began to glide my hands over his length, alternating pressure and twisting at the same time. His chest inflated with each deep breath, and his mouth fell open.

"Ahh, fuck," he moaned. He lifted his hands and dragged them down his face.

I loved knowing I could do this to him. That I could drive him to the edge and give him the utmost level of satisfaction.

I rubbed the head of his cock with my thumb and felt him twitch. His abs tightened, and I was overwhelmed by the magnificent sight. I wanted to memorize every inch of his god-like figure.

Leaning forward, I licked a drop of water from his chest and ran my tongue all the way up his neck. His mouth was already open for me, so I kissed him and twisted my tongue with his.

Pushing up on my knees, I guided his cock to my entrance and eased down on him, savoring every inch. Once I was seated, I began to rock, his length gliding in and out of me as my walls squeezed around him. My hands tangled in his hair, and my nipples brushed against him with each thrust, sending a tingling sensation up my spine.

Water sloshed against the side of the tub, some of it spilling over onto the marble floor. At some point, Ladon began to thrust up into me, driving into me from below. My body shuddered, and I was so close to coming again.

"Ladon," I cried.

Without asking, he knew exactly what I needed. He reached between us and gently rubbed my clit. A few moments later, I was fluttering around him.

I moaned, my head falling forward to rest on his chest. Ladon drove into me a few more times, hard and with everything he had, and then he came too.

I clung to him like my life depended on it, focusing on the way his body expanded and deflated beneath me with each breath. My heart rate slowly returned to normal, matching his.

It took a while to come back to reality, but when I did, I twisted in Ladon's arms so I could see him properly. To my surprise, he was already staring at me, drawing circles on my shoulder.

There was a feeling of anxiety that I hadn't even realized was lingering until it dissolved completely under his gaze. I was completely at home with him. He had all my love and all my devotion, and I knew by the look in his eyes that he understood that.

Just in case he didn't, I told him. "Ladon Castelli, you are my everything. Words cannot describe how much I love you, and I don't think I could ever live without you."

His eyes softened. "You won't have to, princess. I'm not going anywhere."

He looked as though he wanted to say something else but hesitated.

I caressed his neck and held his gaze. "What is it?"

For once, his cheeks turned pink, and that *really* piqued my curiosity. "Ladon... tell me something honest."

He huffed a laugh, knowing he couldn't evade me. His face suddenly became very serious, and he ran his hands along my waist. "Honestly, I'm thinking about how you've changed me for the better. I can't think of a single thing I want more in this life than you."

He licked his lips and nervously looked up before his gaze settled on me once more. "I'm thinking... I'm thinking this life is crazy. How one of the worst things imaginable could lead to something so beautiful. Life is unexpected and could end at any given moment, and all I can think about is how I want to spend the rest of my life, no matter how short or long, with you. Through all the ups and the downs."

My heart skipped a beat, and I raised my eyebrows. "What are you saying?"

He shot me a crooked grin. "I'm saying that I fell in love with you in my darkest nights, but I want you for all my brightest days. Emilie Duval, I want you to be my wife."

I clasped a hand over my mouth, completely speechless. I had to catch my breath before I could give him an answer. My hand moved over my heart, and I replied, "Yes. Gods, yes."

Bonus Chapter

Cyrus

MY DESK WAS AN absolute mess. I tried to focus on organizing it, but it was a useless task. I needed a gods-damned assistant or secretary to take care of all this shit.

Ladon hadn't done much paperwork while I'd been out, but I preferred it that way. There was no way he would've done it to my liking, and I would've had to redo it anyway. That didn't stop me from being frustrated with him, though.

I picked up a folded piece of paper and opened it, reading the first paragraph before sorting it into the trash pile. I carried on with that method for three more pieces of paper before my brain turned fuzzy again.

Sighing, I threw the parchment down and leaned back in my chair. My office was quiet and removed from the commotion in the castle. I couldn't even hear a single person walking out in the hallway or gossiping outside my door, and I liked it that way.

Especially since the past month had been full of party planning.

Ladon and Emilie's engagement party.

I had successfully dodged most of the pandemonium by claiming I needed to work, but I couldn't hide forever. Not since the party was happening this evening.

My eyes flicked to the clock on the wall.

The party was happening in less than ten minutes.

Would they even realize I was missing? Maybe they would, and they'd decide it was for the best. No one wanted a grump around while everyone else was trying to celebrate. Most couples wouldn't bother to invite the bride's ex-fiancé... who also happened to be the groom's brother.

Gods, even thinking it sounded like a fucking mess.

Perhaps I could show up for a few minutes and then escape without anyone realizing. I could pretend I'd fallen ill. My mother might be angry, but she'd get over it. She had another son to dote on all evening, so she didn't need to waste her time on me.

Two minutes to go...

I groaned and leaned forward, elbows on my desk while I buried my head. My mind raced with so many plans to abandon the party that I didn't hear someone approach my door.

There was a knock, and before my head had lifted from my hands, Jade burst through the door, wearing a tight burgundy dress that showed off her muscular arms and more skin than I'd seen since sharing a bunk with her on the Aria.

She stopped abruptly when she caught sight of me, scrunching her face in annoyance. Her dark brows pinched together, and her berry-red lips turned into a frown. "What are you doing?"

"I should be asking you the same thing."

This was not the first time she'd barged into my office without my permission. It was becoming a habit. I blamed it on her lack of friends and basic manners.

She unfroze long enough to sit in the chair on the other side of my desk, propping her feet up on the dark wood—and my mess of papers—like she owned the damn place.

I scoffed, and she feigned an innocent expression, pretending she had no clue why I would be irritated. She had a way of finding all my buttons and pressing them repeatedly.

"Get your fucking feet off my desk, Jade."

She laughed but obliged. "Wow, you are not very nice today, are you? Do you know you're supposed to be at an engagement party right now?"

I looked at the clock and, sure enough, the party had started exactly one minute ago.

My gaze returned to her. "Did you come here just to tell me that?"

"No," she said lightly. Then she reached under the skirt of her dress, exposing a strap around her thigh, and pulled out a small green flask that matched the emerald in her eyes. She opened it, bringing it to her lips for a quick sip, then replaced the cap and handed it to me. "I came here because I knew you would be miserable, and you know how happy that makes me."

"Get out."

"Cheer up, King Crank."

"Jade," I growled.

She pointed at the flask. "Bottoms up. It'll either numb the pain or bring out the worst in you. Either way, it should be interesting for me."

"Do you ever listen?"

"No," she said plainly.

"You're unbelievable."

"Thank you."

She was testing my patience, and I had none left to give.

I missed the days when she hadn't been so chatty. As it turned out, she just needed someone else's misery in order to find her voice. And I was the sad bloke who got to be her muse.

Twisting the flask's cap, I removed it and took a long swig. It tasted like mint and something flowery. Not my favorite, but I took another drink anyway to take off the edge.

"There's more where that came from," she said. "We could ditch this party and I could watch you get wasted. Maybe you'll even cry."

She said it a little too enthusiastically, and to spite her, I finished the liquor in the flask, licking my lips and letting it burn my throat on the way down.

I slammed it down on my desk, surprised that it didn't shatter with the force I'd shown. Then I stood and brushed off my shirt.

Jade appraised me with a look of disgust. "Is that what you're wearing?"

"What's wrong with it?"

She shrugged and shot to her feet. "Nothing. Let's go, King Crank."

My eyes rolled so hard I thought I might lose my vision. "Remind me why you're still here."

"Because we have a treaty, and I need to make sure you hold up your end of the deal."

Right. Another unfortunate mistake of my brother's. I mean, yes, he saved my life, but at what cost?

I crossed the room and opened the door, waving a hand for Jade to walk before me.

She smiled as she passed, saying, "Wow, such a gentleman."

"Don't get used to it," I growled.

"I would never."

Acknowledgements

Wow, I cannot believe this is now the fifth book that I have completed. Thank you so much to everyone who has been with me since day one—my bookish besties, my author pals and my friends and family who have been patient and understanding when author stuff gets in the way and takes up too much time. It means the world that you continue to support me and my dreams even when it's tough.

I have to give a special shoutout to a few bookish influencers because every single time you shared Nights of Obedience, it made a noticeable difference. It wouldn't have that "Best of BookTok" banner without you! Thank you Kylie, Kirsten, Margaret, Lex, Kaila and so many more!

To all my beta readers, editors, street team members and artists—I cannot express my gratitude for you enough!

And to every reader who loves Ladon and Emilie as much as I do, thank you so much for following along. I'll see you in the next one ♥

For a list of titles by Rachel Mays, please visit
www.authorrachelmays.com